A DARK OCEAN'S DESCENT

Heridian Trilogy

Book One

Darryl J. W. Temple

Copyright © 2021 Darryl J. W. Temple All rights reserved.
The characters and events portrayed in this book are fictitious. Any similarity to real persons, living or dead, is coincidental and not intended by the author.

No part of this book may be reproduced, or stored in a retrieval system, or transmitted in any form or by any means, electronic, mechanical, photocopying, recording, or otherwise, without express written permission of the publisher.

Kindle ASIN: B093YQ2DQP
Hardcover (Dust Jacket) ISBN: 9780645185201
Hardcover (Laminate) ISBN: 9798431717062
Paperback ISBN: 9798747377516

Version: 060722

Cover design by: Darryl J. W. Temple. Background image © Yuri_B, © Pixabay.com. Original "Astra" spaceship © Sergeym with kit bash elements © Olegushenok, both © cgTrader.com. Robotic arm © Dries Deryckere, © Sketchfab.com.

Acknowledgements.

First and foremost, I wish to thank my wife Lisa for the constant support and encouragement during the creation of this book. My thanks also to my family for their help, advice, and patience.

If you enjoy this book, please rate or even comment. Cheers!

CHAPTER 1

Dead Man Warping.

Draethus never meant to kill everyone.
    Eyes closed, he let the hot jungle breeze flow over his face. He felt guilt, and a calm acceptance of his fate.
I deserve this.

It had started out so innocently. He was to lead his squad of soldiers and escort a science team to a dig site. Apparently, a piece of technology had been uncovered inside ancient ruins, deep in the jungle. With the enemy's territory on the other side of the world, he never expected an encounter.

His worst expectation was listening to the science teams babbling in their foreign, intellectual language, which always caused Draethus to zone out. Stories about the horrors in the trees always made a great counter however, and the terrified expressions on the men's faces were always welcome.

It's not that Draethus wanted to experience more action. Being a Soldier of the Void, or SOV for short, he expected to fight the Heridian invaders. Growing up on Echelon, a large jungle world on the outskirts of civilized space, fighting creatures wasn't unusual.

On the third day, he received information the enemy was closing in.

It was his decision to stay another twelve hours. Translations of the device, in old Echelonian, suggested the technology was a displacement device. Was it for teleportation? Did it have something to do with space-time traversal?

The war had been raging for fifty years so he had to risk their lives, it was too important a task. How wrong he'd been.

Draethus felt his hand twitch. The dead man's switch he held was primed to activate the explosives they had planted on the device. He couldn't allow for the technology to fall into Heridian hands.

Opening his eyes, he peered into the distance at the Sky-Station, his home and base of operations for SOV. He didn't want to look at the bodies surrounding him, his squad, his friends, and the science team. He felt so guilty.

The Heridians encircled him. Chaotic bio-machines of menace and fury, clicking oversized fangs and flexing serrated claws. The aliens were insect like, except bipedal, walking upright on two legs, with crimson armor plating covering much of their surface. Most of their protection layered over their back, with cogs and pistons shifting underneath. Some even carried hand-held weaponry.

Draethus wondered how many of his friends' physical minds were inside the creatures, enhancing their computational power and intelligence.

Touching the dragon embossed amulet around his neck, he let the trigger slip from his fingers to set off the explosives. He was ready.

The world around him vanished. He expected intense pain and hoped it would only last moments. More than anything, he wanted the enemy to die with him. He sacrificed himself not for heroism, not for any misguided bravado, but for the greater good. He died to protect his people, and killing an enemy detachment was a bonus.

He closed his eyes, welcoming death.

But instead, he felt the sensation of everything, every atom and molecule. He had a sense of creation and destruction, but most curiously, the control over both. As he re-materialized, a surge of pain raced through his body, making his veins tingle.

He staggered, trying to open his eyes and get a bearing on where he was, or what had happened. Rubbing his eyes, he leant against a wall, rubble that wasn't there before, as his vision returned.

Heridian weapons' fire echoed in the distance, causing Draethus to crouch behind the cover. Had the enemy experienced the same displacement? Who were they firing at? His question was answered when he glimpsed a man running through the smoke. The man was screaming, and his panicked expression told Draethus everything he needed to know.

Then he heard it, the high-pitched whine of Heridian servo motors and heavy footsteps from something behind the rubble. Draethus kept silent, pressing himself against the wall and hoping the creature didn't peer over.

The man in the smoke fell to his knees as the Heridian soldier unleashed a salvo from its weapon. The poor soul's eyes glazed over as he toppled.

Draethus felt his heart spike and readied himself to move. As the creature skulked around the rubble, Draethus quietly crept the other way, being careful to keep his head down. He watched on in horror as the Heridian knelt down, collected its kill, and extracted what it needed. Layers of armored plating flipped open on its back carapace, accepting the new biological enhancement, before closing again. The once dormant runes and glyphs across the Heridian's armor pulsed to life as the integration completed.

Draethus knew the enemy soldier would instantly be more intelligent and feared being spotted. He crouched back behind the rubble and hoped the creature would move on. His guilt surfaced again, as he knew it would only be looking for more people to kill. Not him, and not today. If only he could do something, but he lost his weapons during the displacement, or whatever the event was called.

As he closed his eyes, he listened intently for the creature's footsteps and felt relieved they were growing fainter.

Replaying the gory event in his mind, he was reminded of his close friend, who had experienced the same fate as the screaming man.

It happened on a salvaged star vessel called the *Dark Claw*. The ship was unique in that it had survived the fall from orbit, during the initial invasion, landing in the ocean off the populated coast. Even though SOV were prepared and even knew the date of the first wave, they didn't stand a chance. Everything in orbit was gone, so when the opportunity arose to rescue the *Dark Claw*, Draethus and a team of soldiers, including his friend, Johan, volunteered.

The team hadn't made it far when they realized Heridian soldiers were aboard. Johan was the first to fall and through the exiting airlock, Draethus watched him die and integrate. It took Draethus a long time to recover, not that anyone could ever fully heal from such trauma.

Here he sat again, helpless, with no way of saving or rescuing the innocent people around him. He assumed they were probably all dead anyway and then reprimanded himself for the thought. These were scared people, being culled by monsters.

The only thing he could do was reach the Sky-Station and see if SOV could send help. If there even was a Sky-Station. He felt so confused and yearned for answers.

Draethus was snapped out of his thoughts by a Heridian rifle panning over his head from the other side of the rubble. Normally so vigilant, Draethus had missed the enemy walking up to him. He sprinted down the side of the wall and, glancing back, saw the creature begin to chase. Heated bolts whizzed past his head, as the

Heridian opened fire, forcing him to turn a sharp corner where he stopped.

The ruined building was a dead end with no cover. He was out in the open and out of options. Is this how things end for me?

The menacing creature strode confidently into view, its jaws clacking as if trying to speak. Draethus knew the screaming man's mind was inside and wondered how much control he had. Was he still screaming in there? Was he in pain? Is that him trying to talk through the enemy soldier?

Draethus knew the answers didn't matter. This soldier didn't need another biological enhancement, so the only option was obliteration. Not without a fight.

As Draethus charged forward, intent on a final display of defiance, the Heridian was knocked violently off its feet into the side wall. Draethus ducked quickly as shrapnel exploded from the creature and fire erupted across the ground. Before he could see what had caused the blast, the Heridian sprang to its feet and responded with weapons' fire.

Automatic gunfire thundered into the enemy again, blowing off its legs and carapace. Storming into the ruined building, a large, mechanized machine fired again, this time slower and more precise. Draethus froze in shock and wondered if the pilot of the walker was savoring the kill. As the enemy soldier reached up one last time with its weapon, the taller machine stomped on its head, crushing it instantly.

Draethus should have been terrified, or even repulsed by the sight of a Heridian being crushed. The enemy's blood was the same color as his, and he pitied the mind inside. Then again, the screaming man was now at rest.

To Draethus, the machine was magnificent. It stood upright on two heavily armored legs with almost clawed feet. The body was car size and elongated, with a large gatling gun mounted to a stubby arm on the left, and a long-barreled artillery cannon on the right. Draethus couldn't see the pilot through the dark canopy glass, but noticed a variety of twinkling displays. He couldn't shake the idea of a giant metal chicken and suppressed a laugh. The man inside must have noticed because the machine turned, and with loud, angry footsteps, strode over to him.

He instantly raised his arms in the universal sign of surrender, as there was no escape.

'I'm not one of them,' Draethus said, pointing at the dead Heridian soldier in the corner. 'I'm a friendly, do you understand?' He wasn't sure if the man even spoke the same language.

The gatling gun began spooling up, which made Draethus' stomach drop.

'Friendly!' he exclaimed again and stepped back in fear.

In the machine's nose, a tiny array of equipment activated, and a harmless laser shot out, scanning Draethus. He froze and wished the feeling of impending death would finally leave, or just decide and finish him.

When the scan was complete, the machine's gatling gun slowed and then stopped.

'There we go,' Draethus said. 'Good little chicken. Now get lost and go lay some eggs.'

'Who are you?' a voice boomed from hidden speakers in the machine.

Draethus was surprised for a moment before he regained his composure. He recognized the old dialect of Echelonian. 'I'm just a soldier, trying to kill Rids. I'd appreciate if you didn't step on me, though.' The term "Rid" was common throughout known systems, and few would take the time to pronounce the full word. Heridians were not respected, and only feared and hated.

The machine was silent for a moment before asking, 'I asked your name. You will also tell me where you are from and what those creatures are.'

'You're on Echelon. How can you not know what they are?' Draethus questioned. 'The Rids are a scourge, and a menace to all life. They attack without provocation and harvest the living organs of anyone they can find. Is this your first encounter with them?'

'Name!' it yelled, causing Draethus to retreat another step.

'Alright big guy, just calm down. My name is Arcilous Draethus. I serve with the Soldiers of the Void, from the Sky-Station here on Echelon. You know, that big nest in the sky? You may have seen it?'

'If you were from the station, I'd recognize your armor configuration. Your name also sounds ridiculous,' the man in the machine said.

'Oh, it's insults now,' said Draethus, inspecting his storm-colored armor. 'I tell you what, you jump out and trade places. I'll chase you around for a while and ask stupid questions.' He cringed the moment the last words came out. Tick off the psychotic poultry, good job.

'I can't be sure you aren't working with the enemy.'

'You have got to be joking,' said Draethus, trying to keep his cool. 'Look, that dead thing over there, chased me in here and wanted to kill me. So, I guess a thank you is in order.' This isn't going anywhere.

Weapon's fire echoed across the burning sky, and in the distance Draethus could hear people screaming.

'What's your name?' asked Draethus.

The man in the machine didn't answer.

'We need to get out of here,' urged Draethus. 'You can either follow me to the Sky-Station or run off into the fires and save all the lives you can.'

'Or I could kill you.'

Draethus nodded slowly. 'Yes, that is an option, not for me, though. But if you kill me, you will never know how I and the menace were transported here.'

'You brought them here!' the voice boomed through the machine's speakers. 'My city, my town is on fire because of you?'

Not one of my best arguments.

Draethus thought about running, but the machine was too fast. He didn't get a step towards the opening in the ruin before the concussion wave hit. Standard for any walker, the concussion field was normally deployed for crowd control.

Draethus felt weak at the knees. He staggered and, as the second wave hit, saw nothing but dirt.

The walker's canopy flipped open and the pilot, an ex-ganger turned Paladin, named Tremon, climbed down the side of the body, and stood over Draethus. Unclipping his sidearm, he readied himself for any resistance from the semi-conscious soldier.

Tremon crouched down and drew his weapon. Placing the muzzle to the soldier's chest, he pulled back the hammer.

'Your life could end now, you evil bastard,' said Tremon, pushing the gun further into Draethus.

Draethus moaned and tried to push the gun away, but his arms wouldn't move.

Tremon sighed. 'If I kill you now, we'll never find out how you, or these creatures got here.' He stood, holstered his weapon, then tapped Draethus on the head with his boot. 'You'll enjoy what comes next.'

Tremon walked back to his machine and depressed two levers before pulling them out and down. He stepped back as a pod like stretcher slipped down the side, then grabbed his captive and began securing him. When the pod, with Draethus secured, disappeared into the back of the machine, Tremon climbed back in and closed the canopy.

Draethus could feel the machine moving through the city and hoped he was headed for the Sky-Station. As his eyes closed, he wished for answers, and maybe a way to stop passing out.

*

In another section of space, millions of light years away, the dark fleet drifted in a loose formation against a backdrop of blue illumination from a dying star. Hundreds of enormous capital class vessels of various designs waited, a mass of dark fury hungry for war. The lead vessel, the *Wing of Vidar,* floated at the center and cast a shadow across half the force. A city sized monster, it was the flagship of the Cygnian Pirates.

In an abandoned hallway along an old section of the vessel, unused and forgotten, Xain Raeson looked out the viewing window in awe of the metal gods drifting on currents of radiation.

He refocused on his reflection in the glass. His dark hair was messy, and looking into his own hazel-colored eyes, wondered how he was so easily trapped.

'Open the door,' said a heavily modulated voice from behind him.

The cold steel muzzle of a pistol pushed into the back of Raeson's head as the unknown assailant repeated the command.

Xain wanted to rip the weapon from the man's hands and beat him with it, not just for threatening his life but to satisfy the anger in himself for letting someone get so close. He pushed the anger down, remaining calm, and looked for a way to overcome his attacker. They were in a quiet section of the ship and no help was coming.

'It's taken me a long time to get this close to you,' said the assailant, his voice still muffled through the digital modulator. 'Why did it have to be you? Traitor!'

The weapon pressed harder into Raeson's skull, and he knew the passionate hatred in the assailant's voice meant he didn't have long to live.

'Who are you calling a traitor?' Raeson replied with a grin. 'You're the one holding the gun.'

'Your Father...' the assailant began.

'Yes, my father was a traitor, the filth, but I fulfill and honor my family name.'

Xain Raeson, known as Reaper, when in the cockpit of his fighter, was the son of a traitorous human and child to a high-ranking elismorus, alien mother. Considered by the pirates to be a fighter ace, he was almost unmatched.

For centuries, the pirates had been a nomadic force roaming the stars, the largest portion of which comprised elismorus. They were an almost human looking race with slight differences in facial features, with pale skin and dark eyes. The minority was human, recruited from various areas of populated space.

Raeson was born a pirate and raised by both parents. Early in his childhood, Xain's father abandoned the fleet during an escort mission, resulting in the death of one hundred and fifty civilians. Xain remembered standing on the docks and watching the returning pilots basking in victory after hunting down and killing the traitor. That day, Raeson vowed to be better than his father, to prove himself and restore honor to his family name.

No one will ever be above him.

Yet here he stood at the mercy of an unknown assassin, a coward, holding a weapon to the back of his head.

'Few could have pulled this off,' said Raeson. 'I'll give you credit for that.'

'Shut up and do as I ask,' the other man threatened. 'You know nothing of me or who sent me.'

'You're here to kill me obviously, but who sent you, someone I owe money to? Oh, let me guess, Barnes down in the dregs section wants some payback for his loss the other night,' Raeson laughed.

'Your corpse won't be laughing,' the other man growled.

'You do understand how death works, right?'

'Shut it, I said!'

'I mean, if my corpse began laughing, I'd be a little unsettled.'

In the glass reflection, Raeson could see the trigger being pressed and knew he needed to stall.

'So, I'm guessing you are a relation to someone who died under my father's protection?' he replied seriously. He stared out into the dark and knew what lay ahead.

With a prideful reply, the assailant said, 'A great Cygnian leader sent me.'

'Not the Khan?'

The assailant laughed, 'Do you really think you are that important? Your delusions of grandeur are pathetic, traitor.'

'That word again… Traitor… You *will* pay for those words,' warned Raeson.

The assailant shoved him forward, harder this time, as if he were growing impatient. 'I won't ask again.'

Xain laughed and said, 'If you had planned this out thoroughly you wouldn't need me to open the airlock door, would you?'

'I've spent a long-time planning this. I just couldn't gain the access I needed,' the assailant replied.

Xain's mind raced to find a solution, and fast.

How do I overcome this? There aren't many components to his plan. He must want to keep my death quiet, or he would have just shot me already. Then again, he could have just done so and dragged my corpse to the airlock, unless he hasn't the upper body strength. That could just be his backup plan. Where did he even come from?

'There is always a way through,' Raeson said, as he kept his eyes forward. 'My Father's most common saying.'

'Don't you dare quote your father!' the assailant screamed.

That was the opening Raeson needed. The change in the assailant's behavior caused the man to lose concentration, just long enough for Raeson to make his move. With speed, Xain ducked, spun, side stepped and knocked the pistol from the assailant's hands. Without hesitation, the pirate ace followed through with an open-handed strike to his captor's jugular. The assailant was on his knees, incapacitated and with the pistol well out of reach, his hands clasped around the point of injury.

Raeson brushed the assailant's hands aside and grabbed the man's throat. 'Who are you and who sent you?'

The assailant wouldn't speak; not because of the pain, but because he chose not to divulge the information.

'Don't make me ask you again.'

The injured man, his face covered in a nano-fiber mask, connected to a thick cloak, looked up and said, 'My name is Cortane, and I have failed.'

'Yes. Yes, you have,' Raeson replied in a low, threatening tone.

Xain squeezed his grip tighter.

'I thought you would hand me over to the authorities,' the man gurgled in fear. With his calmness now overtaken by terror, his true vulnerability surfaced.

'What authorities?' spat Xain before strengthening his grip again. 'Do you now see who I truly am?'

Raeson dragged the man over to where the weapon had landed, then swooped down and collected it. He waved the pistol hand over a dimly lit crystal on the wall and the airlock opened. He threw the assailant forward with all his aggression, then locked the door with another wave. The man sprawled across the floor, still in pain from the earlier strike. He frantically leaped up and pounded the door with his fists in terror, yelling and screaming something that Xain couldn't hear.

Raeson walked up close to the glass and peered into the dark eye sockets of the assailant's mask.

'You do not know what kind of monster I am,' Xain said.

The airlock's outer door opened like an iris and the semi-conscious assailant launched out into the nothingness of space, his screams unheard.

It may have been a good idea to interrogate him properly, but I enjoyed that.

This was not the first time Raeson had killed, even in cold blood. In the depths of the void, it was easy to lose your morals, especially in a universe torn apart by conflict. He was a cold-blooded killer, and experienced in battle. Most of his victories were from the cockpit of his own fighter craft, his widowmaker.

Killing in person was different, however. Space combat was machine fighting against machine, but in person you have to look your enemy in the eye. If people got in his way, he disposed of them quickly and quietly, as if the person never existed. There was a price to pay, however, as ending someone's life created an empty place in his heart. Although proud of his achievements, even his mother had no desire to associate with him. What drove Xain was the urgency of honor, to restore his family name and prove himself the greatest ace of the Cygnian Pirates; the greatest they had ever known.

He holstered his new pistol and walked back down the corridor. There was a briefing to attend, and his wing would likely be leading the charge. The pirates had been at war for some time now, and the enemy had presented an opening to strike.

CHAPTER 2

An Introduction of One.

Xain Raeson stood with four wing leaders at a circular table in the briefing room. To his right was his long-time friend Amus Zekhal. He'd only ever seen the other three in passing. A holographic display rotated above the table, showing the positions of both friendly and enemy ships spread throughout a small asteroid field. Red blips represented the enemy vessels who lay in wait for an approaching pirate convoy.

'This is the situation,' said the Claw Commander assigned to the mission. Although the man gave his name, Raeson didn't bother to take notice.

The man stood opposite Xain, dressed in the standard colors of black and gray. On his left chest and arm, he wore the insignia of the Cygnian Pirates. It was an elismorus skull struck diagonally through by a sword. The man was slender with downward pointed ears, clearly a mixture of human and elismorus.

'We have leaked information to the enemy,' he said, clasping his hands behind his back, 'of a convoy travelling to the planet, collecting resources for the main fleet. The vessels contain a skeleton crew of courageous pilots with orders to detonate their cargo if the Rids get too close.'

Xain felt fire burning in his chest. *I can finally kill more Rids.* A century ago, the Heridian menace struck the Cygnian pirate homeworld of Cygnus.

There was no warning, and no sign that Cygnus would even be at risk. When the invaders attacked, only a local human fleet responded to the cries for help. The pirate fleet returned to a world ravaged by the monsters and after absorbing the remaining humans into their force, swore vengeance.

'If the convoy sacrificed themselves, what would be the explosion radius, Commander?' a wing leader asked, breaking his formal stance and leaning over the table.

'Approximately ten kilometers,' the Commander replied, raising an eyebrow. 'You will have enough time for your forces to evade.'

'Aye, sir, in that case we should have Raeson's wing at the rear. They will need the extra time to escape,' grinned another, laughing at his own joke.

'Or we could strap you and your teddy bear to a nuke,' Raeson replied with a smirk. 'I know which I'd rather see.'
With a stern look, the Claw Commander cut the man off from making another remark and continued his briefing.

'Your forces will position polar southeast of the convoy, deep in the belt to avoid detection. You will close in ahead of the convoy and attack before the enemy is ready to strike. This will mean fighting in amongst the rocks where the Rids are hiding.'

'It will be fun watching your pilots bounce around them, Raeson,' remarked another wing leader.

'I'm sure the deck crews could install bumper cushions to help,' said another.

Again, with the snide remarks.

Raeson pushed his anger down, being careful not to show any retaliation, and kept his face cold and expressionless. The corner of his mouth curled into a grin as he said, 'I'll make you a deal. You can take point and my wing and I will cover you.'

The color drained from the three wing leaders who knew Xain was serious and what he really meant.

If there had been no leadership in the room, Xain would have dealt with the insults in a darker and more satisfying way. The dead assassin floating in space would have some company.

'We will make sure the convoy is safe, sir,' one man said, giving his superior a nod and trying to shake off the embarrassment. 'Safer than the one Raeson's father abandoned, anyway.'

Raeson spun in anger only to have his arm grabbed by Zekhal, his friend who'd stood silently throughout the briefing. He stepped in between the men and looked into Raeson's fuming eyes.

'Xain, a fight here will not help you,' said Zekhal.

He was a level-headed wing leader and someone Raeson relied on. The pair had served together for most of their training before being promoted to wing leaders.

'You are right, as usual, my friend,' Xain replied, trying to calm himself.

Zekhal released Raeson's arm and gave him a smile.

'Short and sweet, eh Commander?' Zekhal asked playfully.

'When you get to command your own cruiser, don't waste time with idiots either. Plus, I'm too old to handle all of your bullshit.'

Xain couldn't help but laugh and wondered if he would ever reach that rank. He'd be lucky not to be demoted.

'Just remember, we are all here to fight Rids, not each other,' said the Claw Commander, motioning them to leave. 'Get it done.'

Xain gave the other men a death stare and committed their faces to memory. With the briefing over, he and Zekhal headed to the dock area to inspect their fighters and ready their people.

More insects to kill. Anyone who stands against me will suffer the same fate as the Rids.

*

It wasn't long before Raeson and his subordinates were secure in their individual craft and waiting for the command to launch. The WM-01 widowmaker was the preferred fighter of the Cygnians. With rapid thrust and high maneuverability, it proved that capital vessels were not always the answer. The ships were black with forward swept wings and a sleek fuselage edged in sleek paneling.

Positioned in a nosed down state and ready for release into the void, Raeson felt his heart thumping as he watched the stars below rush by. The canopies locked as the fighter's micro reactors pulsed energy into the ship's primary buffer. Raeson gave his orders over the comm to his wing, including a quick rundown on the mission ahead.

His pilots were used to a briefing on the go, but he knew what they really wanted was action. Being ship-side on the Cygnian flagship would drive any pilot stir crazy.

A monotone, digital voice echoed through the docking area. 'Bays pressurized, standby for launch.'

'Here we go, Reaper Wing, let's bury some Rids,' Raeson announced with enthusiasm. He felt centered and strangely at peace with his inner voices. Gripping the flight sticks in each hand, he caressed the triggers. He could feel his heart beating in his head, and it seemed to echo through his helmet.

'Releasing clamps. Antigravity engaged. Confirmed outer doors are open, launch, launch, launch.'

Their engines flared as the fighters burst towards the outer doors. Open space appeared quickly, and Reaper Wing was free of their mother-ship's launch bays.

Pulling back on his right flight stick, Raeson pressed his left foot pedal, causing his fighter to roll and invert. He drifted in a reverse direction and stared back at the fleet. Massive dark vessels moved together in formation like a herd of wandering behemoths. Smaller escort craft filled the gaps in between and the city size flagship, the *Wing of Vidar,* home to thousands of people, sat in the center.

Xain marveled at its sheer size and ran his gaze from the monstrous bow to the sharp wings of the stern. The binary stars behind the fleet covered the vessels in a hue of luminous blue, resembling ghostly apparitions sailing through the night.

'Beautiful,' Raeson whispered to himself, as he took a moment to admire the spectacle. 'Reaper Wing, form up on me,' he commanded over the comm.

After a moment, his subordinates positioned themselves behind in a staggered formation. It was a tactic commonly used to throw off the enemies' perception of range when looking from the front.

'The Sun's End corvette isn't far, so when it initiates translocation make sure you stay in close proximity. If you drift away, I'll leave you here to die. The other fighters to our starboard will join up with their own designated corvette and I don't want them showing us up, understood?'

His pilots knew Xain would leave them behind if needed and rescue craft weren't always available.

Translocation was a method used to traverse the void at great distances, the discovery of which was shrouded in rumors and hearsay. The most commonly accepted theory is it was invented by an unregistered group of scientists on the edge of known space.

Apparently hooking an antimatter reactor to a light switch was not such a great idea, and when the debris was finally found, multiple corporations had to reverse engineer it. They called it the Black Jack Drive, named after an ancient card game that used a similar principle.

It worked by injecting random amounts of energy into the power-banks, also referred to as a "hit". If a commander hit too many times, he or she risked overloading the drive, destroying their ship. Not hitting enough power meant risking a prolonged spooling of the drive. In an emergency, any delay could also be just as fatal.

Once the drive buffer reached full capacity, the energy would then create a field around the host vessel that, when activated, would alter its outer shell to an infinite mass whilst keeping its inner shell normal. The vessel would sink below and break through the fabric of space-time, entering what lay underneath, the spherical universe of non-existence.

By altering the mass of the field at certain points, the ship could shortcut through this spherical universe and re-enter at a different point. If smaller craft were in proximity to a vessel that was translocating, the field would expand and incorporate the additional mass. This made fleet travel much easier to co-ordinate, especially with fighter squadrons like Reaper Wing.

Raeson's wing comprised four other widowmaker class fighters, and were skilled, if not a little strange. They were pilots other flight leaders didn't want, the rejects and insubordinates. He sometimes wondered if that was the reason he commanded a wing, as many amongst the pirate leadership didn't like him.

The first pilot, Slin Naomoka, was regarded as an ace, and almost as skilled as Raeson. He was elismorus, with thin brown eyes and the customary pale skin. The man kept to himself and even though showed leadership potential, never wanted the responsibility.

Tektar Shahath, or Tek, the second pilot, received injuries during a battle years prior, resulting in numerous behavioral issues. An older man, he had a tendency to drift off, mentally absent, and sometimes even pass out. Raeson was reluctant to accept Tek's transfer but needed the numbers.

The third pilot was an elismorus female, Nashek Trian, or Nash. She was the daughter of a merchant and entered the pirate ranks under duress before proving herself capable.

Raeson couldn't get clearance on the fourth pilot. His name was Napier Stark. The man was a shady individual and hadn't earned Raeson's trust. Although an incredibly competent fighter pilot, he was a loner who often ignored commands.

Raeson glanced at his displays and noticed one of his pilots drifting out of position. *At least you idiots aren't boring.*

'You forget where the throttle is again, Tek?' Raeson asked.

'Not at all, sir, because it's a free for all!'

'Hold formation,' Raeson replied angrily. He felt this journey was long enough without the crazy antics of some out-of-date pilot, adding stress and extra time onto the mission.

'Sorry, Raeson, sir, I missed that,' Tektar said cheekily.

'Have you ever experienced latrine duty in zero gravity?'

'What? Ah... still can't hear you.' Tek throttled forward ahead of the formation, erratically rolling and flipping his fighter.

'I think he disabled his coms, sir,' Nash announced angrily. 'I'm going to follow and make sure he doesn't do anything stupid.'

'Confirmed, Nash,' Raeson replied and then, with venom in his voice added, 'Keep him out of trouble but don't put yourself in any danger. If you stray too far from us, let him go. I don't care for the antics of some drunken fool has-been and if he wants to fly away and die somewhere, then let him. Slin and Napier, re-form up on me, two-thirds throttle and watch for bandits.'

'But sir, we are the bandits,' replied Slin.

Raeson watched as the glow from Nash's engines faded into the distance.

*

Nash throttled her widowmaker forward, trying to close the gap between her and Tek. When she saw how far back Raeson was, she wondered if following the old man was a bad call.

'Slow down, you idiot!' yelled Nash over the coms. Checking her instruments, she received an identification and communications ping back from his fighter. 'I know you've enabled your coms.' She never had much tolerance for him. 'Seriously, I can smell the drink on you from here. Are you fueling your fighter with that rubbish?'

'What's the matter, can't the little elis girl keep up?' Tek replied, referring to the elismorus race of people. 'I thought you were good?'

'Keep talking like that old man, and I swear I'm going to ram one of these missiles up your tail.'

Nash activated her targeting reticule and centered the hologram over Tek's fighter. The color tone shifted to red briefly before resetting to the original shade of teal, confirming she'd lost the lock-on.

'Now that's not nice. I doubt you'll ever get a sight on me. In fact, let's find out.'

Tek slowed his fighter, rolled and flipped one hundred and eighty degrees, completing a full twist on the spot to face Nash, his pursuer. Tek accelerated, armed his weapons, and headed on a collision course.

'What are you doing!?!' Nash yelled as she felt her heart rate spike.

Two laser shots streaked past Nash's canopy, causing her to take evasive action. She jinked her craft to the side and narrowly missed the oncoming madman. Both craft rolled and circled each other, attempting to gain a firing sequence. Nash's blood was up and she wanted a taste of victory.

'You're not as bad as I thought,' Tek teased again.

'I'll show you exactly how good I am, you miserable Rid.'

Although neither pilot was in a winning position, Tek was getting what he wanted: a rise from the young pilot.

'Now little elis, no need to be insulting.'

Nash screamed with rage and violently yanked her flight stick back. Her fighter broke out of the entwined battle and shot off. She spun back into her previous position, hoping that Tek had lost her, so she could get behind him. Tek, however, reversed his trajectory and rolled to the side. Nash flew past, her velocity too fast to change course, and Tek rolled back in behind the woman.

'Tough break,' Tek said flatly. 'I wish you were better.'

'If the Rids' don't kill you,' Nash said, 'I will, and that's a promise.'

'That's big talk from you, girl. Maybe one day we'll see you fulfill it.' Tek broke off from his pursuit and slowed his fighter.

'Count on it,' Nash spat in disgust. She thought about continuing the chase until she noticed Raeson's fighter in the distance.

*

'This is Reaper, we have you on visual,' Raeson announced over the coms. He watched his two subordinates dueling below and felt relieved they hadn't killed each other. He took pause and wondered why such a feeling had crossed him, as the idea of worrying for another was a strange sensation.

'Copy that, Reaper,' Tek replied as he headed towards the incoming fighters. Nash trailed slowly behind, defeated, as they flew back into formation. 'Maybe you should all ease up sometime, you know, have a little fun?'

'I have a new game, Tek,' replied Raeson. 'It's called early retirement. Want to play? I'll even let you go first.'

'I think I'll take a pass on that one, sir,' Tek replied. 'Unless there's a prize, and that prize is alcohol, then I'm in.'

Raeson wondered if the man was even worth the oxygen. 'Report to me after the mission, if you're still alive.'

'Sir.'

'The co-ordinates are just ahead. We should be able to see the Sun's End soon.' Raeson said. His patience was growing thin and transferred into his voice.

'I have visual on the Sun's End,' Slin announced. 'I'm sending you its position now. Set your optical zoom to two-thousand.'

'Confirmed, Slin, I see it,' Raeson replied. He checked his displays and noticed Stark was hanging back. 'You've been quiet, Napier. Something troubling you?'

The comm crackled for a moment before Stark replied, 'No, sir, I'm all good. I just misjudged the velocity for a second.'

'Keep that up and I'll start thinking you're checking up on me.'

'Not a chance. I'm a team player, through and through,' Stark said.

'Was there a tone of sarcasm in there?' interrupted Slin with a chuckle. 'Don't think Raeson can't space you just because you're already in space.'

Stark laughed in reply, and for the briefest moment, Raeson wondered if Stark considered the comment a challenge. Better watch my back.

Reaper Wing sped towards the large vessel in the distance, creating a luminous scar across the midnight.

The *Sun's End* corvette appeared in focus, a long vessel of gray and burnt orange. Fins protruded down the length, with streaks of radioactive gas trailing behind. Reaper Wing positioned their craft alongside and prepared for external docking.

Capital ships always impressed Raeson. The immense bulk of the godlike vessels were such a remarkable sight, and truly comprehending their existence was impossible.

He touched his control stick gently and maneuvered his fighter underneath an extended docking clamp, a long mechanical arm with a claw at its end. Raeson watched the over-sized claw hook into his fighter's anchor points and felt a shunt from the locking systems. A voice spoke into his coms, notifying him of a successful connection, as the top half of his fighter was enclosed with a docking collar.

The stars vanished and left Xain with his thoughts.

I wonder if they'll ever find that dead assassin?

*

Further down the *Sun's End* and sitting in the darkness of his cockpit, Napier Stark began deleting his log files. His secret conversation had been heated, and even caused him to lose formation with Reaper Wing. There was no other choice but to comply.

Stark closed his eyes and began planning.

*

Demons screamed and clawed at his face.

Light from the alien sun washed his vision with crimson, transforming the color of his blood to an ash gray. The flashing of claws and teeth surrounded him as the creatures bit and tore into his flesh. The screaming grew louder as Draethus realized there were other victims. Struggling to turn his head, he forced himself to look at two other humans suffering the same fate. There could be no evil greater than this death, this consumption, and he was losing himself to it.

He woke up cold.

I've not dreamt that in a long time.

His head swam in a throbbing vertigo, and he was surprised to be still suffering the effects of the concussion blast. As his vision returned, Draethus realized he was not alone in the room. Someone was silently watching him from the corner.

Draethus tried to stand but was trapped in an anti-gravity field which restricted his movement. Someone had also removed his armor, so he only wore fatigues.

'I thought skydiving lessons were tomorrow,' he said to the stranger in the corner.

'It's called anti-gravity,' the man replied. 'Judging by your armor I expected you to be more sophisticated. I'm also impressed you have learned our language so fast.'

As the man moved into the light, Draethus saw he wore tight fitting, pale blue armor, with strange crests embossed into his shoulders. He spoke with an educated accent.

'I guess I'm just that smart. Who would have thought? If I was that intelligent, I could have vaporized myself better.' He tried flailing his arms about, which caused his body to rotate slowly so he faced the wrong direction. 'You mind telling me what's going on?'

The stranger laughed, unable to hide his surprise. 'You won't be able to break free of those bonds, my friend. Or should I not be calling you that?'

'This is an interrogation, so shouldn't you be answering questions?' Draethus asked with a grin.

Amused, the stranger said calmly, 'We have a lot of questions for you. If you co-operate, we'll release you and return your armor.' The stranger tapped Draethus' shoulder and increased his spin rate then continued. 'If we discover you're an ally, then I apologize for dishonoring you. My suggestion is that you answer the Specters' questions with as much honesty as you can tolerate. If you're an enemy, however, then you'll die and your gear is mine.'

'My armor is prettier than yours anyway,' Draethus said. Ignoring the cheeky comment, the stranger smiled abruptly, then turned and quickly left the room.

As the door slid shut, all noise in the cylindrical room fell silent. Draethus glanced around at his surroundings for anything he could use to escape, but saw none. The only way out was to play their game, whoever they were. His ears popped as the air pressure changed and he rotated upside-down.

The illumination from above shut off unexpectedly and in an instant, Draethus felt nauseous. When the lights returned, he was face to face with a ghost, a Specter that flinched backward as if surprised by what it saw.

'Surely my breath isn't that bad?' Draethus asked through clenched teeth.

The Specter floated a few feet off the ground, was broad, and covered in a black, ragged cloak with a hood covering much of its face. It shifted its gaze as if studying Draethus, before circling around him. Draethus glimpsed inside the creature's hood, which sent shivers up his spine. The Specter didn't have a face, but wore an aged white oval-shaped mask with a dark vertical line carved down the center.

His fear response made the creature pause, as if offended. From its hunched position, it arced back, then glided closer.

'What are you?' Draethus asked, replacing his fear with anger. The Specter raised a claw, triggering an electrical shock that blasted through Draethus. He screamed as his body went into a spasm.

'You will answer, but not ask,' the Specter replied with an icy whisper.

When the electrocution stopped, Draethus regained his composure and tried relaxing his muscles.

'Who are you?' asked the ghost.

Draethus couldn't help himself and replied, 'I'm your disembodied human.'

Electricity ran through him.

'Alright, alright,' Draethus laughed, noticing the pain fade. 'I'll play your little game. My name is Arcilous Draethus. I'm a Soldier of the Void and a protector of Echelon.'

'What is your purpose here?'

'To kill all who threaten us. You may have noticed the big ugly monsters burning the city?'

The Specter seemed to skim over his answers by asking the next question before Draethus could finish. He wondered if the ghost wanted information or just the pleasure of torturing him.

'How did you arrive on Echelon?' it asked.

'So this really *is* Echelon?'

Draethus screamed again as the electric shock intensified. He could see his skin smoking and smell his burning flesh.

The alien repeated the question, *'How did you arrive on Echelon?'*

'I don't know,' Draethus screamed. 'Some device transported me here.'

'What device?' the Specter asked flatly, the volume of its whisper increasing.

It raised its claw again, but Draethus interrupted. 'We found it amongst some ancient ruins, hidden in the jungle. I didn't have a choice and had to destroy it. If the Heridians got a hold of the technology…' The memory of those he sacrificed rose to the surface and it felt wrong to push it down.

The creature circled Draethus again and then darted forward, close to his face.

'What are Heridians?' it asked.

'Heridians are scum and deserve more than a painful death. If I could, I'd revive the menace and kill them again,' Draethus replied, gasping. 'They're some kind of biological machines that steal the minds of other creatures. We think it's their way to evolve and become smarter. They invaded Echelon, and we've fought them now for decades.'

'We?'

'We are SOV, an army of people dedicated to protecting others. We're from the other side of the stars, so we're not giving up.' Draethus almost let slip another question, but bit his lip.

The Specter continued to move around the room, swiftly darting and changed its position. Its long dark cloak shifted in an unseen and otherworldly breeze. The creature moved closer, its position and distance from Draethus relative to the seriousness and intensity of the question.

'How many more are you?' the Specter asked.

'Thousands.'

'Here and now?'

'No. I'm alone here. If you're nice to me, I might even take you out for a drink later.'

The ghostly Specter darted forwards, *'What is your motive?'*

A tingling sensation raced through his chest. 'My motive? I need to kill the Rids and find my way home. Maybe then the fallen will know peace.' He motioned towards the Specter. 'I'll kill anything that gets in my way.'

The Specter drifted back, paused, and stared at its captive before saying, *'Destiny entwines you with others.'*

The lights flickered, and the ethereal interrogator vanished.

'Because that wasn't weird,' Draethus mumbled.

'I would not tempt fate,' the stranger said as he walked back into the chamber. 'If it sensed you were a threat, it would still be here. Be thankful you're alive.'

'What was that apparition?'

'We're not really certain, but we call them Specters. The theory is they've been here all along.' The man walked up to Draethus and inspected his burns, and smiled. 'They make great interrogators though, which is their primary purpose here. But let's not talk about them, let's talk about you.'

Draethus tried to struggle free of his invisible restraints. 'How about you let me down and we'll see about talking?'

The other man laughed, 'Soon my friend, but first I have some questions of my own to ask you. There will be no electrocution this time, honestly.'

'Why not just let the Specter extract the information?'

'They get a little, shall we say, carried away? I can see that you hate these Heridians, as you call them. That makes you an ally from my perspective. Wouldn't you agree?'

Draethus stared at the man as he floated upside-down again.

And I'm supposed to believe you're sincere.

'You want my cooperation as well, then? I told that abomination the truth and I will carry out my word.'

'All on your own?'

'If need be, yes, by myself,' Draethus replied.

'I didn't take you for a fool. However, I will have your armor brought to you and we shall talk as equals, and hopefully, allies. Will you agree to hold off any hostilities until we have spoken further? I will even have the medical staff fix your wounds.'

Draethus was skeptical, but really had no other choice. 'I said I'd take the Specter out for a drink, not you.'

'I'll take that as a yes, then?'

Draethus nodded and replied, 'Just make sure I'm the right way up when you de-activate this thing.'

The stranger looked to the ceiling in acknowledgement, confirming Draethus' theory that he was being observed. He'd watched enough law enforcement vids back home to understand the process.

The door opened and a small lizard ran unsteadily into the chamber, holding Draethus' armor in its small claws. The creature was approximately three feet tall, covered in green scales that reflected the light, which turned shades of purple and orange. It fumbled with the items and at one point almost dropped it. Draethus noticed a scuff mark on the arm that wasn't there before and wondered if someone had been trying it on.

'I've seen these before,' said Draethus as the anti-gravity field lowered him to the floor.

'This is my servant,' the man said cheerfully. 'His name is Livant. I rescued him from the jungles far from here.'

'Rescued?'

'Yes, I found him in a hunter's trap. Was quite amusing actually, watching him swing from a tree with his foot caught in some rope. He was squealing like a banshee, so I think he was enjoying himself.'

'He was lucky,' Draethus said, putting on his armor.

'Quite right. Now, when you're ready, I have some things to show you.'

*

In the observation room above, two figures stood peering at Draethus through a one-way, transparent bulkhead. The taller of the two wore long, forest green robes that flowed from his shoulders. He broke the silence with a murmur.

'Sorry, sir, did you speak?' asked Tremon, the man responsible for Draethus' capture.

'I wonder if this soldier brought the enemy here intentionally,' said the robed man. He was the Great Senechal Praefectus, and responsible for all the residents of the Sky-Station.

'If so, I think the Specter would have extracted the information.'

The Senechal steepled his fingers on the one-sided viewing glass. 'Maybe so, but the Specter's reaction to the captive at the beginning worries me, especially since it said nothing. I hope it's not keeping anything from us.'

'I noticed that. I will speak to the Specter myself and try to piece it altogether.'

'Oh I see,' the Senechal said. 'So you can summon the ghosts on command, can you?'

Tremon felt foolish. *Of course, I can't summon the damn things. It's not like I have a direct line to them.* He looked to the floor and shook his head in silence.

'Thank you for the offer, Tremon, but I will speak to the interrogator myself.'

'I *was* the one to capture him. Have I not earned the right to follow this up?'

The Senechal gripped Tremon's shoulder and replied flatly, 'In normal circumstances, I would agree with you. However, we are losing to these invaders and need all the information we can get.'

'I understand, sir, but I won't just stand back and watch our city burn. If we discover he's an enemy, I'll dispose of him myself.'

'As you wish, Paladin Tremon. But know this: if you overstep the boundaries, I will see you punished. Do you understand?'

'I understand.'

The Senechal turned and swiftly left Tremon by himself. As the door closed, he glanced back to see Draethus exiting the interrogation chamber, followed closely by Livant, the small servant lizard.

'The coming days will be interesting,' Tremon whispered to himself. 'If my race perishes here, at the hands of this menace, I will make sure you die with us.'

CHAPTER 3

Skyward.

Raeson stirred from his deep thoughts as the docking engineer aboard the *Sun's End* spoke into his coms. 'Flight Commander Raeson, we are approaching waypoint and you are clear for release.'

'Confirmed,' Raeson replied. He shifted uncomfortably in his seat and adjusted the environmental controls for his cockpit. It was an automated system that most pilots wouldn't touch, but he preferred a colder setting to stay sharp and alert. 'This is Reaper, all wing begin dock release.'

His subordinates acknowledged the command, and the five widowmaker fighters de-clamped from their docking arms. Each craft fell away from the corvette as a tree would shed its leaves, drifting on invisible currents of the void. Lights flickered into existence, a burning fire followed by trails that ran across the night. The points of light maneuvered together, forming a five-pointed star that traversed as one.

Inside Raeson's cockpit, virtual arrows appeared on his H.U.D, or heads up display, showing a virtual direction that depicted a polar north and south. It was a form of spatial awareness the fleet used to coordinate flight formations. An enemy unit would appear as a red marker, and any friendly ships as blue. He activated a toggle switch and four faces appeared down the sides of his H.U.D.

'Now you have all heard the brief. Hopefully that little stunt of yours, Tektar, hasn't cost us any time,' Raeson said. 'We'll reach the south-east side of the planet in twenty minutes. When I give the order, I want you to disengage your thrusters and quietly drift in behind the asteroid field. The convoy will be a distraction and we'll engage the enemy once the Rids attack. Are there any questions?' He paused. 'Do you remember where your triggers are?'

He saw his subordinates laugh.

'That's these little red lever things, right boss?' Slin joked, twiddling his fingers.

'You should show your girlfriend those,' said Tek.

Anger burned across Nash's face. 'Just give me one reason, you decrepit old...'

The old man laughed and taunted Nash with a point of his finger. 'You've got a lot more than me to worry about, little girl. I doubt you'd last long, anyway.'

'You should concentrate on flying straight, Tek. Now let's kill some Rids,' said Slin enthusiastically.

'Got your back,' Nash said, blowing him a kiss.

'Just stay out of my way, all of you,' was Napier's only response.

Raeson laughed at the dry comment. 'Maybe we could throw your face at the Rids? We'd name it "The Ugly Sticky Bomb", you know, that thing you were hit with at birth?'

'I don't think you're supposed to talk to me like that,' Stark replied.

'I can't take it any longer,' said Xain. 'I have to switch to audio only.' He disconnected from the communication.

The faces on Raeson's display disappeared as he dimmed the illumination in his cockpit. He flipped the safety cap covering a switch on his critical system's panel and cut the engines. As his fighter glided silently through the emptiness of the void, he noticed tiny specks glinting in the distance. They hovered over the blue planet like a halo of fireflies.

He relaxed into his seat. What a sight, so calm and peaceful. It's hard to believe that evil lurks there.

Xain silently browsed over his ship systems. Flying widowmakers had been his dream for years, ever since watching his father fly them, before he disappeared. He thought back to his first solo flight in the widowmaker WM-00 trainer.

The rush of adrenaline as he raced down the launch tube for the first time, feeling the gravities press him into his chair. The exhilaration of being on your own, and the freedom of flight. He could fly anywhere and do anything.

Even with a speed limiter, however, just knowing the dark bird could kill you at any moment, was harrowing. It only took a single wrong turn, stray debris, mechanical fault, or any other variable to die.

Driven by redemption, Xain had a lot to prove and passed his training flights with ease. It didn't take long to be recognized, and he was given Reaper Wing early on.

The shadow of his father never left him, however, and none let him forget the betrayal. Raeson often wondered what rank he would hold now, if it hadn't been for his father. You can't change the past, he always told himself. But you can punish those responsible.

If my father were alive, where would he be right now?

Raeson often thought of such things.

Probably in some far distant exploration vessel, looking for the home-world of the Heridians. He always tried to convince people it existed. Not far to go now, the asteroid field is looking closer.

The menacing silhouettes of the Heridian ships appeared, like ancient creatures of abomination. The red glow of their powerful engines flared, blending into the glow from the world below.

'Almost,' he whispered.

The wing of widowmaker fighters approached quickly. Despite the craft's engines currently inactive, the group streaked through space like missiles approaching a target. Making minor adjustments to the controls, the fighter wing rolled inverted and skimmed past the first asteroid. Raeson could at last see the friendly convoy.

It was time.

'Attack,' Raeson ordered over his coms. 'All fighters engage. Stark, you're with me.'

The fighters split into two groups and targeted the nearest enemy craft. The micro reactors within the heart of each craft burned to life and pumped energy into the systems. Weapons hidden within the hull primed and ran through automated diagnostics as each pilot locked targets.

Holographic displays flooded Raeson's vision as the dark enemy took shape. Before the menace could react, a barrage of missiles slammed into their hulls. They ripped apart the first enemy ship; it burst into a ball of red flame as its ammunition and oxygen exploded, debris colliding into the nearby asteroids. The second enemy ship received a glancing hit but survived the initial attack. A trail of bright fire streaked across the darkness as the pilot ducked into a small cluster of rocks.

'He's mine!' Slin yelled as he engaged the throttle and burned after the wounded craft. His wingmen, Nash and Tek, did their best to keep up.

'Got your back, Slin,' Nash announced.

'Copy that, Nash. I would rather have your back,' Slin replied, transfixed by the target in his sights.

Nash giggled and put her fighter into a full throttle dive, trying to mimic the maneuvers Slin had gracefully performed. Slin expertly shifted out of his target's smoke trail and released a continuous burst from his main laser, trying to finish the job.

Meanwhile, Raeson and Stark repositioned and headed for the next target on the other side of the largest asteroid.

'The plan is working, sir,' Stark said over the coms. 'Only half the Rids are approaching the convoy. We've divided their forces.'

'Time for some payback. I'm in!' Tek shouted, rolling his fighter madly. He broke off from behind Nash and headed off towards the enemy on his own.

'I'm on your wing, Tek,' Stark announced.

'Copy, Stark, just make sure you hit the Rids and not me, got it?'

Stark said nothing, as silence was easier than getting into heated discussions. Raeson followed the two pilots but held back a distance to keep watch for any Heridians trying to outflank them. As the three flew over the asteroid, they discovered something unexpected.

'That's a big one!' Stark yelled.

'I told you not to eat those beans,' joked Tek, throttling forward.

Stark began an explanation, but Xain interrupted. 'Stay together and take on the enemy fighters, avoid the capital ship and stay out of its range.'

The Heridian vessel, which positioned itself in the middle of the fighters, was a frigate and much larger than the corvette *Sun's End,* which was already on its way back to the pirate fleet. The enemy vessel was blood red, with spines running the length of its body and armed with a myriad of weaponry. A predatory monster wasn't a target to be engaged by small fighters.

'Incoming on the right flank!' called Tek.

The three pirates banked sharply to avoid the incoming weapons fire from the Heridian fighters bearing down on their position. It was unavoidable, and Reaper Wing split up to focus on their individual targets. Raeson positioned behind two enemies and with a quick launch of void-to-void or VTV missiles, destroyed both. Wreckage and debris exploded in multiple directions, and before the explosion dissipated, he had already found another target.

An enemy was on Tek's tail, firing wildly, but to no avail. The pirate madly rolled and, throwing his fighter around the asteroid field, he evaded the incoming damage. Most people thought Tek was mad anyway, some even said he would prefer to be the target rather than the pursuer.

Tek's cockpit shook as an enemy exploded beside his ship, causing him to shield his eyes from the brightness.

Stark flew through the debris of the new wreckage and fired a missile at Tek's pursuer. The warhead streaked off into the darkness and hit nothing.

Tek rolled his fighter and frantically tried to shake the enemy off his tail. Again, the enemy fired its weapons as lasers skimmed past his cockpit and cut shards of metal from his fighter's armored plating.

Stark dove his widowmaker down and pulled up on the flight stick. Coming up from underneath the Rid, he fired a second missile, this time with success. The enemy on Tek's tail, his persistent pursuer, broke into three pieces and drifted off into the night.

Tek breathed in relief. 'I told you not to miss.'

'Be thankful that you're still here,' Stark replied in a flat tone. 'I'm sure you were having fun, though.'

Tek laughed, 'Maybe. I felt let down by the lack of explosion. Want to go again?'

Before Stark could respond, they were in a rolling and diving fight once again with yet more enemy fighters.

The Heridian frigate, its engines now a flare of burning exhaust, moved through the asteroid field toward the ongoing mass of entwined fighters. Raeson glanced out of his cockpit display, whilst being careful not to collide with an oncoming rock, and noticed enemy fighters docking, flying into large holes beneath the beast.

'The fighters are retreating,' he announced to his wingman. 'But the frigate is heading our way.'

'I say we take it on!' the old man shouted.

Raeson, although not one to retreat, knew when to pick his fights. 'Negative, Tek, we are ill-equipped to destroy the vessel. Our weaponry won't penetrate that much armor.'

'Sir, if we...' Tek replied before being cut off by his flight leader.

'Go ahead, Stark,' Xain asked.

'I'm picking up Slin's ejection beacon nearby,' Stark said.

'Slin, the mighty ace of aces, Slin Naomoka, shot out of the dark skies!? Ha!' Tek laughed.

'Shut it, Tek,' Raeson spat, his patience reaching an end. 'Lead the way, Stark. We need to get some distance between us and that frigate.'

The three pilots throttled forward, each dodging debris and rock alike. The enemy capital ship, although carefully navigating the asteroids, began disappearing in the distance.

'The pulse from the beacon is getting stronger, but I can't get a fix on his exact location,' Stark announced.

'Keep trying,' Xain asked. 'That frigate is not far away.'

His stomach felt sick with nerves, a sensation he was unaccustomed to. He altered his radar and hoped to receive the same signal that Stark was tracing before his coms crackled with static.

'Over there!' Stark yelled.

Rounding two chucks of rock that had recently clashed, the three pirates found Nash's fighter clinging to an asteroid. She had it anchored by reinforced titanium cables normally used to grapple enemy ships during boarding actions. Nash had left her ship, and attired in protective space armor, was investigating wreckage embedded into the rock.

'Nash, what's going on?' Raeson asked over the coms.

'They shot Slin down, sir. His ejection pod jammed as his ship crashed into this damn rock. I can't get him out,' the woman exclaimed. 'Raeson, my system says he's alive. Please help me, we can't abandon him.'

Stark's voice chimed in, 'The frigate is almost on us, and we have to go.'

'Nash, I'm ordering you to get back into your fighter. I'm going to have to blast him out.'

'What? But you might kill him,' she cried.

'Weapons armed.'

With the enemy closing, there was no other choice.

Nash hurried back to her fighter, sealed her canopy, and took off immediately. The flame from her engines exploded off the rock and she shot upward and away from her trapped lover. The hulking menace of the enemy frigate cast a shadow over the fighters and in a display of crackling electricity fired a massive beam that crashed into the asteroid, shattering it into large fragments.

'Break!' Raeson screamed into his coms, directed at the pilots under his command.

To his surprise that is exactly what the enemy frigate did. It broke, broke into thousands of tiny pieces as pulse cannons from behind ripped it apart. Fires, explosions, and debris launched away from Reaper Wing as the resulting shock wave rippled outward.

'This is the Dying Nova to Reaper Wing,' said a voice over coms.

'We copy Dying Nova. Thank you for the warning,' Raeson replied sarcastically.

The Talon Commander of the vessel continued, 'I would have you show more gratitude, pilot. But then I guess you are the son of that...' He didn't finish his sentence.

'Just pure luck then, finding yourself on the rear end of that frigate,' Xain said. 'Nothing to do with the convoy softening it up?'

The *Dying Nova,* whilst also being a frigate class capital vessel, was smaller than the frigate it had destroyed.

'We heard there was a capital involved,' said the Commander, 'and thought you made good bait. Luckily for you, the convoy managed to escape, so dock your fighters. We've killed a nice amount of Rids today.'

'Confirmed,' Xain replied before slamming his fist against the cockpit and said, 'Reaper out.'

'Sir, Slin's life monitor is still active. He must be still out there,' Nash announced.

'It's probably just malfunctioning, Nashy,' Tek said in a rarely heard sympathetic voice.

'You three dock with the Dying Nova. I'll spend some time searching and if I find anything I'll contact you. Just make sure you stay alert in case more enemy appear, understand?' Raeson ordered. He ran his eyes over the frigate that just saved him and his team and then said, 'Oh, and make sure that dust eater of a talon commander doesn't leave without me.'

Raeson swiveled his fighter and accessed his ship's sensors. If Nash were correct and Slin was alive, his beacon would still be active and locatable.

I may have to upgrade my sensors with life sign statistics.

Raeson never used them in the past, as they always seemed redundant. His pilots were dead or flying. Why worry about the in between?

His heads-up display, or HUD, chimed as it located the faint signal of an emergency beacon. It was a quiet notification in his ears and grew louder the further he maneuvered through the asteroid field. He jinked his fighter to avoid some debris and followed a wide arcing curve that led to the night side of a medium-sized rock.

After a while, his coms crackled. 'Raeson, I order you to dock with the Dying Nova. Why have you not complied?'

'Copy that, I'm returning now… wait, I can see Slin's ejection pod. It's damaged but intact.'

'Understood, Reaper,' the voice replied. 'Send us the co-ordinates and we will retrieve him.'

'Received and understood,' replied Xain. 'You are actually going to retrieve my pilot, aren't you?'

There was a pause over the channel before the voice replied, 'Of course, the retrieval team is on its way.'

Raeson felt a small amount of relief and turned his craft around. 'Docking now.'

Within minutes, a rescue craft had discovered Slin's emergency pod and taken it back to the frigate. Nash was waiting anxiously in the docking bay to see if he was still alive, surrounded by the medical team who rushed him away. With the mission complete, the *Dying Nova* translocated and headed for the main fleet.

*

As the doors opened, Draethus shielded his face from the glare and took a few moments to adjust his eyes. Hundreds of people were rushing in random directions carrying supplies, weapons, and equipment. A small red lizard carrying a pile of paperwork bumped into his leg and fell onto its back with a squeak. It stood up angrily, was about to attack the obstruction until it saw the height of Draethus, and decided against the idea. The creature quickly cleared up the mess and ran off, muttering under its breath.

Draethus smiled and with a curious look said, 'Interesting place.'

'Yes, I agree. Is it the same where you are from?' the stranger from earlier asked. He still wore the pale blue armor and Draethus wondered if he slept in it.

'No, we are more disciplined,' Draethus replied. 'Strange, though, we have a few of these lizard servant creatures. Can they fetch drinks as well?'

The stranger laughed and looked flustered. 'That *is* interesting, but no, they help where they can. Come, my friend, follow.'

The hall they walked was enormous, with white curved walls arching towards a clear tall ceiling. Intricate patterns and grooves snaked their way through pillars that stretched the full height of the area. Draethus noticed the blue sky beyond and remembered his youth, staring up at clusters of clouds slowly drifting on the warm breeze. Even as a soldier, he took the time to appreciate the beauty of his surroundings.

'Through here,' the stranger said.

'Are you ever going to tell me your name?' Draethus asked, feeling a little foolish he hadn't asked earlier.

The stranger nodded, smiled, and kept walking.

The two men entered through another door. It hissed open automatically as they approached, and a gush of hot and muggy air washed over Draethus. He rushed forwards and stared out over the balcony.

'How am I still on Echelon?' Draethus asked. 'My people should be here, not whatever you are.'

'I suspect it has something to do with the displacement device you mentioned during your interrogation. Maybe you're a distant time traveler here to make me rich?' The stranger grinned, then said, 'There is a person who can help.'

'Then we must go,' Draethus said, eager for answers.

The stranger held up a hand. 'In good time. My reason for bringing you here is for something different.'

The nameless man looked out over the balcony and took a moment to take in the sight. The fortress they stood on floated two kilometers above the surface.

'Look out further beyond the jungle below, out towards the city,' the man asked.

Draethus pressed a button on the neck of his armor that activated his helmet to flip over and cover his head. It clamped shut to seal him inside, then activated optic sensors and zoomed in on the horizon above the tree line. 'Those are the buildings I found myself in a few days ago. They're still burning,' he said.

'That's right, the Heridians have taken the city. We've lost many troops and the civilian population is all but wiped out. The only question I have for you, warrior, is where did you and this menace come from and why?'

'Like I answered the interrogator,' Draethus started. 'The Heridians invaded our world, the Echelon where I am from, and we have been at war ever since. I was guarding a device hidden inside some ruins when the Rids attacked. They breached all our defenses and killed everyone in my squad. I was the last standing.'

'So how did you end up in the city?'

'Before the attack, one of our technical staff told me where to place explosive charges on the device to do the most damage.'

'You intended to detonate this device even though it would cost you your life?'

'I have incredible life insurance,' Draethus shrugged.

'I have no idea what that is,' said the stranger.

A man carrying equipment walked onto the balcony, saw it was occupied, tipped his head in apology and retreated by closing the door behind him.

The stranger returned the politeness then continued, 'So you were successful in activating the device?'

'If by activating you mean blowing myself up along with a Rid detachment, then kind of,' Draethus replied. 'All I remember is a blinding light, roaring noise, and then it was like every particle in my body was being ripped apart. The next thing I recall, I was in the city surrounded by screaming civilians, Heridians and that robot that brought me here.'

'So you brought the enemy here?'

Draethus marveled at how far away the surface was below and sighed, 'It was not my intention, stranger.'

There was a silence between the two warriors. The stranger looked into the glowing green eyes of Draethus' helmet but could not see the warrior's face.

'What will your superiors do when they find out I'm responsible?' asked Draethus.

The stranger let out a sigh and shrugged his shoulders. 'I don't know, my friend. Some will hate you for it because we have lost our city, not to mention the casualties.'

'And the others?'

'They will see you as an ally against this enemy and will request your help, I would imagine.'

'I understand, so there is still hope of a resolution.' Draethus disengaged his helmet and let it fold back into his armor. 'If I help you defeat this menace, will you help me return?'

'That is what I had planned. May I refer to you by first name?' the stranger asked.

'My name is Arcilous Draethus. You may refer to me as the latter,' he replied, looking down at his new comrade. 'You have helped me so far, and for that I am grateful. What is your position here?'

'I am a Paladin Captain in the Home Guard Legion. At the Great Senechal's request, I am to retrieve as much information from you as possible. Primarily, I need to learn the enemy's weakness.'

'I see, and your name?'

'My name is Varican.'

'Varican?' Draethus said in surprise.

'You look shocked. Do you know this name?'

'I do. Although I have never met him, there is a Soldier of the Void with that name.'

'That is interesting, warrior Draethus.'

'Draethus will be fine, Captain.'

Varican laughed, 'As you wish, Arcilous Draethus. Now we need to locate a scientist by the name of Spectalin. With the information you possess, we may discover some answers. It will be an excellent opportunity for you to share any Heridian weakness that you are aware of and of course their tactics.'

'Understood, Captain Varican. Lead the way.'

Varican took one last look over the balcony. The massive fortress, floating in the sky, could make one feel small amongst the many wonders of Echelon. Far below the Sky-Station, on the distant horizon, the fires in the city still burned. Smoke belched clouds of darkness and turned the beautiful Echelon into a twisted, nightmarish creation.

'If it's alright with you, Arcilous Draethus,' he said in a less enthusiastic tone, 'our commander would like to meet you.'

'You called him Senechal, correct?' Draethus replied, joining Varican in watching the atrocities happening in the distance.

'That's right, Great Senechal Praefectus.'

'That would be an honor, especially if he's willing to forget the hitchhikers I picked up along the way.'

'I wouldn't count on that,' Varican replied with a chuckle. 'If you're lucky, he might feed only half of you to the reptiles in the jungles.'

'My upper half is the nicest.'

The two warriors walked back through the corridors of the Sky-Station. Their conversation became lighter with brief mention of the stressful events that had taken place since the enemy had arrived.

'You spoke of a blinding light before?' Varican asked.

'That's right. I would think the city illuminated in the same manner when I arrived?' Draethus was curious to know where his new friend was going with his question.

'When you first arrived,' Varican said inquisitively, 'there were multiple flashes of light as more of the menace appeared in the city, but not all at once.'

'As the device affected us simultaneously, I assumed we arrived together. Maybe we shared the end destination but at variations in time.' Draethus was careful to not injure any of the people that were rushing around him. 'When I appeared here, the battle had already begun, so that would make sense.'

'It was the light itself that makes me curious,' said Varican, waving at someone he knew in the crowd. 'I'm sure that I have seen it somewhere before.'

CHAPTER 4

Intentions of Matter.

Standing on the deck, high above the docking bay, the Great Khan, leader of the Cygnian Pirates, gazed upon the small fighter entering his vessel. He had been in command of the pirate forces for decades, and the fury of his people's slaughter drove him onward with a passionate hatred. Single-minded, meticulous and utterly obsessed, the Khan had led his fleet to rampage any foe that stood before them. The Heridian menace was the enemy at the forefront of his mind, as no other threat could match such a malicious race. He stepped away from the window and ran his hand through his dark beard.

'Have that pilot report to me immediately,' he said over his coms, using a small communication device that clipped on his lower jaw.

'Yes, my Lord,' a voice replied.

'So, what of my son?' a female voice from the corner spoke out to him.

'I have further plans for your son.'

'You always have plans, Alexon Hayreddin, even before you were the Khan,' she replied.

The pirate Khan laughed, stretched out his hands and placing them on the woman's shoulders. 'That is the reason I lead the fleet, Zelene Raeson.'

He took a step back and looked into the elismorus woman's icy white eyes. Even though she was at least eighty to ninety years old, she still looked young and vibrant. Hayreddin had known the woman from the time he was a fighter pilot and had competed for her affections many times. However, she chose another.

'Some despise your son amongst the pirates. I wish to put him in a position of power so he can earn their respect.'

'Few will follow him into battle.'

'You are right, Zelene. But with each successful mission he has achieved, I have no reason not to give him a greater command.'

'Like his father?'

The Khan nodded and then said, 'There is a corvette in the fleet that needs a good crew and I think it would be a way for him to earn some respect from the fleet.'

The older man walked over to the viewing window and folded his hands behind his back. The vessels outside were repositioning themselves into a unique formation, whilst smaller ships raced past the view port and began docking.

'We both know what the associate did for this fleet and the sacrifices he made. It is unfortunate that Xain has to pay the price for it,' said the Khan.

Zelene dropped her head and stared at the floor. 'Yes, I live with that price and it's better Xain live with his, the way he does.'

'He will be here soon. You should leave.'

'As you wish, Alexon, and thank you.'

'Thank you?' the Khan said, confused.

'Yes, for helping my son when most would not have.'

'If most men were like me, there would be too many Khans, yes?'

Zelene gave a little laugh, turned, and left.

*

Slin was still. His body was in agony as he lay on the medical recovery bed. He gradually opened his eyes and tried to let light in from the ceiling above. Something stirred next to him, followed by a muffled voice.

'Slin, are you awake? Slin?' said the voice.

His lips were dry and all he could manage was the word, 'Who?'

'It's Nash, it's me.'

'Nash, what happened? I remember going after a Rid but…'

'Another Rid hit you from the flank. It doesn't matter now, you're safe. I was so scared that we'd never find you.'

'I can't feel all of my body,' he replied as he peered under the sheet.

Slin had seen many atrocities in his life, but what the Rids inflicted was incomparable. His body was a mess, skin torn from muscle, and he barely recognized himself. Cybernetic enhanced limbs had replaced his arms and left leg, and his skin had begun to grow over them.

'This can't be,' he said in horror. 'My face, I can't touch my face.'

Nash quickly leant over him.

'It's alright, there's no damage there. They did have to replace your eye, though. It was full of shrapnel from the canopy.'

Slin tried again to move his new arms. 'Were we successful? Did the convoy survive?'

'Yes. Don't worry about the details. For now, you need to rest.'

She stood over him and gently placed her hand on his chest until his eyes closed and relaxed. The floating orbs at the head of his bed dimmed to a soft light to signal that he was falling asleep. When the light completely faded, Nash gave him a kiss on his forehead and sat back down in the chair beside him.

'Rest my Slin, tomorrow will be a hard day.'

*

The small lizard jumped to another desk as the scientist, Spectalin, chased after him, trying to hit the reptile with his long measuring device.

'You annoying little creature!' he yelled. 'Stand still so I can swat you!'

Livant, the name given to the lizard, giggled, and hissed in hysterics as he bounced around the room holding the plans that Spectalin had been working on. Livant jumped to the top of a bookshelf at the end of the room and hopped from foot to foot. Sticking his forked tongue out, the creature taunted. Spectalin gave him a death stare and felt like he was going to explode. He darted over to the bench and with a heavy gasp, picked up an oversized rifle that he'd been working on. He flicked a switch, and it began charging. Spectalin's face changed to an evil smile.

With his finger poised on the trigger, he took aim, but was interrupted as the door burst open, making Livant yelp. In a snowfall of paperwork, the lizard threw the plans on the floor and jumped down onto the shoulder of the visitor.

'It seems I was just in time,' Varican said with a smile, looking across at his small servant creature cowering behind his head.

'He stole my plans, Varican. He's always stealing my things!'

'He means no harm, he's just being… playful.'

'Well, I was about to be… playful,' Spectalin replied as he struggled to lift the rifle back on the bench.

Draethus stepped into the room and watched the scientist struggle with the enormous gun. He walked over and with one hand, lifted the weapon from the white lab coated man and gently placed it on the bench.

'That armor? You're the man who appeared with the creatures in the city, right?' Spectalin took a step back to admire the soldier.

Draethus walked over to a large blueprint encased in glass that hung on the wall, and closely studied its contents. 'You studied my armor?' he asked.

'That's right, during your interrogation. I was trying to determine where you came from and if we could benefit from the technology,' Spectalin replied as he slid a finger over the top of his glasses. 'The blueprints you see on the wall are my findings. I guess you could shed some light on how close I am in the design.'

Draethus grunted, 'It may as well be a map to my heart.' Taking his armored glove off, he touched the glass and said, 'It feels cold enough, but who knows?'

'Oh, I see,' Spectalin said, disappointed. He hoped with the soldiers' co-operation he could discover more about the design and technology.

Livant hopped onto a desk, picked up a shiny tool and examined it with great fascination. The halogen from above created a reflection in the lizard's eyes. Spectalin watched him intensely, was about to leap after the little creature before Varican waved his attention back and continued speaking. 'We are about to meet with the Senechal soon and before I do, I would like some answers first.'

After a brief pause, a second death stare aimed at Livant, Spectalin responded. 'Of course, I am as curious as anyone about the matter.' He turned to Draethus, and looking up, he introduced himself.

'My name is Spectalin. I'm the lead scientist and research developer here on the Sky-Station. You can refer to me as "Spect" if you like.'

'This is Draethus,' said Varican.

'Are you the only scientist here?' Draethus asked, ignoring the introduction.

'At the moment I am, all the other scientists are down on the surface, working on the machine. Well, they *were* working on it,' he said. He turned away and his shoulders dropped. 'They are probably dead by now, though.'

'Heridians,' Draethus said.

'Is that what you call the creatures you brought back with you? I haven't viewed your interrogation logs yet, so I'm a little behind on the latest news.'

'What machine are you talking about?' asked Draethus.

'We are calling it the Chronological Displacement Device,' replied Varican.

'Displacement Device?' Draethus repeated as he motioned forward, taking the others by surprise and causing them to retreat a step. 'You mean to tell me, you have known all along what brought me here? If the Rids capture that machine, they will have access to anywhere of their choosing!'

Varican held his hand up and interrupted, 'The machine is not complete, and the enemy cannot use it. We are still wondering if you appeared here through the device, even though it's inactive.'

Draethus straightened and looked down at the two. 'If this machine is the same, then we have to destroy it now.'

'It doesn't operate,' Spect added. 'I've been overseeing the development of the device and it's not even close to complete. What I need from you, Draethus, however, is the details of where you came from.'

Reaching into his armor, near to where his helmet folded into his back, Draethus pulled out a slim crystal. It was pale green and illuminated at his touch. 'This is a low-grade mapping unit of Echelon and the surrounding star systems. Maybe you could use this and figure out what you need.'

'That's perfect!' Spect exclaimed before asking, 'Where did you appear?'

'He was in the city,' Varican interrupted.

Draethus handed over the crystal and said, 'It seems likely that I am from your future, and you may have triggered my displacement. If you need to know when that is, well, you have fun with that. Otherwise, I want to know your plan to destroy the device and how to help me return. If the Rids get it working, they will have access to more innocents.'

'What makes you think you're from the future and not our past?' asked Varican.

'The Sky-Station is different here. You could lick the walls with how clean it is, and it's undamaged.'

Spect gasped and asked, 'Why would you lick the walls and how is it damaged?'

'Let's just say that something big took a chunk out of it at some stage, but that was before we settled here.'

Varican collected his lizard, turned and walked out the door. 'We need to go.'

'I guess we'll see what this great leader has to say,' Draethus said.

*

It wasn't long before Draethus and Varican were nearing the home command of the Senechal. The two men walked along a large walkway suspended by giant black rails above the key area of the marketplace.

Dark transparent marble covered the floor and as Draethus looked down, he noticed other walkways branching in multiple directions, flooded with hundreds of busily rushing people.

The pair walked off the gantry and approached a door guarded by two soldiers standing on either side. Draethus made note of their armor, heavy and covered in pictograms. One soldier held a large axe weapon which connected to his armor via a cable. The other was armed with a laser rifle Draethus had seen equipped on similar men along the way.

'I am here to see Great Senechal Praefectus as requested by the Senechal himself,' Varican announced to the guards as he put his arm across his chest in a salute like gesture. The guard held the Paladin Captains' gaze then spoke. 'You have authorization. Proceed.'

They walked through and, as the door closed, the elevator quickly ascended. Looking up, Draethus could see the destination through the transparent ceiling.

'It's quite the sight, don't you think?' Varican asked, staring out of the clear walls.

'The Sky-Station contains wonders and secrets,' Draethus replied, staring out in the same direction. 'I've spent years exploring the many walkways and passages. It's hard to imagine this pristine structure is the same fortress I know.'

'What is the station like where you are from?'

'Much the same, but like I said, different.'

'I believe you,' Varican stated. 'Seems hard to believe, but time would explain the cosmetic differences, if it has aged like you say. What of us, however? Is there any sign about what happened to the civilization here?'

Draethus paused and considered how much information he should keep to himself. If he divulged too many details, it may affect future events. He instead turned to face the curious man. 'If you tell me what the Senechal needs from me and what I am to expect, I'll answer your questions. Then again, I do like surprises. Except my twelfth birthday when I asked for a pet dinosaur. That thing had seriously sharp teeth and I think it ate someone.'

Varican's expression betrayed a little shock as he considered the proposal. 'I am a negotiable person, so why not? The Senechal is in charge of the Sky-Station and also the world below. He is going to want information from you about this new enemy and if there's more.'

'I told you what I knew in the interrogation,' Draethus added with a frown.

'Yes, however, the Senechal has a way of finding out… more from you. I don't mean that threateningly, just that he is our leader for a reason. I believe he wants guidance on how to beat this threat. He knows you are not one of them.'

The elevator neared the top level and Draethus could sense Varican wanted to finish the conversation.

'Why not bombard them from orbit? I saw space faring vessels in the docks on the way here,' Draethus asked.

'Those vessels are nothing but transports, merchants trying to make a living. Even if we could convert one into a warship, an accidental hit on the device could have dire consequences.' The elevator came to a halt. 'We've arrived. Please leave the talking to me at first until the Senechal asks you to speak. We will talk later about my query.'

The elevator doors opened into an expansive circular area bordered by tapestries and arcane statues. Draethus noticed Paladin soldiers in formal stance against the walls, armed with a variety of projectile weaponry.

As he stepped forward, the walkway beneath illuminated with elegant symbols that traced his feet. When he glanced to the ceiling, Draethus knew exactly where he was. In his time, the room was used as the gardens, a place where people could mix, socialize, and enjoy a relaxing moment away from the war. Even though there were no plants or fauna now, he felt calm as someone walked into the center from the outer edge.

The first thing Draethus noticed was the newcomers' heavy forest green robes, inlaid with golden thread that wound its way down into interesting symbols. Large ornate buttons held the cloak together offset from center and reminded Draethus of an ancient warrior knight or king. A shrouded collar surrounded the older man's face, and he guessed him to be around fifty years of age. It had to be the Senechal.

'So, you're the one causing us all this trouble?' the Senechal said, his voice booming around the room.

A second man walked up from behind the Senechal, attired in similar armor to Varican except white with black edging. His iconography was simpler and sparse.

Varican bowed to his leader then said, 'I'd like you to meet Arcilous Draethus, my Lord.'

'I'm sure the pleasure is mine, of course,' the Senechal said. 'Have you anything to say?'

Draethus cleared his throat and answered, 'I like your coat.'

A soldier behind a tapestry giggled, which earned him a harsh look from the white armored man, followed by instant silence.

'Indeed,' the Senechal said. 'But we are not here to discuss fashion.'

'Why are we here?' Draethus asked. 'With respect,' he said, nodding his head slightly, 'I told your strange interrogator everything I know. As honored as I am to meet you, it feels pointless rehashing everything.'

'You will address Senechal Praefectus as "Lord" when you speak,' said the other man with disdain.

'How nice, you have a little minion,' Draethus said. The man's face turned to fire and Draethus could tell he was spoiling for a fight.

'That is quite enough Tremon, you are my new bodyguard, not my spokesperson,' the Senechal replied, adjusting his collar.

'How did you like the concussion shot?' Tremon asked Draethus. 'Want to go another round?'

Draethus laughed and replied, 'So it was you in the robot. I should have known. Is your cockpit tinted to hide your ugly face or do you pilot that thing because you're compensating for something?'

He could see Tremon's nostrils flaring.

'I wish I'd used the artillery gun now.'

'Do you make a habit of stunning men unconscious and dragging them home?' Draethus grinned.

Tremon angrily lowered his head as his Lord silenced them with outstretched hands.

'We are here to discuss solutions to the monsters plaguing our borders, not infighting,' the Senechal stated.

'The solution would be to nuke the monsters from orbit,' said Draethus. 'Though that may be bad for the future of Echelon.'

'Ah yes, the future,' the Senechal said. 'I don't completely believe in your claim of time displacement. The idea of something or someone shifting through time sounds ridiculous.'

'As ridiculous as a ship translocation beneath the fabric of space, only to reappear, incomprehensibly, in another area of the galaxy? I'm no scientist, but it sounds plausible to me,' Draethus said.

The Senechal grinned and with a slight nod replied, 'You make a good point. But there is the other matter of who you are exactly. Do you expect me to take your word that you're one of these... what did you call yourselves?'

'Soldier of the Void.'

'That's right, a SOV, for short. Now I remember.'

Draethus felt he was being manipulated, and the Senechal was smarter than he projected. You don't command an army of Paladins and rule over an entire world by being stupid. 'Let's just cut right to it, Lord Senechal. What exactly do you want from me?'

The Senechal laughed deeply and eyed the Paladins around the room. 'This man is direct. If only I had more people like him. You are right, there is something I want from you. I desire you to take these evil creatures back through the device and leave us.'

'That isn't something I have control of,' Draethus said. 'I'm here completely by accident and was hoping you would help me return.'

'In exchange for?'

'My help fighting the Heridians,' Draethus replied.

The Senechal approached Draethus with enthusiasm, causing the Paladins around the room to step forward and raise their weapons.

'And what help can a single man do against the enemy? Did you help your former people against them by bringing them here? Are you someone so special that you can annihilate the threat with a click of your fingers? What good have you even done for your people?'

The last question sent a pang of regret through Draethus as he pictured the faces of his squad and science team that perished at his orders. 'I wanted to do more.'

'Good intentions do not win wars, Arcilous Draethus. The only reason we haven't executed you, apart from being the good-natured people we are, is I see a genuine intent to fight the enemy.' The Senechal clasped his hands behind him, glanced down at the floor, then said, 'Do you know how long we have been on Echelon?'

Draethus shook his head.

'We settled here, centuries ago, on a colony ship from the origin planet. In fact, you are standing on the remnants of that ship, repurposed into the Sky-Station. A people will always face hardships, but the one you have brought down on us, I fear, will be the end. What you can do is explain every Heridian weakness and help formulate a plan to send them back.'

'It was my intention to blow up the Rid's, not send them back to hurt my people,' Draethus stated.

'But it is acceptable for the enemy to murder ours?'

'No, of course not. I never intended to even survive. But now the Rids are in control of the device and if they get it working…'

'They will have access to anywhere and anytime of their choosing, if in fact it can displace people through time. How will you prove yourself to me?' asked the Senechal. 'What are you going to do to make things right?'

Draethus didn't hesitate and replied, 'Give me some soldiers and we'll destroy the device. It's the only way.'

The great leader laughed and said, 'You haven't earned my trust, yet you expect to lead my people? Tell me, was exploding yourself your plan or are you just dim?'

Tremon sniggered and seemed satisfied that Draethus had said something foolish.

The Senechal looked at Tremon, and with a wide grin said, 'I think you should lead a team to destroy the device. It won't kill them all, but at least we can limit their capability.'

'I'd be honored, my Lord,' replied Tremon. 'I think an aerial insertion would be best, so we don't have to break through the lines.'

'I agree,' the Senechal replied. 'Draethus seems to want to prove himself, so take him with you.'

Tremon was about to object, but the Senechal cut him off. 'Show him the drop fighters and pick out volunteers for the insertion. You cannot fail at this, do you understand?'

With a grimace, Tremon acknowledged the command, then to Varican said, 'Please show him to the bays and I'll join you soon.'

'Of course,' Varican replied.

'Thank you, Lord Senechal,' Draethus said. 'I will make this right and avenge the fallen.'

Draethus and Varican headed for the elevator and once out of earshot of the Senechal, Varican asked, 'Did you really have a pet dinosaur, and did it actually eat someone?'

As the doors closed, Draethus watched Tremon in a heated discussion with the Senechal, then replied, 'His teeth were tiny and blunt, but I woke up to find him gnawing on my arm once.'

'Adorable.'

*

'Is this a good idea, my Lord?' Tremon asked as his sandy hair flicked across his face. 'I don't trust him, so don't be surprised if he doesn't make it back.'

'What matters is that you secure the device,' the Senechal replied. He watched the elevator doors close and said, 'I need you to do something for me in the meantime.'

'I am at your command.'

'The device was reverse engineered from what appeared on the dock many years ago. You know of this, I expect?' The Senechal gazed sternly into Tremon's eyes as he continued. 'I need you to assign a detachment of men to reinforce the docks. If the planet side device is important to the enemy, then I suspect what we are guarding is as well.'

'As you wish my Lord Senechal. There is no way for the creatures to reach the Sky-Station, is there? And should we keep this information from the newcomer?'

'I don't know what to expect from Draethus, so for the moment just focus on the mission ahead. As for the monsters, the creator only knows their potential. It is possible for the enemy to capture the lifters and maybe even figure out how to operate them.'

'Understood,' Tremon finished. He bowed and left for the drop bays, daydreaming about killing the monsters. It wasn't just Draethus who had something to prove.

CHAPTER 5

Craft of Despair.

Of the many wonders in the universe, the pirate flagship was among the greatest. Tens of kilometers across and twice in length, it silently slipped through space, dark sails extended, capturing the solar energy from a nearby sun. Known by many names depending on which world it plundered, other races learned to fear it.

To the pirates it was the heart of the fleet, the *Wing of Vidar,* and the center of military force. An undermined class of capital vessel, hybrid carrier, super dreadnought and world ship, it bristled with thousands of weapons and could hold a myriad of fighters and escorts.

Raeson gently maneuvered his fighter using holographic docking lines displayed in his eyes, generated from small lasers attached to his helmet. As he shifted the control stick, the lines displayed his course and suggested correction. In the distance, he could see the docking bay doors of the great ship open, ready to receive his widowmaker.

'This is Reaper to dock 412, I am on course, and estimate time of arrival is one minute. Do you receive?'

A lively feminine voice, full of energy, replied over the coms. 'Raeson is that you? I was wondering when you would come back and visit!'

Raeson smiled to himself as the voice triggered memories of his childhood friend. They were both inducted into the pirates together but followed different paths after being assigned different roles. Her name was Rel, and she had always loved the mechanical working of machines, following the technician path, as opposed to Raeson who chose the fighter pilot.

Raeson spoke into the coms again, 'Rel? What is a tech doing answering a docking call?'

'The docking chief got called away, and I was the only one available to take command... me taking command, strange don't you think?' Rel replied.

'As long as you don't close the doors on me, I'm sure you'll be fine.'

The coms crackled again as Rel continued, 'I've changed a lot, I'll have you know, and that was an accident! Anyway, your path and trajectory are confirmed, and you have the all clear to dock.'

'Acknowledged,' Raeson replied.

His fighter slipped through the open doors and into an enormous open area filled with bustling activity and hundreds of craft. As he flew parallel with his designated dock, the guiding lights changed, went blue, and four large docking clamps dropped down, connecting with the craft. Pulling the fighter closer, it clicked into place, and on a rail, carried Raeson further into the pirate flagship.

Raeson could see light emanating from the far end of the tunnel as the mechanism paused, then diverted ninety degrees sideways towards his destination. The robotic arms extended again and placed the ship in the docking bay, lowering it down to the platform below.

He popped the canopy and before he could finish climbing down, Rel greeted him with a big hug, which almost threw him to the ground.

'Still the same Rel, I see,' he said.

'Still the same brooding warrior, I see,' Rel teased back.

She wore olive drab technician clothes that looked old and worn, with grease and oil covering her skin. Despite her attire, the male crew of the ship regarded the girl with affection. She was half human and elismorus like Raeson himself, except with ears and facial features more human than his. Long, bright red hair flowed behind and down the sides of her ears, with a fringe covering soft eyes. Headgear, comprising a microphone and optical lenses, poked through the long strands.

'I can't believe you still have the hair,' Raeson said, pulling away from her arms. 'Surely it's clogged enough air intakes by now?'

'No, smart guy, they let me keep it. I'm not really sure why, though,' she replied curiously.

'Give it time. We'll have to get together after my meeting,' he suggested.

'What is the meeting about?'

To her surprise, Raeson tapped her cheek twice. He knew it irritated his friend, and only he could get away with it. 'I've not been told, probably something connected with the last mission. So how did you end up on the Vidar, anyway?' he asked, changing the subject.

'They transferred me here after a minor incident I had with a commander. He was escorting the vessel I was on.'

'Really?' Raeson replied, his grin growing with every word.

'Don't look at me like that, Mr. Broody, I can shoot down anything that's in front of me.' It was common knowledge that Rel had a fiery temper and to run if it was directed at you.

'And behind and next to me,' he said with a grin.

'You love this a little too much, I think...' Rel stopped mid-sentence as Raeson held his hands up as if surrendering.

'Well,' she continued. 'This commander ordered his men to take off from the docking bay in an emergency scramble, even though half of the ships were not ready. Some were barely even functional.'

'I think I know the commander you speak of,' added Raeson.

'I wouldn't let some rookie pilots die because of a power stupid commander, so I gave him a piece of my mind, and my fist,' she said, holding her fist up in rage.

'And the big heavy tool you were using, I heard,' replied a voice, walking up behind the two laughing.

'Zekhal, my friend!' Raeson exclaimed, turning to greet his long-time comrade at arms. The two mutually clasped each other's wrists and shook hands.

'Good to see you too,' Zekhal said. 'They sent me to escort you to see… someone.'

Rel spoke up again, never one to be quiet. 'Good to see you as well Zekhal, who are you going to see?'

Zekhal turned, looked down on Rel and just smiled, knowing she would understand what his silence meant.

'Alright,' she said. 'Just come and see me before you leave Raeson, you promise?'

'I promise Rel, I *will* come and see you.'

'You better, because I haven't cooked for anyone in a long time.'

'I haven't had food poisoning in a long time,' Raeson joked. Raeson and Zekhal left quickly, avoiding her gaze, and expecting a flying tool that never came. As they exited the docking bay, Raeson turned and watched as Rel began working on his ship. He knew she would check over every molecule of his fighter to make sure it was safe.

A short while later, Raeson and Zekhal stood at the doors leading to Khan Alexon Hayreddin's strategic observatory. The room was reserved for tactical planning and official meetings, and it was unlike the Khan to summon a pair of flight leaders. As the steel doors slid open, they were instantly met with a battle-hardened gaze, and both silently stared down at the floor.

'You may enter,' the Khan bellowed, his voice deep.

'My Khan,' the men said in unison.

'You are wondering why I summoned you both, yes?' the Khan said.

He tilted his head in curiosity and with a low snigger said, 'So you've heard that looking into my eyes will turn you to stone?' Raeson stuttered as he tried to speak before the Khan continued. 'For creator's sake, stop acting like a bunch of green idiots and look up when I speak to you.'

The Khan motioned the men further into the room with a low wave of his hand and cleared his throat. 'It feels like a year ago I was in your position. So young and stupid, full of dreams and hope.' He approached Raeson and then said, 'I called you here to promote you both.'

'Thank you, sir!' Zekhal blurted out, so excited he couldn't hold it in. Zekhal had been after a greater command since his days as a rookie. Raeson remembered his babbling about the capital ships and always talked about the rare dreadnaught class vessels.

'I would not thank me yet, however I admire your enthusiasm,' the Khan smiled. 'You, Amus Zekhal, will command the Dying Nova. I believe you had an experience with this ship, Xain?'

'Yes, my Khan,' Raeson replied. 'It saved my wing in the last mission, a vessel worthy of commanding.' He turned to his longtime friend and with a small nod of his head said, 'Congratulations.'

Zekhal couldn't hide his excitement. Finally, the commander of his own capital ship, not the size of a dreadnaught, but a step closer to his goal.

The Khan turned to Raeson and continued. 'And you, Xain, will command the Arvernus.' He studied the look on Raeson's face as he broke the news. There was no change in Raeson's expression, no look of dread or fear. Zekhal appeared to have seen death itself, with his eyes wide and face pale. He tried his best to cover up his emotion for the sake of his friend.

'The Arvernus, my Khan? You would have me command such a famous ship?'

The Khan turned his back, walked over to the large window at the rear of his observation room, and took a moment of thought before he spoke.

'Congratulations again Amus, on your promotion to talon commander. You may leave.'

'Yes, my Khan,' Zekhal replied. He locked eye contact with Raeson before turning and leaving the room.

The doors slid shut, prompting the Khan to alter the direction of the conversation. 'Most races considered the flagship cursed before we captured it. Where this vessel would go, war followed and death was not far behind. When we plundered the home-world of the ship's builders, many of them were happy to see it leave.'

Raeson could see the Khan smiling and reminiscing about his prideful past, the *Wing of Vidar,* and how it became the flagship of the pirates.

'When I saw the Vidar, I knew it was the vessel I would command, despite the hearsay and rumours. The technology was similar to our own, even down to the solar sails, yet so much bigger than anything I'd ever seen. It was and still is, the gem of our fleet, even though others constructed it.'

'It's an incredible vessel, my Khan,' Raeson said.

'Yet if you told a version of me that was ten years younger, before I captured it, I may have not believed that.' The Khan went silent for a few moments. 'Tell me Raeson,' the Khan asked. 'What do you know of the Arvernus?'

'I know that it's a corvette class vessel, smaller than a frigate, capable of harboring five fighters and can translocate further than other ships of its size.' He paused for a few seconds, thinking about how to continue. 'I also know that almost every pilot considers the vessel cursed, because all its commanders have vanished during its jumps, without explanation.'

'Does that bother you, Commander?' the Khan asked, putting an emphasis on Raeson's new rank. 'Join me for this view Raeson, few people get the privilege.'

He followed his Khan's request and was curious why he was still in the room.

'Do you believe that my decision is an injustice to you because of your past?' the Khan asked, his gaze not leaving the armada of ships in formation outside the large window.

'No sir, but I think it's because of someone else.'

'Oh yes, your father, the one that abandoned us, causing hundreds to lose their lives,' the Khan said flatly. He turned and looked into Raeson's face, giving him his full attention. 'It's because of your father that I give you command of this ship.'

Raeson could feel his anger rising inside him. I shouldn't have to carry his burden.

'It's not for the reason you believe. I'm giving you this vessel so you can prove yourself. If you can tame and master this great ship, then none have reason to doubt you.'

Raeson's anger vanished as quickly as it had begun. 'You honor me and offer me a solution to something that has plagued me for so long? Thank you, but why are you helping me?'

The Khan's body language seemed less formal. 'Because no person should live under the dark, repentant shadow of another's deeds. I know this like I knew your father.'

'You knew him? I didn't know that... Please tell me you punched him out at least a dozen times?'

'Oh, more than that,' the Khan laughed. 'I even spaced him once but the damn fool was too stubborn to die, but that's a story for another day. You didn't need to be told, and the past is just that.'

'What was he like, my father?'

'He was a great man, a skilled pilot and a brilliant commander. I grew up with him through our military career, much like you and Zekhal, so I hear.'

Raeson had many questions and wanted to ask them all at once. 'Zekhal and I are close. If you knew my father, the way I know my friend, then you can tell me why he abandoned us?'

'I've asked myself that question for years, my boy, and I am still no closer to an answer.'

'I see,' Raeson added. 'Where can I find more information?'

'He erased everything,' replied the Khan. 'It was all premeditated. Your father was a very smart man, and he knew how to cover his tracks.'

'Still not smart enough to avoid the hunters you sent after him,' Raeson said hatefully.

'Yes, you're right, and the hunters ended everything for him.' The Khan motioned to Raeson and escorted him to the door. 'That's all I have time for, Talon Commander Raeson. Look after the Arvernus. Despite the hearsay she is a good ship, like the Dying Nova, worthy of an excellent commander.'

'Thank you, my Khan, and I will prove myself.'

'I know you will. Watch your back out there and keep your eye on the dark corners,' the Khan finished as Raeson left, the doors closing behind him.

Raeson headed down the corridor towards the briefing room. A large-scale attack on a Heridian fleet was about to take place and he needed to familiarize himself with his new role.

I can't believe the Khan knew my father. There's more to the story, and I'm not going to stop until I find out, not that the traitor is worth it.

Raeson froze in the middle of the busy corridor before he realized something.

I always watch the dark corners, ever since the assassination attempts started. Does he know about the killers? He shook his head and felt stupid. There's no way he's involved, right?

*

On the Sky-Station, Tremon and Draethus reached the hangar and launching bays. It was of an unusual design with fighters and troop carrier craft pointed downward, towards the floor. Draethus could see fourteen craft at first, with more in the background. He walked over to the first fighter and peered into the open cockpit.

'That's a vampire drop fighter,' Tremon said as Draethus began studying the weapons attached to the forward swept wings. 'We designed them as aerial support fighters to escort the bigger drakon drop ships, over there,' Tremon said, pointing to a larger craft resembling a flying lizard that Draethus had seen on the planet.

'You launch them downward?' Draethus asked, examining the mechanism underneath.

'Did the word "Drop" give it away?' Tremon asked with a smug expression.

'It's all fun and games until someone trips and falls,' replied Draethus. He began walking towards Tremon when another man stepped in from the side. Covered in oil and smelling like he hadn't bathed in years, he shook a large tool in his hand.

'The squadron is ready, sir!' said the man with enthusiasm.

'Thank you, mechanic,' Tremon said. 'Please notify the squad leader and perform preliminary checks. We'll launch in an hour.'

The mechanic was about to leave when Tremon added, 'If I die from mechanical failure, I'll return and haunt you.'
The mechanic replied with a nervous smile, backed away and then hurried off.

'You better know what you're doing, or more people, good people, will die because of you,' Tremon warned Draethus as his smile faded.

'More people will die if the menace gets that device working, perhaps even billions in the long run,' Draethus said, putting aside his thoughts of tearing the man apart. 'Tell me, Tremon, why don't you trust me? I'm dedicated to destroying the Heridians, yet you treat me with such disdain.'

'Because you're an outsider, a stranger to our cause, and it worries me the lengths you'll go for victory. Would you sacrifice everyone to rid Echelon of this threat?'

Draethus thought about his answer, which was yes, of course. A SOV's purpose is the greater good. Sometimes that involves extreme actions in order to achieve it. He would sacrifice an entire world if it meant saving everyone else. Looking down at the floor, the guilt surfaced as he remembered his old team. 'Let's hope it never comes to that.'

'Get yourself ready, Draethus, we're going in,' Tremon said with a scowl.

An hour later, the aerial craft was ready for launch. Draethus sat in a drakon drop ship, and because of his height, had to duck his head to avoid a hand railing behind him.

The craft was bustling with activity, with paladin soldiers checking equipment, weapons, and safety gear. He checked his own harness and found it difficult because of the vertical position of the dropship. Glancing back at the soldiers, he mimicked their foot position on the chair's base, so as not to dangle freely.

A voice sounded over the intercom in the hangar, 'Ready to launch in five...'

'Shouldn't the engines be spooling up?' Draethus asked, looking over at Tremon who sat opposite. He noticed his armor still fit well in the cramped space, though the man looked unwell.

'No, it's free fall, until we clear the electromagnetic pulse field that protects the underside of the Sky-Station,' Tremon replied.

'Wait, we're going to drop from the sky with no power or engines?' Draethus was a little surprised. 'What happens if the systems don't power back on?'

'Then we die, of course,' Varican replied from behind, grinning profusely. 'Isn't it exciting?'

'Good of you to join us,' Draethus said, then turning to Tremon added, 'If you spew on me...'

'Drop, drop, drop!' the voice announced.

With a loud rush of air, the hangar bay doors below opened, sending all the ships into free-fall and plummeting to the surface. The troops held onto the rail above as the craft nosed downward, spiraling out of control. Draethus felt his stomach meet his spine as vertigo overcame his senses. Shaking his head, he focused on the view through the cockpit and could make out the ground rapidly approaching.

He listened to the pilots talking over the coms. 'Out of interference in three, two, one... engage power systems and light up the controls.'

At first, the controls didn't respond, and holding onto the rail even tighter, he thought death was near. The moments passed slowly, and Draethus imagined himself crossing the event horizon of a black hole, minus the crushing part. Without warning, the consoles sprung to life and were covered in activity.

The engines spun up and harsh vibrations rattled the interior so much that Draethus thought they were under fire. As his stomach said its farewell to his spine, his ears popped and the roaring of engines became clearer. All the craft leveled out smoothly into formation, with the Drakon drop ships in the center, surrounded by the Vampire fighters as escort. Tremon looked worse than before.

The squadron flew east first and then north, approaching the city from a different angle, hoping to confuse the enemy. Draethus remembered seeing the city from the balcony on the Sky-Station, with the fire and smoke rising into the distance. It wouldn't be long until they reached their destination, and he could once again kill the enemy.

Like he was reading Draethus' mind, Varican asked, 'Have they given you any weapons yet?'

Draethus felt a little foolish for not asking already. He assumed they would be given to him on arrival. 'My mind is the sharpest weapon,' he grinned.

Varican laughed before looking over to Tremon and saying, 'Make sure he gets the standard issue rifle and blade when we land.'

Tremon nodded and said, 'We could just use him as a shield instead, maybe even landing gear.'

Sitting back, Draethus ignored the comment and instead, remembered the sensation of his vibration sword slicing into the enemy. Not long now.

The coms crackled again as the squadron leader gave the orders, 'Drop to level two and begin insertion.'

Draethus felt the drop ship make a quick dip in altitude as it prepared to make a lightning-fast landing. Without warning, a massive explosion detonated off the side of the craft's armor, causing it to veer off course. The pilot did well to keep control and pulled it back to approach vector.

'That was a close one!' Draethus heard over the coms chatter.

The noise from the explosions grew louder, and Draethus knew the origin. He had seen it before, a large walking tank resembling a hunched over cockroach, carrying a massive rail gun on its back, atop of four legs. It doubled as anti-aircraft and anti-ground assault, and used in great numbers, made a formidable opponent.

Another explosion ignited off the armor, sending vibrations rippling through the hull as the drop ship neared destruction.

Looking out the window, Draethus could see the ship next to them was not so lucky, receiving a glancing hit to the cockpit. The ship spun wildly out of control and almost collided with a vampire escort as it careened to the ground, exploding before impact.

'Get ready, men!' Tremon yelled over the explosions. 'The moment we land, I want everyone out fast and following my lead!'

'Understood!' the soldiers replied in unison.

The paladin soldiers seemed disciplined and courageous, and Draethus could sense their experience.

The drop ships decreased their altitude again and fired their afterburners. Bright orange flame trailed as they flew over the ruined buildings below. Escort fighters fired salvos of air-to-surface rockets to clear the landing zone, before climbing high into the sky.

'Looping back, you are clear to drop your troops,' the escorts reported over the coms.

'We copy,' replied the dropship pilots.

The two remaining drop ships nosed up, their engines pivoting on the sides, then fired retro rockets towards the ground to slow the heavy craft's descent. The back doors sprung open to release the occupants, and the team rushed out, shooting at an enemy Heridian soldier. Anti-personnel guns mounted on the top of the craft, swept a ring of automatic laser fire around the landing site, clearing a path.

Then, just as quickly as they landed, the ships took off on a plume of fire, heading away from the battle, in a new direction out of the city.

'You are on your own,' a pilot voiced over the coms.

'Affirmative, just be ready for extraction,' Tremon ordered the pilot.

'Copy that.'

The insertion team had successfully dropped behind Heridian lines, regrettably losing a single drop ship. Draethus couldn't help but see the parallel between himself and Tremon.

CHAPTER 6

Times of Shrike.

It had been three days since Slin's surgery, having the robotic limbs and mechanisms implanted into his body. During his recovery, Nash had never left his side, and repeatedly played the events of his crash in her mind. Could she have done more? Was it her fault that Slin was trapped in his cockpit for so long? Is that the reason he lost so much of his physical self? She looked into the large liquid filled tube and tried to make out the blurred figure of her lover through the glass inside.

'Is he in there?' asked a voice from behind her.

She turned to see Tek, the aging fighter pilot, walking through the door, looking as if he hadn't cleaned himself for days. As he approached, she struck out her hand and slapped his face as hard as she could.

'What were you thinking?' she screamed. 'You were shooting at me instead of the enemy!' She aggressed towards him, more intent on taking out her anger.

'That was a few days ago. I thought you would have been over that by now, little one,' Tek replied as he crept back, feeling the rage emanating from the woman.

'You are part of our squad. You're supposed to help us and watch our backs, not play around like a child!' She angrily swept her sweaty dark fringe aside, and it merged with her short cropped hair. Tek froze and glanced at the floor. He was ashamed, and a dark shadow crossed his face as he said, 'That word again.'

'What word? You mean help each other, or acting like children!?' Nash still hadn't calmed.

'Squad,' he whispered, 'I had one of those once.'

'And did you shoot at them too? I'm surprised you've lasted this long, Tek.' She turned her back on him and walked over to the tube. Putting her hand on the glass, she felt the cold condensation dripping down its surface.

Trying to calm herself, she said, 'Do you know what's happening to him in there?' Her voice was softer as sadness replaced the anger.

The old man looked up, his face a mirror of regret. 'No,' he replied.

'In this tank, Slin's skin will grow over his mechanical implants. The machines inside are currently adjusting them, and if the cybernetics suit their host, provided the body doesn't reject them, no one would know they existed. But Slin will know and never forget, and he may never feel a whole person again.'

Tek walked over to the woman and put his hand on her shoulder. 'He will be alright,' he said. 'He'll be alright because he has you to look after him.'

Nash smiled a little. 'They say the pain you feel inside the tube can lead to mental breakdowns, feeling every molecule of skin growing back at an accelerated rate. I hope you're right Tek, for Slin's sake.'

'You must be hungry, waiting by his side like this. I'll be back with some food soon.' Tek paused and waited for her acknowledgement before exiting the room.

As the door closed, Nash watched him through the small window and noticed a great sadness. He reached into his pocket for a small flask, unscrewed the lid, and took a drink.

'My squad,' she heard him mutter. 'Why did it have to be that way? Food, better get some before she gets angry again.'

*

The briefing was long, tiresome, and involved a quarter of the fleet's commanders. War strategists labeled the upcoming mission as a surgical strike, targeting the heart of a newly discovered enemy supply line. The Heridians had been using a small cluster of planets as a mid-point, launching attacks on nearby systems and drawing back to repair and rearm.

Intelligence suggested that some Heridian soldiers required sources of food to remain functional. They deduced these troops to be the creatures containing the biological components, or minds, captured from other forms of life. Without food, the humanoid organs contained within, degenerated and died.

The science teams also speculated the enemy harboring these humanoid parts to be smarter and more devious, and therefore a greater threat than their counterparts.

The primary goal of the mission was to destroy the food source stored at the cluster of planets, to cripple the Heridian fleet.

Raeson exited the briefing, followed closely by Zekhal, who quickly joined his side.

'You think this mission will be successful?' Zekhal asked, running his fingers back through his thick brown hair.

'I think we'll pull it off,' Raeson replied. 'I don't think cutting off supplies to one fleet will make a difference, though.'

'Minor victories will eventually add up,' Zekhal said a little stunned with Raeson's response. 'It's not like we can just press the "win" button.'

'There are so many Rid fleets out there,' Raeson replied. 'Cutting off the food supply to one fleet will not stop them.'

'And what would you suggest?'

Raeson stopped and looked at him. 'We track one enemy fleet back to its home-world and bombard the menace from space. I think I'd enjoy looking down on them while they die.' He grinned profusely at his friend and added, 'Might even sell tickets and get rich in the process.'

'Brilliant plan, but how do you track something that large without being detected? Especially when it translocates, and you can't track it. That's if they even return to their home-world, if that even exists.'

'Minor details,' Raeson said. 'My point is we need to destroy the head of the menace and cut it off from the source. With no leadership, they cannot co-ordinate strikes. If we create a power vacuum during the reselection of leadership, we can cause chaos during the confusion.'

Zekhal scratched his head. 'Why don't you put a plan together and present it to the Khan? Speaking of which, did you find out why he gave you the Arvernus?'

'That I did my friend. He gave me that ship so I can prove myself, because of my family's past.'

'I see,' said Zekhal, 'Tame the beast and you tame everyone's doubt and restore pride to your family name.'

A group of soldiers ran past the two men in the corridor, all of which gave a quick acknowledgment when they realized what rank they were.

'There's a lot to do. I better get back to my fighter,' Raeson said.

'I think Rel will have it so shiny it could be the next jump beacon,' laughed Zekhal. 'And I discovered why she could keep that extra-long hair of hers.'

As his time was limited, Raeson was about to cut the conversation short but couldn't shake the curiosity.

'Apparently,' Zekhal continued, keeping up with Raeson, 'Rel received an ordered to cut it shorter by the master technician, but she cried in front of the entire maintenance crew. The master tech didn't know what to do. He just flushed crimson embarrassment and gave in to the stares from his men.'

'That sounds like Rel,' Raeson laughed.

'I can't believe that someone can get away with crying on a pirate vessel. What would you even do if a crew member responded to an order like that? Speaking of which, I better go introduce myself to them. I haven't even been aboard my new command yet,' replied Zekhal, giving a quick informal salute and heading in a different direction.

Zekhal is right. If I know Rel, my fighter will be in perfect condition. Tears or not, though, there better not be a purple flower in my cockpit again.

*

Far from the Sky-Station, on Echelon's surface, the large Heridian creature glanced up at the smoke-filled sky above. Ash from the distant fires drifted through the air and landed on the complex's glass ceiling, ash created from the battles taking place in the city.

The menace turned and scanned the displacement device with its alien eyes. Digital enhancements displayed readings of dimension and mass alongside other anomalies. The device was attached to a large platform like structure, capable of transferring matter to another time and space, the same device that brought them here.

Other smaller Heridians, hunched over and the size of a small human, attempted to repair the damage caused during their shifting to this instance.

The large Heridian walked up the platform, illuminated red runes covering its armored body, leaving light trails following behind. The runes signified bio-intelligence inside its core, a living brain and spinal column taken from an organic life form. In a standard Heridian soldier, this would make it smarter, faster, and stronger.

This Heridian however was different; this was a leader amongst the menace even before it gained biological internals. It not only possessed the skill of leadership but also free will, ambition and above all, a great sense of self-awareness.

Its orders had been simple. Lead a force of Heridians to the device's location and seize control, regardless of opposition. After obtaining the objective, the creature was to return it back to base, on the far side of the planet. If the Heridians could accomplish this task, they could access any location at any point in time they choose. They could even go as far as sending resources back to the past and infinitely increase the size of their army. However, the mission did not go as straightforward as it sounded. The Heridians faced a squad of dark gray armored warriors, The Soldiers of the Void. It was the soldier's curiosity that powered the device to begin with that notified the Heridians of its existence and location.

The device had never meant to activate the way it had. That blame falls on the one soldier that stood alone at the end. The Heridian leader hadn't seen the soldier since the event, despite dispatching the many scout hunters at its disposal. It was not wise to assume the soldier had perished.

*

Five kilometers away, the human scout zoomed in closer with her sniper rifle, being careful not to give away her concealed position. She had hidden away whilst the Heridians first attacked the city and felt puzzled by how they appeared. For days, the sniper silently watched the menace at work on the device through the transparent ceiling of the complex. The large Heridian leader moved over to the device as she tracked it with her scope. She could take the shot and kill the creature, with one well-placed bullet, if she hit the mark. The only drawback would be her death, as the menace would be onto her position in minutes, and the exit strategy was too slow, too exposed.

She had to live.

Her self-imposed mission was to track the movements of the enemy and feed the information back to the paladin units on the front line. Without this information, the Heridians would dominate and eventually win against the ground forces. They had lost many human lives during the initial battle, and she wanted no more blood spilled, human blood, anyway.

The communication device on her head vibrated softly, to notify her of an incoming message. With a thought, the message opened and displayed on the digital lens covering her eye. She was to contact a Captain Wrath, and scout ahead for a group across a nearby bridge. Cursing, she moved from her hiding place, turned, and silently slipped away from the area. Although her orders were frustrating, she had no choice but to obey.

*

Draethus and the paladin squad moved quietly through the burnt-out buildings as fires smoldered and rubble fell from the ceilings.

Sneaking was not something Draethus was used to, as SOV soldiers preferred a more head on approach. Bringing up the tactical map inside his helmet, he reviewed the estimated enemy positions and the direction of their objective. Much of the information was hours old data relayed from ground forces and the odd street level scanner hidden away.

He stopped, crouched, and held up his fist in a silent command to halt the team. Tremon moved quietly up to his position and made sure he didn't surprise the soldier.

'What is it?' Tremon whispered.

'I saw movement up ahead,' Draethus replied.

'Are you seeing ghosts?'

'Your future ghost, maybe,' Draethus grinned. Stress rolled off his mind like a waterfall when he saw Tremon's angry expression.

'Like you'll live long enough to see it,' Tremon replied bitterly, then moved across to another building, roughly twenty meters to the left of the squad.

Tremon reached behind him and pulled out a small visual device that he put to his face. He zoomed in to where Draethus thought he saw movement, and within seconds was alerted to hostile contacts. The enemy was approaching down the road leading to the squad's position. Rushing back to the squad, he whispered a harsh warning and immediately the men went to ground, finding hiding places under the rubble.

The Heridian patrol, although few, comprised enough firepower to wipe out the squad. Four standard Heridian creatures walked in formation, carrying rifles whilst scanning the ruins. Behind them skulked their armored escort, a large four-legged abomination with a body the size of a small tank. Attached to the walker's carapace were anti-infantry gatling cannons that seemed to pivot of their own accord on gimbaled fixtures. Draethus couldn't see any glowing runes on the enemy, signifying they were not overly clever, however still dangerous.

The world around them fell silent. The enemy patrol ceased movement as Draethus lowered his face under the concrete rubble.

They must be on top of us. Even if we fought, they would only call reinforcements and it would compromise our position.

The wind blew sand over the back of his head as the sound of his heartbeat thrummed in his throat. He could almost feel the Heridian's eyes staring towards his hiding place. A straightforward fight would have been so much easier had it not been for the mission. The Heridian patrol began moving towards them, slowly and purposefully. Something had caught their attention.

Suddenly there was a colossal explosion off in the distance, and the resulting tremors shook the surrounding buildings. The Heridians changed their heading to investigate, the walker leading the way. Draethus looked up, shook off the powdered concrete in his hair, and surveyed the area to make sure it was safe for the squad to continue forward.

Tremon, with Varican trailing behind, ran over to him. 'You need to look at this,' he said, tapping his helmet.

The message transferred to Draethus and appeared on his own display. It gave details of a distraction and co-ordinates to meet with a forward scout.

'Where is this position?' Draethus asked. 'It's not on our path to the device?'

A Paladin in the squad, an older man covered in facial scars, moved up to the three. 'It's probably an over-watch position near the bridge. Whoever sent this message might know a better way to the device.'

Draethus checked the ammunition level on his rifle and said, 'You're the mission leader, so it's your call, Tremon. We can't advance from this position, and my map information suggests enemy forces have us cut off. How reliable would this person be? Can we trust him?'

'We don't really have an option,' Tremon replied. 'Do we?'

*

Swirls of smoke spun like mini tornados down the desolate street as dim sunlight struggled to penetrate the ash clouds. The fighting in the city had decreased, as what remained of the population had fled into the jungles, hunted by small animal sized Heridians. Even the engagements on the front line had lessened.

The small squad of paladins, led by Tremon, advanced through the remnants of buildings parallel to the road. He signaled that the bridge was up ahead and pointed to a tall structure visible over the ruins. Draethus zoomed in with the optic lens in his helmet and could make out a little red dot on a top floor.

Varican moved up next to him. 'Our scout is up ahead in that building. We need to reach his position to get an overview of the way through.'

'Agreed,' Draethus replied. 'That guy may as well send up a flare with how visible his laser sight is.'

'If you see his sights, then you'll be dead before you could alert anyone,' Varican chuckled. 'Maybe you don't need your head?'

Varican was defensive of his forces, and his paladins had been loyal to him for many years. His off-world operations had been so successful that he reached the rank of captain quickly. Tremon, however, although not in a captaincy position, still held a higher rank because of his status as honor guard for the Senechal.
Tremon signaled the go ahead to his men, and they took advantage of nearby cover to conceal themselves on the path to the structure. Draethus followed behind with Tremon at his back, sidestepping through a tangle of wires and debris. Passing through a narrow alley created by a fallen building, the squad walked ankle deep in muddy water.

'Blood,' whispered Tremon.

Draethus looked over and knew the comment was directed at him.

'That's blood we're walking through,' Tremon continued. 'That's blood caused by your actions.' From the moment Tremon found Draethus, he harbored a relentless distrust.

'Just be thankful it's not yours,' said Draethus. 'I mean, it could be if you wanted?'

As the two warriors exchanged words, the squad came to a halt. A paladin soldier, running point, scouted ahead alone into the entrance of the tall structure.

Running his armored glove along the wall, Draethus drew a line in blood seeping from a corpse pinned by debris above. He lifted it to eye level in front of Tremon and said, 'This is a reminder of what we're fighting for. These remnants were real people and lived real lives. I don't take their deaths lightly and I'll do whatever I can to prevent more loss in the future.'

Draethus could see Tremon's anger rising, and felt inclined to fight it out, but knew they couldn't risk it.

'Left unchecked,' continued Draethus, 'the Rids would take you all. When no humans remain, they will turn their attention to the wildlife. They will share the same fate, harvested for their biological internals, and the Heridian force would grow. If they activate the displacement device, the Heridians will bring in an infinite number of reinforcements and spread throughout your known space. Your solar system will burn. Whether this happens here in your instance of time or in mine, the result is the same: everything is at risk. Be thankful you are part of the solution.'

The paladin running point returned and whispered, 'It's clear,' as the squad began filling the lower level of the structure.

It was a large and dimly lit room with stairs ascending the center before spreading both ways at the top to adjoin the next level. Residue from gunfire charred the walls, and scorch marks reached a high ceiling.

The group moved in haste and covered both sides of the stairs, assault rifles at the ready, as they advanced. Taking the direction to the right, they sprinted along the broken tiled floor to a stairwell, leading to the upper floors. Within minutes, the squad had passed twenty-two levels and arrived at the highest room, close to where

Draethus spotted the red scope.

The soldier who ran point, the man to the front, stopped and with a quick swipe across his eye, brought down a digital display over his retina. A large marking was visible through his lens on the nearby wall, and geometric patterns informed the paladin that a friendly combatant was in the next room, but to approach with caution. As he flicked the lens back from over his eye, a red beam appeared on his forehead, from a gap in the doors ahead.

Quickly, the squad raised their weapons and crouched to take aim. The paladin, however, dared not move, as his life was now at the mercy of another. The beam from the sniper rifle vanished as the doors slowly opened, flooding the corridor with volumetric light as the scout purposefully approached. As a friendly gesture, she pointed her sniper rifle to the side. The woman wore camouflaged clothing in shades of urban grays, with shoulder length dark hair, streaked with blonde highlights that flicked outwards at their ends.
Assassin.

'I heard you coming from the other-side of the planet,' the scout said, holstering the pistol concealed behind her back. 'These creatures have better hearing than I do, so I suggest you show more caution next time.'

Draethus approached the woman, towered over her and asked, 'Nice rifle. Can I have it?'

'No, of course you can't!' the scout exclaimed. 'What kind of person would ask such a stupid…'

Varican stepped towards her and interrupted. 'Excuse our friend here. Sometimes I don't know if he wants to be taken seriously.'

The scout looked Draethus up and down. 'So you're the guy that appeared with the creatures. I thought you'd be more intimidating.'

'You haven't seen me in the daylight yet.'

'We haven't time for this,' Tremon said impatiently. 'Scout, show us the bridge and the way past.'

'Very well,' she huffed, spinning on her heal and turning her back. 'This way.'

'Back where you're from, is there a line of people wanting to kill you? Like there is here, I mean?' finished Tremon with a smirk.

The scout led the squad back through the doors in which she arrived and, as they entered, found themselves surrounded by the familiar ruins of the city. Half the floor was missing, the roof only partially covered the group, and the entire side of the building lay on the street below.

'Stick to the wall and for all our benefit, be silent,' whispered the scout, staring at Draethus.

Draethus neared the edge where a wall once stood and peered over. Soot rested like a blanket of ocean and covered everything beneath them.

'There,' the scout stated, pointing to a distant structure that was barely visible through the clouds of haze over the ruins.

'It's too open to cross, they would discover us in seconds,' said Draethus. He may have preferred a straightforward fight to all the sneaking around, but he wasn't about to risk a mission for a glorified bridge crossing.

'What other path is there?' Tremon asked. He moved closer, trying to get a better view of the surrounding terrain.

'As you're probably aware, the device is secured within the complex on the small urban island, north of the city,' the scout said. 'What most people don't realize is that aside from water, carnivorous and amphibious jungle plants protect the island as well. The only access is that bridge, normally.' She made sure all the squad were listening and backed away from the ledge. 'There is an underwater cable supplying power to the island that we can use as a zip line. Provided we find something to propel us fast enough, we should be safe from the dangers in the water.'

'Interesting idea,' Varican said, as if looking forward to the adventure.

'I say we send Draethus first,' Tremon suggested. 'It's not like any of us would miss him.'

'Your girlfriend might,' Draethus laughed. 'But seriously, I'm all for showing you how things are done.'

'I was a day away from attempting it myself, before I got the call to rescue this team of yours,' the scout said.

'Rescue?' Draethus chuckled. 'Only some of us needed rescuing.' He glared at Tremon, hoping to see his anger flare again.

'What do you suggest we use for the propulsion? It will have to be something fast,' Varican asked. 'Those underwater plants are bloody quick. I ran across some of them on my exploration trips through the jungle.'

'The power line begins at an underground facility on the edge of the lake. I found some old maintenance equipment we can use that should be sufficient, and there is enough for all of us. Heridian soldiers guard the facility, so we'll have to eliminate them first. I've scouted the area plenty of times so I can get us there undetected. The rest will be up to you,' she said.

'Understood,' Draethus said with a smirk. 'I look forward to a straight-out fight. I'll leave the sneaking around to you, assassin.'

'My name is Shade, not assassin, you idiot.'

*

Fire lit up the skyline as another shell burst from the massive cannon atop the great tank. From the open hatch towards the front, Captain Wrath, Lead Armor Commander of the ground forces, listened to the sound of his crew reloading another shell. He lowered his optical enhancing device and took in the view.

The exhaust from his armored group blotted out the moons above and the remaining light shone onto the wet muddy ground, flickering in their reflection. Rain fell softly and created ripples, making the surrounding area shimmer and dance.

Wrath could feel the steam emanating from the machine's weapon as the water cooled the metal behemoth. The Arbalest class command tank, the pride of the paladin forces, sat at the head of the group's formation. Covered in jungle camouflage, the patterns of brush and vines, it fired again. The shot sent a shock wave into the ground and created a clap of thunder.

'Hold fire.' Wrath commanded into his coms unit. Looking through his optic enhancer, he could see the Heridians pulling back. His tank group had positioned on the edge of the city atop a ridge that gave them a wide field of view.

'I want scouts on the lookout for any approaching forces surrounding our area,' he continued. 'Have forward infiltrators hide on the city line.'

'At once, sir,' replied one of Wrath's lieutenants.

Wrath was an experienced tank commander and had led many battles before the Heridian invasion. The armored division was his life and would always be until it became his tomb.

He rubbed his square jaw and took one last look around.

Far too quiet.

Grabbing the hatch handle, he lowered himself into the arbalest and sealed the lock behind him. He slid down the ladder and made his way through the narrow corridor and into the command room. It was here that Captain Wrath planned the group's strategies alongside the other armor lieutenants of his division. Sitting down at the large table, in the middle of the command room, he greeted his men, some of which were his closest friends.

'Sir,' the men said, almost in unison.

The table illuminated and a holographic image of the battlefield hovered above, with green markers at its edge representing their own forces. Scattered in the city rested three dimensional spheres displaying enemy ground troops with the enemy armored walkers in orange.

'So far,' Wrath began, 'we are just keeping the Rids at bay.'

'We should launch an offensive into the enemies' heart I say!' exclaimed Lieutenant Camerous, eager for engagement and hungry for action. 'None of this sitting around picking off the odd Rid from the ridge.'

Wrath stirred in his seat. 'I would agree, Camerous, however we shouldn't act rashly. We have a more immediate task to accomplish.'

He could see his men's eyes widen at the possibility of getting into action. Sitting around all day created a culture of laziness, the fear of any lieutenant.

'The infiltration force has almost reached their destination, and it's our mission now to create a distraction for them to gain access to the device.'

'You mean the squad with the man claiming to be from Echelon, but not from Echelon?' asked one of his men.

'Yeah, that's the one. When we receive the message from our contact, this is what will happen…'

CHAPTER 7

Swarms of Iron.

'Fire, full broadside!' Raeson screamed to the crew of the *Arvernus* as the Heridian transport ship tried desperately to escape, burning its engines to reach maximum velocity. The lasers from the pirate corvette ripped into the enemy, blasting armor into the blackness of space. Small fires erupted along the enemy vessel before a gigantic explosion rippled outward and split the ship into three large pieces. The crew cheered at their first kill under the command of Raeson.

'Turn to port, full burn,' Raeson ordered, trying to keep his excitement down.

The pilot on the lower level acknowledged the command, and gripping hold of the large control handles, began the maneuver.

The bridge of the *Arvernus* was not large compared to other capital vessels. It complimented a crew of five, plus the commander who sat in the center, elevated on a large chair. Holographic screens levitated to the front, relaying tactical data to the crew.

Outside the vessel, the fighters of Reaper Wing protected the corvette, destroying incoming projectiles and intercepting enemy craft. The battlefield was a chaotic clash between the pirates and Heridian forces, lit with weapons' fire and explosions. Enemy transport ships disappeared in great flashes of plasma as their support fighters failed to compete with overwhelming numbers. The frigate, *Dying Nova,* had been firing its weapons without pause, cutting a swath of debris and destruction, proving that Talon Commander Zekhal was a competent leader. Raeson almost wished his ship comprised the same weapon load out, so he could match Zekhal's kill count. The battle was taking place in an area of space far from any celestial body, with zero points of interest and nothing to block incoming fire such as asteroids or debris.

The *Arvernus* charged toward a group of five enemy ships attempting to escape.

'These ships are short range and have no ability to translocate. How are they here?' Raeson whispered to himself. He noticed some of the crew glance in his direction and wondered if they thought he was crazy. 'That's right, I talk to myself. Now make sure you hit something,' he finished, loud enough for the others to hear clearly.

An enemy fighter exploded near the starboard viewing window on the bridge. A flash of fire forced Xain to sheer away and caused the ship to shudder.

'That was a close one,' Tek said over the coms from his fighter outside. 'You almost had the pleasure of smelling what it had for breakfast.'

'Keep it going Reaper Wing, they are down twenty-one transports,' Raeson replied. He turned to his newly appointed crewman. 'Gunner, focus fire on those ships.'

Frontal lasers lashed out at the fleeing Heridian transports and carved a fiery arc across two of them. The vessels collided with a third and erupted as the oxygen ignited within the hulls. The remaining two vessels split off into different directions only to transform into raging fireballs from a lance of energy, cast from the frigate *Dying Nova,* kilometers away to the port side.

'Blood thirsty today, Zekhal?' Raeson said over the coms with a laugh.

'Finally, some payback,' his friend replied. 'The firepower of this frigate is incredible for its size.'

'Reaper Wing, clean up what's left of the Heridian fighters and return.'

'Confirmed, Commander Raeson,' Nash replied, her coms hissing with static. 'I must admit it's strange not having you and Slin out here with us.'

'You won't see me sitting in this chair all the time,' Raeson said, brushing his flight armor.

'You got to sleep, eat and shi…' interjected Tek, laughing over the coms.

'And reprimand old subordinates who drink too much,' Raeson said. He stared out into the void at the large pirate fleet trading fire with the enemy. Crimson and violet laser flashed and crisscrossed on the display in a brilliant light show, joined by enormous explosions. A send off for the dead.

It didn't take the pirate fleet long to wipe the Heridian convoy from the empty and salvage what data and technology remained. They had won the day with minimal losses, and there was hope of discovering further information from the wrecks.

The three pilots of Reaper Wing maneuvered into docking position behind the *Arvernus*. They approached slowly and when their fighters were in range, the corvettes' docking arms grabbed hold and clamped the craft down. A large mechanical object protruded from the corvette, then covered the fighter's cockpit in order for its pilot to climb out and enter the parent ship.

'Translocation in progress. Crew is to proceed to designated positions,' the automated voice announced over the *Arvernus* intercom. Nash, Stark and Tek raced down the narrow corridor from the docking hatches to find a secure seat, in an area attached to the bridge, ready for the jump.

'I never thought I'd be on this cursed ship,' said Tek. 'If we are still here on the other side, it'll be a miracle.'

'Nonsense,' Stark replied in a condescending tone, as he often did. 'There is no curse on any ship.'

'Every commander of this vessel has vanished,' added Nash. 'Translocating.'

The *Arvernus* disappeared from the fabric of space, entering the non-existence underneath, and with the short jump, reappeared at the rendezvous point.

The area around the two ships warped like manipulated light around a lens. Electricity arced as remaining energy from the travel released, and both vessels flared their engines, maneuvering towards the allocated position. A blue hue trailed as glowing plasma streamed behind, forming patterns that swirled and interwove. They had arrived a short distance from the Cygnian fleet.

'Translocation spike detected!' yelled a crew member on the *Arvernus*.

'Get back out there,' ordered Raeson to his pilots, who didn't hesitate and sprinted back to their fighters.

Red lightning streaked across the void as a massive Heridian fleet appeared behind them. At its center, a large menacing vessel, asymmetrical and adorned with jagged spines, vectored in on the pirate location and opened fire. Purple arcing lasers cut into the unsuspecting pirates as three ships exploded, illuminating other nearby vessels.

The pirates immediately scattered, burning away in all directions, launching fighters and support craft. Smaller craft began splitting off from the Heridian ship comprising fighters, bombers and corvette sized ships. They immediately began swarming the closest pirate ship, a destroyer class, cutting through its hull in seconds.

'This is Khan Hayreddin. Form up on the Vidar and keep in formation. All capital ships focus fire on the large Rid ship at the center. Fighters and support craft, emergency launch, and keep the Heridian ships distracted from the main fleet!'

Like two rival swarms of iron locusts, the fighters of both sides raced towards each other and merged into a cloud of engine flare. The pilots of Reaper Wing were experienced, but even they would be lucky to survive.

Nash threw her fighter into a roll, trailing a Heridian ship she had marked as her primary target. Tek formed up on her wing and they both fired off volleys of laser fire. Two concealed weapons on each fighter spun in a blur and tore into the enemy, ripping it apart in a hail of energy. Systematically, the pair worked as one, dodging nearby ships, both friendly and rival. Purple laser fire arced from their starboard side and hit Tek on his back wing. The reverse delta fin launched off into the night, but wasn't enough to cause catastrophic damage.

'Where is Stark!?!' Nash yelled over the coms to Tek.

'I can't see him anywhere,' the old man replied, out of breath. 'There must be hundreds of fighters in this brawl. Rid to the left!'

The pair rolled and banked towards the incoming fighter, causing it to over-shoot, its weapon's fire streaked off into the darkness. Both pirate fighters turned in a sweeping move, which positioned them behind the Heridian fighter. As they unleased their lasers, the enemy exploded, debris launched itself into the fray of fighting ships.

'Damn him! He knows to be in formation with us,' Nash said angrily.

'Forget him, Nash,' said Tek. 'He's probably dead.'

*

Sitting in his fighter, high above the battle, Stark watched in darkness. With his systems powered down, he drifted slowly and silently. It looked to him like a ball of multicolored fireflies trailing luminous lines. He zoomed in on the *Vidar*, using the optics in his helmet.

Such a majestic behemoth.

Violet laser was striking the pirate flagship, causing its nanite armor to ripple and spark. It returned fire with missiles that were so large it made the surrounding fighters appear like insects. The projectiles slammed into the enemy capital ship, causing damage to the hull and metal fragments to break away. It was an even battle so far, with losses on both sides approaching the hundreds.

A Heridian destroyer class ship broke formation and burnt away from the battle, trailing a white dust cloud from its engines and rolling uncontrollably. One of the *Vidar's* capital missiles had struck it in the side, knocking it out of the battle and crippling the weapons and propulsion. Capsule like pods ejected from ports around the vessel's front and slowly, under their own propulsion, moved their way towards the large Heridian ship at the center of battle.

'Go now,' read the message inside Stark's helmet.

Switching on his systems, Stark fired up his fighter's engines. The cockpit came to life with lights and holographic displays. With a flick of his flight stick, he rolled his fighter over and headed towards the gaping hole in the crippled enemy destroyer.

*

On the bridge of the *Wing of Vidar*, Khan Hayreddin viewed the data displayed above a glass-topped table. Blue and red points floated and moved as the holographic display relayed vital tactical information on the battle raging outside. He turned and looked out the large viewing window to see the massive Heridian vessel in the distance being lit up by the missiles he just fired.

'Reload the next wave of missiles,' he commanded to one of his crew. 'I want that disgraceful Rid ship out of my sky.'

'Sir!' replied a crew member from the forward gunnery section.

Gunfire continually exchanged between both fleets. Being a mixture of human and elismorus weaponry, some pirate destroyers fired large projectile cannons instead of the traditional capital lasers. The shells impacted with the enemy fleet in great devastation; explosions engulfing the vessels in red plasma clouds and shearing off armor and componentry. Caught in a blast, a Heridian corvette veered off uncontrollably, colliding with a pirate fighter before exploding.

'Seven corvettes on an intercept course with us!' warned a member of the bridge crew.

'I want them intercepted…' before the Khan could finish his sentence, all seven of the enemy vessels exploded as the *Dying Nova* threw itself in their path, a suicidal attempt to save the *Vidar*. It easily sliced through the enemy but, as a result, caused immense damage to itself. Fire and plasma clouds streamed behind as the crew tried to regain control.

'Brave commander that one,' the Khan said, hoping the ship would survive and not succumb to the other threats in the battle.

*

Back on Echelon, and looking over the waterline, Varican kept watch as the team of infiltrators crept towards the power station below. He could see the gray waters, still and motionless, like a plain of glass sitting atop a depthless color.

In the distance, small luminous points moved back and forwards along the large bridge that joined the island to the mainland. Large pillars rose out of the water and towered above, keeping the bridge from touching the wide river. Statues of reptile creatures spiraled around the pillars, looking to the heavens, mouths open as if calling out to each other. The team was far enough away from the enemy's position to lower the possibility of detection.

'Still clear.' he whispered over the coms.

When the team had been close to their objective, Shade, the assassin, as Draethus called her, had vanished and not returned. Untrustworthy had been the Soldiers' words and Varican remembered seeing, again, that fire and aggression in his new friends' eyes. He was sure he would see that fire a lot more before this war was over.

'Varican, I need you here.' Draethus' voice was not the whisper he would have expected or preferred. He sprinted down the path to the power station and burst through the open hatchway, expecting the worst. There in front of him lay a dead Heridian soldier, face up, surrounded by a pool of dark red blood.

'There's more, there and over there,' Tremon said, pointing at positions in the large room. Steam hissed and the noises of the power-plant made clunking sounds as it generated the electrical life the island needed.

'You're too slow,' said a familiar voice mockingly from somewhere in the room. Shade dropped from a dark place above, hidden by pipes and valves.

'Start running and we'll see who's fastest,' Draethus said, arming his rifle with a clack of steel before marching towards the women. 'Ladies first.'

'Calm down,' Shade laughed, backing away, and keeping her gaze on the soldier. 'I snuck away to take down the Rid soldiers quick and quiet, and there was less than expected. Your squad here wouldn't have been so silent.'

Varican, who forever felt like the mediator, said, 'Let's get to these propulsion machines you spoke of, Shade. I'm looking forward to a rematch with these plant things.'

The propulsion units were roughly three feet long, with one end a stubbed nozzle and the other a propeller. A handle sat behind the nozzle and flow pipes connected the intake to the prop. The units resembled a torpedo and were normally used for underwater maintenance. Shade helped the squad find the units and gave them all a quick brief on how it worked.

They each wore a breathing apparatus with a harness strapped around their waist that clipped onto the underwater power cable. With enclosed armor, Draethus didn't require a breathing module and relied on a limited oxygen supply within.

Making their way down grated steps, they entered the pool of water where the power cable started its journey to the island. A paladin reached into his backpack, pulled out an explosive device and placed it at the base of the cable.

'That's charge number five,' he said, looking around. 'We placed the other four around the compound.'

The nine squad members clipped themselves to the cable, checked their breathing apparatus worked, then launched into the water. Draethus led from the front and gave Varican a nod as he disappeared under the surface.

*

Algae covered the underwater cable, slimy and slippery, and made the clips almost frictionless as the squad propelled forwards. Now and then the odd piece of weed would cause the clip to stick, before it cut through and continued onto its destination.

Draethus looked down into the murky depths. The gray water made it impossible to see anything over a few meters ahead, and he was sure they were being watched. Only his vibration sword was available, as his other hand held the propulsion unit. Looking back over his shoulder, he signaled to the paladin behind him, nodding in a downward direction. One by one, the squad drew their blades and readied themselves.

The creatures were completely silent and moved like lightning, slipping through the water as green spears darting in all directions. A paladin was the first to go, dragged into the depths right in front of Tremon, who let out a muffled roar through his breather. The squad aggressively slashed the empty water around them, hoping to catch one of the amphibious plants as they struck.

Draethus could see a blur below him, moving rapidly upwards. He kicked down in time and contacted the plant's head. The creature floated in front of him, its large weed like limbs trailing off from its multiple pod like body. One limb held the soldier's leg as he propelled forward. He could see rows of teeth on the mouth of the head, large enough to envelope a human size limb before it slipped away.

Not far now.

The creatures had stopped their darting attacks and circled the group. Draethus could swear he saw a smile on Varican's face under his apparatus.

He would make a great SOV warrior.

The propulsion units continued pulling them forwards as the plants snapped their jaws, the circling predators striking from different sides, baiting, and switching the group's attention. With his blade facing inward, Varican outstretched his arm, offering the limb as a sacrifice. As a creature neared, he retracted his arm, causing the creature to pause, then reversed his hand, spearing it through the bulbous head. Two, three, and four more fell to his blade as the squad emulated his tactic. A trail of dead vegetative carcass floated behind them, but still the rest circled.

It came up fast, almost fast enough to catch the squad unawares. The cable passed through a large net with just enough room for the team to slip through, and because of the net's repelling pulse, left the animals behind. The end of the cable rose out of the water and disappeared into a structure. As the team unclipped, they kept low on the rocky shore, looking for cover.

'You were having way too much fun,' Draethus said to Varican, shaking vegetation off his gloves.

Varican brushed something imaginary off his shoulder. 'I think we should go back that way.' His grin was infectious until the pair noticed Tremon.

'We lost one,' Tremon mumbled, disappointed he couldn't save the man.

Draethus placed his hand on his rival's shoulder and said, 'And we could have lost more.' He knew exactly what Tremon was feeling at that very moment, and it caused him to question his opinion of the man. Tremon wasn't much different to himself and also struggled with the loss of those around him. He cared and also shared the same hatred for the Heridians.

Nodding, Tremon moved forward up to Shade's position. She was scanning the island for sentries and a way to the compound.

'If we take the ridge line,' she said, pointing at a group of rocks along the shore. 'It will get us closer to the entrance.'

Overhearing, Draethus and Varican moved up. 'What about those sentries at the end of the ridge?' Varican asked, pointing.

Draethus could see two towers on the ridgeline, and the faint movement of Heridian forces.

'That will be Wrath's turn,' she replied with a grin.

'Who is this Wrath?' Draethus asked.

*

'Forward!' Captain Wrath ordered as the large tank group began its high-speed run down the ridge and into the city. The massive, tracked monsters roared, spitting black smoke from vents attached to the rear armor, crushing their way onto the ruined streets. The high-pitched squeal of axles echoed through the fallen concrete.

'Formation Serpent, keep your speed at high; we need to reach the waypoint within five minutes.'

He pulled out his small data-pad and re-read over the message he received moments earlier. Wrath knew his task, and there wasn't much time. Racing into the city lines was suicide, but necessary for the infiltration team to achieve their goal.

'Sir,' a voice crackled over Wrath's coms unit. 'We are approaching the way point with minimal resistance.'

'Understood,' he replied, adjusting the microphone unit on his helmet. 'When we reach the position, hold the line, shoot anything hostile and wait for further orders.'

'Copy that, Captain,' the man replied as the coms shut off.

The waypoint rested on the maximum range the tanks could land their shells. To Wrath's right, positioned a formation of smaller artillery tanks, used for sorties with no line-of-sight. Unlike the heavy arbalests, the artillery tanks were lightly armored and housed an enormous cylindrical cannon. Slowly, the artillery weapon atop each tank adjusted its angle towards the sky.

'Fire!' commanded Wrath, before fury unleashed onto the enemy in the distance. Twelve artillery tanks launched a barrage of shell after shell, a blanket of devastation that created streaking smoke trails over the remnants of buildings and ending in an apocalyptic mushroom cloud.

'Here they come!' yelled one of the crew.

The arbalest tanks supporting the artillery opened fire. Automated guns roared projectiles at the red menace, and shell casings littered the ground as they cut down the infantry charging their position.

Pieces of Heridian soldiers sprawled to the ground as their dark blood exploded, splattering the ground with bio-metal.

The Heridian armor support was not far behind. Striding through the carnage on six legs, the giant insect like machines unleashed crimson lasers over the paladin's tanks. One of the enemy machines stumbled as an arbalest tank blasted a shell into one of its legs. The shock wave was enough to knock it to the ground before it clumsily regained its footing and returned fire. The tank's armor glowed red hot as the other Heridian walkers focused fire, causing the ammo to explode and rip the tank apart. Losing the crew was enough for Wrath to call a retreat, as he only needed to create a distraction. He would mourn the loss later.

'Reverse to the next waypoint,' Wrath ordered. 'Lieutenants, call your targets and focus fire.'

*

Hearing the battle raging in the city, the Heridian soldiers took their gaze off the rocky coastline just long enough for Draethus and the paladins to slip past unnoticed.

The complex was vast, comprising many small structures roughly four meters in height, that hummed and pulsated with energy.

The team snaked their way towards the island's middle and planted charges on random structures as they went. Ahead was the center complex, a small white tower protruding from an octagonal building at its base. Large white doors seemed the only access, and looked heavily secured, even without the squad of six Heridians standing guard. Normally an infiltration squad would keep quiet, however the area to the complex was open ground with no cover.

Keeping crouched behind one of the pulsing generator structures, Draethus surveyed the entrance. The enhanced optics in his helmet provided a closer look and provided more information.

'It looks different,' he said in a hushed voice.

'What does?' Tremon asked as he slid into cover, being careful that his armor didn't touch the structure and alert the guards nearby.

'When we found this place, back where I came from, this complex wasn't here. It was just ruins, surrounded by four, fallen pillars. The area around here is unfamiliar, even the lake is new to me,' replied Draethus as he backed further into cover.

'Your entire squad died, right?' asked Tremon skeptically. 'I'm happy you're not leading this one.'

'Off you go then, lead the way,' Draethus said dryly.

Before Tremon could respond, Shade snuck up from behind. 'I have a plan,' she said, catching her breath.

'Of course you do, assassin,' Draethus added.

As the three joined the rest of the squad, Tremon grabbed Draethus by the shoulder and asked, 'How did only you survive, anyway?'

Taking one last look at their objective, he replied, 'Just unlucky, I guess.'

CHAPTER 8

With Loss of Conflict.

The bullet blew the Heridian's neck out, spraying blood across the facility's doors. The creature tried to turn towards the shots direction before falling to the ground in a heap of blood-stained viscera.

The alarm klaxons sounded and the towers surrounding the complex changed to an alert status. Another Heridian fell to the ground, but this time the shot didn't penetrate the armored head of the menace and it stumbled to gain its footing.

Enemy guards stalked in the shooter's direction, trying to pin down a visual target to relay to the above towers. Shade performed her role perfectly; the paladin squad was already halfway across the open area before any Heridians realized something had distracted them. Draethus reached the doors first, unsheathed his vibration sword, and began hacking at the remaining enemy soldiers with all the fury he could muster. The rest of the paladins drew their blades and followed his example.

Within minutes the guards were dead and the soldiers manning the towers lay unseen thanks to Shade's almost unnatural sniping ability.

Draethus Inspected his long-bladed weapon, impressed how

something weighing so little could cut through armor like paper. The cobalt, silver shine and the faint vibrations it created caused the enemy blood to splash away, giving the weapon a pristine appearance. He thought back to his old weaponry, a laser rifle, a mid-sized blade, and his electro enhanced sword. He had lost all during the charge for the complex, forced to lighten his equipment to run the gauntlet of enemy gunfire.

'Stand back,' a paladin said as he attached two mechanisms to each door. He flicked a few switches, and a burning hot laser joined the two, creating a flare so bright the men had to look away. When the laser finished, the door's locks were disabled, and one door pushed forward, causing the two mechanisms to fall away and smolder on the ground. With weapons drawn, the warriors walked inside and into a long hallway.

'Close it,' ordered Varican.

The hallway was wide enough for an arbalest tank to fit and twice as tall. Along the sides, pillars and pipes stretched from floor to ceiling, lights glowed and pulsated, showing electrical activity that fed into the circuit like pattern above. At the end of the hallway, some two hundred meters back, an impressive device stood atop a platform suspended by anti-gravity. Arcane stairs joined the floating platform to the ground whilst statues of reptilian creatures stood on either side at the base.

So, this is what it looks like.

Originally, Draethus had only seen the control mechanism which now stood at the top of the stairs. The device itself was only now visible to him, encased in a cylindrical force field with large metal clawed arms at each end. Within the field, two dark objects rotated erratically, with azure runes illuminated across the surface of the dark and oily metal.

The team advanced down the corridor and planted explosive charges along the walls, whilst keeping a lookout for enemies nearby.

'An obvious trap,' Varican said to Draethus as they led from the front.

'You're right, there should be Rids here,' Draethus replied.

They reached the stairs with no sign of the Heridians. The team was at the edge of their nerves and knew the complex should have been far more protected. Then, as expected, they were ambushed. Heridian forces had left a guardian to protect the displacement device. The massive creature fell from the ceiling and landed at the top of the stairs, causing the group to lose footing and fall back to the ground. The monster towered over the recovering soldiers, measuring nine feet in height, with large illuminated crimson runes across its armored, insect like body.

Draethus noticed massive armor plates on its left side and assumed they were an addition to the normal Heridian leader he'd witnessed in the past. Its hands were giant serrated claws, with a third claw protruding from a left upper arm. The tail was long, and its jaws elongated with multiple rows of nightmarish teeth.

It took a few steps towards the soldiers with its reverse jointed legs, breaking part of the stone stairs as it did so.

'Draethus,' it said in a deep, echoing voice, full of hatred and bloodlust.

'How do you know who I am?'

Draethus, blade drawn, knew the mechanical beast was more than his match. He had been lucky during the first battle to secure the device, and a feeling of closure whispered in the back of his mind. Something stirred in that point of darkness within him, and he wondered why he wasn't afraid. Was he ready to die and accepted his last moments? Even if he failed here, the charges in the complex would destroy the building and bury the machine. Guilt surfaced, for he knew the paladins shared his fate.

'I have already won this battle,' he said under his breath.

Gazing down the hall, the creature laughed at the small devices on the walls. It raised a claw and in a display of sparks, they sizzled and fried, falling to the floor.

'Do you really think our preparation is so lax, soldier?' it cackled, looking down at the human.

'You still haven't answered my question, beast,' Draethus said, his hand tightening on his blade. The paladins behind him readied themselves for the fight.

Howling in laughter, the beast's jaws were wide, displaying rows of murderous teeth before it said, 'This is not the first time we have fought.' It stalked forward and glared at the proud warrior encased in his dark gray armor. 'They sent me to bury you, soldier Draethus.'

Draethus struck first, launching forward with his sword, and slashing upward, aiming for the creature's throat, only to have it parried by the enormous claws. The menace struck down with full force as the soldier leapt to the side, slicing again with his blade at the base of the claw. The sound of grinding metal echoed through the long open corridor as Varican gave the command to open fire. Red and blue lasers lit up the Heridian creature, who only laughed as it continued its duel with Draethus. Dodging and parrying, Draethus was no match for the utter mass of the beast, his vibrating sword inflicting only light gashes in its armor.

A Soldier of the Void trained to be fast and resilient. Even encased in a lightweight graphene composite, with a thin layer of laser reflecting coating, he was weak compared to the creature. Its right arm came from nowhere and backhanded Draethus, sending him sprawling down the stairs to the floor below.

Both Tremon and Varican raced over to give him cover as they continued their non-effective firing. They struggled to drag Draethus back to the group as the creature launched itself into the air, landing in the center of the paladins. Two of the warriors died instantly, their armor crushed below its feet as their bodies exploded into multiple pieces. A third was screaming with his lower body pinned down.

The Heridian slowly reached down, savoring the moment, and with his claw, ripped the top half of the human away. It held the upper torso in the air, letting the blood flood over its face, howling in laughter before throwing it at Draethus. The torso skimmed past the three warriors, who froze in horror. Draethus regained consciousness, picked up his sword and through throbbing pain, assessed the situation. We die here today.

The paladins circled the monster, choosing their vibrating blades over their ineffective laser weapons. Slashing and stabbing, they swarmed, trying to take down the large prey. The odd paladin became the focus of attacks, succumbing to death in the blood painted corridor and one by one, the team grew smaller.

'We have to destroy the device!' yelled Draethus as he turned and ran towards the stairs.

'I'll stay and fight,' Varican replied. 'My paladins are my blood.'

'Tremon with me,' Draethus yelled, hoping the man would set aside his anger for the greater good, at least for the battle. Draethus lifted his sword above his head and with all his force struck down at the device, aiming to shatter the re-enforced glass. His blade deflected as an electrical current arced away, revealing a dark, lit force-field protecting the core. Continuously, both Draethus and Tremon slashed and hacked at the device, only to find they had no effect.

'There must be a better way,' Tremon said, trying to catch his breath.

'We are out of explosives and out of options.' Draethus had never been one for giving up. As a young recruit, before he became a full-fledged soldier, he endured harsh trials in the feral jungles of Echelon. Fighting man, beast, and gigantic monster, he always prevailed. When it looked like he was going to fail, something surfaced from the depths of his mind, and helped to conquer everything standing in his way.

'Creator knows I could use some explosives right now,' roared the soldier, stabbing again against the force-field.

The paladin team was dying. The device was too well protected and beyond the destructive means of their weapons, and there was nothing they could do. It betrayed the honor he felt in his heart, but Draethus knew what they must do.

'Fall back!' he yelled, racing down the stairs. 'We don't possess the weapons to destroy the device and dying here means nothing.'

As if experiencing surprise, the Heridian creature arced up and bellowed out a screech so evil, so horrific, it made Draethus' skin crawl. Howling with laughter, it stormed towards him with long fangs covered in paladin blood. Alongside pulsing runes, its mechanized joints whirred and spun.

Draethus jumped back as darkness flashed in front of him. Smoke filled the fighting area of the corridor and visibility vanished. He activated his helmet optics and saw the female figure of Shade, helping Tremon move down the long passage followed by one other paladin. He grabbed Varican and broke into a run and followed. Dishonor filled his chest, and he experienced the mental pain of failure for the first time.

'Draethus!' the creature screamed.

The Heridian leader slashed out in a crazed frenzy, looking for its nemesis, hoping to catch a lucky strike that would satisfy its bloodlust.

A guttural growl escaped the creature's jaws as its warning echoed violently down the corridor. 'We will finish this battle, coward.'

*

In his lab, on the Sky-Station, Spectalin moved his instruments over the containment cell, positioning them to closer inspect the prisoner. Restrained to a horizontal steel slab, the Heridian could only watch as small optical devices and surgical tools began cutting into it, learning the hidden anatomy beneath the unusual bio-metal plating.

'I heard Captain Wrath brought back a specimen of interest,' said the Great Senechal Praefectus, walking up behind the scientist.

'Yes, my Lord and a magnificent specimen at that,' Spect replied, looking up surprised. 'This is one of the commanding Rids, the soldiers that seem more intelligent and covered in those glowing runes.'

'Ah yes, the runes, have you figured out what they are?'

'It will take some time, but I will have more answers soon.'

'Excellent. If we can…'

The enemy strapped to the table thrashed about violently and interrupted the Senechal, howling the same word repeatedly.

'Draethus!'

*

Flashes of red and white flickered in the dark as ships from both sides tumbled and exploded. From a distance, the battle would have resembled shining insects, swarming amongst a cloud of explosive gases. The pirates had put up a brave fight against numbers far superior to their own.

The huge Heridian destroyer rolled gently as the trail of smoke, now shades of gray mixed with greens and purples, expelled superheated particles. Fires erupted down its side as molten metal armor plates peeled off, ejecting into its trail.

The *Arvernus'* engines burned brightly as they matched the velocity of the doomed capital ship, mimicking the roll to enter the gaping hole in the side. Sliding ever so elegantly into the cavernous void that was now their entry point, the *Arvernus* corvette disengaged from the chaotic battle and latched onto the stricken vessel. Harpoons shot out with a ping of magnetic discharge, connecting with a bulkhead.

Talon Commander Reaper's fighter squadron had since docked their craft and joined the *Arvernus'* crew in their new, on the fly, exploration mission. If they could find critical information about the Heridians, their bases, flight paths and weakness, then the war could be that little step closer to ending. Finding out what Stark was doing in there would be a bonus.

'Breathers on, watch the corners and stay together,' ordered Xain to his squad.

Raeson was no stranger to boarding actions. During the war, he had captured and boarded many ships, from an average trader running goods, to other pirate factions and even the local military. The outcome was always the same; he took what he wanted for the survival of his brethren. If the original owner of the vessel was co-operative, they normally lived. To ensure the cycle of goods and supplies was frequent, however, he handed back the vessels to their original owners for the opportunity of capture again.

The outer lasers finished cutting through the destroyer's bulkhead, joining the *Arvernus'* airlock to the capital ship, and with a loud blast and hiss of explosive dust the bulkhead blew inward. The boarding team rushed forward and set up near the entrance. Raeson, Tek and Nash, all with assault rifles in hand, hurried down the destroyer's corridor in the bow's direction. The airlock closed behind and locked, guarded by two crew members on the inside.

'We head to the bridge,' Raeson commanded as he scouted round a corridor junction and waved his team through.

'You know Commander, I'm not really cut out for this soldier dirt,' Tek said, slapping his own rifle on the way past. 'Don't mind the guns, though.' Dirt was a negative term to describe planet dwellers. Boring, unadventurous, and stable.

'I'm picking up movement!' Nash yelled.

Heridian drones zoomed in from the dark corridor ahead and began firing small lasers at Raeson's team. Like daemonic wasps, they kept their distance, wings unmoving, fangs clicking, and red glowing runes pulsating down their bodies. The three pirates dove in opposite directions, taking cover behind scrap metal that had peeled off the walls. Nash fired a burst from her rifle and half the face of a drone melted as it plunged headfirst into the grated floor below. It exploded like a firework into small chunks of metal and sinew.

'Shot girly,' Tek yelled across, met only with a look of disgust from the woman.

Two more drones exploded as Raeson destroyed the others. Leaping over the scrap, he swiftly secured the dead by kicking the biomass across the floor, creating blood spatters, like an abstract painting.

'What you think?' asked Raeson dryly. 'Am I the next artist to grace the Cygnians with my presence?'

'You're weird enough, boss,' Nash chuckled, walking up behind. 'Where are you, old man?'

Stumbling forward, Tek used his rifle as a crutch. Blood trickled down the side of his face as he said, 'One of those bastards got lucky.'

'Move out of the way, next time,' Raeson said. 'Let's get going. This vessel won't be whole for much longer.'

Raeson never knew if his words had reached the old man. The grinding of steel drowned out his voice and a quaking death erupted beneath their feet. When he refocused his eyes, a fresh fear gripped him. A bottomless pit replaced the corridor, still within the confines of the destroyer, but far from sight.

Tek had fallen.

Nash stood staring. Shock crept up her spine as the reality of what had happened dawned on her.

'He's gone,' she whispered.

'There's nothing we can do for him. He's dead,' Raeson said, grabbing her shoulder and forcing her along.

'I hate the man, so why am I upset?' she said under her breath. Closing her eyes and refocusing her vision, she added, 'Harden the fuck up.'

Raeson looked over his shoulder but said nothing.

*

Stark stared in amazement at the behemoth of pillars that stood before him. Never had he seen such a sight, let alone a monument within a space faring vessel. On the destroyer, in the hall from which he stood, metallic sculptures depicted Heridians fighting creatures Stark didn't recognize.

As he moved forward, the shadows danced on the walls, making the sculptures almost come alive in frightful motion. At the end of the hall, a terrifying monster of a Heridian statue, stood at attention like a military soldier. In one hand was a giant spear, and the other a skeleton of an unknown creature.

'That's got to be fifty meters tall,' he said under his breath. 'That thing better not move…'

The doors at the monster's base slid open as Stark approached cautiously, flicking his gaze between the statue and what was ahead. Weapon drawn, he proceeded towards his objective.

*

'This piece of crap ship!' Raeson swore. 'Show me the cheese.'

Time was against the pair, and the corridors were leading them around in circles.

'We passed this turn already,' Nash said, frustrated. 'This isn't how I imagined my life to be, you know, Boss,' she said, running her hand along one of the smooth walls of the corridor.

'Is that right? And what exactly did you think Pirates did?' Raeson was beyond caring.

'If you lived on some backwater planet, you would want excitement, too. I mean sure my father used to tell me stories of people trying to attack him during his trade runs, but I wanted to see for myself.' Nash daydreamed as she remembered. 'He always painted himself as the gallant space trader, dodging pirates and making his fortune.'

'So why did you become a pirate then? Isn't that what your father hated?' Raeson asked.

Nash's expression darkened. 'You know damn well why.'

'Look out!' Raeson dived at her, throwing them both to the ground. Lasers burnt and ricochet off the walls around them as they scrambled in the opposite direction. The sound of footsteps grew closer; the Heridian sentinels left to guard the ship had found them.

'Faster!' he yelled as they kept low, sprinting blindly down the hallway. 'Stick together.'

The sentinels were closing in and looking back, Raeson could see their silhouette. Unlike other Heridians, they were extremely tall, thin, yet agile. Each carried a weapon attached to their arms that spun as its laser fired.

Light ahead of them reflected off the sentinels armor, displaying the dark crimson tinge Raeson recognised. As they scrambled, they found themselves in a massive open chamber covered in exotic statues of creatures in battle, long since passed.

'This way,' yelled Nash as she headed to a pair of doors at the base of a large, towering Heridian statue.

Weapon's fire ricocheted and lit up the air around them as they dodged, choosing to flee instead of retaliate. Their assault rifles were powerful, but couldn't penetrate the sentinel's armor. As the pair ran through the doors, the last enemy fire fell short and out of range. The sentinel's efforts to protect the ship and purge the biological virus had failed.

Walking cautiously, Raeson and Nash, weapons at the ready, crept silently over the narrow-suspended walkway connecting the entrance to what appeared to be a control center. Holograms floated and rotated around computer consoles covered in strange symbols as a blue glow lit the railing.

'Check your corners,' ordered Raeson as they secured the room.

'Something's missing from the center of this machine,' Nash said, prodding the floating glyphs. Her finger reacted to the haptic feedback as if she'd received an electric shock. At the machine's center sat a claw, larger than a man's head, reaching vertically to the ceiling with illuminated wires hanging ripped from its fingers.

'Central core maybe?' she asked.

'Not our problem right now,' Raeson replied. 'Grab whatever information you can. This ship is far too big to find one person.'

Shocked, Nash asked, 'We're giving up? Tek lost his life so we could get here, and you want to bail out?'

'That was not a suggestion, soldier. Put your damn memory adapter into that console and don't make me repeat myself.' Raeson was angry. One man down, another with his own agenda stuck on an enemy ship, and it was a long way back to the *Arvernus*.

'Hell fell from the sky and I never wished for our extinction more,' Nash whispered.

'I told you…' Raeson said and stopped when he saw Nash's reaction.

Frantically waving him over, Nash's focus was transfixed on writing, repeating itself on a display screen. Raeson viewed the sentence, in their own language, as if placed there specifically for them.

'This ship creeps me out,' Raeson said, before the room faded into darkness. His limbs felt the pull of intense gravity as his body slumped to the floor. The last thing he saw was Nash lying next to him, covered in a strange, thin steel filament.

'Wake up,' droned a deep, monstrous voice, the sound of nightmare and terror.

Raeson and Nash shot to consciousness. Struggling and thrashing, they tried to fight off whatever ailment was keeping them bound. Suspended from the ceiling of a hexagonal room by fine steel filament, wires covered them like a web.

Towering over the pirates sat the embodiment of fear itself. Dark crimson gears and cogs spun under jagged armor plates as the Heridian moved and studied its captured prey. Twice the size of a normal Heridian, giant claws at arm's end and a mammoth jaw laced with fangs filled Xain's view. He could see movement in between its external ribs that acted as an armored chest plate.

'What are you supposed to be?' spat Raeson. The venomous tone of his voice hid no hatred for his captor.

'Such a bite from a tiny insect. You are a virus on my ship and the only reason you are breathing is I want to know what you did with my core.' The Heridian leaned in and Raeson could feel the fiery breath between its fangs. 'How about I pull your female friend here apart until you tell me?' The monster grinned and then added, 'I am Skylord Theradin, ancient among our race and captain of this vessel.'

It leaned back into its enormous chair like a king settling on his throne. Illuminated wires connected the chair to the wall behind it and disappeared behind a strange, extruded symbol. Raeson assumed it was Theradin's own personal mark.

'What have you done with my core!?!' the Skylord roared as he thrust his claw out, pausing in front of Nash's face, and watched her flinch. He grinned; rows of razor-sharp teeth caught the glow of the surrounding wires, turning its mouth red as if it recently consuming the blood of a human. It leaned back again and laughed, motioning with a single claw. The binding filament wrapped itself around her neck and squeezed. Nash let out a gurgling cry of pain as it pulled her in opposite directions.

'We saw no core.' Raeson's voice was loud but could not hide his panic. How had he become so attached? He'd been the subject of so much hate and resentment growing up because of his father betraying the fleet, so he had to reciprocate. Friends, although he had few, were scarce, and it was not like him to care for a member of his team.

'Unlikely, elismorus. As grand as you believe your race to be, I would never trust the word of a pirate,' the Skylord replied. 'What proof would you have of this?'

'A race and ship so sophisticated as yours would have some kind of security footage, correct?' Raeson's binding became tighter, almost cutting off the circulation to his arms that secured behind his back.

'Destroyed… By your attack on my ship.' Theradin shifted on his giant throne.

The bindings around Nash's neck loosened as she gasped for air.

'Not us,' she whispered.

The dark, terrifying creature grinned as he began moving his claws as if scratching an invisible animal in his palm. The filament released further, only to snake its way around Xain's forehead. One length of filament rose into the air and struck into his neck at the base of his skull. He screamed as it forced its way into his brain.

'No more!' Raeson cried out to the enjoyment of the Skylord.

'Let me show you something, pirate. Let me show you what will become of all your worlds.'

He felt so sick, nauseated, as the filament tendril squirmed inside, looking for the correct part of his brain. A small buzz of electricity pulsed through the filament and the surrounding room faded. As if by magic, the walls flew away into the distance, the metal floor melted into ash gray stone, and a strange substance covered the land. Storm clouds bellowed in, bringing lightning and loud crashes of thunder. A heavy rain fell from above and lightly singed Raeson's skin as he realized it wasn't just acidic, but red. He tried desperately to shake the vision.

'Look to your right,' a loud voice bellowed from the sky above.

It terrified Raeson.

'Look!' it roared again.

Slowly, he obeyed and turned to see a structure, barely visible at first. As he squinted to focus, he realized it touched every dark, fearful corner of his soul. It was a weapon pointed to the heavens, a long barrel extended outward covered in the same runes he had seen on the Heridian soldiers before. What powered this weapon sickened Xain, for he knew, somehow, the sentient beings nailed, tied and fused to the outside of its iron skin was the source.

'You see those poor insects fused to the weapons skin, human? That's what will become of all your kind. Harvest is your race's future. You all are below us.'

'Where is this?' Raeson cried, trying to cover his eyes, but found he could no longer move.

'This is my world.' As Theradin's giant face appeared inches from his. 'This is the world of Heridia!'

The surrounding room materialized again, and Raeson glanced across to see Nash's panicked face struggling against her bindings.

'Where is that world?' Raeson asked. 'In what part of this galaxy is it?'

'It isn't,' the menacing creature laughed. 'Now, where is my core?'

Raeson spat in the Skylord's direction. 'We took it right from under you! If you were half the race you claim, you wouldn't have let us get this far. Maybe if you weren't so focused on playing with your gears...'

'Insects!' The Skylord bellowed as he leaned forward, intensity burning a fire inside his eye sockets.
His claw slammed down on the arm of the great chair. The runes over his armored carapace of a body flickered and the gears underneath spun wildly. He stood towering over the two pirates. Steam hissed from his back as liquid began dripping from the ceiling, only to evaporate as it landed on the armor. The jaws belonging to the ancient Heridian Captain clicked as he moved in for the kill. Rage enveloped the creature as he pulled back his arm and lurched towards his captured prey.

Night fell on both pirates.

Raeson could feel the cold, the cold only the emptiness of space could provide, and wondered where he was. Dead maybe? Worse, was his mind ripped from his carcass and now living in the creature calling himself Skylord Theradin? Was he now part of the internal systems of the menace he had been fighting for most of his life?

'Do not question,' came a whisper from the dark, 'but sense.'

'Sense what?' Raeson asked, not knowing if he was talking or thinking about it. 'You make no sense.'

There was a long pause before the voice, which Raeson now considered being in his head, spoke again.

'Sense with your mind, a droplet in an ocean of your being, an echo of your true self reaching for the surface of reality.'

When Raeson regained consciousness, he, along with Nash, were laying on the floor outside the room of their imprisonment. Roaring screams came from the other side of the locked doors, with yells of monster, menace, and evil from the Heridian itself. Something crashed against the massive door and the sounds of a battle ceased.

'Time to go,' Raeson said, quickly helping Nash to her feet and checking her injuries. 'Back to the Arvernus.'

Entering the bridge of the *Arvernus*, Raeson stormed past the line of consoles and fell into his command chair. 'Begin de-clamp sequence, match our velocity and vectors with the destroyer.'

'Yes, sir,' replied the pilot sitting in front on the lower level. Engines whined and manoeuvring thrusters stirred as the corvette matched the roll of the damaged capital ship, creating slack in the grapples.

'Grapples released,' a voice said behind him.

'Matching speed and vector,' said another.

The sleek ship lit its engines and shot out of the damaged destroyer's hull, leaving it to tumble into the blackness, away from the battle.

'Open coms with the Vidar. I want a direct and secure channel to the Khan,' ordered Raeson.

Moments later, the Khans face appeared on a floating screen in front of the corvettes commander.

'My Khan,' Raeson started, 'my apologies for distracting you from the battle.'

'What is it, Xain?' Khan Hayreddin was short and to the point.

'I believe a member of our team has gone rogue, stolen something valuable from the destroyer you see hurtling out of control. We couldn't find him and request his arrest if he docks with the fleet.'

The image of the Khan flickered as the *Vidar* took a direct hit to the top of the port-side armor.

'Request it from somewhere else,' the Khan snapped and closed the connection.

Raeson sat silent for a moment and contemplated what happened. He felt annoyed that his request was so easily brushed off and it wasn't like the Khan to talk to him that way. Maybe he could have picked a better moment to make a request, though.

Orders appeared on his screen as retreat announcements broadcast from the Khan to the fleet. Slamming his fist down, Raeson stood and with fury burning his chest said, 'Head for the Vidar, our mission is over.'

*

The battle outside the doomed tumbling destroyer raged on as the Heridian forces overwhelmed the pirate fleet. There was a large flash of light and another capital Heridian ship appeared, opening up its front armored claw like doors and infesting the battlefield with more waves of fighters.

Squadrons of pirate craft banked around on an intercept course, knowing their chances of success were low, if not zero, and clashed in a storm of confusing aerial manoeuvres. Rolling, diving, jinking, and strafing, they fought for survival and, most of all, revenge.

Every pilot had lost someone, family, friends, lovers, associates, and hatred had consumed most into a selfless rage quenched only by Heridian blood. A fighter burned, its pilot on the brink of death only to crash himself into a Heridian craft, ricocheting off and colliding with another, taking two enemies down with him. From high above Stark watched, his fighter a safe distance from the battle, powered down and silent.

Helpless or safe, I wonder?

He sat quietly in the dark like a fly on the wall, watching his comrades perish in a battle that he could have been a part of.

'No matter, I need to get moving.'

Powering on only the minimalist of systems, he fired his manoeuvring thrusters towards the *Vidar* flagship. Slowly but patiently, he edged forward.

*

The largest of the Heridian capital ships, seven kilometres across and named in their language no human or elismorus could understand, sat in the center of the menacing fleet.

The face of the monstrosity resembled an ancient aquatic predatory creature crossed with an insect, covered in scale like armor plates and glistening with weaponry. Two large tail like structures attached themselves behind and arced up over the back, forming massive capital rail guns.

The pirates classified the vessel as the Heridian flagship, as no other resembled its size. The behemoth served as a fighter carrier and destroyer, the bringer of genocide to many worlds. Around it, escort vessels, large and small, swarmed like a school of fish, some spiralling chaotically and others drifting lazily alongside.

The area in front of the enemy flagship shimmered and stretched as light warped and enveloped it. An azure glow appeared as the fabric of space tore open in an incredible display that caused pulses of illumination to smother both forces.

Khan Hayreddin, standing on the bridge of the *Vidar*, shielded his eyes as one of the blinding lights hit the armored transparency before automatically dimming to protect the occupants.

'Is that a weapon?' he asked, knowing his bridge crew wouldn't have an answer.

The Heridian flagship flared its engines and disappeared through the tear.

CHAPTER 9

The Edge of Comprehension.

Livant scuttled across the desk, knocking over a beaker, and before it fell to the floor, caught it with his tail. With a relieved sigh, he carefully placed the glass back to its initial position. The small lizard flicked his tongue out, tasting the strange metallic odor lingering in the air of oil, metal, and blood. The scales on his back glistened as the skylight reflected the teal shine protecting his body.

Looking over, he stared at the abomination that lay close to death, bound and chained to the examination table in the middle of the room. Levitating on glass plates around the room, the creature's armor lay surrounded by a small force field, preventing contamination to the outside.

The menace moved, stirred, then struggled against its bindings. Livant bared his teeth and hissed as the door to the room slid open. Spect rushed in to find what the commotion was about, followed closely by two armed paladin guards.

'So, the creature wakes. Did you wake it, you little devil?' Spect asked, pointing a finger at Livant, almost expecting him to reply.

The lizard just stared at the scientist, mockery in his grin. As he neared, Spect noticed the gears of the captured Heridian spinning and whirring, its pistons pumping, and muscle fibres contracting under the dark red, almost translucent skin. Its insect like head glared at Spect as its jaws opened, revealing lines of damaged teeth. The creature thrashed again, trying to break free of its restraints, causing the paladin guards to prime their weapons.

'Don't get too close, sir,' one of them said.

Spect ignored him and waved a hand in dismissal. 'He's not going anywhere, soldier. Look at that.'

Scattered runes began glowing over the creature's body, but not as concentrated as before. On closer inspection, Spect could see into the menace's skull where he had forcefully removed the armor plating. Inside and barely visible, a brain pulsed, surrounded by a strange liquid and a clear oily substance with dark tendrils with a mind of their own.

The creature stared back at the ceiling and screamed, 'Destined one!'

*

The drop ship's engines screamed as it flew above the Sky-Station's magnetic interference, then spinning one-hundred and eighty degrees, touched down on a landing pad. Smoke streamed out from damaged areas of the craft as crews sprayed foam, trying to douse the flames. Armor peeled and melted to the floor, charred paint flecked in the wind, and the exiting soldiers kicked empty ammo casings from the deck.

'That was a severe waste of time,' Tremon yelled over the sound of spooling down engines and commotion. He threw his helmet and asked, 'How many more paladins do you want to kill, Draethus?'

Varican stepped between the men, trying to pull Tremon away.

'We all chose to be there, you know that.'

'Why don't you get in your big chicken and go shoot some Rids to cool off?' Draethus said.

'When the Senechal hears of our failure, he'll put you to death,' Tremon said. He bent down, and collecting his helmet added, 'During his prime, he was a thousand times the soldier you are.'

'You really have a thing for your great leader, don't you?' Draethus asked, watching the anger spread over Tremon's face. Draethus knew he shouldn't push the man further, but couldn't resist. 'How about we go find some green robes and play dress up? I'll even let you be the Senechal?' Draethus was furious, but he knew on some level Tremon was right. What really was the mission's outcome? Only failure?

Tremon was about to leave as a deck crewman ran up to them.

'Scientist Spectalin requests your presence in the examination room. Captain Wrath has captured something you might be interested in seeing,' the man reported, sweat pouring down his face.

'We'll continue this conversation later, Tremon.' Draethus said. 'And if you need help to get off the station, just let me know.'

Tremon was already halfway off the landing platform.

*

The dark faded as the Heridian opened its eyes, letting in the brightness of the hanging halogens above. The digital display icons flickered in its eyes and took readings from the blurry humanoids standing over.

It felt something prod into its side as electrical impulses surged through its system. It could hear someone screaming in the distance and realized it was probably its own. The display readouts suddenly ceased their flickering, and the captors came into focus.

A skinny male with fluffy hair and glasses was tinkering with the armor on a countertop nearby. His white lab coat flapped around, whipping into the face of a small scaly creature. The lizard, its eyes wide, seemed to reach into the coat pockets as if looking for something. Two others stood staring at the Heridian, one of which he recognised as wearing the colors of the local soldiers, however more intricate. A cloak covered one shoulder, pinned across the chest. The other man was taller, in blue gray armor, holding a sword that glimmered and vibrated with a high-pitched whine.

'Is the thing awake?' Draethus asked in disgust.

'Oh yes.' Spect put down the armor, greeting the two soldiers. 'Thank you for coming, and yes, welcome to my lab.' He shuffled over to the Heridian with a taser-rod in hand and said, 'It is awake. I don't think he'll be in a welcoming mood, however.'

'So Captain Wrath picked this thing up?' Varican asked, walking around the table. 'It's ugly. I bet you had fun cutting its armor off.'

'It was very satisfying,' Spec laughed. 'I rarely get to engage in such methods against any enemy. Captain Wrath disengaged from the distraction and got his forces to safety, but took a few losses. He inflicted some damage though, but as a gunner told me, he dragged this sorry excuse into his own tank. It's only because of an unexploded round that this Rid even survived. The gunner said he'd never seen a crew so shocked. Captain Wrath is just a tough case, in my honest opinion.' Spect pressed the trigger and electricity arced to the ceiling.

Draethus sheathed his sword, walked over to the Heridian, and heavily tapped its head with the back of his glove. The creature flicked open its eyes and, with jagged teeth, snapped at him.

'This guy needs a tooth clean, Spect,' Draethus said.

The heads up display in the creature's eyes changed color, the reds and blues melded into a purple, and the description of the human changed from unknown to something else.

'Destined one!' it screamed, staring at a confused Draethus before repeating the term.

Livant, the little lizard, scampered across the room in fear and jumped up onto Varican's shoulder.

'Why do you call me that?' Draethus asked, puzzled. 'Where do you even come from?'

The creature laughed. 'You do not know the home-world of Heridia? It surprises this one. I thought being from the future of this world you would have knowledge of such things.' It stirred in its restraints in a show of non-submission, its face twisted with hatred. 'We come from a world that exists, yet it does not.' The creature coughed and sputtered, spitting out a strange oil over itself and the table. 'Exist to harvest, to grow and survive. Feed until we have extinguished all biological life. We will consume your higher function organs for our own benefit, implanted into ourselves to become stronger and smarter. This is how we evolve. This is how we win.'

'Now look who's the talkative one?' Draethus said through gritted teeth, glaring at the enemy he'd known most of his life. 'You will never win, menace. We will kill you, maim you, all the way back to your world, this Heridia.'

Clenching his fist, he felt like beating the Heridian until it died, died in all the pain and anguish he had experienced. Draethus calmed himself and looked at Varican, then said, 'The Heridian fleet was first detected on extended range planetary scanners from a direction of nothingness, with no stars. Knowing they have a world could help us.'

'Can I ask something?' Spect asked.

'Only if you put your hand up,' Draethus said, with a serious expression.

The scientist flushed red as Varican said, 'He's not serious.'

'Oh, I see. You're a little strange.'

'Says the weird bush-haired scientist,' laughed Draethus.

'Why not attack the Rids from space if you had interstellar capabilities?' Spect asked. He had been listening profusely in the background. 'Why not fly over their landing zone and bombard them from the safety of orbit?'

'The Rids planted a defensive grid, creating an orbital interference from ground-based structures that originally detached from their capital ships,' replied Draethus. 'We could only reach the structures from the ground, but not with enough firepower to take them out. We tried, of course with our own fleet on the outside of the barrier and eventually lost them to Heridian forces. The boundaries and front lines changed often, but we held our own, which is what led me to this point, well that and the displacement device.'

'The device,' the Heridian stammered. 'Must take the device, must complete it.'

Draethus grabbed the creature by the throat, and it spattered more oil like blood onto his arm. 'What are your plans for it, Rid?' He squeezed further.

'The lords need it. They command and we obey. We can give them access to more of our forces throughout time and space. Untrap them, release them. You can release them, destined one!' The creature spasmed as its blood spilled out of the cogs, now spinning out of control over its body. The soldiers stood back and watched the last dying throws of their enemy's life.

'Heridia!' it screamed. 'It exists, but does not. Timeless, it burns cold in the stellar winds. You must find the Link that leads to it, destined one, find the Link!'

The spasms ceased as the creature came to rest, the display inside its eyes faded to darkness once more with only one command.

TELL HIM.

*

There was silence as the three men processed the Heridian's last words.

'That was fun,' said Varican, then asked, 'What is this Link, Draethus? A gateway maybe? Have you heard of this before?' He patted his scared lizard helper who then jumped onto a countertop.

'A few times,' Draethus replied. 'Over the years, we've captured Rids and coerced information from them. The Link is a location in space that opens a gateway to the Rid's home. We assume it's a natural phenomenon but aren't sure where it is, but at least now we know it leads to an actual world. I just wish he told me where to mail the thank-you card. Dear lords, it is with great pleasure I invite myself to your annihilation.'

Varican flicked his cloak back over his shoulder, 'So the Rids trapped on the other side, could they use that time device to escape?'

'I believe so,' interrupted Spect. 'Though it would only give them access to a time-shift, so to speak, and not a movement in space… oh.' He turned and looked at the floor in deep thought, face flushed like they had caught him out with something.

Draethus continued. 'We believe the Link opened, bringing the first Heridian wave to Echelon, so it makes sense they would be after something that could release the rest of the Rids. What's strange is that our leadership knew when the first wave would hit, and even of a second wave on its way.' He stared at Spect and noticed a drastic change in his behavior, then added, 'Teams were dispatched into the void, before the destruction of our fleet, to locate the Link. Some of those teams returned, and others were lost to the depths. If we can find these co-ordinates, we could take the fight to them.'

'On their home-world?' asked Varican.

'This so called Heridia, yes.' Draethus looked over at Spect, who was busy shuffling papers. 'What's wrong with you, scientist? Why are you acting strange?'

Spect couldn't make eye contact. 'Well,' he stuttered, feeling something stuck in his throat. He paused for a moment and continued when Varican gave him a hurrying motion with his hand. 'I might know why the Rids came to Echelon, and what caused the first wave of your war.'

'They wanted the displacement device, I know this,' Draethus replied. 'You're not telling me anything I don't already know.'

'That's true, but I only developed that a short while ago, based on the, um, how you say, original.'

'Original? What do you mean, original? Is there another one?' Draethus asked, astounded.

'Think of the displacement device as a scent, a trail. When you activated it on your end, you and the force of Rids appeared here in our time, but in the same space, the same area. The amount of energy used to activate the device is vast and temporal displacement would scream a signal in all directions for any capital ship's sensors.' The scientist ran a finger across the top of his thick glasses. 'So, when the enemy fleet in your time escaped through the Link, they would have detected residual traces of the device from our present, from right now. They landed and attacked your world, trying to search and pinpoint the device's location. But the machine I built can only displace bodies back in time, not space, as I could only reverse engineer some of it.'

'Reverse engineer from what exactly?' Draethus asked, on edge. He brought the Heridians to this era, causing all this devastation, but it was Spect who built the device. He could say Scientist Spectalin caused the first wave, but they may have attacked Echelon, regardless. By the creator, by appearing here did I attract the Rids to invade in my time? Are they now, at this very moment, following the energy trail and becoming the first wave?

'I call her the Dawn Eclipse,' Spect said enthusiastically, raising his voice and throwing his arms into the air, proud of his announcement.

'You didn't!' exclaimed Varican.

'Sorry Paladin Captain, but I'm a scientist and the lead engineer. Of course, I'm going to create technology that I believe will help our race.'

'What is this Dawn Eclipse?' Draethus asked, flicking the Heridian blood off his glove.

'It's a ship, of course.' The glee in Spect's voice was unmistakable as he added, 'And not just any ship, but a vessel of mystery and intrigue.' He steepled his fingers, hunched his back and in a deep and creepy voice said, 'Our race has occupied Echelon for centuries, and we even built the amazing Sky-Station you're standing in. Our technology has progressed immensely since we awoke here from our slumber pods.'

'Pods?' asked Draethus.

'Yes pods,' Spect continued. 'We don't really know where our race originates from, but we came from a colony ship that landed here thousands of years ago, sent out to populate other worlds. Over time, we dismantled it and built the station.'

Draethus was getting frustrated and asked, 'What has this got to do with the ship?'

'The vessel just appeared in one of the Sky-Station docks as if by magic and no one even saw it fly in. Security footage shows one frame the dock is empty, and the next the ship is moored. How fascinating!'

'Take me there, take me there now,' Draethus ordered. He was SOV, a Soldier of the Void, from an era locked in a constant war, and finally he was getting answers.

Spect looked over to where Livant was busy sniffing a piece of armor. The little reptile turned, feeling the scientist's eyes on him, and locked him in a stare. Livant slowly nudged the item off and sprinted for the door with a reptilian grin.

Minutes later Draethus, Varican and Spect were rushing through the crowds of people swarming the busy docking areas. Market place keepers called to passers-by, promising exotic goods from the jungles below at the lowest prices, their stalls covered in colorful tapestry. Some offered self-protection, weaponry, and other strange foods.

One man reached out and grabbed Draethus by the arm, trying to coerce him into his stall for some off world delicacies, found nowhere else, so he said. As they moved, Draethus marvelled at the high arched ceilings, lined with the carvings he remembered, over enormous windows with a view of the world below.

'Ignore them,' Varican said, pushing the stall keeper away. 'They will hound you until your pockets are empty.'

'They normally are,' Draethus replied.

They came into a clearing that opened into a large arc of levitating stairs, joining an above walkway horizontally across. Once up, they veered to the right, and as he looked over his shoulder, Draethus could see docked ships in the distance.

Most looked like merchant craft of various shapes and sizes, beaten up, aged, and overworked. One vessel looked so rusty he wondered how it even flew. Attached were panels of metal sheeting covering structural holes and looked to fall apart at any moment. Spect noticed the soldier's curiosity and, being the bearer of all knowledge, in his head at least, was glad to fill in the pieces.

'That's the dockyards, well part of it anyway. There are twenty-three docks in total and house all kinds of vessels, most being the merchants. That's where a lot of our food comes from, off world from other colonies, as the jungles below are too dangerous. You get the odd supplier that will try his luck at collecting the dangerous goods, but they don't normally last long. Even the people that live, excuse me, lived in the city below wouldn't be game enough to venture too deep into the jungles. The jungles, are they still there in your era, Draethus?'

Draethus continued walking, then glanced over his shoulder and answered, 'Haven't changed. If the viruses don't kill you and you survive the carnivorous plants, the giant reptiles will finish you.'

'And is our race still here?' Varican asked.

Draethus gave him a blank expression, which was more than enough to answer his question.

'I see,' was all Varican could manage.

The men arrived at a large door sealed by yellow and black warning signs, with two paladin soldiers standing guard on either side. Both stared ahead in rigid discipline, their weapons in hand, and made Draethus recall the statues in the main courtyard, back in his era.

'Gentleman,' Spect said, waving his hand forward, motioning to open the doors.

Annoyance crossed the face of one guard, and then begrudgingly he turned and accessed the panel behind him. The large security doors slid apart, and light blinded the group for a moment as the most amazing sight anchored before them.

When his eyes adjusted, Draethus was awestruck at the visual beauty of the mysterious vessel, the *Dawn Eclipse*. It resembled a majestic dragon of old, menacing, and omnipotent, nesting in the dock. So much unlike any craft ever seen, it reflected shades of gold and bronze like an ancient treasure at the bottom of the ocean.

Smooth curves travelled the length from bow to stern, with sleek armor plating, layered in stylish patterns crisscrossing over each other, creating visual illusions. Multiple tail fins protruded from the rear and sides, adding to the angelic appearance. It levitated, sat motionless, soundless, massive though sleek and all Draethus could do was stare.

He could feel it calling him, reaching out, and luring him to come closer. Darkness and light entangled and interwoven into something his mind could barely understand on the edge of comprehension. Draethus could barely make out what those around him were saying as he approached. He felt himself answering the ship's call and ignored the muffled warnings.

'Let him pass!' Varican ordered the guards, breaking Draethus from his trance.

Now aware of the commotion, Draethus found himself on the walkway next to the *Eclipse*. The guards nearby had weapons drawn and aimed at him.

Spect ran up and inspected the soldier who, with a look of disgust, pushed the smaller man aside.

'What are you doing, scientist?' Draethus asked, brushing the pesky white coated man away as he again attempted to breach his personal space.

'That was very interesting behavior. Very interesting,' Spect replied, backing away.

The guards nearby lowered their weapons as Draethus walked up the gangway that linked to the great ship, ending at its hull.

'How do I enter?' Draethus yelled to Spect who was eagerly waiting at the base of the gantry like an excited child. 'You can design a displacement device but not a door key? You're that kind of genius that can calculate the square root of the universe but can't tie his shoelaces, right?'

Running a finger over the top of his glasses, Spect shrugged. 'No one has entered, or found a door. We even tried cutting through, but nothing breached the hull, like I said a mystery. It wasn't impenetrable to my scans though, which is how I reverse engineered part of it.'

Turning back to the ship, the vessel still called to Draethus. It was like an electric impulse in his head, a siren calling over the waters of consciousness, a dark ocean descending into an endless madness.

Ever so closer he approached, the impulse increasing, and the once hushed voices grew louder, surrounding him in whispers. Frightful yet enticing, this vessel of uncertainty seemed alive.

Before he realized, Draethus reached out to it, connecting with something so ancient it may even predate the stars themselves.

Through his armored glove, the ship felt warm to the touch, vibrating with an exotic energy that now flowed through his body.

He closed his eyes and for the briefest moment could feel everything in the universe, every molecule, every particle, and the power to destroy or create with it.

The ship's hull activated with pulsing, golden runes, weaving patterns of intricate lines that appeared and flashed over the armor plates. Great engines roared and illuminated, sending ripples of heat and shock waves over the docks, knocking the nearby guards to the ground.

The ancient beast awoke from its slumber.

Plating around Draethus' hand shifted like a puzzle, creating an entranceway at the end of the platform. Without a word or hesitation, the soldier walked through and the world around him vanished. Screams filled his ears, burning his nostrils and the pain, the pain in his mind was unbearable. Collapsing to the floor, Draethus clutched his head and roared in agony.

'Make it stop!'

Flashes of crimson blinded his eyes as creatures clawed at his sanity, threatening to breach his soul. Scraping and scratching, he tore at his skull and let the pieces float into his hands as if by magic.

The ground beneath him transformed to soil as the surrounding darkness drew closer, trapping him into the smallest of spaces. Still, he clawed at his flesh. The screams grew louder, the blood in his hands fuller and his sanity on the verge of breaking. As quickly as it started, the visions subsided.

Draethus lay on the floor in the *Eclipse's* entranceway, being helped up by Tremon.

'You really are trouble,' Tremon said.

*

The enormous engines of the *Vidar* flared as the pirate flagship raced away from the battle. Fires burned across its gigantic hull, pieces of armor fragmenting and blistering away, and hot plasma streamed behind like a disconnected tail. Burn marks painted dark patterns across the vessel's port side as its weapons engaged the pursuing Heridian force.

The pirate fleet, minus fifteen percent of its original number, was on the retreat and keeping its distance. Destroyers, battleships, cruisers and other escort craft kept pace, valiantly taking damage, acting as shields from enemy fire in a disciplined formation. The enemy, a wave of dark reds, kept up the pressure as the smaller, faster craft persisted, trying to slow the pirates so their main capital ships could get into range.

On the bridge of the *Vidar,* the Khan stood calmly, his hands clasped behind his back, looking out into the darkness, through the transparent armor screen. A purple and pink nebula filled most of his view, stretching across the void like an eel through the water. The ship rocked again as a laser from a Heridian cruiser glanced off around the docking bay.

'Status on the nanite shielding?' Khan Hayreddin asked in a level tone to his bridge crew.

This wasn't the first full scale battle he'd seen and hopefully not the last. From his raids on the Common Worlds, the interception of merchant fleets in the Trade Cluster, to increasing his numbers by breaking out thousands of prisoners on Colman.

The Heridians had always proven the most horrific. Inhuman, insect like and robotic monstrosities, the creatures inflicted the greatest death toll. The pirate fleet had resorted to hit-and-run tactics as opposed to full scale assaults because of the overwhelming numbers and firepower presented by their enemy.

He didn't enjoy running.

He hated running.

After a few moments, one of the crew checked the damage report, fed to him by the live system integrated through his ear implant to the panels in front. 'Systems report we are at sixty percent nanite capacity overall, although the port side is at thirty and slowly dropping with the Rids faster craft close by.'

'Any breaches?' The Khan asked, looking over.

'None so far, my Khan, and engines are still functioning correctly.'

The gunnery station of the bridge was at a raised level to the back left. Its staff were busy controlling and manipulating holographic controls as they focused on fending away the attackers.

One of the crew stood and barked orders. 'Get someone down to the port side gunnery array and get eyes on why it's not responding!'

The man then turned to the Khan and with panic on his face stated, 'The side guns are malfunctioning.'

'Move a destroyer to our port side and get it between us and the enemy.' When the Khan gave an order, his crew were compliant.

'Talon Commander Raeson to see the Khan,' a voice from a crew member yelled out from the background.

'Approved. He may enter.'

*

Raeson was furious, enhanced by his elevated heart rate from the run through the flagship and questions relating to Stark. As he entered the bridge, he composed himself, slowed and steadied.

'Commander Raeson,' the look on the Khan's face was flat and emotionless as the younger commander walked out onto the massive platform.

Xain felt truly out of his depth, surrounded by dozens of people operating on different levels behind large panels and controls.

'My Khan,' Xain gestured with a small bow of the head and noticed the nebula in the view behind.

'What do you have for me, Talon Commander?'

'We encountered a Heridian leader aboard the damaged destroyer. He gave us information regarding their home-world, information I would rather tell you in private.'

'Very well,' replied the Khan, turning his back and looking out into the void once more. 'What was this Rid leader like?'

Raeson felt sick as the memory of his encounter surfaced back into the front of his thoughts. 'Huge, violent, sadistic and called himself Skylord Theradin. He tortured one of my crew and I for information about some core I believe was stolen by Stark.' Xain ran his fingers through his messy dark hair and said, 'I wish to have him placed in holding, for acting against the interests of the fleet.'

'Leave this to me, and I will see that he receives his dues. How did you escape this Skylord?'

Raeson was surprised with the bitter replies from the Khan and wondered if he'd picked the wrong time for his request. *Maybe I've failed? You idiot, we're in the middle of one of the largest battles we've seen in years and you bother him with this rubbish.*

'I'm... uncertain. We awoke outside the Skylord's domain to the sound of fighting inside.'

'Interesting,' the Khan replied abruptly. 'I want a report on this urgently. It could turn the tide of the war.'

'Yes, my Khan,' Raeson gestured.

His vision blurred, and he thought the Khan said something incoherent. Then, without warning, Raeson collapsed. Darkness filled his head, a crimson crossed his mind's eye, and pain roared

through him.
The screams were too much…

Raeson stirred as a medic jabbed a large needle into his arm.

'That should keep you going, sir,' the man said, his bedside manner dull. 'You might consider more sleep. You're exhausted.'

Raeson nodded. 'Couldn't you find a bigger syringe?'

The medic huffed, fiddled with some tools on his tray, and walked off.

Lying back, Xain stared at the ceiling and recalled what he'd seen. Such death and pain had flooded his mind, causing him to collapse. Those noises, the screaming, was he hearing himself?

What did that Skylord Rid do to me? To collapse in front of the Khan. How embarrassing.

CHAPTER 10

To Fell a Leviathan.

Gazing up at the gray clouds of the heavens, Captain Wrath felt the icy rain against his face as droplets fell into his eyes. The cool breeze merged with the warm exhaust from the arbalest tank as he sat, a moment of bliss before the battle ahead. There was always a calm eeriness before a fight that Wrath loved, a strange serenity. His tank company was motionless, hidden in the tall grass and mud, waiting for his command to power up and strike.

Even though the machines were massive, Wrath could make out only a few under his command, as the mixture of camouflage and submersion in the mud worked perfectly to plan. He took in another breath and another moment.

It was time. Wrath shook the water off his face and lowered the hatch.

'Forward scouts report a Heridian patrol approaching from the west sector, sir,' Lieutenant Camerous stated as Wrath strapped himself into his command chair.

'Perfectly on time. Notify the rest of the group but keep primary systems powered down,' Wrath ordered.

In the darkness of the arbalest tank, the captain switched on his forward monitor and saw a large squad of Heridian soldiers approaching, escorted by an array of walking armor, guns on legs.

'We'll make quick work of these,' he said, glancing around the dark at his men manning the drive and guns.

His crew on the lower level looked around, nodding as they readied themselves and began a quick diagnostic of their station's systems. Serenity of the pre-battle vanished, replaced by fury and a taste of anxiety, then silence. The only sound was the rain hammering down from above. The men waited.

'Power up! All armor is to engage the Rids to the front and focus fire on the lead walker,' Wrath roared, now in his element.

Thunder replaced the sound of falling water as sixty-seven of the largest tanks ever to roll the surface of Echelon, fired their guns at the unsuspecting Heridian squad. Armor plating, wires, gears and blood erupted from the enemy forces as they scrambled in response.

The lead five walkers evaporated in an instant, covering the landscape in red metal debris before turning the road into a smouldering mess. The ground troops at the rear of the enemy column veered towards the tank group and fired aimlessly at the mass of armor. They cut the remaining Heridians down with anti-infantry fire.

'Time to get this done, boys,' Wrath said over the coms. 'Fall in.'

The behemoth armored tanks drove forwards, lifting themselves out of the mud. Stopping at the tip of the spear formation, Wrath exited through the top hatch and made his way over the vehicle and down to the surface. Inspecting a torn up Heridian wreck, he ran his gloved fingers over some armor and felt the bloodied oil, smooth, frictionless, and wet.

'Have as many of these parts strapped to each tank as you can,' he ordered over the coms. 'If these things have some sort of identification system, maybe we can mask our approach.'

Wrath peered down the road and took in the smell of mechanical death around him.

We'll need every advantage possible if we're going to win this fight.

*

Its long metallic claws tapped across the steel railing, creating sparks that lit up the dark control room in the complex housing the displacement device. Silently, though quickly, Heridian soldiers busied around the different computer panels pressing holographic buttons that changed color and vibrated to the touch with haptic feedback.

'How long?' the giant Heridian leader asked impatiently. 'I want it done now…'

A soldier below looked up. 'Three half cycles, my Lord,' it said, then in fear of retribution, twisted its attention back to the consoles.

A screen to the right of the Heridian Lord illuminated and came to life, showing a large group of red blips overlay onto a map of the local area.

The Heridian lord laughed. 'Like insects, they keep coming. Maybe this time they will stay and fight, unlike the last cowards, so disappointing. Let them in close. I want all of their force engaged in this fight. Send word to our forces they are to feign surprise and die if they have to.' The soldiers in the room acknowledged in the standard Heridian language. 'When the cycle count down is complete, this pathetic enemy will burn,' the Lord grinned. 'Wherever you are Draethus, I call to you now. See this fire as a beacon and fight me once more!'

*

'Open fire!' roared the order over the coms from Captain Wrath to his tank formation.

The landscape exploded with hundreds of bright orange and yellow streaks of light, connecting with the large complex over the water. Concrete and steel ruptured, sending dust and debris into the air with pieces crashing into the murky liquid surrounding the area. The tank force had masked its signature perfectly and surprised the Heridian enemy guarding the displacement device.

Enemy troops quickly took up positions across the other side and returned the onslaught. One tank bore the focus of enemy fire and exploded, causing vibrations through the ground. Repeatedly, the thunder of guns rocked the landscape in a dance of violent confusion. Heridian walkers exploded as the tank group shifted focus to reduce the incoming damage and where one died, another would take its place in a never-ending battle.

'I want twenty guns on that complex at all times,' Wrath yelled. 'The rest take care of that enemy armor. Gunners target the Rids on the ground. They might be small, but they add up. Any sign of their ground artillery, Camerous?'

'No, sir,' the Lieutenant replied. 'No sign at all, which is strange. Forward scouts reported seeing them in this area days ago. It wouldn't make sense to leave the complex unprotected.'

'No matter, just keep at them. All units spread out in case that artillery makes an appearance.' Wrath tapped a few keys on his console. 'This is Captain Wrath to Sky-Station. We have engaged the complex and require aerial assistance. If we win this fight, the complex will be ours for the taking.'

The coms crackled and a gruff voice replied, 'We didn't expect you to engage. Why did you not notify…' the voice cut out abruptly, replaced by someone more superior.

'This is the Praefectus. I commend you on getting so close to the complex, you must have caught them off guard. You will have aerial support shortly, Captain.'

'Thank you, sir,' Wrath replied, fighting the urge to solute over the coms.

Another thunderous shudder rocked the command tank as a friendly unit exploded unexpectedly, killing all the crew on board. Wrath turned his external cameras to his force and saw the extent of the damage. Fires covered most of the monstrous vehicles, and armor on some were melting, however they continued their onslaught. For the first time they were winning, a fact Wrath knew, but losing people dulled the excitement. All under his command were his responsibility, his pride, and his fault.

The enemy lines had piled up with twisted metal debris that the Heridians took advantage of for cover. The once murky water turned black with whatever ran through their veins. A Heridian walker scaled over a wall, let off a blast from its over-shoulder cannon that landed in the dirt, before reeling back from return fire and breaking into pieces in a smouldering explosion. Sparks ignited the fuel-soaked ground nearby and burnt a blue fire, sending gray smoke into the already clouded area. Wrath's gaze followed it skyward, and he noticed something shimmering above the battle.

The ground shook violently as the battle-damaged complex transformed and opened, flooding the surrounding area with intense light. Wrath could feel the air around him tingle with electricity as the hairs on his arms stood up.

This isn't good.

A single laser reached into the sky from the complex and hit the shimmering clouds above. A terrifying crack of sound ripped across the heavens, tearing the fabric of time itself in a show of amazing illumination. For a moment, all Wrath could see was white as he shielded his eyes, then all faded to darkness as a star vessel of immense size emerged from the tear in the sky and blocked out the sun.

*

'This way!' Draethus yelled to his colleagues behind him.

He was in a wide passageway of whites and grays, with an illuminated blue underfloor that increased in intensity as he walked on the different sections. At every few meters, the bulkheads seemed to come alive with mechanical activity, reacting to his presence. He stopped at the base of some stairs leading up to a double doorway of smooth, white metal.

After finding a way in, the team had been exploring the ship, and although they'd discovered some remarkable rooms, the bridge or command section had evaded them. Spect ran up from behind and hugged the door like a friend he hadn't seen in a lifetime.

'This has to be it!' he screamed. 'This has to be the control bridge. Can we cut through it?'

'Move aside,' Draethus said, clamping his hand on the scientist's shoulder. 'That panel on the side has the same markings as before.'

He lifted his hand up, a beam of light appeared, and the doors phased out of existence. Walking onto the command deck, the equipment activated, panels sparked to life, holograms flickered and morphed, and the floor once again illuminated a soft azure. Six panels with flight chairs rested on both sides of the center, leading out onto a ledge overlooking a lower section. Bulkheads lined the room shaped with curvatures, soft edges, and thin lines.

Tremon and Varican excitedly entered the command deck and joined the others.

Noticing the expressions on their faces, Draethus asked, 'What do you think of my new ship?'

Varican's grin was infectious as he answered, 'I think it would be a great donation to our cause, considering what you brought here.'

'Thanks for reminding me.'

'What do you make of that?' Tremon asked as the team looked over the ledge.

Below the group rested a liquid of dark reflection, a metallic substance that shifted like an ocean stretching the entire length of the bottom level.

'Is that supposed to be there? It doesn't look right,' Varican asked.

'It's a little unsettling, isn't it?' Spect was almost dancing with excitement. 'I'm sure you can see the stars in it too!'

A section of liquid splashed up against a bulkhead and separated like a wave crashing on rocks. Draethus could see a nebula shining a multitude of colors in the shimmer's surface.

Unsettling.

Spect danced around the consoles like a child exploring his new toy, pushing the holographic keys, and smiling when they vibrated in response to his touch. One console displayed a disc that the scientist subsequently grabbed hold of and rotated, ending in a clicking sound.

'Maybe you touch nothing, Spect,' said Draethus, feeling an anxiety brought on by their unfamiliar surroundings and the fear of some defence system killing them all. Pushing buttons can be dangerous.

The lights on the bridge faded to red as a digital warning klaxon sounded, and the strange liquid below became a still, dark reflective lake once more.

'I didn't do that, I swear,' the scientist said as they all stared at him. 'Wait, what's that?'

A three-dimensional scene appeared in the air over the liquid, depicting almost a hundred massive tanks fighting a battle across a large lake against hordes of Heridian armor and infantry.

'That's the complex,' said Varican, gripping hold of the guardrail. 'Is that happening right now? How can the ship see this?'

'I want one of these hologram machines…' Spect said sheepishly, slinking away after he realized, he spoke aloud.

The lead tank moved to the front of the line and destroyed an enemy walker that exploded and fell into the lake.

'That's got to be Captain Wrath.' Tremon had been in the paladins long enough to recognise the markings. 'I wasn't aware there was an assault on the complex?'

'We should be…' Draethus said, interrupted.

A light blinded them all, followed by a dark tear that opened over the battle. It shimmered, like the liquid below, and illuminated the edges of the surrounding space. A massive Heridian vessel emerged and cast a shadow over the carnage below as the payload of weapons it carried unleased an inferno through the lines of tanks. Clusters of the paladin war machines exploded as the huge capital lasers bombarded them with streaks of plasma, transforming the battlefield into a molten mess.

'What is that?' asked Varican, mouth wide open.

'The Rids,' Draethus said, rushing over to the consoles. 'How do we get this ship moving!' he screamed, pushing buttons, trying to get a response. 'Spect…'

'I'm on it,' the scientist replied, reverting to his previous behavior of twisting holograms and dials, though in a more serious and determined manner.

The rest of the team followed their example, choosing a console each and hoping blind luck could help them. Draethus slammed his fist down in frustration, his voice drowned out by the battle still raging on the hologram. The surviving tanks scattered in all directions to avoid the aerial bombardment, racing full pace away from the complex, most of them damaged and on fire in some respect.

The ship's audio system activated in a strange language, a deep mechanical voice that sounded inquisitive, then it paused…*Commander?*

'You speak our language?' Draethus exclaimed, feeling hope flood his mind, and rushed over to the hologram battle. The three other men looked at him, puzzled.

'Who speaks our language? What are you talking about?' asked Tremon, bewildered.

'The ship spoke Echelonian, did you not hear it? Ship, take us to that battle.'

Those around you cannot hear this voice, Commander Draethus, from the Soldiers of the Void. The voice in his mind felt warm, yet somewhat ominous.

I knew something felt unsettling, well the screams in my head should have given that away. What do you call yourself, ship? Draethus thought, feeling crazy more than curious.

Known by many names over the eons and in many languages. Your scientist referred to the name the Dawn Eclipse, which will suffice.

Alright, Eclipse, take us to the battle.

This can't be real.

Step over to the ledge… the voice faded in Draethus' mind, and he felt its presence drifting and lingering in the background.

The railing phased out, like the door earlier, and a platform levitated from beneath the dark metallic waves and floated to the edge of where the soldier was standing.

'What's going on?' Varican asked him as Draethus stepped onto the platform. It dipped in the air with his weight.

'I think the ship likes me,' Draethus said. 'It accepts the name you gave it as well, Spect.'

The scientist's face brightened as if he had just received the greatest compliment of his life.

The platform floated out over the dark liquid lake and without warning plummeted into the middle. Draethus hadn't the time to react to the panic of drowning before he found himself in an unworldly place. The surrounding area was a dim red, with floating patches of black cloud that gradually swirled around him like ink in water. His mind couldn't comprehend what suspended him, but he relinquished and breathed. The fluid entered his lungs as his heart pounded in fear and subsided after a few breaths.

We are as one, Commander Draethus, the dark voice said into his mind.

His thoughts washed over with a strange yet familiar feeling of being, as he could feel the ship's systems coursing through his veins. In his mind's eye, he could see himself as the sleek golden ship, berthed at the dock. He willed the exotic vessel to move and felt controls manifest in his hands. He thrust the throttle forward and from his view of the outside watched the vessel's engines flare a hot white, and the ship propel forward.

'Pick a console,' Draethus said over the coms to the confused team on the bridge, which was about to climb down to the bottom level to rescue him. Shocked at first, they complied.

'I will guide you throughout your systems as we need it,' Draethus finished.

His mind was everywhere through the ship, but with help he could multitask easier. Somehow, by being one with the ship, he just knew how to operate the systems.

'Here we go, ready yourselves,' Draethus said again.

The golden ship's engines flared even brighter, before accelerating and leaving the Sky-Station.

*

Looking out over the lake, the giant Heridian, leader and guardian of the displacement device, stared at the flames that burned into the sky. The creature's long serrated tail slapped the dirt in amusement, knowing how much death the vessel above had just inflicted on the paladin armored force.

The smell of burnt flesh wafted through its senses as the wind changed direction. Smaller Heridian soldiers rushed around carrying supplies and tools, loading them into large platforms dropped by the ship above.

One such platform had finished being loaded as four thick cables lowered down, attached themselves, then lifted the structure into the ship. Every surface of the ground had something ready to haul as the complex was stripped and transported onto the ship.

'Drop the tethers and take the device,' the lead Heridian communicated to the massive carrier above. 'Take care. If it falls, so do you.'

Within moments, more tethers lowered and began lifting the section of the complex housing the displacement device.

'Your transportation is ready to proceed,' notified the carrier.

The leader stepped onto a platform, sent a notification to the ship above, and as it lifted saw a flash and commanded, 'Tether faster, the device needs to reach the carrier now!'

The creature looked across to the other platform and screamed.

*

The golden vessel, the *Dawn Eclipse,* burst into the skies above the battlefield with a crack of thunder and a flash of light. It vectored high, rolled over, and dived into the shadow of the now rising carrier above.

'By the creator, what is that vessel?' Varican asked in horror. 'Is it alive?'

'And what are those structures being lifted?' Tremon asked as he fiddled around with his console, pushing highlighted buttons as he ran through a brief training exercise started by the ship's new commander.

After a brief pause, some puzzled looks from Spect and a shrug of shoulders from Varican, the voice spoke again over the coms from Draethus. 'They're stripping the complex and taking the displacement device aboard that giant Rid vessel. We can't let that happen. If that device is operational, and that ship escapes, there will be no way to halt the Heridian forces.'

'Let's shoot it down then.' Tremon's hands hovered over the holographic weapon hilt that controlled the weapons. 'Target the device and let's end this. I'm sorry, Draethus, I know that means you can't return home.'

Reflecting on Draethus' actions and seeing the hatred he had for the menace, Tremon, for the first time, displayed compassion for the man.

The ship levelled, entered a firing pattern before jinking off to the side as a laser from the above carrier caused it to break off its run.

'Circling back around,' Draethus notified the already focused crew.

The golden vessel banked back around, shifted from side to side, and locked onto the signature of the displacement device. Tremon's controls lit green as he squeezed the three triggers in both hands. Six lasers pulsed out from the smooth sides of the ship, smashing into the rising platform causing the tethers to buckle then snap. Tumbling, the device and its structure fell. Its sheer mass pounded the ground and buried it deep beneath the surface, leaving a crater and incapacitating enemy soldiers.

'The mass of the device must have been immensely dense to cause a crater that large,' said Spect, abandoning his console and leaning over the railing for a closer look.

'Forget about that for now and get back to your console.' Draethus ordered, enjoying his new command. 'Follow your training and mark the Sky-Station as the next destination.'

'Copy that… Commander Draethus,' Spect replied with a smile. 'Sounds good, doesn't it? The Heridian vessel is on course for the Sky-Station. I think we made it angry. Oh, and by the way, what's it like in that metal liquid… stuff?'

'You can ask questions later,' Draethus replied. 'I'm only interested in cracking that space crab open and tasting its juicy contents.'

'Have we got enough firepower to take on that vessel?' asked Varican with worry in his voice.

'I'm not sure. I locked the waypoint in and are flaring engines. We'll do all we can.'

Draethus initiated the burn to the station.

*

'I know Draethus is piloting that ship. How did he learn to control it so quickly?' The Heridian leader roared furiously, as he paced the length of the command bridge on the enormous Heridian carrier.

Its tail scraped along the metal flooring behind, causing it to spark before flicking up and scratching the viewing window that stretched the length of the bridge.

A voice from the shadows in the corner warned, 'Don't mistake your status as one able to damage my ship without punishment.' The source of the voice was stern, but not insulting.

'That attack was far too fast. He must have had help, and he's destroyed the displacement device.' The leader stopped itself from lashing out again, pulling its third claw from the viewing window.

The voice from the dark continued, 'The Lords need that golden ship, you know this.' It moved about and shuffled in the dark. 'The device existed only for the purpose it now served.'

The leader growled like a wild animal challenging another, 'I know its purpose. With that device, we would not need that ship and the lords could be free.'

'And if the device never fell, you would not be here now, would you?' the dark voice laughed.

The Heridian leader, angry, was not in any mood to be told what he already knew. 'When we reach the Sky-Station, open fire with everything you have. I want it crashing to the ground before we leave.'

*

The *Dawn Eclipse* slid quickly sideways into the dock of the Sky-Station. Upon arrival, the side hatch opened, and Paladin Captain Varican exited. He turned to face the ship's new commander, the soldier Draethus.

'The Sky-Station is my home and my responsibility. I need to get my people to safety before that enemy ship arrives,' Varican said, gripping forearms with his friend. 'If I don't see you after this, I wish you all the best in your next endeavours.'

'And you, my friend, may the creator watch over you,' replied Draethus as Varican turned and walked down the levitating gangway. 'We'll have a drink when we meet again.'

The Paladin Captain laughed.

A short time later, back on the bridge of the *Eclipse,* both Tremon and Spect stood next to their consoles, and greeted their commander as he walked between. The stern expression on Tremon's face told Draethus that he was finally warming to him.

'You've both stayed, then?' Draethus said with a grin.

Spect was beaming. 'Have you seen the science bay here? It's massive! I could spend months just learning how to use the equipment. Plus, I don't need to endure the taunting of that little animal, unless it gets onboard of course.'

'And you Tremon, what's your reason? I thought you would have stayed with the paladins.'

'It's a privilege to serve with a ship such as this. I protect my people with the best methods possible, so an exotic vessel with guns, lots of them, would better suit me. I may also have to redeem myself with how I treated you in the beginning.'

Draethus slapped Tremon on the shoulder and said, 'You're not going to start crying, are you?'

Tremon laughed and replied, 'You could be so lucky.'

'No, I see a tear… right there…' Draethus pointed to the man's face and had his finger brushed away.

'Don't push it.'

'Well then, let's get to it. Get to your stations and let's try drawing away that Rid monstrosity. It will give the people time to evacuate the Sky-Station.'

Spect looked uncomfortable. 'Can the ship operate with only the three of us?'

'Don't worry,' replied Tremon. 'I'm sure we will manage, what with our amazing gunner.'

*

The Heridian carrier was half the size of the Sky-Station, but twice as deadly. The station's anti-air defences pummelled the opposing vessel with projectiles and lasers but couldn't breach the nanite coated armor of the brutish vessel.

Enormous shell casings dropped into the jungle below like metal rain, splashing into the wet mud and scaring the wildlife which fled into the depths. The smoke of weapons fire concealed the towers of the station, with only the large guns visible, their recoil sending visible shock waves through the superstructure.

Watching from under the liquid of the lower-level command deck, Draethus felt small and powerless. The only plan they had was to distract the enemy vessel long enough for the trade and drop ships to ferry people down to the surface or flee. Some trade ships had already left, seeking profits somewhere a little less hostile, and others still loaded their cargo. The *Eclipse* strafed the bridge of the enemy carrier repeatedly, trying to entice it to follow and lead it away.

'Wish we had bigger guns,' Tremon said, clutching his controls and firing another salvo of lasers at the enemy vessel.

Incoming signal, the *Eclipse* announced into the mind of its commander.

Display on the main hologram, Draethus replied, still uncomfortable, speaking inside his own head with another voice.

A large image of the Heridian leader they fought previously appeared as a three-dimensional image hovering over the liquid. Its face occupied the front of the top level, causing Spect to jump.

'You... You fought that?' Spect asked in astonishment.

'That's right,' Tremon whispered across. 'It's even uglier in person.'

'Draethus!' the Heridian leader roared. 'I see you've come back to face me again.'

'And you are just as putrid as before, menace,' replied Draethus, now tired of the game the creature thought it was playing.

'So, here's how this is going to play out, insect,' the Heridian leader began. 'You are going to land your ship inside one of my carrier's docking bays and surrender your golden vessel. If you do not, I will wipe that station from existence.' It smiled, revealing rows of metallic razor-sharp teeth. 'Can you justify the loss of so many people just for your pride?'

Can he see me? Draethus asked the *Eclipse*.

Yes, this is a two-way connection. The words washed over his mind.

'You see this face, menace?' the Commander said, pointing. 'The next time you see it will be when the lights dim, from your soon to be, cold dead eyes. I will not surrender a vessel that you can use to benefit your race or release your lords.'

The Heridian leader couldn't hide its shock that Draethus had knowledge of its masters, or their imprisonment. It laughed, 'Then how about you treat my offer as redemption for leaving me to die on the *Dark claw,* old friend?' The Heridian paused and let the words sink in. 'You left me in the torturous claws of our enemies, to become one of them, and I swear I will make you suffer the same fate.'

Draethus couldn't believe what he was hearing. He felt dumb founded, and shock filled his chest, revealed by the look in his eyes. 'It can't be… No, you died?'

'Yet here I stand before you, more powerful than I could ever be in the flesh, an officer among the mightiest species that ever existed!' The Heridian leader cut the communication with a swipe of its claw.

The Heridian super capital weapons ignited, creating rings around the two large tail weapons that arced over the massive vessel. Forced to shield their eyes and block their ears, the residents of the Sky-Station panicked as an immense energy beam fired from the carrier.

A huge chunk of structure broke off the station, a corner that slid like water on glass and fell. Rubble, twisted metal, girders and bodies followed the large piece down and crashed onto the surface, throwing dust into the air and covering the landscape in a shroud of destruction.

'You filthy menace!' screamed Draethus as tears flowed from his face. 'Johan, how could you do this?'

He is one of them. He will follow their commands. His mind corrupted and turned against everything he ever loved. The release of death can only save him. The ship's voice in his mind was soft, knowing how much mental pain Draethus was in.

Draethus wondered if the ship could read his thoughts or just hear the words he projected.

The carrier is turning and vectoring back to the tear which is closing. We haven't much time. What are your commands, Draethus?

Follow it through, Draethus thought. *Follow it through so we can end my friend's existence.*

CHAPTER 11

The Precursory Eleven.

The corner of Sky-Station had torn away, like a ravaged island falling to the depths, dragging unwilling souls whose only motivation was escape.

On the station, Paladin Captain Varican, along with soldiers and some civilians, searched the rubble for survivors, hoping to finish the evacuation using ships untouched by the destruction.

'Varican!' a man yelled from the other side of a twisted walkway that had fallen across the main dock area.

Varican glanced over to see a collapsed section covering some food stands. As he ran up, he could hear faint and familiar cries, reminding him of the first time meeting Livant, the small lizard. Back then Livant was happily swinging from a tree with his foot caught in a trap. The tone of his voice this time however, was full of panic and fear.

'I'm coming little one, are you hurt!?!' Varican yelled. Squeezing through the dangerous remnants, Varican caught sight of the lizard, who was squirming in agony. 'Just a bit further, hang on!' The man from earlier, a gruff and hairy mechanic, in full coveralls and covered in dust, came from behind them. 'Lift from here,' he said as the two men levered the girder, letting the small creature drag itself out of the rubble. They let it drop as Varican scooped up his lizard.

'Thank you,' Varican said, bowing his head. 'I don't know what I'd do without this one.'

'Very welcome, Captain. I need to keep going, but I'd suggest taking your friend to the infirmary, although it's really crowded.'

'I will, and thank you again.'

One of Varican's greatest fears was losing his little helper Livant, and he felt guilty for leaving him in the infirmary. Was he abandoning him? He knew that fear was manipulating his senses and pushed the feeling down. Duty called.

He stood amongst others in a briefing room on the Sky-Station. Emergency lighting shone from the floor, illuminating the Praefectus, who appeared dark, as opposed to his normal, bright demeanour. The gathering of people around him comprised the greatest leaders and commanders of Echelon, and was curious about their summons. Murmurs echoed around the small room as they wondered why, during such an ominous time, would their leader waste time assembling people when they should be fighting the enemy.

Lead Armor Commander, Captain Wrath, stood to the front, with a newly acquired slash across his face from the recent battle he barely escaped. His subordinate, Lieutenant Camerous, leaned on a chair at Wrath's side, clutching a broken arm as he swayed from a concussion. The rest of the group, Varican, knew mainly by reputation only.

'You may wonder why I've called you all here to this meeting,' Senechal Praefectus began. 'The battle against the Heridians has tested our strengths and shown how fierce and determined we are as a people. I commend all of you here today for your bravery and tenacity against overwhelming odds.'

He took a moment to look everyone in the eye before continuing. 'These invaders are the greatest threat we have ever faced.' The group stirred with a reaction the Senechal expected. 'Our war against the Heridians has been short-lived compared to how long our descendants shall fight.'

'We will never give up!' someone yelled from the group as others added their agreement, with nods and cheers.

'You're right, we *won't* give up,' he said with a smile, 'which is why I have selected you all here in this room. Our people are leaving the Sky-Station and abandoning Echelon.'

Varican felt confused and noticed identical expressions on everyone's faces.

'After the recent invasion and the threat of further conflict, traders will never again make their fortunes here. With the destruction of the city below, it isn't viable for our people to inhabit this world. It will only be a matter of time before commerce in this solar system fades permanently and Echelon will be a dead world. We must think of our long-term goals and remaining here will only see our race perish. The Heridians are here to stay, and there is nothing we can do about that right now. However, the fight is not over. As you all know, the information provided to us by the soldier known as Arcilous Draethus tells us the war continues far from now. It is this war that requires the same heroics all of you have shown.'

Wrath was the first to question, 'What do you require of us, Senechal Praefectus?'

'I require,' he answered, 'volunteers to continue the fight in the next war for Echelon. I understand that some of you have families and will wish to leave, and that is expected. This is a great ask, and something I don't want you to feel forced into doing as we'll need soldiers for the years ahead, anyway.'

'You've piqued our curiosity,' Varican said, looking around at the crowd. 'If we stay, what then?'

The Senechal straightened his green robes and replied, 'Deep within the Sky-Station exists hidden vaults containing left over hibernation chambers from the colony ship that landed here hundreds of years ago. You will sleep for thousands of years until awoken by the next inhabitants of this world, the people Draethus referred to as the Soldiers of the Void. Help them, fight alongside them, and protect this world from the coming threat of the next invasion. With your knowledge and expertise, they will stand a chance against the Heridians.'

There was silence at first, followed by a mixture of acceptance and angry grumbling in the group.

'This sounds ridiculous. Why can't we stay and fight them?' asked a man from the back. 'If we're going to stay here, why not fight?'

Another man joined the protest and asked, 'How do we know the Heridians won't find us in the vaults and kill us? Who will protect the fleet?'

The Senechal nodded in acknowledgment. 'You are free, of course, to make your own decision, as I cannot force you to follow the plan.'

'As you wish, Great Senechal,' Wrath said with a raised voice and stared down the men against the idea. Bowing his head, he added, 'I will continue the fight.'

'Any others?' the Senechal asked. 'Like I said, if you have a family, I understand. This will be a drastic change to your life and I know it's an enormous decision. Our descendants need your help and leadership.'

The prospect of leaving Echelon permanently wasn't something Varican ever wanted to consider. He felt duty bound to fulfill his leader's request, and it didn't take long to decide. 'I'll volunteer,' he said gracefully. 'If it helps fight this menace, then I'm all in.'

A few other men raised their hands to volunteer, some shook heads in rejection and others stated they needed time to consider.

As the gathering headed for the exit, the Senechal stepped forward.

'Camerous.'

'Yes, Lord?' Camerous was not accustomed to dealing with his leader directly.

'Or should I say, Captain Camerous?'

The newly appointed captain beamed before the Senechal continued, 'It has been a long time coming. You've fought well alongside Wrath and your promotion is well deserved.'

'Thank you, my Lord Senechal,' Camerous replied with a big smile before Varican slapped him on the back in congratulations.

Acknowledging the Senechal, Varican exited the room and headed for the infirmary to collect Livant and then his possessions. He felt excited about the new chapter in his life and wondered what adventures lay ahead.

After much debate and deliberation, eleven captains volunteered for the life-changing assignment, forever know as The Precursory Eleven.

*

The *Arvernus* appeared from translocation in a bright flash, with sparks that quickly faded, shimmering into non-existence. Immediately its engines flared, and the pirate corvette traversed the emptiness of space, its matt black armor dulling any reflections from the nearby star.

With the pirate fleet on the run from Heridian forces, the Khan had tasked Raeson with infiltrating enemy lines and monitoring their traffic. The anomalous tear from earlier, that had swallowed an enemy vessel, had been slowly closing, and the Khan, concerned, needed more information.

Raeson wondered if this task was simply punishment for his behavior against Stark, or just a way to stop him from asking more questions. Rumors spread quickly and were never in the fleet's best interest. Was he just in the way?

'Get me a heading to the tear and keep systems running at minimum,' ordered Raeson. 'I don't want an engagement this far out with no backup.'

Their previous pilot, Tektar, had been killed on the Heridian destroyer, in their last battle. The new pilot was young and Raeson wondered what he'd done to deserve his new position.

'Yes, sir,' the youngster replied. 'Power down weapons as well?'

'Everything.'

From the back of the command deck, Slin, now recovered from surgery, moved his robotic arm across his panel and powered down most of the ship's systems. He gave Nash a small grin and, looking up, enjoyed watching her blush a little. Nash had been through hell, tortured by a psychotic Heridian Skylord, and almost lost her love and partner, who now seemed to enjoy his cybernetic implants. Yet still she remained strong willed, a trait no doubt inherited from her father.

The bridge of the *Arvernus* felt strange without the humorous, and sometimes annoying, Tektar. He had been a drunkard, self-loathing joker of an old man that Nash had hated, but admired. Replaced by a red-haired, green nosed youngster whose name no one ever seemed to remember.

Xain Raeson stood at the front of the bridge, staring out into the darkness, still haunted by the demonic visions he encountered. Ever since that moment, his perception of the world was different, like something was calling to him and it felt stronger the closer they got to the tear.

'Estimated time to the over watch point on the tear, Nash?' Raeson asked.

'Three hours, sir,' she replied. 'If need be, we can flare the engines again, which will cut that time in half, though we'll run loud.'

Raeson turned and walked to the bridge exit. 'Keep her on quiet run. We have time.'

*

On the command deck of the golden vessel, Tremon and Spect stood with their commander.

'So, I guess you know that Heridian,' Tremon started, referring to the conversation he witnessed during the fight above the Sky-Station. 'Considering it cut down a squad of Paladins, men I knew, I wouldn't mind an answer... Commander,' he finished with a respectful nod.

Draethus was still in shock with the knowledge of his friend's capture, and felt he could have done something, helped him. Although the term captured was a very loose term for his demise.

'He was my friend, Johan, Johan Servatus. We trained together to become SOV, and fought by each other's side for a long time. He saved my life many times, and I his.'

Spect sat back at his console. 'So he changed into that creature during a battle? Like a Rid would have grabbed him and...' he made a ripping motion with his hands.

'Yeah, something like that. I lost him on a vessel we tried salvaging under the ocean, and I thought he died.' Draethus ran his hand through his hair and rubbed his forehead. 'Something else that's my fault. I should have done something, but it doesn't make sense. We designed a failsafe into every soldier, to counter any Rid that tried to take a mind.' He pointed to the back of his neck to a disc under the surface of his skin. 'If a Rid tries anything...'

'An explosive device?' Tremon asked, surprised.

Spect started approaching his commander to investigate but held off, not so much out of etiquette but concern for his own well-being.

'Remind me not to stand too close if a Rid gets you,' Tremon said.

The comment forced a smile on the Commander's face before he said, 'If I die, the explosive device will sever my spine, making it impossible for a Rid to take my mind, drastic but essential.'

'I understand, but we've seen Heridians do that before, though none of them end up looking like whatever creature we encountered in the complex. I mean sure they glow with the runes, but Johan was something else entirely,' Tremon said.

'My understanding,' Draethus continued, 'is the Rids have a hierarchy. If a Rid with a higher status takes a mind, it moves up that hierarchy and the mind gains control under the corruption of the machine. They meld together as one entity.'

Spect rubbed his chin, mumbled to himself, and started fidgeting.

'You have something to say, scientist?' Draethus shot him a look.

'I was just wondering,' Spect said nervously. 'Would the stronger the mind taken equate to how high in the hierarchy that machine would place? I mean he was SOV, strong willed, so is that why he is a leader amongst them? Or was that by his choice?' He looked down, 'I don't mean…'

'You're asking me if he sold out and became a Rid through fear, death or pain?' Draethus felt his blood rising.

'No, no, no, I don't mean that, just if his personality measured his level of hierarchy.'

Draethus paused.

The warmth flooded his head again as the ship spoke to him through his mind. *He means well.*

'We might never know, Spect,' Draethus smiled. 'Let's hope none of us experience it. Then again, you like to tinker. Care to try it out?'

'That was a joke, right?'

A warning klaxon blared before Draethus could respond, and he walked over to the railing.

Commander, we are approaching the Heridian flagship, the *Eclipse* said in his mind.

Adjust our trajectory to approach from below. Can we get into the tear before it? Draethus questioned.

No, we will trail through behind. In order to pass through the tear, we would need to be in proximity.

At least we might get under its big guns, would give us a fighting chance. Get us there, Eclipse.

Yes, Commander.

'Strap in men, we're going in under the Rid's guns. Spect, keep our shields forward and above, but our speed high. Tremon, I want weapon power diverted to engines. We're going to need a boost.' Draethus headed for the liquid lake as both his crew acknowledged his commands.

The *Dawn Eclipses'* engines screamed as the golden vessel accelerated towards the Heridian flagship once more. Anti-air flooded the sky with violet streaks of plasma as the enemy ship fired its guns at the incoming vessel.

The ship rolled and banked over, weaving from side to side, navigating through the maze of death. A cluster of missiles headed towards them, leaving behind a trail of white smoke, then separated into smaller pieces. Each small warhead homed in on its intended target, spinning and twisting, calculating its attack trajectory. A burst of laser fire from the *Eclipse* lit up the area in front of the ship, blanketing the enemy missiles with a mixture of heat and electromagnetic pulses that disabled the projectiles.

'Excellent work, Tremon,' Draethus said over the coms.

'I wondered what that button did,' Tremon said to himself, smiling.

The ship rose sharply into the shadow of the behemoth and matched the speed and heading of the Heridian carrier, nestling in a dark crevice inside the gun's turning circle. Without the support of the enemy fighters, the carrier couldn't locate or fire upon the attacker.

We are in position, Commander, the *Eclipse* communicated to Draethus.

The tear came up quickly, a shimmer of something Draethus could only perceive as blue electricity. Both vessels dove through the tear in reality, the rip in space-time that defied the known laws of physics and traversed to another place. The Heridian Carrier was once again back where it belonged.

*

'Something's coming through!' the young pilot on board the *Arvernus* yelled.

'Alright, keep it down,' Raeson commanded back to him. 'I'm looking at the same screen as you, boy.'

The enormous carrier entered the fabric of space, slowly and patiently, a predator taking its time to stalk its prey. Its hull bristled with guns and other weaponry, and then finally the world ending tails emerged, signalling its complete materialization. The tear, now depleted of energy, vanished without the light show Raeson expected. An anticlimax to the rarest of objects in the universe.

'The vessel is altering its course, sir,' Slin said from his chair behind. 'Look's like it's heading for the rest of the Rid fleets last known location.'

'Alright, let's shadow this thing for a while, after all the tears…' Raeson cut his command short as laser fire rocked the *Arvernus* from below, as three Heridian fighters launched from the carrier, sensing a kill.

'All turrets open fire! Get me a lock onto those bastards and change heading back to the fleet. I want this sky clear.' Raeson's blood was pumping under the pressure of combat.

'They've launched more fighters, sir!' the youngster called out.

'Nash, get us out of here,' Raeson ordered, almost louder than the enemy weapons fire slashing into their nanite armored hull.

'We have eight, no twelve more fighters inbound.' Slin was marking them with his hands as the small holographic blips floated over his console. 'Estimate, they will be on us in twenty seconds. With that firepower, Commander, not even the Arvernus can withstand…'

'I realize, Slin,' Raeson replied with a grimace from his command chair. He finished buckling his straps and flicked away data floating in his face. 'How are we looking, Nash?'

'Engines are over flaring, but we don't have the initial speed to outrun those fighters.' Nash was hectically pulling out power from every system she could find that could get them away just that little faster.

Fifteen fighters buzzed and strafed the *Arvernus* as it rolled and dodged erratically, trying not to lose speed whilst keeping to a heading away from the Heridian flagship. One enemy fighter got too close and disappeared in a flash of explosion, taking a direct hit from the forward guns.

The turrets of the defending corvette fired in all directions as the on-board computers did their best to track the fast-moving Heridian craft to little avail. Two fighters appeared on the rear of the pirate vessel and launched a ferocious volley that vanished into the bright flares of the engines. A minor explosion signalled the demise of the corvette's continued acceleration. The *Arvernus*' engines activated emergency systems and shut off, though the ship continued to move forward through the void.

'We are adrift,' Nash said hopelessly from the now dimly lit control panel at the back of the bridge section.

'Sir, we have another blip heading our way from beneath us, a lot bigger than the fighters,' Slin reported.

Raeson stared out of the transparent armor of the forward section and wondered what he could have done differently.

If we hadn't needed the speed, we could have brought the defence fighters along.

'The larger blip is almost on us,' Slin whispered.

Like a school of scared fish, the Heridian fighters scattered in multiple directions, trying to evade a greater threat. Two fighters exploded instantly, showering the *Arvernus* in debris and molten metal. A third trailed off into the distance, spinning out of control, leaving behind a trail of venting plasma.

The golden vessel, burst into Raeson's view from below, a flash of light across his mind. He staggered back, surprised, and unsure of what was happening. 'What beast is this?' he asked in Slin's general direction.

'Ah, that was the blip, not sure if it's friendly but it doesn't like the Rids.'

'Well, let's not anger it.' Raeson walked over to the group of consoles. 'Keep firing, but don't hit that ship.'

The *Dawn Eclipse* rocketed high above, before falling onto its back to fly another pass at the attacking Heridian fighters. Streaks of light burst from the bow of the ship again and sent another fighter to its death, ripping its wings apart. The remaining hostiles scattered away from the battle and fled back in the flagship's direction. As the enemy carrier translocated from known space, the fighters vanished within its proximity.

Slowly, the *Dawn Eclipse* approached the stricken pirate vessel, gliding up beside and keeping away from the *Arvernus'* front weaponry. The golden vessel was five times the corvette's size, mostly in length, and differed in design. Where the *Eclipse* shined in elegant golden layers of intricate waves and trailing fins, the *Arvernus* was black, slim and sleek.

The youngster aboard the pirate vessel brought up a three-dimensional image of the other vessel and let it rotate on the bridge. 'Impressive,' he said, making sure not to meet his commander's eyes.

'Very,' Raeson replied, walking to the side display screen. 'Anymore outbursts and you can see it up close and personal.'

The young pilot flushed red and focused back on his systems.

'The vessel is opening communications with us,' Nash announced. 'Should I accept the connection?'

'Not much else we can do, accept the link, Nash,' Raeson ordered.

There was a brief pause as white noise sounded over the coms, followed by a deep voice of authority, with an accent Raeson couldn't place.

'Stricken vessel, my name is Arcilous Draethus of the *Dawn Eclipse*. State your damage status and intent.'

'Sounds like law enforcement,' Slin said. 'I haven't seen one of those in years.'

Raeson touched the device on his ear to reply to the faceless voice. 'My name is Talon Commander Xain Raeson of the corvette Arvernus.' He thought about hiding who they were and decided against it. Some truths now might just build the trust they needed. 'They disabled our engines with no means of self-repair, but weapons systems are working to normal standards.'

'And your intent?' Draethus asked.

'We were here to monitor the anomaly, the tear, and Heridian movements in this area. We are enemies of the Rids, as you seem to be also, and request docking rights and haulage back to our main fleet.' Raeson shifted on his feet, knowing what question was coming.

Draethus' voice over the coms paused for a moment, then asked, 'And what fleet might that be?'

'This is bad, sir,' Nash whispered. 'What if he thinks we're a threat and just vaporises us like he did the Rid fighters? Shouldn't we make up a story, then board and take his ship?'

'Look at you being all pirate like,' grinned Slin.

Raeson was already ahead of her. It would make sense. Dock, meet the *Dawn Eclipses'* crew, take them out and steal the ship. After all, it was big, deadly, and looked amazing. There was something causing him to hesitate however, and not because of the other crew's help. Something had been calling him, a whisper in the back of his mind ever since that flagship entered the tear.

Raeson smiled and said, 'My crew thinks I should make up a story and convince you we're harmless individuals scouting the area.'

'I see,' the voice replied.

'As you seem to be enemies of the Heridians, I will extend a trust to you normally only reserved for our allies.' Raeson could see his crew's anxiety as they knew what his words meant.

'We also saved your lives, and you are sitting dead in space, so you really don't have any choice but to trust us, Commander Raeson,' Draethus warned.

'Yes, I suppose you're right.' Raeson could almost visualise a finger on the trigger with him firmly in its crosshairs, begging for a reason to blow them out of space. 'We belong to the Cygnian Pirates, a force focused on the destruction of the Heridian race and anyone who allies with them.'

Pirate.

The word hovered in the air for what felt like an eternity to the crew of the *Arvernus*. The youngster was sweating profusely, his hands shaking and feeling his last moments were upon him. He didn't want to die. Nash sat, her face buried in her hands whilst Slin just kept watch on his commander. Xain Raeson, Talon Commander, stood as always unshaken in front of his crew.

'Pirate,' replied the voice of Draethus, again over the coms. 'So, time travel, assassins and now pirates? What should I expect next, ninjas?' There was a brief static as Draethus pondered his next move. 'Tell me pirate, if I hauled you back to your fleet, would you ally with me to fight against the Rids on their home-world?'

The question shocked Raeson. 'No one has ever found a Heridian home-world. It's a myth, laughable!'

'It's real, and we are currently hunting it, which is how we ended up here. There is a Heridian leader on-board that flagship you just saw that can give us the information we need.' Raeson wondered why the man would share so much information so freely. One ship won't last against them. He needs us.

Draethus continued, 'Before that Rid carrier left, he, or it I should say, sent me the co-ordinates of a meeting place it wishes us to converge on. It intends to capture the *Dawn Eclipse* and release their home-world, and he wants the pleasure of killing me. I will take on his challenge and finish what I started. This abomination will die, by my hand.'

'So, what are your demands, Commander Draethus?' Raeson asked.

'It's more of an agreement than a demand. We'll haul your ship to the safety of your fleet and you can help us locate a point of interest, the meeting place, for our duel.' The logic made sense and Raeson knew the man was desperate to trust a pirate, or stupid.

'Understood,' Raeson replied. 'Consider the agreement well and true, and if you can locate the home-world of the menace, we will be in debt to you.'

'Happy to help. Begin docking procedures and let's meet face to face, and Commander Raeson?' Draethus asked.

'Yes?'

'If you cross me, I will make sure you never get that location.' Knowing Draethus had the leverage he needed, Raeson began having second thoughts about trying to take the other ship.

'Consider us allies. So, what is this point of interest called exactly?' Raeson asked, glancing at his crew.

'Tiberous.'

The crew of the *Arvernus* looked at each other with dread.

CHAPTER 12

A Meeting of Morality.

The pirate vessel *Arvernus* sat motionless against the hull of the *Dawn Eclipse*, tethered by an invisible array of lasers strengthened by the tethering cables of the corvette itself. A docking collar extended from the golden ship, creating an air seal for the *Eclipses'* crew to cross over.

On the bridge of the *Arvernus,* its Talon Commander, Xain Raeson, stood with his crew beside him, facing their rescuers. Draethus took center, tall encased in his dark gray armor with his helm collapsed back. On his right was his rival, Tremon, and behind to his left, the scientist, Spectalin. Silence ensued for a few moments before Draethus started.

'I'm disappointed,' Draethus said. The pirates looked confused before he added, 'I expected eye patches.'

Slin laughed, but quickly stopped when he noticed Raeson's gaze.

'You must be Draethus?' Raeson asked.

'I am. You are all unarmed, I take it?'

Raeson turned his palms outward as a sign of trust. 'We are and have no intention of engagement here, especially with what's at stake. In the end, it's our race against the Rids. There is no greater threat, right?'

Tremon, with his ever-untrusting personality, squinted and scanned the pirates in front of him. 'Can't trust pirates, if you give me a reason…'

'We don't need to fight you,' Nash replied. 'You saved us, and we're in your debt after all.'

'What race are you exactly?' Draethus had the tendency to be a little blunt and hoped they didn't take offence.

'The Cygnian Pirates are a mixture of human and a race you obviously haven't met before, called elismorus.' Raeson slid a finger over the side of his head, joining his ears. 'We're a little different from humans, but not that different. The elismorus are mostly space faring and doesn't like the dirt much. Slin, over here is full Elis, I'm half.'

'Then we have full humans like me and…' Nash pointed to the young crewman next to her, 'him.'

'I have a name, you know,' the young pilot said, running his fingers through his thick red hair.

'And maybe one day we'll remember it,' Slin laughed, lightly punching him in the shoulder.

'So how did you come about fighting the Rids?' asked Draethus.

'A long tale of death,' Raeson grimaced. He leaned back against his command console to ease the tension in the room. 'The Rids hit us hard, took down our stations before wiping out our families on our home-planet. That was long before I was born, of course. My father used to tell me the tale when I was a child. The fleet was away in another sector of space and came home to find our world on fire, with nothing left. Since then, we've been a nomadic race collecting allies who experienced similar fates, of their own free will or not. That's how the humans came to live amongst us, driven by the same thirst for vengeance.' Raeson motioned for the newcomers to sit, pointing at the nearby console stations near the door. 'So, what's your story?' he asked.

Oh, it's story time is it?' Draethus asked sarcastically.

Spect tapped his fingers across the new controls in front of him and said, 'We were minding our own business on our home-world when this guy appeared from nowhere with an army of Rids hunting him down. We fought, lost, found a golden spaceship and followed them through a tear in space-time. Quite simple, really.'

Slin chuckled. 'Well, you're a special one, aren't you?'

'Scientist actually,' Spect replied.

'Very special,' Tremon dropped in with a grin.

'When you appeared from the tear, dusted the Rids and saved our arses, our inclination is to trust you,' Raeson said. 'But we need more information if we're to trust you, Draethus.'

I have co-ordinates locked Commander, do you want to proceed to translocate? the *Eclipse* said into Draethus' mind.

Proceed.

There was a flash in the eyes of both crews as the *Dawn Eclipse*, with the *Arvernus* attached, translocated out of normal space and headed to the location of the pirate fleet provided by Raeson.

'We are underway, roughly ten hours to reach the location of your fleet,' Draethus said, seeing the pirates' concerned expressions. 'My story, I haven't really talked about it much, I guess, even to my crew. I'm also from Echelon, the same jungle planet as these two, although at a different point, forward in time.'

'What, like the future?' the red-haired youngster said before realising he spoke out of turn.

'Yeah, the future, hard to believe even for me. I'm a Soldier of the Void. I shoot things, explode Rids and fly an ancient star vessel that might someday eat me.' Draethus could sense he had the pirate's full attention and felt the last of the tension lift. 'The SOV, as we call ourselves, arrived on Echelon when I was young, which is how I came to be in their service. The first wave of Heridians attacked us, wiping out all our space faring vessels and left us stranded planet-side. When I vanished from there, the war had been raging for decades, although in our favor. We downed the last of their orbiting vessels and even killed their leader. I believe I took most of the remaining enemy with me when I activated the displacement device and ended up in your present... well, on the other side of the tear before it closed.'

'You beat them?' Raeson asked, surprised. 'Hundreds of Rid capital space craft accompanied by thousands of fighters, escorts and ground troops?'

'Creator, no,' Draethus laughed. 'Three orbiting capital vessels, nothing like the size of that flagship you just saw, cruisers at most. I'd estimate ten thousand ground troops with armor support remained.'

'What hit you must have only been a small section of their primary force.' Raeson said, troubled. 'Why send only a small portion when the main body of their armies could have defeated you in mere hours?'

Nash approached the new crew, put down three glasses and poured a dark liquid into each, then repeated the same for her own crew mates. 'It's a common drink brewed in our fleet,' she said, drinking. 'See, it's not poisonous.'

Tremon tried first, sipped before closing his eyes, enjoying the burning sensation down his throat. 'Hope you have more of that,' he coughed.

Spect took one smell, realized it contained alcohol and pushed it away.

'What's the matter... Spect, was it? You don't drink?' Slin said, taking a sip of his own.

'I like nothing that clouds my thoughts. My brain is useful, and I can't afford to kill it with toxins.'

'That's why Slin loves the stuff,' Nash said, twisting the glass in her fingers. 'He killed those brain cells years ago.'

'Is that why I'm with you?' Slin asked mockingly as Nash pretended to throw the glass at him.

Draethus held the glass to the light and continued. 'When the SOV arrived on Echelon, they found something on its moon revealing when the Rids would appear. They thought they were ready for the first wave but underestimated the Rids firepower. There's a second wave coming, though, but we're not sure how large. The SOV leaders are aware of when but are unclear to the co-ordinates of their origin. If we can discover that location, rebuild our space vessels, we can wait and hit them as they arrive, hopefully a great distance from Echelon.'

'What did your leaders do to find it, this location?' Slin asked.

'They sent out teams to search for information from other worlds, races, stations, even following old stories, clues and artefacts. None, as yet, have found anything confirming the location, and most teams are still looking.' Draethus tried the drink for the first time, approved and continued. 'With your help we can find Heridia, the Rid home-world, and destroy them before the next wave could even start. It may even prevent the first wave from even happening.'

'I see. Well, when we reach the fleet, I'd like you to meet the Khan, the leader of all Cygnians.' Raeson said as he knocked back the drink. 'I'll draw up the report explaining everything that you've told us and request your help. He might even provide you with more information. He's been around a long, long time.'

'Don't let the Khan hear you say that,' said Slin. 'He'd space you in a heartbeat.'

'No doubt.'

'I'm surprised,' said Draethus, with a smile.

'That we haven't tried to capture you, or is this about the eye patch thing again?' asked Raeson.

'Oh, the latter.' Draethus placed the glass gently on the console then said, 'I expected you to overpower us the moment we came aboard.'

'We thought about it, but I guess we're just lazy pirates,' Raeson chuckled. 'In all seriousness, if you can give us the location of the Rid home-world, you can keep any ship you want.'

'And I'm bigger than you,' Draethus said. 'That's the real reason.'

'And uglier,' retorted Raeson.

'Now boys…' interjected Nash. 'Let's not get off track here…'

Draethus didn't trust these new men and women, but felt he had no other choice. He knew that his decision to translocate to the pirate fleet might end in the death of his crew, and again he felt at a crossroads. The leverage he held, however, the duel with the Heridian leader, was the only plan he had. Draethus felt as if the fates were aligning and giving him the opportunity to make a difference in the war, and hoped it would turn out better than his last decision. The liquid ran warm through his system and a fresh sense of calm washed over his mind and senses.

Tremon was right, this stuff was good.

*

With the crews now introduced to each other, and a plan actioned, the sense of anxiety passed for both parties. The night had been relaxing and Spect, the only truly sober person now aboard, finally got the chance he needed to go exploring.

Previously, the golden ship had sat in the docks of the Sky-Station for months and the curiosity was unyielding. It was during this time that Spect had scanned the vessel's internals and decoded a portion of its secrets, which is how he built the device that caused so much trouble. But to get full access now to the ship itself, he was like a child given his dream toy to do whatever he wanted.

The ship felt even bigger inside than he imagined, with endless corridors stretching down its lengths, connected by an everlasting labyrinth of junctions. Spect stopped to catch his breath, leaned up against one of the smooth glossy white bulkheads, and pulled a device from his dirty lab coat.

'Forgot I had this,' he said out loud to himself. 'Bringing you along wasn't a waste of time.'

He held a metallic ball about the size of his palm, and twisted the top, causing it to click and come alive with lights and a low-level buzzing. He threw it into the air where it stayed and hovered. 'I want you to fly around and scan all these corridors, make me a map so I can find something interesting… and no, I am not lost.'

The floating metal ball zipped off down the corridor and started three dimensionally mapping out the ship, much faster than Spect could have done it manually. He sat down against the wall, pulled out some food he saved for an emergency, and began munching.

'I'm not lost,' he said again.

Fifteen minutes later, Spect stared at the massive smooth, white metal doors as his small drone reached his location. He reached up, took the floating ball, twisted it, and put it back in his pocket.

'You did well, little guy,' he said to the non-sentient machine. 'Now what do we have behind these doors, you think?'

He ran his hands across the cold steel, trying to find a panel to gain access. 'Maybe only the Commander can enter, like how he entered the ship.'

Walking around the locked section, Spect took the time to investigate the walls, then ended back at the large doors.

'I bet this is it, the core that powers the ship and its displacement device,' he mumbled to himself. 'The scan I took on the Sky-Station suggests it's the right size. I really need to get in there.'

He stroked the white doors softly. 'I'll find your secrets soon, Eclipse, don't you worry.'

*

Back on the *Arvernus,* Slin stepped into the upright medical pod and let the machine's mechanical arms go to work on his cybernetics. Since the battle that robbed him of his arms and left leg, he had to undergo regular check-ups and adjustments to make sure they were operating correctly.

A small laser emanated from one of the surgical devices and seared one component in his artificial leg that had been seizing. He winced with the pain and could smell burning.

'Still painful?' Nash asked, sitting across from him and nursing the last of the alcohol, swirling it in her glass.

'I'm getting used to it, even liking it better than the originals.'

'I don't think I could ever get used to that, my poor Slin. I was a wreck when you were missing.'

One of the surgical arms reached up and removed a small panel on the side of his face, placed it on a tray and began working on the internals.

'Will you tell me about where you grew up, Slin? I mean, I know you don't like to talk about it, and you don't have to tell me, but at least it will take your mind off the pain?'

'You want to know about Colman, the prison planet?' Slin's faced darkened.

'What was it like there?'

Slin paused for a moment and considered how much he should say, as he didn't want her perception of him to change. 'I was born there from parents I never knew, criminals I expect, and sold to whoever would have me. Passed from person to person, used like a servant fetching things for whatever group I belonged to. I became good at acquiring objects, stealing, so proved my worth.' The surgical instruments began working on his other leg.

'That's horrible,' Nash said. 'You had no one?'

'None, but I never knew the difference. The world of Colman existed as a dumping ground for the unwanted criminals, a place to offload the rubbish. Entire cities towered into the skies where the gang-lords operated. Scum and low-lives would live on the surface outside of the towers. If you were lucky, they recruited you into a gang where you're looked after. They kill the unlucky, exploited them as slave labour or in some areas, even ate them.'

'They eat people!?!' gasped Nash. 'That's awful. So how did you escape? It wasn't during the great breakout of Colman, was it? My father used those as bedtime stories when I was a child.'

'That's exactly when,' Slin smiled, although with a great deal of effort considering the pain he was going through. 'I was twelve when I got caught stealing from a small group of bandits operating out of an underground junk town outside the principal city.'

'No, it couldn't have been,' she yelled with excitement.

'Yeah, it was, the infamous Second Skulls, led by the great Latronis Skull himself.' Slin felt a great deal of pride flood his system and mix with the drugs being pumped into him from the medical pod. 'You know the stories I'd say. Latronis and his men were planning an escape in secret and owned a certain component another gang leader needed, which is where I came in.'

Nash leaned forward intently, excitement in her eyes as Slin continued. 'I snuck in under the cover of darkness, grabbed the component, but was never told how heavy it was. Damn, it was heavy. I tripped and fell onto a card table on a lower level. I thought they would execute me on the spot, but Latronis said I had balls of iron and recruited me.' Slin laughed again. 'I must have been a sight.'

'So, you escaped the planet with the Skulls, then the stories were true?' Nash asked.

'That was true, yes,' Slin added. 'The orbiting guard stations around Colman never even saw us leave, or they didn't care. We made it to one of the free trading stations, bargained our way onto a transport, and the story of the Skulls continued from there.'

'That's amazing,' Nash laughed. 'What was he like, Latronis Skull?'

'He was a tough son of a bitch, a little crazy, fair, but ruthless. Taught me how to fly, everything from transports to fighters and even operating capital ships. He mentored me in the bandit's art, plundering, looting, and salvaging.'

'And how did you come to be in the Cygnian Pirates? Were you captured like me?' Nash asked in a harsh tone. She never let that go.

'After I was out of the Skulls, I looked for targets mining the belts, ships that were far enough away from anywhere, so help couldn't arrive to get in my way. I killed none of them, mind you. Latronis had taught me the ways of chivalry. I just ransomed them a little. I guess word of my exploits spread because the Cygnian Pirates had set a trap. Seven fighters sprung from powered down locations around an unmanned miner. I took down five, damaged the other two and if it wasn't for a corvette that landed on me, I probably would have escaped, but then would never had met you.'

Nash blushed, then put her glass away on the table behind her.

'I didn't take too much convincing to join,' Slin said, 'even though it was more of a military by then, unlike the bandits I knew. What about you? I know your father was a trader, but how did you end up here?'

'Typical pirate fashion.' A look of anger crossed her face. 'My father operated a merchant transport vessel out of this backwater planet no one has heard of or cared to know. The pirates used the system as a refuel and rearm point, appeared one day and told everyone they either join or leave.'

'Sounds typical of the Cygnians,' Slin added.

'We fought instead, stupidly. I mean some rickety space vessels against an organised pirate fleet. What were we thinking? You can imagine the outcome. My father died during that battle, and they captured me hugging his lifeless body. Before he passed, he told me to survive, to make a life for myself no matter what it took. It was those words that made me decide to join the pirates in the end, despite how much I hated them.'

'I'm glad you don't hate me.'

'Of course not, my Slin,' she sighed. 'I was a prisoner then a pirate and over time have made friends here.'

'What was your father like? I always imagined him to be the gentle kind, being a trader and all.'

'He was kind, always had a story to tell. Some of my fondest memories were sitting by the view screens on the trade ship, the planet below filling the room with an orange glow while he told me bedtime stories from across the galaxy. He was always a legitimate trader, never stepped a foot outside the law.'

'Sounds like a great man,' Slin said as the surgical instruments finished their work on his cybernetic limbs. 'Wish I could have met him.'

'I'm not sure he would have liked you Slin, being a pirate after all, or who I've become.'

'But you're happy and have made a life for yourself? I'm sure he would have been proud.'

*

The huge flagship sat motionless in the center of the enormous Heridian fleet. Thousands upon thousands of smaller craft buzzed and orbited, dodging each other and filling the gaps between their leader and the multitude of other capital class vessels. It was a sea of crimson, like a weed festering and intertwining, a corruption of sight.

The solid doors to the bridge of the flagship slammed open as a pair of claws forced them aside. Servatus, the Heridian leader tasked with finding and protecting the displacement device, Draethus' lost friend, stormed into the large room and confronted the dark figure at its center.

'What have you done!?!' Servatus yelled, noticing the escort ships flying by through the transparent bulkheads.

The flagship's commander hovered, taller than Servatus, covered in the same armor plates, however darker and more intricate. Large cables from the ship crisscrossed the floor and connected into the creature's back. Lights flickered and cascaded through them, carrying signals and commands. Servatus could see fragments of cloth that had worn away and knew them to be the remnants of a cloak.

'What have you done!?!' He roared again, demanding an answer. 'Don't regard me as your subordinate, Commander.'

The dark figure hovered above the floor as the cables helped it move about. Multiple mandibles opened as it spoke, the audio sounding from vocal cords deep inside with no movement of its mouth. 'I've done what you should have completed already.' It floated closer to the Heridian leader and said, 'I set about events that will lead the Dawn Eclipse to a destination of my choosing.'

Servatus was furious. 'The lords charged me with its capture, and I have already set it on a path and into a pre-set trap. You have corrupted those plans!'

'You sent it to Tiberous, you fool, the ancient war ground.' The Commander's movement became quicker and more threatening. 'You know what they could find there!'

Servatus flexed his claws, feeling the urge to swipe the creature for its insubordination before being interrupted.

'The lords never specified the method of capture or by whom. I have followed your orders; I collected you from Echelon and brought you to the fleet. If I capture the ship, then so be it.' The flagships commander floated back into the center of the dark bridge before continuing. 'If you fail, the lords will strip you of your command, and your existence.'

'And if your actions have compromised my plans, I will wipe you from existence as well,' Servatus replied. 'What did you do?'

The dark figure laughed. 'I left something for them to find on their way to Tiberous.'

*

The technician fumbled with a gadget before reaching into the fighter's open engine assembly and continued his work. The fighter deck on the *Wing of Vidar*, one of many, littered the area with disassembled parts from damaged craft of the last battle. Thousands of people frantically busied themselves with tasks, an organised mayhem to ready the fighters for flight.

The *Vidar* also comprised machine-controlled repair and replace systems that could service a multitude of craft at once, creating an efficient process. Robotic arms craned large replacement pieces, workers guiding them into place as sparks from handheld equipment sealed them together. Again, the technician dropped the gadget and cursed under his breath as he heard a movement behind him.

'Having some trouble?' Rel asked in a sarcastic tone, enjoying getting one over on a fellow crew member. The man huffed and walked away whilst throwing down a second tool from his belt.

'Well fine, I was just seeing if you wanted help,' she said, a little shocked at his response. Being one of the few female fighter technicians had its problems however they normally showed her more respect, or even some banter. She picked up the gadget he dropped, leant into the same opening on the fighter, and looked.

'This isn't right,' she said with gritted teeth, holding onto a small torch. 'None of this is right.'

Looking back, Rel tried to remember the other tech's name but didn't read the name tag. She made a mental note to request he receive more training if she worked out his identity. She went back to work on the fighter engine, undoing all the incorrect work.

I wonder how Xain is going on his mission. He's been a long time, I'm getting worried.

The latest music started playing in her headset as she worked. It always made the time pass easier and the work more enjoyable. The last time the fleet docked with civilization, she purchased new music created by some unspeakable sounding race that was orchestral and powerful. It used the sounds of their world's enormous underwater marine life as the vocals mixed with a strange variety of instruments.

'The Arvernus,' she said out loud. 'That's a ship I would love to get my hands into. I mean a cursed ship. What a load of nonsense. Just needs a talented mechanic, I bet.'

She wrenched a component out and threw it over her shoulder.

'I'm worried about him though, especially lately, and he's so stubborn. I hear he collapsed on the bridge, in front of the Khan of all things, and didn't tell me. Me, of all people, his best friend since we were children, and he doesn't tell me.'

She huffed and hammered the new component into the engine before twisting the locking mechanism and connecting with a group of luminous wires.

'He's probably so stubborn that he will fly that ship into the damn sun just to prove he's the best commander in the fleet. All because his father was a traitor, he thinks he has something to prove, and he doesn't.'

She stopped and looked up at the ceiling of the fighter deck. 'He's also got me talking to myself.'

I'm going to have some serious words to that man when he gets back.

She completed a last check of her work and ran a diagnostic with a hand-held device that clipped to her belt. The engine repair displayed a success on the device with a green light. She checked the engine bay for any tools or debris, closed its hatch and looked around.

'Why couldn't he have just been a mechanic like me? It's so much safer, but *no,* he has to go jetting off trying to get himself killed.'

The music in her ears hit a peak and filled her with emotion. 'I wonder if his mother feels the same way?'

She shuffled over to the next piece of equipment and started work again, a mangled avionics module contained inside a damaged unit.

'Probably not,' she said, answering her own question. 'I bet she's proud of him, especially reaching the rank of talon commander and after what her husband did to the fleet… son of a,' a component sparked and zapped her finger. 'Hate that.'

She shook off the pain, waved away the smoke, and continued. 'Anyway, the Arvernus,' although she tried not to make a habit of it, she enjoyed talking to herself.

'There's been nothing mechanically wrong with the ship, not found anyway. It's just that its commanders keep vanishing. Maybe they got bored or just went crazy and used the cursed ship to escape the pirate life.'

She paused in thought as a soothing part of music started.

'I guess the fleet would have investigated the disappearances, so if it was that simple, we would know about it. I heard one tale from an actual crew member that served on the ship. One moment the commander was standing in front of his crew, the *Arvernus* translocated, and when it re-emerged into normal space, the guy just wasn't there, like vanished. A little spooky, I guess.'

Emotion flooded over her again, 'I hope that doesn't happen to Xain, I'd miss him too much.'

Rel wiped a tear from her cheek and packed up her equipment.

That's it for today. This unit is ready for active service, so I'll give the go ahead for its release.

She walked across the large bay to a service elevator that would take her to the living section of the ship, entered a passcode and boarded.

'Living section, floor eight-nine-five please,' she commanded.

The elevator rose into the air on its rail and as it disappeared into the body of the ship, the emergency lighting activated, turning everything into a shade of red. Flashing yellow lights animated on every corner of the fighter deck and a bellowing klaxon echoed through the vessel. The *Vidar* was on battle stations.

CHAPTER 13

Creation of the Infinite.

'Cut the klaxon,' Khan Hayreddin ordered as he walked onto the command deck of the pirate flagship, the *Wing of Vidar*. 'What have we got?'

'New vessel appeared from the sun, sir, its holding position,' one of the crew members replied as he brought an image up on the viewing display that stretched the entire length of the forward bridge.

'Holding position? Interesting, get me a magnification on that.' The Khan clasped his hands behind his back as he watched the display flicker and zoom in. A smile crept its way into the corner of his mouth before he put the crew's curiosity at ease.

'Keep nanite shielding active but drop the active response level.'

'Sir?' the man operating the visuals replied, surprised.

'This ship is no threat to us. I've waited a long time for this.' The Khan sat in his command chair and ran his fingers through his beard.

This must be it, after so many years.

The golden ship reflected light rays from behind, shining like a beacon on a backdrop of endless night. The curvatures of the vessel were sleek and smooth, armor plates with sharp edges created a fire of illumination. No weapons were visible on the display.

'Ping a communication to that ship,' ordered the Khan.

The crew busied themselves with the coms before they signalled the mystery ship.

A face appeared as a three-dimensional image in front of the viewing display. A man, battle worn with a scar running down his face, stared out onto the command deck of the pirate flagship. He brushed his messy brown fringe aside and began. 'My name is Arcilous Draethus, Commander of the Dawn Eclipse. We are here on behalf of one of your own commanders, Xain Raeson of the Arvernus.'

The Khan motioned the soldier in charge of the display to move the lens in closer to the golden ship's port side.

'I see you have our corvette tethered. Have you captured my vessel, Draethus of the Eclipse?'

Draethus smiled and replied, 'We rescued it from the Heridian flagship near the tear you sent it to monitor. Raeson and his crew are safe and we wish to deliver them under an agreement we have bargained.'

The Khan lifted an eyebrow. 'What agreement might that be?'

'We return the Arvernus and its crew back to your fleet and you help us reach Tiberous so we might locate the Heridian home-world.'

'Heridian home-world,' laughed the Khan. 'That's a children's story. You possess our crew, however, so I'll grant you tethering rights to the Vidar. Proceed to the route presented to you and we will talk further.'

'And the agreement?'

'That is between you and the Talon Commander of the Arvernus, though I will respect it for the moment. Besides, anyone wanting to go to Tiberous won't be a threat for very long, regardless of your motives.' The Khan had the communication cut and the viewing screen returned to the image of the exotic vessel.

*

On board the *Dawn Eclipse,* Tremon looked through the holographic scope that protruded from his console. 'That pirate vessel is massive. I mean I can't even see it all on zero magnification.'

'Bigger than the Heridian carrier, I bet,' Spect replied, sitting at the console directly across.

Tremon adjusted the display with a twist of his fingers, trying again to get a full visual. 'Commander,' he said, 'are you sure we can trust these people? Using the trail to find the location of the Rid home-world is one thing, but you heard that bearded guy, he doesn't even believe it exists.'

Static buzzed on the coms for a moment. 'We still have the message sent from that carrier as proof.' Draethus paused for a moment as he moved the ship along the path laid out by the pirates. 'It sounds to me that these pirates have been fighting the Rids for as long as the SOV, if not longer. If the SOV are looking for just the location of the Link where the next Heridian wave will appear, imagine how important the location of the Rid home-world would be to the pirates. This gives us massive leverage and a platform for negotiation.'

'Unless they torture us for the information.' Spect laughed nervously. 'Although they would need us to fly the Eclipse, as that's what the Rids are after.'

'Exactly,' said Draethus, 'these pirates will do anything to annihilate the Rids and we can help that happen. This is a win - win situation provided of course they believe the evidence I'll put forward. They don't really have anything to lose, yet anyway. Just be ready to run like your thrusters are on fire… And don't be surprised if they actually are.'

The *Eclipse* side shifted into the invisible passageway lit up by the *Vidar's* docking lasers off the pirate flagship's starboard side. A tunnel of light, circular, shot out from the pirate vessel's hull, showing the ship was to fly inside it and through the open outer doors.

'Into the mouth of the beast,' said Spect, almost cowering as their vessel passed through. The docking lights on the screen created a green hue on the command deck, then vanished as the pirate flagship swallowed their ship. For a moment, the viewing display over the liquid lake was blank and then filled with the outside world.

A myriad of metal bulkheads, girders, scaffolding, and levels stretched far into the distance. The *Wing of Vidar*, being the flagship of the Cygnian Pirates, was a floating city of a vessel containing not only a defence force of fighters and corvettes but the main population of the fleet.

The *Eclipse* cut its engines and floated in the large, wide-open space of the docking area before using its manoeuvring thrusters to position itself near the required bay. Tethering cables extended down from a multitude of directions and attached, keeping the ship stable and motionless.

The golden ship's own laser tethering extended outward and clamped themselves onto the side of the docking bay. A group of repair ships floated over to the port side, detached the *Arvernus'* own cables, grabbed hold of the large corvette class vessel, and drifted further into the body of the *Vidar*.

'There goes some of our leverage,' Tremon said, sitting back in his chair. 'Not feeling great about this one.'

'You didn't feel great about me at first and look how that turned out,' Draethus said.

'We're about to be captured and tortured by pirates. I'd say it's about equal.'

Raeson's face appeared on the screen. 'Eclipse crew, a small group of our soldiers will escort you to meet the Khan. Our agreement still holds, and we will give you the opportunity to present yourself to the fleet. You are to be unarmed and we will tolerate no form of aggressive behavior. Do we have an understanding?'

Draethus' voice from under the metallic liquid lake sounded over the loudspeakers, 'We do Raeson, just remember our agreement and everything will go smoothly.'

The platform from under the liquid levitated and Draethus stepped off onto the top level of the bridge.

Until your return, Commander, the ship is on lockdown, the *Eclipse* said in his mind.

Draethus gave a mental acknowledgment and turned to his crew. 'I'll meet the two of you at the docking doors.'

The Commander of the golden ship followed the ship's directions through the winding corridors to the living section of the vessel. Small doors sealed either side of a suspended walkway with the end finishing in the Commander's own personal quarters. The large door phased out of existence as Draethus walked up to it. The room was large, sunken into the floor to give a larger impression of size and contained a small amount of furniture. Once inside, he walked over to the desk and drew his vibration sword. The blade shimmered with electricity, and he could feel the minute vibrations from tip to hilt.

He placed it down on the desk, after clicking the switch to turn it off, and pulled his pistol from the holster.

This better be worth the risk.

It's your best chance, said the *Eclipse*, with a warm and reassuring tone.

He took one last look around his private living quarters before leaving, then followed the directions to the docking portal without getting lost.

What exactly are you Eclipse, an artificial intelligence or a life form maybe? Draethus asked in his mind as he made his way through the winding corridors.

There was a long pause, like the ship was deliberating before it replied.

Sentient would be the best explanation to help you understand.

Sentient, right so you could be a robot mind, alien or both. Will I ever fully understand?

You will Commander Draethus, certainly.

Draethus was reaching the end of the corridors and could see the docking entrance.

And what of your age? Who built you?

Again, the ship took its time to answer.

Infinite, built by the same.

Draethus entered the dock area to see his two crew members looking nervous.

That makes no sense, Eclipse, he thought as the ship fell silent. As he walked up to his crew, he whispered to the ship, 'I meant what I said earlier. If you eat me, I'm going to be very unhappy with you.'

'We are unarmed and ready to get captured by blood thirsty pirates that would love to torture us and steal our ship,' Tremon announced with a smile on his face.

Spect, with a terrified expression, said, 'Please don't give them any ideas.'

'You can guarantee they have already thought of it.'
Draethus put his hand to the wall, and the airlock door phased out of existence. 'Let's go then. Keep your eyes sharp and stay together.' He clasped a hand on Spect's shoulder, 'Stay together, no getting lost exploring, right Spect?'

The scientist flushed red. 'Did the ship tell you I got lost? I totally knew where I was…'

Both soldiers gave a chuckle before walking through the door and onto the dock. A squad of pirates was waiting at the bottom of the walkway, armed with assault rifles. Their black armor was uniform and Draethus could make out close combat weapons on their back. He looked over his shoulder as the *Eclipse* sealed the ship, phasing back in the door.

A woman walked in between the pirate guards, brown hair cut at the shoulders outfitted in the same gear.

'Welcome to the Wing of Vidar,' she said with a small bow of the head, 'the flagship of the Cygnian Pirates, home to our craft and our race.'

'Greetings again, Nash,' Draethus replied. 'I hope your crew fared well.'

'Indeed, Commander Draethus, we thank you.' She ran her fingers over the grip of her holstered automatic projectile pistol. 'Raeson has briefed you to what will happen now, I believe?'

Tremon stepped forward. 'As long as you keep your weapons to yourself, everything will be fine.'

Nash laughed and spun on her heal, 'As long as you keep your hands to yourself, you will be fine. This way.'

*

'Xain!' Rel yelled as she ran over to the Talon Commander of the *Arvernus*. 'Where have you been?'

Raeson took a step back as the fighter mechanic flew into his chest and gave him a big hug. Some nearby dock workers laughed, which quickly vanished after receiving a death stare from the pirate commander.

'Someone told me you got captured by a Rid lord and tortured, you didn't even tell me!' She punched him in the chest, 'and now I find out they nearly destroyed you at that tear thingy.'

Raeson looked away with a shrug of the shoulders, 'It's what I do, and it's a dangerous life.'

Rel was angry, her face red with fury. 'You could at least have told me, we're supposed to be best friends, right?'

'We are Rel, I just don't want you to worry and…' he cut off his sentence, 'excuse me…'

Raeson ran off to the docking area to the disgust of his childhood friend, yelling at him from behind.

'Stark!' Xain yelled, sprinting through the corridor.

Stark, the member of his crew who vanished during a previous battle, stopped and spun around, ducked the oncoming fist and returned Raeson's punch. Raeson tapped the fist aside before launching an elbow, only to miss as Stark side stepped and jumped back.

'The Khan told you to leave the subject alone, Xain.'

Raeson, now even more furious, launched himself forward with a flurry of strikes. Ducking and dodging, Stark parried again and finished with a spinning kick that caught Raeson off guard. The pirate commander staggered for a moment, caught his composure, and readied his next attack.

'Someone taught you to fight well, Stark.'

It was Starks' turn to strike. He was fast, too fast for Raeson to parry or counter as knife hands landed around his head and neck. Xain bounced off a wall and hit the ground hard. He took a moment to catch his breath and said, 'That Rid lord could have killed us, Stark, and for what? So, you could steal Rid tech for yourself?' He slowly got to his feet, 'How much did you make, a small fortune?'

Stark fixed his charcoal dark uniform. 'The Khan told you to leave the subject alone, Xain,' he repeated. 'We needed something on that Heridian destroyer.'

Raeson wiped the blood from his forehead and readied himself before being interrupted by the coms in his ear.

'The crew of the Eclipse are five minutes out, please proceed to area seven five, training section level nine.' The coms went silent as the announcement finished.

When Raeson looked back at Stark, the warrior had vanished.

*

They primarily used the training section as a conference location when meeting with other races in a civilian part of the *Vidar,* away from any sensitive systems. The area comprised a higher and lower tier where diplomatic discussions could take place, surrounded by a multitude of plants, twisting trees, and greenery.

As he stood on the lower tier, Draethus understood the use of the forestry to create a calming atmosphere, although he didn't enjoy being on a lower level. On the higher tier stood the pirates, people known to him, with the addition of some unfamiliar faces.

He ran his fingers down the scar on his face and glanced at his two crew members. Tremon, as always, looked stern and unimpressed. Spect, his scientist, had a look of terror and curiosity that only he could have even made possible.

Raeson and his crew, all of which were on the top tier, stood to one side of the bearded man the *Eclipses'* crew had seen before.

'Crew of the Dawn Eclipse,' Raeson started. 'Standing before you is the lord and leader of the Cygnian Pirates, Khan Hayreddin. To my left is fellow Talon Commander Amus Zekhal, of the frigate the *Dying Nova* and I am Commander Xain "Reaper" Raeson of the Arvernus.' He motioned to the soldiers behind him. 'You have already met my other crew, Slin Naomoka and Nashek Trian, both excellent fighter pilots.'

Draethus took a step forward. 'It is an honor to meet you and I thank you for taking the time to hear our offer, Khan Hayreddin.'

The large, bearded man, attired in ceremonial dark armor, stood firm. An expressionless look on his face betrayed no emotion.

'We have granted you free and safe harbor in our fleet, Commander Draethus, only so you can present your request that may favor our motives.' The Khans' voice was deep and loud, which caused Spect to startle. 'If your request is not to our motives, you may not like the consequences,' the Khan finished.

Tremon held his temper as he shot Draethus a look of disgust.

'We are enemies of the Heridian race and originate from a world called Echelon, a large jungle planet, in two instances of time,' Draethus stated. 'My two crew members are from your current time, so we believe, and I from a future.' He let the words settle on the minds of the pirates, proving its plausibility would be hard.

Zekhal, a man the same age as Raeson, in his mid-twenties, spoke up for the first time. 'You expect us to believe you are from another time? What proof is there and how did you travel?'

'I travelled well, thank you,' Draethus replied with a wide grin. He noticed the unimpressed expressions on the pirate's face and decided that now wasn't a great time for banter. 'Excuse my humor, I tend to diffuse situations with it.' He looked over at Spect and found he was trying not to make eye contact with his commander. 'Spect…'

The scientist looked around for a moment and ran his finger across the frame of his glasses. 'Your honors, um, highnesses.'

'Speak,' Zekhal ordered.

Spect steadied himself, straightened his back and put a hand in his pocket and without warning threw a metallic ball into the air. The pirates quickly drew their weapons and were about to fire when a hologram of the golden vessel shone out, and all but filled the area.

'By the creator, Spect…' Tremon said, covering his forehead with his hand.

The pirates eased their weapons as Draethus threw a shrug toward Raeson, who returned with words assumed to be prayers or curses.

'This is the Dawn Eclipse,' Spect announced as he started his grand speech. 'Just over one year ago it appeared in the docks of our Sky-Station on Echelon, as if from know where, like a ghost.'

Zekhal holstered his weapon, 'and it is now on our docks, get to the point.'

'Well, Commander… wow, there are a lot of commanders here… ships just don't appear from nowhere. They either fly or translocate. This ship on the security cameras was absent in one frame and present in the next, meaning there was another method. I ran a scan of the ship and could piece together part of what I thought was a drive but was, in fact, a time device.'

He changed the hologram to a three-dimensional blueprint of the device as the Khan nodded to his men to put away their weapons.

'I'll shorten the story. Commander Draethus activated the device I designed, from our future, which then time-shifted him to his past along with the Rids he was fighting. I made that word up. I think we should use it.'

Tremon stepped forward, 'What Spect here is trying to say is we have a ship capable of shifting through time…'

'Time-shifting,' interrupted Spect.

The hologram changed to a massive red glowing vessel, the Heridian flagship.

'This abomination attacked the Sky-Station, and we followed it back through that tear in space the Rids created after they captured and repaired the displacement device.' Draethus added.

'That explains where the tear came from,' Raeson replied. 'We thought that maybe the Rid flagship had created it.'

'No, that was from our end,' Draethus smiled. 'We destroyed the device when they tried to capture it, then followed the Rid flagship through the tear. We don't even know what point in space we are in right now.'

'So, the Heridians want access to time displacement?' the Khan asked bluntly.

'Time-shift…' Spect said before being interrupted with a shoulder nudge from Tremon.

'Yes Khan, that is correct.' Draethus ran his fingers over the scar on his face again. 'Where I'm from, the Heridian forces are close to defeat, though this is just a small force, a first wave. We believe the second wave to be much larger and know when they are coming, but not from where. If we can find this location, or Link as it's known, we can be ready and waiting.'

'A Link, you say?' said the Khan, eyeing the Heridian flagship hologram that now replaced the golden ship, and stroking his dark beard.

Draethus could see the curiosity in his eyes and knew he had struck the interest needed. 'The Link is the gateway to their home-world, the path to Heridia.'

There were gasps from Zekhal and some guards behind him. The pirates had been fighting the Heridians for generations, with no proof of a Heridian home-world.

'So why Tiberous?' Zekhal asked, throwing his hand up in the air. 'Is the Link to Heridia there?'

Draethus stared him in the eye. 'It's a possibility. Before the Rid flagship translocated, a Heridian leader going by the name Servatus, sent me an invitation to a duel, one on one.'

'A duel? Why would he want to duel you?' Zekhal was getting agitated.

Spect waved his hand at the floating metal ball as Draethus dropped what he thought might break the negotiations.

'Servatus, before becoming a Heridian, was once a Soldier of the Void, like myself. He and I were friends, and he feels he has a score to settle. If we win, he'll give us the co-ordinates to the Link we need.'

'And if we lose?' the Khan asked.

'If we lose, the Rids get the ship and the time-shifting device inside it.'

A smile reached the corner of Spect's cheek at hearing his new word was catching on.

'The Heridian leaders can only traverse the Link in rare circumstances,' Draethus continued. 'If they have access to the time device, they can escape and even call on reinforcements from any space-time period. They will be unstoppable, with access to any place and an infinite number of forces.'

Raeson, after quietly listening, stepped forward. 'How do we know this isn't just your personal vendetta against your old friend?'

Spect waved his hand again at his floating ball. The image of Servatus appeared to loom over the meeting, and he set the message to play. Draethus wondered if the pirates had even seen a Heridian up close after seeing the lock of terror on their faces.

The terrifying message finished after a few minutes and the Khan walked to the edge of the higher tier. 'This could, of course be a trap, leading you to Tiberous, although it gives us an opportunity as we know where they will be. But if this is indeed an invitation that may lead to the co-ordinates of the Link and therefore Heridia, I will take that chance.'

A wave of relief flooded over Draethus and his crew, but the Commander reeled himself back in as there was still a lot of work ahead.

'Your ship, Commander Draethus,' the Khan announced, 'cannot fall in the hands of the Heridian forces, even if you are to lose the duel. Therefore, I will send an escort of pirate vessels, who will be there for your safety. They will also be your ship's executioner if you lose to this Servatus filth.'

Upon hearing the Khans' words, Draethus felt a fear deep in the pit of his stomach, although he knew the pirate was right. The Heridians could not under any circumstances gain access to the vessel, and neither could the pirates.

The Khan continued. 'I will also send Raeson with you; he will report directly to me and have full access to the ship. Slin will command the Arvernus in his stead and be part of the escort.'

Slin's ears tweaked at the new promotion.

'So you will show us the way to Tiberous, good, and I thank you, Khan,' Draethus said with a slight bow of the head. 'And when we find this pathway to Heridia, you will take the fight to them?'

The Khan smiled for the first time during the meeting. 'When we find their home-world, the Rids will burn and they will never again plague our skies.'

*

The conference doors opened as Draethus and his crew exited the meeting, followed by the pirate guards, whose role it was to escort them back to the *Eclipse*. Rel, who had been waiting patiently by the doors, sprang out. 'Raeson? Where's Raeson?'

The guards ignored her and kept walking. Draethus however, paused as the girl ran up to him.

'Is he back in there?' she asked, trying to glimpse the meeting room through the now closing doors.

'He was, but left with the rest of the pirate leaders,' Draethus said, trying to hide the surprised look in his eyes. 'And who might you be?'

Rel paused, embarrassed that she hadn't introduced herself. 'I'm Rel, the resident fighter mechanic around here, one of anyway.'

'Well, Rel, I'm Draethus, Commander of the Dawn Eclipse.'

Tremon made a coughing sound, as if he were trying to clear his throat, which snapped Draethus out of his daze.

'Oh... um... This is my crew, Tremon and Spect,' Draethus responded.

The two crew members waved. Tremon grinned at his commander before they started walking again.

'Well, I was going to give this to Raeson, but he's hard to get hold of sometimes, so...' Rel handed Draethus a purple flower, looked down and blushed. 'It was nice to meet you, Draethus. I hope we can meet again.' She stood there for a moment as the two of them smiled before deciding that running off was in order.

Draethus watched her leave and caught up with the rest of the group.

'So...' started Tremon.

'I don't want to hear it,' Draethus replied, red faced.

Spect, after watching the entire encounter, had a puzzled look on his face.

'Don't worry, Spect,' Tremon smiled, 'you might understand, one day.'

As the group entered the elevator, Draethus noticed movement back in the direction they came. A dark shadow was exiting the conference area, almost drifting.

Is that a Specter?

Curiosity, surprise, nervousness, and fear enveloped him.

This feeling... is this the shadow? Or Rel?

CHAPTER 14

The Darkness that Follows.

Darkness with a full sense of everything, all that occurred, and the probability of what will occur. The Lords of Heridia knew every thought, sensation, molecule, feeling and conversation on their world. Two Heridian soldiers mined a fallen rock on the plains of nothingness. An insect walked across a dead carcass under its blood oceans, and the minds of the lords were present.

The crimson world they lived sat suspended, locked in place and imprisoned because of a long-ago war. Black clouds drifted, emptying their contents of acidic rain onto the barren wastelands across its surface. The oceans of blood, thousands of years of collection from other species, covered a third of its surface, home to a variety of monstrous creatures.

The centerpiece of this menacing world was a city, a massive construct built with the same materials as the Heridian space faring vessels. It housed the many thousands of soldiers that were the world's protectors, a force capable enough to defend it from the ground. In the middle of the city, stretching high into the dark clouds, was the Heridian spire and the central command. The structure resembled an enormous spear thrust into the ground, protruding into the atmosphere of the planet. Hidden at the base of the spire, deep underground and connected to the planet's core, lay the physical bodies of the lords themselves. It was from here they plotted for their freedom, and the future of the Heridian race.

Heridia existed in a pocket disconnected from normal space-time, trapped and the only exit was a Link that had briefly opened many millennia ago. The Lords took this opportunity to send their ships out and continue their plans of genocide against all opposing races. This gateway, however, had never opened since that day and the lords, if their plan was successful, would gain enough control to open and close it at will.

The three lords, all of which melded into the spire, were motionless in the darkness of their self-containment. Being linked to the spire meant the communication between them was digital, and in the Heridian language rather than outwardly vocal.

Third Lord: Initiate conversation, subject is the ongoing plans to gain access to the surrounding space.
Fifth Lord: Last reports our main fleet has engaged the pirates and is pursuing with outstanding success. Our flagship almost recovered a time device thanks to Servatus and created a breach in space, proving a partial validity of the device.
Fourth Lord: Servatus lost us this opportunity because of his personal vendetta against a combatant. Suggest purging it from our lines and redirecting responsibility to another.
Third Lord: Noted, however, we should communicate with Servatus to discover any plans currently in motion.
Fifth Lord: Agreed.
Fourth Lord: Agreed, under caution, not to be overconfident with its abilities.
Fifth Lord: If Servatus fails?
Fourth Lord: Purge him.
Third Lord: Agreed, however, we do not have another protagonist placed so well. Connecting with the array…

From the light of an unspecified, unimportant nebula, an abandoned array station sat motionless, forgotten by time and its creators. The giant antenna stretched for kilometres and attached to an extensive structure, resembling a cluster of asteroids. To someone searching, it would be hard to spot even from inside the nebula.

The array pulsed and drew in the swirling particles from the surrounding anomaly, charging the antenna with exotic matter. It was only by chance the Heridian race found the array during its quick exodus through the Link and discovered they could use it to communicate with their home-world.

Using quantum entanglement powered by the strange matter of the nebula, a probable reason for its location, Heridians could communicate with the spire. The edges of the spire back on Heridia illuminated with a bright white that caused static in the surrounding air, charged particles that crackled and sparked.

Third Lord: Connection to the array established, locating Servatus…

The image in the mind's eye of the three lords faded from black to the face of Servatus, the Heridian leader tasked with capturing the displacement device.

'My Lords,' Servatus growled with a slight bow of the head. 'You wish for an update on my mission?'

The Fourth Lord, who had never been an advocate of the leader tasked with their escape, spoke first. 'Have you captured the Dawn Eclipse yet, grunt?'

A flash of anger crossed Servatus' face. 'Plans are in place, my Lords. I have divulged the rendezvous coordinates to the Eclipses' Commander, and a duel issued.'

'Duel?' the Third Lord said in surprise.

The Fifth Lord interrupted, 'Why would the commander accept a duel when he knows for certain it would be a trap?'

Servatus smiled and said, 'I've offered the co-ordinates to the Link as a reward for defeating me, along with the death of his friend's mind inside me of course.'

'So you have created a situation where you win, you gain control of the ship, if you lose he brings the ship to us?' the Third Lord asked.

'Correct, my lords,' Servatus replied.

The Fourth Lord was not so understanding. 'When this commander loses, his crew will not just hand the ship over, they will have precautions in place as they possibly know our motives for its capture. You should lose the duel and sacrifice yourself so that it will lead the ship here.'

Servatus paused for a moment and considered the options. 'If I am required, so be it, however I am confident that even with the duel won, I will capture that ship.'

'We will purge you if failed,' the Fifth Lord warned. 'Let nothing stop you.'

*

The night life aboard the pirate flagship, the *Wing of Vidar*, although it was always night in the void, was a constant buzz of drunken activity.

Though the pirates were a more military force because of the war against the Heridians, their old ways of drunken behavior remained while off duty. Various clubs and bars littered the city sized vessel with entire areas dedicated to the social life the enormous crew needed. One such bar, the Junkers Retreat, was positioned on a long section of such establishments and was popular because of its no ranks, no rules policy.

'I don't know about this,' Spect said as he sauntered through the front doors.

A fight was taking place in a far corner between officers and non-ranked pirates. The officers weren't winning.

Slin slapped the scientist on the shoulder and pulled him along. 'You'll be fine, my friend. Come, let's drink!'

The two men, followed by Slin's lover Nash and the ex-Paladin Tremon, wound their way through the crowd and sat at the head of the bar.

'Tender!' Slin yelled, 'My friend here and I will have some Sludge to calm his nerves.'

The bar man, a huge half breed of human and eismorus, covered in tattoos, reached up and grabbed a dark bottle.

'And the lady?' the Tender asked.

'No, this is Tremon, he's...' Slin laughed painfully as Nash punched him in the back.

'Don't mind him,' Nash said, smiling to Tremon before answering the Tender herself. 'Just Spirit Jack for me, Tender.'

Tremon, now finally in the mood to relax, refused to give in. 'Try not to spill any of that on your arms, Slin. You might blow a circuit.'

Slin laughed again as he put the glass of green alcohol into Spect's hand. 'You like to explore and experiment, right?'

The scientist hesitated before knocking the whole thing back in one go.

'Maybe you should take it easy on that,' said Tremon, smiling. 'Tender, what's that on the wall?'

The Tender grinned, evilly, and pulled down a long glass bottle shaped like a reptile head. 'This comes from the fermented brain of the swamp creatures living on a certain trade world. It's called Fang. Think you have the stomach for it?'

Slin gestured cut off signs with his hand against his neck, showing it wasn't a good idea. Tremon, never the one to back down, wasn't going to.

'Pour me one, let's go, all of this is on Slin's tab by the way.'

He sipped the black liquid out of the special skull glass given to those who dare try the drink. 'What a kick!' Tremon yelled. 'I think I found my drink of the night.'

The music blared as the fight from earlier spewed out onto the street, joined by more people outside.

'Is it always like this here?' Spect asked.

Nash reset herself on the bar stool. 'Of course! Best way to blow off steam, other than killing Rids, that is. There are places like this all over the ship, as people need a place to relax when they aren't on duty.'

'And the Junkers Retreat? Weird name. Where's it from?' Tremon asked, trying to hide the effect the Fang was having on him. A small line of drool escaped the corner of his lips.

Slin raised his glass to the Tender, who was listening in. 'The Junkers was a salvage ship that took us ages to hunt and chase down, like ages. Whenever we got close, it would retreat, hence the name.'

The bar man smiled to himself as he quietly cleaned the glasses.

'What's your story, Tremon? How did you end up with that commander of yours?' Nash asked.

Tremon, now slurring, knocked the rest of the Fang back and signalled the Tender to pour another. 'I grew up in the gangs on my world, on Echelon.'

'A ganger, how interesting,' Slin said.

'Well, it's a longer story,' Tremon continued, 'but the short version is I helped take back some territory, which is when the Paladins recruited me. They're the soldiers who protected the planet. Years later I captured Draethus.'

'You captured the man that's now your commander,' Slin laughed.

'That's right,' Tremon smiled, 'then got mixed up in this war.'

'So noble,' Nash laughed. 'What about you, Spect?'

Spect, after four drinks of what Slin referred to as Sludge, was not so coherent. 'I grew up on the Sky-Station, like to take things apart, and hate small lizards that mess with my stuff.'

The other three watched as he slumped over the bar and started murmuring, much to the group's amusement.

'And the two of you, what's your story? How did you meet Raeson?' Tremon asked.

Slin jumped out of his chair, threw his arms into the air as he prepared to make a giant speech only to have Nash pull him down, keeping him grounded.

'Where do I start?' Slin yelled, giving Nash a kiss on the cheek. 'My life started when I met this fine woman.'

Nash flushed a bright shade of scarlet. 'You suck up,' she giggled, 'answer his question.'

Slin, now a drunken pirate with his guard down, started. 'I was a prisoner on a forsaken planet, got free and became a pirate. The end.'

'So modest,' Nash added then said, 'I was a trader before being forced to join… this bunch of degenerates.'

'So, the pirates recruit from everywhere. You're not just born amongst them?' asked the ex-ganger turned Paladin.

'That's right,' said Nash, 'but there are many people that are born here, like Raeson, for instance.'

She threw back more of her drink. 'Now his story is long, but I will say this. Never cross him. His father was a traitor to the pirates, so he has a lot to prove. That is one commander that won't hesitate to space you out the nearest airlock. He has a dark personality, that's for sure, but he is loyal to the fleet. Stay honorable and you won't have any problem.'

Spect sat up for a moment. 'What about that scary bearded leader of yours, the Khan? What makes him so important?'

'The Khan you say?' Slin exclaimed, completely uncaring to how loud he was being. 'Now that's a story. Let me see.' He leaned back against the bar. 'On the day the Rids hit us, the all mighty Cygnian Pirates, we lost our chain of command. All the Pirate lords died in one sweep, the largest of our capital ships destroyed.

Years later, Hayreddin and his small frigate unified us. Under his command we recruited the neighbouring military, that we used to fight against by the way, and won our first battle against the Rids.' Slin felt like the storyteller of the hour. 'They elected him Khan not long after, and he even found the Wing of Vidar himself, although it had another name originally. In short, the man is one scary bad arse leader that has all our interests in mind. He hates the Rids more than anyone.'

Slin sat back on his stool as the Tender refilled his glass. 'Just water for this one here for a while,' he said, patting Spect on the back. 'They assigned Nash, Tektar and I to Raeson because we were troublemakers. Not being liked by the fleet meant Raeson inherited all the scum, so to speak.'

'I see, so we're associated with the unpopular pirates,' Tremon laughed. 'I'm in the right place, then. Who is Tektar?'

A frown crossed both pirates' faces.

'Tektar,' Slin started, 'was the craziest, ever drunken, most degenerate of all, but he was one of us, one of Reaper Squadron.'

They both raised their glasses in salute and took a drink before a random man wearing a standard pirate uniform walked up to the group. 'I know that name, Tektar. Was he assigned to you lot?'

'That's right, he was one of us,' Nash replied. 'What of it?'

The man put his hands in the air, as if to say he wasn't a threat, and continued. 'I was the pilot who picked him and another up after some mission went horribly wrong a few years ago.'

'Before he joined Reaper Squadron, you mean?' Slin asked.

'That's right,' the man replied. 'I got information that two fighters were drifting away from a Heridian unmanned trap, and they needed rescuing.' He put his arms down and motioned the Tender to pour him a drink. 'When I got there, all I saw was carnage, seen nothing like it. The Rids had placed six gravity devices in such a way that created a sphere, a bubble, so to speak. The design worked to repulse any ship into the center and then crushed by the shear mass.'

'A Rid made black hole?' Tremon asked in surprise. 'An inverted one, anyway.'

'Yeah,' the man replied, 'and they placed it in the fleet's path. Tektar and his squad were the forward scouts, charged with flying ahead and making sure the path was safe. Our forces would have been easy pickings for the Rid fleet had we fallen into it, the survivors anyway.'

'So how did Tek escape?' asked Nash as tears started welling up in her eyes.

'Tek worked out a way to disable the trap by setting six of their eight fighter's engines to critical. Timed right, the blast created a feedback loop that would overload and destroy the gravity generators, or at least disable them. The only problem was his men weren't willing to sacrifice themselves to fulfil the plan and instead turned on him.' The man looked down at the floor as he relived the visions of the twisted craft in his mind. 'Tek won the fight and killed all but one of his squad, who then agreed to position the cores of the wrecks and set them to detonate.'

'By the creator, he saved thousands of lives,' Slin said, astonished.

'All our lives. He was a hero, and his story was barely even told. I think leadership wanted to keep silent the fact one of our own had to murder his own squad. But yes, he saved us all.'

The man raised his glass, along with everyone else in the bar who had listened to his story. 'Tektar Shahath... Shahath!'

As the night progressed, Spect eventually regained consciousness, although still inebriated, and came to his senses long enough to hold some decent conversation with his new friends. Slin and Nash were happy knowing they had crewed with a hero such as Tek. Tremon was finally feeling like he belonged somewhere that was making a difference, more than even the Paladins could offer.

*

Sat in his ornate wooden chair, the Khan ran his fingers along the base of a thick drinking glass. The condensation from the cold blue liquid inside it formed droplets that slowly ran down the outside, causing an icy sensation on his pale gray skin.

'The Heridians are close on our tail, not enough to be of a concern,' the pirate leader said, running his eyes over the long, frosted blue hair of his guest.

Zelene Raeson, experienced in the art of knowledge and manipulation, as the Khan was in warfare, sat at the other end of the glass table and smiled.

'There's too many to fight head on, isn't there?' she replied, wondering how she could finish the last of her drink without looking like an alcoholic.

'Far too many, but we may have found the break we need. Do you remember the reason your husband abandoned us all those years ago?'

Zelene snapped into focus as the pain of betrayal filled her heart and replied, 'How can I forget?'

The Khan shifted in his seat. 'Another opportunity has surfaced that might give us the location of the Rid home-world. It means risking an asset the Rids could use against us if we fail.'

Zelene's focus drifted off to the large viewing window they dined next to in the Khans' quarters. The stars outside blurred and distorted because of the sheer speed the fleet was travelling at. One cruiser in the fleet stretched and contracted as it neared the *Vidar* but kept enough distance as to not cause any alarm. Space travel was dangerous, so the capital vessels kept to a generic formation where collisions were almost unheard of.

'How well do you remember my husband?' she asked softly.

'The Associate? I think about him from time to time, and wish things could have gone differently.'

'I don't like when you call him that,' she said with a frown. 'You both were close once.'

With his dinner finished, the Khan stood and walked over to the window. 'Once, yes, but he chose his path, and that didn't include our way of life, despite his motives.'

'You know his motives were true Alexon. It's not fair that the fleet thinks him the traitor when you and I both know what he did was for a greater good.' A tear fell from Zelene's cheek. 'I just wish he was back with us.' She got out of her chair, glass in hand, and walked up the small stairs to the viewing window next to the great Khan.

The stars streaked across her view, a field of bright lasers glistening amongst a dark nothingness.

'You didn't have to send out an assassination team. You could have just exiled him,' she continued.

'And look weak to the rest of the fleet? What example would that have set, that one of our own could sacrifice so many with no consequence? Where would the fleet be now if I had done so?' His tone was harsh, but he held his composure knowing she was talking from a place of sadness, not logic.

'Part of me always wondered if you did that for selfish reasons,' Zelene said, unable to make eye contact.

'I've always acted in the best interest of the fleet, never myself. The Associate...' he cut off mid-word to correct himself. 'Your husband won your affection instead of I. That I will always regret, but I would never have given the order based on that. His actions caused the death of hundreds of civilians on the vessel he was escorting, because he abandoned it. If he had followed his orders, his mission, the Rids would never have captured it and slaughtered everyone on board. It was his negligence that led to my order and therefore his sacrifice. Even if his reasons were true, I would imagine the people lost would disagree and be of the opinion there could have been another way.'

The Khan had reviewed his orders many times over the years and still believed his decision was the correct one. There was no other way to deal with it without further and more severe repercussions to the pirate fleet. Zelene and her son, Xain, were the ones that had suffered the most, but that still didn't make the Khan feel any better about it.

'I wish I could see him again, and maybe there could have been another way,' Zelene whispered. 'But that still doesn't make it any easier. Tell me something,' she placed her hand on the viewing glass, 'why have you never tried for my affections since that day?'

The Khan felt pain in his chest, the type of ache with no release. 'I ordered his death and by doing so killed a part of you as well. Whether it was the right call, I'm still responsible for that and can never forgive myself. I could never dishonor you or Xain in that way.'

She wiped a tear from her eye and gave a small smile, 'My son looks up to you, respects you more than anyone else.'

'That he does,' said the Khan, 'and he reminds me a lot of his father, sometimes too much. He's hot-headed, stubborn, and feels he always has something to prove. A darkness follows him everywhere. He's a better pilot than his father. I'll give him that much. A better ship commander, though, we will have to see.'

'I'm glad you have looked after him,' she said, 'though I wish we could tell him what really happened.'

'It's the least I can do considering, though I haven't needed to do very much,' he replied. 'Xain can never find out the events of what really happened that day, for his sake and the rest of the fleet.'

Zelene gave the Khan a hug and a kiss on the cheek, 'You're right of course and it hasn't been easy keeping that from him. Thank you for dinner. It was enjoyable as always.'

The Khan gave a bow of the head, escorted his guest to the door and said, 'It was good to see you again, Ms. Raeson.'

*

Xain Raeson stood aboard the *Arvernus* and noted his surroundings. His crew busied themselves with their tasks, running commands over holographic displays from flight chairs positioned at a level just below him. The command deck stretched in an oval shape with his command chair at the center, surrounded by visual equipment to give him spatial awareness of the environment around the ship. Even though it was technically his ship, for the next mission Slin, his best pilot, would command it.

'Going to miss her already?' Slin asked as he walked up from behind him.

'Who would have thought it, me missing a cursed ship?'

'And now I get to command it,' Slin said with a laugh. 'Maybe you will find my cybernetics left over the day I go missing.'

Raeson slapped his hand on Slin's shoulder as he walked off the bridge, laughing.

A short time later, Xain was at the docks in front of the golden vessel and marvelled at the sheer size. So much unlike the rest of the pirate fleet, it stood out as a gold coin would against a backdrop of dark metal. The large door phased open to reveal its commander, Draethus, in full dark gray armor, complete with a sheathed sword.

'Permission to board,' Raeson said in a formal tone.

'Permission granted, Xain Raeson.'

Raeson walked up the ramp and stopped as the soldier held up his palm and said, 'Know this, if you cause any trouble on my ship, pirate, I will space you the first chance I get. Is that understood?'

Raeson smiled with a darkness behind his eyes. 'I will respect the chain of command, Draethus. We are all on the same side, right?'

'Which is my side.'

'Of course,' grinned Raeson. 'The side that's inside the ship's airlock.'

The pirate stepped into the portal opening before pain ripped through his mind. He fell to the ground as a thousand voices screamed into his mind, clawing at his sanity. His vision flashed a clouded red, as he rolled over to see Draethus suffering the same fate.

'What are these visions?' Raeson screamed, 'and why are you getting them as well?'

CHAPTER 15

The Whispering Invasion of Guilt.

'Coming up on the vessel,' Nash reported from the back of the bridge on the *Arvernus*.

Earlier both vessels, the pirate corvette flying in formation with the *Dawn Eclipse,* before translocation, detected the signature of a Heridian craft. The sensors determined it to be drifting under low power and in the path to Tiberous, so Draethus decided upon investigation.

From inside the liquid lake on the lower section command deck of his ship, Draethus, now recovered from the visions, gave the command. 'Both ships drop out of translocate and get a bearing on that Rid vessel,' he ordered, running his fingers down the scar on his face. It always seemed to hurt him more after the visions tore at his mind.

With an ejection of sparks, the two ships dropped out of translocation, hoping to get a fix on the enemy ship's location. The Heridian vessel, roughly the size of the *Dawn Eclipse* itself, spun slowly from bow to stern and tumbled through the empty. The golden ship lit its engines in a haze of glow and headed for the stricken vessel with the *Arvernus* not far behind.

'What's the status of that vessel, Spect?' Draethus asked.

Tremon, sitting at his gunnery station, gave the update. 'Spect is down in that room again, not on the command deck.' He swallowed the tense lump in his throat. 'From the forward display, I can see the Rid ship shows signs of physical damage and its systems are offline. Could this be a trap?'

Not at his station? We could fly into a trap and Spect is off exploring again. What is it with scientists?

He is very interested in the workings of your ship, Commander, the *Eclipse* said into his mind, *mainly with the section he once scanned to create the displacement device.*

Displacement Device… I was glad to see an end to that.

He waved his arm across the area in front of him to create a viewing screen of the ship outside. Although he hadn't been in command of the ship for long, Draethus had worked out several physical commands thanks to the help of the *Eclipse* itself. He could see the enemy ship, cartwheeling through space slowly, and every instinct in his body felt wrong.

'Raeson, where on the ship are you right now?' he asked into the coms.

'I'm in the corridors on the way to the fighter bay. That's if I am going in the right direction. I plan on boarding that Rid vessel to see what secrets it holds.'

'Understood. Slin, do you copy?' replied Draethus.

'I copy Commander. I'm sending a fighter wing out as an escort. A couple of them will join Commander Raeson on the enemy ship as back up.'

'Make this quick people. We don't want to be here longer than necessary,' Draethus ordered sternly. The pirates needed to know who was in charge.

*

Raeson, after stumbling in the right direction, found the fighter bay of the *Dawn Eclipse* and with it, his widowmaker pirate fighter. Under permission from Draethus, the pirates equipped the ship with a small contingent of fighters for any emergency situations. An enemy vessel drifting through space was one such situation Raeson couldn't ignore, especially after the last incident.

He activated the cockpit canopy by placing his palm on the reader and climbed in. The leather seat felt cold through the cloth of his black uniform and the dual flight sticks icy to the touch. The canopy lowered as his systems came online and lit up the small area around him. Raeson flicked some switches above him for pre-start and entered his personal code on the holographic control panel.

His personal profile loaded, the engine fired to life and vibrations coursed through the dark warbird and begged to be let loose. As the anti-gravity activated, the landing gear retracted into the fighter's body, the wings swept forward and down, ready for flight.

Weapons check out fine.

'Commander Draethus, please open the docking bay doors. Reaper is ready,' Raeson said over the coms, his voice echoing in the small cockpit.

The docking doors phased out of existence, making Raeson wonder if they existed to begin with. Putting the thought aside, he throttled forward, grabbed hold of both flight sticks and shot out of the larger ship like a large missile. It had been a long time since he'd flown the pirate fighter, and it gave him an incredible sense of freedom. Rolling on his back, Raeson headed for the enemy vessel, joining three other fighters.

'It's been a while since we have flown together,' said a familiar voice.

Raeson, knowing exactly who had spoken, felt raging fire and anger. 'Stark. Here to steal everything that isn't welded down?'

Stark flew up beside his wing leader and looked at him through his cockpit. 'You are my talon commander after all Raeson, why would I not be here?' he smiled knowing how much he infuriated his leader.

'And the other two fighters?' Raeson asked.

Stark's fighter dropped back into formation, 'New grunts assigned personally by the Khan, still to earn their wings.'

'I see. Well Stark, you can run guard duty once we reach the Rid vessel. You other two are to tether your fighters to the Rid and board with me. Is that understood?'

Stark, along with the two new pilots, gave their confirmation of orders and fell in line.

*

Spectalin's curiosity enveloped the scientist into obsession. His fascination with the locked room since boarding the *Eclipse* had stolen all his attention. For what seemed the hundredth time, he ran his hand over the smooth white door again, hoping for it to open. His coms unit, embedded in his ear, crackled.

'Spect, where are you?' his commander asked.

By his tone, Spect knew he was angry with him, but a scientist must do what a scientist does. Spect considered not answering but thought against it.

'I'm at that place again. There must be a way in, I know it.'

'We are about to board a Heridian vessel that's adrift. I need you on the command deck. Is that clear?'

The scientist put his hands on his head, still aching from drinking the previous night, and replied, 'Yes, sir, but can you please get into this room?'

Draethus paused, which confirmed he was angry. 'Very well,' Draethus replied bitterly. 'Eclipse, can you open the door in question please so my scientist can fulfil his curiosity and return to his post?' The coms crackled offline.

Spect stood for a moment and watched his reflection in the door.

'He was joking. There is no way into this room, is there?' he said to himself out loud.

As the frustrated scientist turned, the white door phased out of existence, and he frantically raced into the room. It was hexagonal, with white floor lights illuminating the walls and the space in the center. The ceiling was high, as if built to hold something tall and a blank white, like the door.

'It's empty?' Spect screamed. 'I've been trying to get entrance to this massive room, and it's empty! How could this be?' He slumped to the ground and held his head again, which now pulsed with anger alongside the hangover. 'This isn't possible. I scanned this room from the Sky-Station, which is how I got the plans for the displacement device. None of this makes any sense… what was that?' he said, startled as he heard a whisper from the corner of the room. 'Is someone there?'

For a moment, there was silence before the whisper returned, louder and closer. The now spooked scientist shuffled in retreat on his backside towards the door and stared at the corner.

'If something is there, show yourself!' he yelled.

Again, something whispered, followed by another from a different direction, closer and louder still. More voices followed; a room of whispers that grew louder, stronger, and most frighteningly closer.

'Whatever you are, stay back!'

The voices were on top of Spect, loud, violent, and oppressive. He sprung to his feet and sprinted back down the corridor.

'Commander Draethus,' he stuttered into his coms, 'please close the door now.'

*

The inner door fell with a violent crash as the cutting torch finished its work. The wingman stepped back as Raeson stormed in, assault rifle at eye level, and checked the corners.

'You, down that way,' he ordered, 'and you with me.'

The first wingman made his way down one section of the corridor whilst Raeson and his follower down the other.

The Heridian vessel, with pirate fighters attached, continued to tumble bow over stern. Sporadically, the internal systems would start up, causing the engines to fire for a few moments before shorting out. The enemy vessel revealed its internal framework in a display of mayhem, battle damage with trailing pieces. The ship wasn't large compared to other capital vessels, sizing between a pirate frigate and corvette class.

Raeson kept his head low as he quickly but quietly stalked down the dark corridor, dodging the fallen debris. Pieces of twisted metal lay scattered across their path with sparking wires on the ceiling, creating strange shadows on the bulkhead walls. They rounded a corner only to find it collapsed with no way through.

Raeson's coms buzzed. 'Sir, you will want to see this,' the lone wingman said from the other side of the ship.

'This way is blocked,' Raeson replied. 'We'll be right there.'

It didn't take Raeson long to reach the other pirate and see his puzzled expression.

'Sir, it's the most bizarre thing,' the man said, laughing.

Raeson took the lead and rounded the corner. Startled, he fired his weapon into a Heridian soldier and then jumped back behind cover.

'I did that as well, sir,' the wingman said, still trying to hide his smirk. 'The thing's already dead.'

Puzzled, the pirate commander stepped out again with weapon drawn.

The armored Heridian jiggled on the spot. 'Is that the way to greet the captain of this ship?' a voice said from a speaker hanging around its neck. 'I demand more respect. It will take me ages to buff those bullet holes out.'

It dumbfounded Raeson as his two wingmen approached from behind. 'What?' Xain began.

'You see? The most bizarre thing!' the wingman said again.

Another armored puppet, seven feet high like the first, swung out of the dark. 'You still think you are the captain?' it laughed in a fake manner. 'I have always captained this vessel.'

'Which is why it is in disrepair,' said a third that appeared from an above section.

Tracing the wires, the giant alien puppets were hanging from, Raeson could see they were being controlled from nearby. 'This way,' he ordered. 'Try not to trip over anything.'

'You do not have permission to board my ship,' one puppet yelled.

'Or mine,' said the other.

The three men followed the wire trail on the ceiling, crossing into a large open section, which appeared to be the main junction of the vessel.

'Move quickly and keep...' Raeson began saying before being interrupted. A massive Heridian leader burst out of the centerpiece of the area, a large body of liquid on the floor.

The men fired their automatic weapons at the enormous head, followed by the chest as vermilion liquid fell from its armor. The creature roared from jaws filled with lines of teeth, then slashed at the air with long rusted claws. Like oil, the dark blood covered its entire body, hiding most of what was underneath.

'Who dares enter my ship?' it exclaimed, the echoes of which sounded down the corridors behind.

Raeson could hear the puppets they passed earlier chattering among themselves. 'Oh, they've done it now. Jeffrex is mad.'

'He doesn't like it when you call him that!' the other said.

'Hold fire!' Raeson ordered. 'Look, it has cables and wires.'

The enormous Heridian, or armored puppet, began speaking again. 'What business do you have aboard my ship?' It left its jaws open in threat.

Alright, I'll play along.

'I left my personality on this ship. Have you seen it?' Raeson asked.

'What does it look like?'

With a wicked grin, Raeson replied, 'It's dark and murderous. Perhaps you've seen it?'

The strange puppet started to reply when Raeson interrupted. 'We're really here to help you.'

'Help, you say. Me? The great Rid, I mean, Heridian leader and Captain of this vessel?' it laughed hysterically before slamming a claw down on a nearby piece of rubble.

'Your ship is hurtling out of control. Did you mean for this to happen, great one?' Raeson asked with a smirk.

'Everything you see here was by my design. Of course, it is part of my plan.'

Raeson felt curious and asked, 'Plan, what plan is that exactly?'

The Heridian puppet laughed again, 'Why to lure insects like you in!'

The wingman behind Raeson laughed along as well, more at the strange situation than threats from something absurd. As the liquid fell away from the creation, the boarding team could see the strung together pieces of Heridian soldiers. Chest plates were wired together to resemble armor plates combined with leg and arm pieces.

'You're constructed well, I'll give you that,' one wingman shouted, 'for a puppet.'

'Puppet!' the monstrosity screamed. 'Who are you calling a puppet?' It slammed down both arms, frantically swiping in all directions, hoping to catch the men who were far out of reach.

'I've had enough of this charade,' Raeson said. 'Let's find the owner of these things.'

The creation threw its head back in laughter. 'You better be quick about it. The ship is about to start translocation.'

Raeson's eyes went wide with realisation. The puppets were stalling them. 'There is only one other way to the bridge, this way,' he commanded as his men trailed behind him. The creation's howling laugh echoed through the ship.

The corridors at the bow showed extensive damaged, more than the stern where they had entered. Bulkheads peeled back, creating pockets of darkness the team had to check along the way.

'Boarding crew, status please.' Draethus asked over the coms. 'Do you read?'

Raeson finished checking a ruined section of floor they avoided to reach the next section. 'I read Draethus, we don't have long. This ship is about to translocate. We're going to the bridge to stop it.'

'I suggest you turn back before it does. What timeframe do you think you have?'

'Unclear, but we are closer to the bridge than our exit point. It's our best chance,' Raeson replied. 'If we vanish it won't be your problem, will it?'

'That is true pirate, proceed to the bridge and report back when you can. Draethus out.'

The coms crackled off and Raeson signalled his men forward again, increasing his pace. One of his men stumbled over a small piece of debris and almost fell into a dark hole in the floor before regaining his balance.

'Sorry,' he said to his commander, red faced.

'Watch your step or I'll leave you behind,' replied Raeson, never the one for sympathy.

Since his promotion to talon commander, Raeson discovered himself valuing the life of his comrades, a new and unsettling feeling. When he was younger, if someone fell in battle, he wouldn't consider helping them. If they weren't skilled enough, it was their failure. That was that. If a comrade betrayed him, something that happened regularly because of his father's past, Raeson had ways to make that person disappear. Such was the life he led. Now, however, the lives of those under his command were his responsibility. His superiors held him accountable and if his team failed, so did he.

'I think this is the door, Commander,' one wingman stated, running his weapon light up the scorched markings at the end of the corridor.

'Cut it down, pilot.'

The man dropped to one knee and opened the rugged backpack containing the torch cutter. Within seconds, flames began sparking off the thick door as the tool did its work. The metal fell inwards as Raeson kicked it, being careful to avoid the molten edges dripping onto the floor.

Raeson burst through first and yelled, 'Put your weapon down and step away from the console!'

Ahead of Xain, another armored puppet stood, similar to the first three they encountered, but painted blue with a clumsy white stripe on the shoulders.

'Very good, invader, you have made it this far and passed all of my tests,' a voice sounded.

Raeson raised his weapon and was about to fire when he noticed this creation had no wires or cables. It neither jiggled nor moved as the previous puppets. Something was different. It looked like a Heridian soldier, despite the color and adorned the same armor.

'Who or what are you?' Raeson asked.

'Your death!' it screamed as it produced a hidden weapon and began blasting away wildly at the boarding party.

The pirates dived to the sides behind old burnt-out consoles and set up their firing positions.

'Do we fire, Commander Raeson?' one wingman shouted out from across the bridge.

As Xain responded, the blue creation threw down its weapon in surprise.

'Is that Commander Xain Raeson, the Reaper!?!' it stuttered.

Raeson, seeing the weapon lying on the floor, stood and swiftly moved over to kick the gun away.

He raised his assault rifle at the creation, 'How do you know my name, great one?'

The creation slowly lifted its arms towards its helmet, the whole time being tracked by the weapon Raeson was holding. The helmet lifted off and revealed something Xain never thought he'd see again.

'Tek?' Raeson yelled, lowering his weapon. 'But how, you were dead?'

Tek smiled intensely as he choked back the tears. 'I've been alone on this vessel for so many years, and I thought you abandoned me.'

'We saw you fall away with the section of Rid ship months ago. How are you alive and how can it be years?'

Tek walked up to his commander of long ago and clasps arms. 'I guess time works differently out here. As for how I survived, that's a lot hazier. I've been alone on this ship for so long it's hard to remember much of anything that happened after that day. As you can see, I kept myself busy, though. Oh, the translocation.' Tek rushed over to the center console, his armor clinking together, causing the pirates to cringe at the sound, and deactivated the translocate sequence.

'I don't remember how I ended up on this ship,' he began again. 'All I know is its systems activate at predictable intervals and cause the vessel to translocate, jumping to random places. Only that function, life support, and food reserves work. From what I can tell, the blasted thing just cartwheels through space, out of control.'

'You can turn off the translocate systems, though?' Raeson asked.

Tek smiled. 'And that's about all I can do. Would you like to try some Rid food? It's really nasty, but you get used to it?'

'I'll pass thanks, but hey, I'll buy you a drink back on the Vidar. We need to get going.'

'I can't wait. Oh, I almost forgot, I found this scratched into a panel on the bridge.' Tek handed over a small piece of flat metal shard inscribed with numbers and a name.

'You found this here?' Xain asked.

'Yeah, any idea what it means?'

Raeson frowned, 'Draethus,' he said out loud, 'the word means trouble, but how by the creator did it end up on this ship?'

'I don't even know how I ended up on this ship,' Tek laughed, stumbling over his dropped helmet and almost tripping. 'Well, I'm going to go say goodbye to my friends. If you'll excuse me, Jeffrex needs some attention.'

Tek, adorned in his blue Heridian armor, clumsily strode off the bridge and disappeared down the corridor.

'See what else you can find on these consoles, and then we head back,' Raeson ordered.

The wingmen acknowledged his command and got to work.

Raeson walked off the bridge to follow his old comrade. Tek wasn't looking in the best health, physically or mentally, and was unshaven and malnourished. He watched as the man bent down and started talking to his largest creation, dubbed Jeffrex, and felt a pain in his heart.

Guilt. It's rare I feel guilty about something.

In his mind, Xain knew he had left Tek to die and didn't even search for him. Did Tek watch them fly away? The image of their ship leaving was painful.

He walked over to a dark corner and touched the coms in his ear. 'Draethus, are you there?'

'I read you Xain, status?'

'We stopped the ship from translocating and found something interesting, well a couple of things, really.'

'I see, go on.'

Raeson paused for a moment as he watched Tek walk off, looking for his other creations, then over the com added, 'There was a shard of metal with a group of co-ordinates scratched into it, alongside some writing.'

'Writing, you say? Bring it aboard and we'll pinpoint the location. Wait, have you been into the crayons again?'

'Do me a favor. Direct your coms into the cold of space and see if anyone is laughing.' Raeson adjusted the com unit attached to his jaw line then added, 'It's your name inscribed on the shard.'

There was silence for a moment before Draethus answered, 'Well, that is interesting.'

'Trouble seems to follow you. I'm also bringing aboard an old friend. He will be my responsibility.'

'You found someone on the ship?' Draethus sounded surprised.

'That's right, but like I said, he will be my responsibility.'

'Understood. Speaking of old friends, I hear Rel is serving aboard the Arvernus now, for this mission at least?'

'What importance does that serve?' Raeson replied with a defensive tone.

'Just keeping track of who is serving with you, nothing more,' Draethus finished as he closed the coms.

The wingman walked out of the bridge and joined their commander.

'Tek!' Raeson yelled. 'Finish your goodbyes. It's time to go.'

'And this ship, sir, what will become of it?' asked a wingman.

Raeson stared at him and replied, 'Let it vanish.'

CHAPTER 16

Scrounging for Answers.

Spectalin leant nervously against a bulkhead, opposite the room that had plagued so much of his curiosity. He stared at his reflection, remembering what he felt after finally accessing the other side. The fear, the unseen presence that surrounded him, the way it spoke causing his retreat. His hands trembled as sweat poured down his forehead, a gut-wrenching panic forming in the pit of his stomach.

'Found you,' Tremon said as he ran down the corridor. 'It's so easy to get lost in this ship.'

He stopped at the doors and watched his own reflection join the scientist. 'Are you alright Spect? You look a little pale.'

The scientist cleared his throat and looked down. 'I'm scared out of my mind, Tremon. Whatever is in that room isn't human or even of this reality, I think.'

'Well then, are you going to open it? We don't have to wait for Draethus, he can catch up.'

'I'm not sure,' Spect replied.

'I'm tough. I can handle it. Be brave!' Tremon was itching to find out what was so spooky on the other side.

Timidly placing his palm to the side of the bulkhead, Spect opened the room. The door phased out of existence to reveal the same empty hexagon shaped room as before.

'Wow, looks really spooky,' Tremon laughed as he walked in. 'I was expecting something dark and foreboding.'

The whispers around the room started again, beginning at one of the far corners, and approaching Tremon. He took a few steps inside, only to freeze as if blocked by an unknown force. The volume of the voices increased and surrounded him, like an unseen group of spirits swirling in a vortex ready to consume the man. Tremon quickly stepped back out of the room and fumbled for the unseen panel Spect had used to open the door. The white metal phased back into existence and created a barrier between Tremon and whatever force he felt threatened by.

'Right, there may be something to your theory then Spect,' Tremon grimaced.

*

'What's all the noise?' Draethus asked, walking up to the pair.

Tremon got in first and said, 'There's something in that room and it's well, not of this reality and we can't see it.'

Draethus looked puzzled and said, 'Alright, let's see what's there. Spect, open it.'

'Yes, Commander,' the scientist acknowledged, his hands shaking again.

Draethus walked up to the doors as they phased out of existence, then took a step into the room. For a moment, there was no activity. His two crewmen behind him looked anxious. The lights flickered, a vibration in the air caused their ear drums to pulse from the pressure and something stirred. It started with a faint word, a shadow on the edge of the visual spectrum, and a darkness in the center of the room manifested. A small cloud began forming at Draethus' eye level, joined by something swirling, first around the manifestation, then through it. Colors of magenta flashed like lightning as the entity grew until it occupied half the room.

Un-phased, the Commander of the *Dawn Eclipse* stood firm, listening to the voices, both around him and in his head. As he looked into the manifestation, Draethus swore he could see faces, twisted and warped. They swirled amongst the clouds as comets would streak through a solar system.

The visions that had plagued the soldier began again, but this time without the agonising pain and played back as a series of flashes instead. The creatures that clawed at him, the ground that seared and the world that burned. It was as if Draethus was experiencing a vision of what was to come. The entity's growth stopped just short of his face, and the vibrations in the air ceased.

'What is this darkness, Eclipse?' he asked out loud, for the benefit of his crew.

The warm sensation entered his mind and replaced the voices that had grown more intense. *This is the heart of the Dawn Eclipse. It is everything and nothing.*

'You talk in riddles. I need a more direct answer, Eclipse.'

'What is it?' Spect asked as Tremon nudged him to wait for the answer.

This ship links to the threads of time, and what lays beyond, called the Tether Source.

'So, what we are seeing here is how this ship can travel through space-time?'

It does, in a way. What you are seeing is a glimpse into the Tether, its power.

Draethus backed away from the manifestation and shut the door.

'What you are sensing, scientist Spectalin,' Draethus began, 'is what links this ship with space-time, but not in the same way as translocation. The ship called it the Tether Source, which powers the drives and gives us the ability to travel by it.'

'The Tether Source? I like how that sounds, but why does it have to be so frightening? And how if I scanned the ship back on Echelon, did I get the plans for the device instead of this manifestation?'

Tremon interrupted. 'I'd imagine this ship gave you the plans you needed to start this mess.'

The scientist rubbed his chin in thought. 'I guess that makes sense.'

Draethus turned and walked away. 'Maybe this ship started our path, but we will finish it.'

*

The floor was cold against Xain Raeson's face. His vision blurred and his head pounded. Rel was sitting up next to him talking, saying something he couldn't understand as pain overtook his senses. He struggled to his feet whilst being helped by the small mechanic.

'Xain!' she yelled, 'Xain, what's wrong?'

He fell back against the wall of the Commander's room on the *Arvernus* and grabbed his head. 'What happened?' he asked through gritted teeth.

'We were having dinner, talking about your mother and how you don't really talk, the nicest dinner I've ever made you, by the way. You just screamed and collapsed.' She frowned and asked, 'Not that bad, was it?'

'No, not that I remember.'

'Not that you remember!' Rel's eyes flared. 'What do you mean, not that you remember? It was excellent!'

'Help me up, will you?' Xain wasn't in a fit state. Each set of visions seemed to be more intense, and he feared for how deadly they might become.

'I've been getting these visions from time to time, and they knock me out.'

'Visions?' she said. 'What are you seeing and why?'

Raeson stumbled over to the table and sat on the small, padded silver chair. 'I don't know why I get them. It started a couple of months ago and they are getting worse, more painful.'

'Have you seen anyone about them? Actually, go to the infirmary, there is a doctor on the Arvernus at the moment, and he's been helping Slin with his cybernetics.'

'I'll be fine. I've been told that Draethus has been receiving visions as well since he boarded the Eclipse, so I think it may be connected. Not sure why I would get them, though.' He took a sip of his wine before knocking the whole drink back.

'So Draethus has this pain too?' the girl asked, putting her hand to her lips.

Raeson looked at her strangely for a moment. 'Yeah, he does. Why would that make a difference?'

Rel looked away and changed the subject. 'So what do you see when it happens?'

'I see crimson oceans and the flood of pain. I see creatures that claw and slash at me, cutting away my flesh. Sometimes there are storms, acid rain melting my skin and other times a world on fire, burning my body into ash.'

The look on Rel's face was one of terror mixed with sorrow. 'How can you stand that? How can you sleep with those memories?'

Raeson smiled. 'If it weren't for the headache, I don't think they'd be all that bad.'

Rel got out of her chair and punched him. 'You shouldn't joke about these things, and it's not funny.'

'No, I guess it isn't.' He got up and escorted Rel to the door. 'Thank you for making this for me, as always.'

She collected her things and made her way out of the commander's quarters, turned, and gave him a harsh stare. 'You should take better care of yourself, because no one else will. That doctor could do something for you. I know he could.'

Raeson smiled, leaned up against the door, then saw something move at the end of the corridor.

'What is it?' Rel asked.

'I'm not sure,' he replied, craning his neck in curiosity. 'I swear something just walked through that wall. Stay here.'

Xain reached into his quarters, grabbed a sidearm from its holster near the door, and proceeded quickly after whatever he saw. He approached with weapon at the ready and opened the door to a room he thought the shadow moved into.

Just a storage room, nothing here.

He walked back to Rel, now hiding behind the door. 'All clear,' he assured her.

'You're acting weird tonight, Xain, I don't like it and I'm worried.'

He put the gun back into its holster and said, 'You should worry more about yourself than other people. That always was your weakness, Rel. Pirates are cold-hearted, ruthless survivors and look after themselves. Maybe you should be more like that and less dependent on other people?'

Tears welled up in her eyes as she pointed her finger up into Raeson's face angrily. 'And if I were like that, where would you be? Someone around here needs to think of others instead of themselves. As for being depended, well, we can't all be Mr Commander of Darkness, can we, Xain?'

A smile crept into the corner of his mouth as he realized he'd hit a nerve.

'You're fooling with me again, aren't you? Seriously, one of these days I'm going to cut the life support on your fighter and then we'll see who's smirking.'

She turned in a huff and stormed off down the corridor.

'See you again,' Raeson yelled after her.

He shut the door, walked over to the table, and poured himself another wine.

I wonder what type of person I would be if Rel wasn't in my life? I hope that day never comes.

*

The three widowmaker fighters streaked across the endless night towards the co-ordinates found earlier, marked on the metal shard alongside the name, Draethus. As the point of interest wasn't far off course, they had deviated from their path to Tiberous.

The *Dawn Eclipse* and the *Arvernus* lay in anchor on the edge of visual and sensor range, a distance away from the point, to stay hidden in case of a trap. The pirate fighters, led by Stark, raced ahead to scout the area, and discover what lay ahead.

'All fighters, full burn for twenty seconds in three, two, one, burn now.' Stark commanded over the coms.

The engines flared an impressive blue fire like a small comet's ice trail, and the nozzles heated and sparked with the sustained action.

Stark looked over each shoulder to make sure both wingmen had complied, counted down from twenty in his head, and gave the order.

'Cut all engines and power down, keep current trajectory and velocity so we can go in with minimal to no signature. Clear coms.'

The men on each wing gave their reply by visual salute and went dark.

I've seen many things in my time, but never something like that. He shielded his eyes from the intense rays of the star to his front. The three craft were approaching a sun like no other, not round like most, but oval and tilted on a thirty-degree angle. Purple flames spun like wildfire across the star's surface and coated the fighters in an eerie glow. Every now and again, solar flares would stretch out like tentacles searching for prey.

As they got closer, Stark could make out a reflection glinting in the distance and deduced it must be something metallic. He activated the zoom function on his heads-up display connected with his eyes and targeted the area in question, without turning on the rest of his systems.

At first, he could see nothing, just purple flames emanating from the star, until he panned right and found what they were looking for.

An orbital station, how interesting. What would some random platform be doing way out here, I wonder? Studying the star, maybe? Refuel point?

He reached into the side compartment, grabbed a small handheld light, and signalled his wingman to keep watch on him. He knew they would wait for his fighter to power up before mirroring the action.

Just a little further.

He felt a pulse of nervousness. Because he had been in combat for most of his life, he rarely got nervous before a battle. This situation, though, was different. Something wasn't right.

Stark's cockpit glowed with a violet hue cast by the star and felt himself calm. He flicked the red switch above him and lit up his systems. For a moment, they glowed as bright as the sun ahead. His engine roared back to life as the micro reactor injected power into the buffers. Weapons and navigation systems activated, and his flight sticks became responsive.

'Full burn at that station for five, maximum throttle, let's go!' Stark commanded, watching the other two craft power up.

It didn't take long for the orbital station to fill his view. It was long, roughly three kilometres and stood on its end. The top comprised a cluster of viewing windows he thought maybe a control section where people could get visual recognition of any incoming ships. From the middle of the station, on a right angle, protruded an enormous platform that stretched out two-thirds of the station's entire length. Covered in markings, it was large enough to land a frigate squadron, or an army of fighters.

'What does that say, I wonder?' one wingman asked as the pirate fighters flew past the main body section. Letters in an unknown language appeared from top to bottom.

'No idea,' replied Stark. 'The station name, I'd imagine. This place looks old though, abandoned.'

'Agreed,' the other wingman said. 'Should we land and inspect? I'd love to see what's inside it.'

'I've run a sound echo scan on the interior and there doesn't seem to be anything there, but yes, we need a closer look,' said Stark.

*

Draethus grinned profusely at Raeson.
On Draethus' request, the pirate had transferred over to the *Dawn Eclipse,* and stood in disbelief, staring out over the ledge of the liquid lake.

'What's it like inside that stuff?' Xain asked.

Draethus joined him on the rail. 'Hard to explain really, it's like being under water, but not at the same time. It gives you a good tactical view of everything around the ship. Once you get over the panic of drowning under a lake of liquid metal, that is.'

Raeson returned his smile and said, 'Maybe I could try it one day.'

'For my sake I hope you don't have to,' Draethus laughed. 'Are you curious about what's under there, or is there more to it?'

'The visions, Draethus, it's the visions that I'm wondering about. I know you get them as well and I want to know why that is?'

Draethus turned to look at his crew, who were busy manning their consoles behind the pair of commanders. 'What do you see when it happens?'

'I see death. I see the death of me, of thousands of others on a world of fire. Acid melts my skin and evil creatures consume all the surrounding people, feeding.'

'Then they are the same visions,' Draethus replied. He thought for a moment, before deciding to let the pirate know of what he learned earlier. 'The visions originate from this ship and what powers it.'

'The Eclipse?' Raeson said, surprised. 'How could a ship cause me to have crippling visions?'

'Earlier, we discovered this vessel taps into power using something called the Tether Source. It's a link to whatever enables the ship to jump through space-time.' A flash of uneasiness crossed Draethus' face. 'When I looked into the source, I saw the same visions but without the pain.'

'That doesn't explain why I would receive the same visions, though.'

'No, it doesn't, but maybe I can show you this source later and we can get some answers.'

'Agreed. I'd like to understand what it is. The headaches are a killer.'

Both men laughed before Tremon called out, 'The scout team has missed their scheduled communication.'

Draethus called for the platform to lower him into the liquid lake before Raeson interrupted. 'I recommend leaving them. We can't risk this ship and the mission.'

'Leave them?' replied Draethus. 'You would leave your own men to die out there? What if they are just delayed and there is no risk?'

'Can you justify this ship falling into the hands of the Rids for the sake of three men, one of which I would gladly sacrifice either way?'

'I will leave no one behind, even if they are just pirates,' Draethus replied, remembering the people he'd lost back on Echelon.

The platform lowered him into the liquid metal and Spect opened a communication to the *Arvernus*.

'This is Commander Draethus to Slin; we are going in at full speed, adjust heading to suit, and we will investigate what's happened to the scouts.'

'Is that wise Commander? What does Raeson say?' Slin replied before being cut off.

'Raeson has his own opinion, however I am in command of this mission so you will fall into formation, is that clear?'

There was a pause for a moment as Slin gave the matter some thought before replying, 'Yes, Commander.'

Both the *Dawn Eclipse* and the *Arvernus* engaged their engines and sped towards the co-ordinates. It took a few minutes for the pirate corvette to fall into the formation Draethus desired, but considering the size and velocity of the vessels, he let it slide. The purple star came up quickly as the warships went into a battle readiness, their nanite plated armor primed and weapons online. Tremon, a little trigger-happy as he had shot nothing for a while, was leaning into the hologram of his console and searching for any reason to unleash havoc.

'We are inside scanning range of the co-ordinates,' Spect announced. 'I'm detecting a large signature orbiting the star, but no sign of the fighters.'

'Enemy activity?' Draethus questioned.

'None, sir. The signature, however, will be in visual range within the next few minutes,' Spect replied.

The moment we have a visual on that signature, please display it on the bridge, Eclipse, Draethus asked the ship in his mind.

As you wish, Commander. You should know I am detecting a source of power from the signature, nuclear energy to be exact.

From above the bridge, the image of the orbital platform appeared and began rendering into a three-dimensional hologram. Once the digital bones of the structure completed, the real-time visual overlay activated to give the crew an in-depth look at the situation.

'Zoom in on the platform, near where it joins the primary structure,' Draethus ordered.

The cylindrical space station zoomed in to reveal the three fighters landed in formation on the platform.

'They landed?' observed Spect. 'Why would they land?'

'So they can loot whatever's in that orbital station, that's why,' Raeson replied angrily. 'We should have just left them behind.'

'Seems to be the pirate way, doesn't it?' Draethus said over the coms. 'Remind me to never let you fly me anywhere.'

'Open communications, get them back here now,' Raeson ordered. 'Give them a time limit. If they exceed, they're left behind.'

A visual display appeared behind the hologram of a man's face and flickered with static. 'Crew of the Eclipse, do not approach, the station is a trap. I repeat, do not approach, the station is a trap,' said the man before gunfire blew him away from the screen. A splash of blood covered half of the video feed as the man slumped back onto the wall behind him. A creature, thin with brownish yellow skin and ragged clothes, walked in front of him and fired again to make sure the pirate was dead.

From the platform, two of the pirate fighters launched and headed toward the awaiting vessels.

'Adjust trajectory down to our six, full burn, get us away from the station, now!' Draethus commanded. 'Tremon, target those fighters, but hold fire until we can identify the pilots.'

The two fighters were in full burn, screaming away from the station, flying erratically.

'This is Stark to Eclipse. We are both wounded and request landing. You are in the middle of a minefield. I suggest halting engines.'

'Confirmed, dock with the Arvernus. We will have a medic meet you at the dock,' Slin replied.

With a quick wave of his hand, Draethus cut engines and used the manoeuvring thrusters to begin deceleration.

Can he be right, Eclipse? are we in a minefield? He asked in his mind.

It took a moment for the warmth of the voice to surface. *It could be possible, however, I am not detecting any objects in our immediate vicinity.*

I see.

'Stark, where exactly are these mines, you speak of?' Raeson asked over the coms.

'They are low level, long distance grapplers like the ones we used in the past, in our more pirate days,' Stark replied.

'Spect, can you scan for any signatures on the edge of our range that are distorting the surrounding light?' Raeson inquired.

'You think these mines would create a gravity effect?' the scientist asked, with an obvious expression of panic.

'Correct. If Stark is right, they'll be at extreme range and…' Raeson stopped as the *Eclipse* performed an emergency stop, causing the crew to stagger as the artificial gravity compensated.

'They've got us!' Spect yelled. 'Twenty-nine, no thirty-two mines have us snared.'

From hundreds of kilometres away, invisible against the backdrop of night, the mines surrounded both capital vessels and held them in place with a focussed beam of gravity. Unable to manoeuvre, both the ships, despite being at full power, couldn't escape such a force.

'We're on board, Raeson,' Stark notified over the coms.

'Good. I'm so glad you could make it even though you led us into a trap,' Raeson replied bitterly. 'Why did you land and what could you have hoped to accomplish?'

'First, know that I do not need to explain my actions to you,' Stark replied. 'But we explored the station, which is how we discovered the mines. We also disabled most of the mines as the station held the command point for them.'

'There were more?' Draethus asked.

'Yes, Commander. If we hadn't boarded the platform, there would also be the explosive type in the mix as well,' Stark said.

'Well, we are thankful that you did. That doesn't solve our predicament, though. Also,' Draethus added, 'what was that creature that killed the pirate?'

'We call them Scroungers. They are a poorly organised and nomadic race who sells their services to the highest bidder. Here I'm guessing it was the Rids, wouldn't be the first time either,' Raeson added in.

'I see,' Draethus replied, 'yet another enemy to add to the list, but we'll deal with that later.'

Eclipse, how do we escape this?

I'm sorry Commander, but I am detecting multiple signatures emerging from translocation and am activating emergency contingency, the *Eclipse* replied.

'By the creator, eleven Rid cruisers just appeared on the grid, and they have weapons primed,' exclaimed Spect.

What contingency is this?

The golden armor plates covering the *Dawn Eclipse* separated like a flower in bloom. Sharp edges glistened with light, reflecting purple fire from the star behind. Blue energy burst from the vessel like smoke engulfing a building, covering both ships, and a flash of white vaporized them into nothingness. The crew, alongside their new pirate allies, had made their first jump through space-time.

CHAPTER 17

Emerging From Shadows.

It started with a spark of immense light, seen for thousands of kilometres in all directions, if there was anyone or anything present to witness. Fire erupted from its center as the spark increased in size as a tear in the fabric of space-time ripped open, materializing the two vessels.

The *Dawn Eclipse*, now covered in a blue haze adding to its golden splendour, contracted its armor plates and began spooling down the power of its time drive. The *Arvernus,* however, not being a ship designed for such travel, had small fires running down the length of its body.

'I need a systems damage report, Nash,' Slin ordered, 'and an explanation to what the hell happened.'

'Yes, sir,' she responded, then added, 'as for what happened, I think that glowing ship out there might have an answer.'

Looking out of the forward display, Slin marvelled at the majestic sight.

How could something like that even exist, let alone be a star vessel?

The young pirate, sitting in the active pilot's chair, whose name Slin still couldn't remember, piped up and said, 'I don't think that's the only vision of awe. I'd suggest we manoeuvre sixty-five degrees to starboard.'

'This isn't your private pleasure yacht,' Slin replied, 'but go ahead, show us where we are.'

The *Arvernus* adjusted its heading and spun to starboard. The crew looked on in curiosity as the most immense structure filled the screens, causing a unified gasp.

'By the creator, what is that?' Nash asked, her question trailing off into a whisper.

Standing before both ships was a pair of statues, both identical and roughly a thousand kilometres in height. Resembling an armored man with the head of a reptile, they both held a staff in one claw and a shield in the other. The gap between the two megaliths measured approximately two hundred kilometres and gave the crew the impression they were standing guard.

'Are they gods?' Slin asked.

The coms crackled to life as Nash redirected the incoming voice to the loudspeaker.

'Slin, what is your ship status? I see fires erupting on your main armor,' Raeson asked from the bridge of the *Eclipse*.

Nash swiped her screen, and it appeared on the acting commander's console.

'Minor damage, Commander Raeson. The fires will burn out soon. The nanites are doing their job nicely,' Slin replied. 'What happened and what are those statues out there?'

'I can answer that one,' Draethus interrupted, over the coms. 'The Eclipse activated a contingency reserved for imminent capture.'

The image of Draethus appeared on the front display and replaced the towering gods.

'We had no choice but to engage the time drive and jump ourselves, along with the Arvernus, out of danger. It only made sense to land at our intended destination, or so the ship has told me,' Draethus continued.

'So why couldn't we have just time jumped here in the first place?' Slin asked.

'Because time-shifting is dangerous for the ship and us.'

Slin nodded his head in acknowledgement. 'So your ship talks to you then?'

'I thought a bookshelf was talking to me once, turned out to be the guy next door,' said the red-headed pilot from below. The crew tried their best to ignore him, but Slin managed a snigger.

'In a manner of speaking it does,' Draethus said with a smile, 'and those megaliths out there, the ship tells me, are the Pillars of Vanquish. Beyond them are exotic particles from the nearby anomaly, a Nebula Stream that we can sail, if you will, to Tiberous.'

'Like gods, they guard the dark ocean entry to the mysterious Tiberous,' the young pirate called out.

'Quite a dramatic way to put it, but yes, they mark the entrance,' Raeson added.

Slin watched on the display as Raeson stood up from his console and walked closer to the viewing hologram. The talon commander manipulated the photons displaying the enormous guardians.

'I've heard of Tiberous since I was a child,' said Xain, 'but never knew of such a sight. Who built them?'

'The only information the Eclipse will relinquish is they're in the image of its builders, obviously not to scale. As to the name of the ancient race, that would have faded with their extinction.' Draethus touched the scar on his face, 'I'm told they lived on Tiberous, and we are probably lucky not to have met them.'

'Crew of the Arvernus,' Draethus ordered, 'we are on a strict schedule. Please dock with the Eclipse to speed up repairs.'

The pirate corvette activated its manoeuvring thrusters, spun and gently made its way towards its sister ship. Once closer, the *Arvernus* triggered its grappling wires and latched onto the golden vessel. Both ships anchored motionless in full view of the towering gods, as insects would to giants.

*

The doors phased out of existence as the entrance to the golden vessel joined with the *Arvernus*. Nash stood at attention, ready to welcome their allies aboard, which was normally the custom, as someone came up from behind her.

'Rel, what are you doing here?' Nash asked. 'I thought you were repairing the fighters.'

The small red-haired girl only laughed. 'They were easy to fix, only minor damage. Are they here yet?'

'Commander Raeson, you mean? Not yet.'

'No, I meant, um,' Rel cut her sentence short as the crew of the *Eclipse* appeared in the doorway.

'Permission to board,' Draethus asked formally.

'Permission granted, Commander.'

Draethus, adorned in his dark gray armor, strode onto the pirate corvette, followed by Raeson, Tremon and Spect.

'Hi Commander,' Rel said, red faced with a smile and a small wave.

Raeson almost replied, realized the greeting wasn't for him, and nodded instead. He headed to the bridge to see Slin and Nash followed closely behind.

Draethus smiled at the small mechanic and said, 'It's good to see you again, Rel. I hope you've been keeping out of trouble?'

The girl giggled, 'I'm not sure what you mean Draethus, and I never get into any trouble. I was wondering though if you would like to see where I work.'

Draethus looked at his crew, thought about declining because of his workload, then saw Tremon smirking. 'That sounds like a great idea, Rel. Lead the way.'

Tremon, who had changed his opinion of Draethus since they first met, yelled after them. 'We won't wait up, Commander.'

'What are we supposed to do, then?' Spect asked.

'I guess we find Slin and ask for a guided or unguided tour of the corvette,' Tremon replied. 'We didn't get to see all of it last time, did we?'

Spect's face lit up. 'I wonder what their translocation drive looks like and...'

Tremon headed for the command deck, followed by the scientist who began babbling to himself about what he could discover.

*

In another part of the *Arvernus*, Draethus and Rel entered the small docking bay. An extensive collection of mechanical pieces was scattered about the ground, with dark liquids dripping through mechanisms that pooled excessively. The underside of the widowmaker fighters was attached to the ceiling, with their topside covered by retractable armor from the corvette.

'Well, this is it. What do you think, Draethus?' Rel asked.

Draethus, who was used to discipline and structure, looked around the dock area and tried to hide his surprise. 'Do you work with explosives?'

'You think it's messy, don't you?' she said with a sarcastic pout. 'Well, all this is necessary to repair craft efficiently, where everything gets inspected. You wouldn't want to be in the depths of space and run out of life support, would you?'

Draethus looked down at the girl who was standing with hands on hips. 'I can't think of anything worse,' he laughed. 'You obviously enjoy taking machines apart. Do you normally work on the Arvernus, though?'

'I'm only here for this mission to monitor Talon Commander Raeson and make sure he does nothing stupid. We don't want him dying,' she replied.

'What stupid things?' Draethus asked. 'Besides running out of fuel before we found him, or did he forget his keys again?'

Rel laughed, 'That sounds like him, but I'm pretty sure he was hit by Rids that time.'

'A nice coverup. This might sound abrupt, but is there something between the two of you?'

A look of shock crossed Rel's face. 'Oh no it's nothing like that. We're just childhood friends, and grew up together.'

Draethus smiled, 'That's good to hear. Was that the only reason you came on this mission?'

The girl blushed, more than she had ever done in her life, before replying, 'No reason.'

She looked away.

'I'm happy you came.' Draethus said with a genuine smile, and then added, 'I was wondering when I could see you again.'

He found a flat piece of equipment and sat down. Rel sat on the bay floor and leaned back against a rail at his feet.

'So how does a beautiful woman end up being a pirate, let alone a mechanic?'

Rel glanced up and smiled. 'My aunt was a boarding soldier for the pirates and raised me. She was one bad arse woman; had to be.'

'I see,' Draethus said, 'what happened to your parents?'

'My aunt never talked about them much, but I know they died during the war against the Rids. They weren't soldiers or anything, but they had something to do with freighters, ferrying goods to different sectors of pirate space.'

'Logistics is an important part of any fleet.'

'They were important, yes, and I never knew them. I was only a baby.' Rel shifted uncomfortably. 'My aunt was my guardian, and I'm glad to have met her. She died not that long ago, and not even against the Rids. She captured a hauling vessel from the Common World's Alliance, full of priceless goods, and died leading the boarding party. Those ships don't always have escorts, but they're full of heavily armored personnel. It was a risk, and she knew it. Her crew captured the ship in the end though and I got to say my farewells.'

Draethus frowned. 'I'm sorry to hear that, Rel, this way of life is dangerous.'

She blushed again. 'Another reason I came on this mission was to keep an eye on you as well.'

Draethus' smile reached his eyes this time, and he never imagined meeting anyone special. He always imagined the end of his life would be on some long-forgotten battlefield.

'What about you, Commander Draethus of the Dawn Eclipse,' Rel said playfully. 'Where did you grow up?'

'There's a planet called Echelon where I was born. It's a massive jungle world populated by carnivorous creatures, plants and thousands of other animals that try to eat you.'

'By the creator!'

'It's as bad as it sounds,' Draethus laughed. 'But growing up in the jungles you don't know any other way of life. Then one day the Soldiers of the Void arrived from the heavens and laid claim to the planet. I left my tribe, as many others did, and learnt their language and customs. I proved my worth quickly, alongside a childhood friend, and became one of them. Not long after, the Rids invaded, which is how I gained my combat experience over the years.'

'That doesn't sound like a great way to grow up,' the girl said. 'What of your parents?'

'The tribes of the jungles don't work that way. You're born, and then raised as a group of children, kind of like training future hunters for the tribe. There's no concept of parents, just tribal upbringing.'

'That's horrible, so you're an orphan, but you're not.'

'That's life on Echelon, and it continues to this day. The toughest of young fighters earn their way into the ranks, which replenishes the SOV, the trial and errors of life.'

Rel stood up and moved into Draethus's personal space, so close he could feel her breath.

'I've been thinking a lot about you, Draethus,' she said, looking up into his eyes. 'I know that your way of life is dangerous, but I just want nothing bad to happen to you.'

The soldier smiled and said, 'I've shifted to another time, fought Rids at every corner, adopted a mysterious telepathic star vessel, allied myself with pirates and the best part has been meeting you.'

Rel blushed as Draethus leaned in and kissed her for the first time. The nervousness, excitement and feelings washed over the pair of them as they embraced. Slowly and passionately, they became as one and after a few minutes, parted. Draethus, who would normally run his fingers down the scar on his face, instead caressed Rel and cupped her cheek in his hand.

'You'll have to come aboard more often.'

She smiled with delight and said, 'I will. I could even make you dinner sometime and you could tell me the story of how you got here.'

Draethus played with the dragon embossed amulet hidden between his armor plates on his chest.

'What's that?' Rel asked.

He looked down, unaware he was holding it. 'They give this amulet to all SOV on the day of induction. It contains information on the individual's achievements.'

'Can I see?'

He unclipped the clasp at the back of his neck and handed it to her. 'If you press here,' he said, showing the hidden button, 'a hologram appears, and you can select the achievements. This one is when I defeated a carnosaur in a trial to become a soldier.'

The hologram illuminated the dock area and showed a video of a young Draethus, not armored, fighting a giant lizard with a primitive sword.

'That's so dangerous!' she yelled. 'How can anyone expect you to defeat that!?!'

Draethus laughed, 'The trials are harsh to become a soldier and the challenges you face after induction are even harder still.'

She pressed the amulet again to shut the recording off, then unclipped her own locket. The gold reflected off her skin and was round with a crest embossed on the front.

'This belonged to my mother. My aunt gifted it to me when I came of age and has some small pictures of my family.'

'What's the crest on the front?' he asked.

'I think it's the crest of my family, but I'm unsure. I want you to have it.'

Draethus looked shocked. 'Are you sure? I don't know what to say.'

'Say you will keep it with you always and think of me in times of need.'

'It would honor me, Rel,' he replied, clipping it around his neck. 'I promise I won't fence it.'

'You promise what exactly?' Rel replied with a huff as a smile reached the corner of her lips. 'If you think being hunted by a giant lizard was bad, I'd be worse!'

He looked into her eyes and said with a laugh, 'Then you can look after my amulet.' He placed it around her neck and added, 'It looks really large on you.'

Rel giggled. 'It really does. If it's alright with you, I might keep it in a safe place. After all, you are the one running into danger all the time.'

'I seem to fly more than run lately, or is it sailing? The space thing is new to me.'

*

Raeson walked into the entrance of the dock and froze when he saw the pair standing in each other's arms. A feeling of resentment coursed through his blood. Rel was his childhood friend.

Why am I angry? It's not like we were ever a couple, or ever going to be.

He turned and left quickly, hoping the pair hadn't noticed.

*

Tektar Shahath, or Tek to his friends, sat on the edge of the infirmary bed and looked around the room.

'Such a clinical space. Where is the junk, the colors, the darkness?' he said to himself. 'I wonder what the guys are doing now?'

'What people are you talking about?' Nash asked as she walked through the door.

She faced him with a big smile on her face, and a tear dropped from her cheek.

'My friends on the ship I just left. I miss them,' he replied.

'We missed you too, Tek. Watching you fall away like that and disappearing in the dark broke my heart. I never should have been so hard on you. I'm so sorry.'

The man looked ragged, aged, and to Nash it seemed like his mind had given up.

'I don't blame you for how you felt towards me, girl. I was an arse and, worst of all, I was dangerous. The best thing that could have happened was my death on the Rid destroyer.'

'Please don't talk like that, Tek. If we knew you were still alive, we would have come back for you. I didn't think anyone could have survived that.'

'I wouldn't have either, yet here I am alive in the flesh and no recollection of how. I don't even know how I ended up on that vessel Raeson found me on.'

'I'm just happy you are safe and here, alive,' she said, her smile beaming with a second chance to talk to her old wing mate.

Nash sat on the bed next to him. 'We all heard about what you did to save the fleet in your past.'

'Did you,' Tek replied, 'and who did you hear that from?'

'The pilot that rescued you, who saw what you did.' She frowned. 'It's a terrible decision to make, but I believe what you did was the correct one. You saved the fleet when others put themselves first and would have let us all burn.'

'Doesn't make living with it any easier, I can tell you,' he said.

'No, but you're a hero and everyone in the fleet knows the story now. It spread like crazy.'

'I don't want that exposure. I killed my own and should have paid the price.'

'You've carried the guilt with you for years. What more of a price would you want to pay? Don't you think your fellow brothers and sisters in arms should decide that?' Nash replied, rubbing his shoulder.

Tek zoned out for a moment before he realized Nash was still in the room. 'Yes, yes, of course, that makes sense.'

'We should go for a walk around the Vidar when we get back. Stretch your legs. I think it will surprise you at what you see. There is even writing on the walls welcoming back the hero of the fleet.'

For the first time, Tek smiled. A genuine sense of happiness that maybe everything he'd endured had been worth it.

'I would like that,' he said, gripping the sheets. 'I haven't had a drop of alcohol in what must be years. But it would be good to do something that doesn't involve staring at walls.'

'Then it's settled,' Nash replied as she gave her old friend a powerful hug. 'I'm so glad you're back with us. Oh, who were the friends you were talking about as I came in? Were there other people on that ship too?'

'No, I was alone,' Tek replied as he looked around for his boots.

*

The black capital cruisers sat motionless amongst the large fleet of Cygnian Pirates. Anchored around a nameless star, the god-like vessels cast shadows over the nearby asteroids, sheltering them from the ever-watching eyes of the dark heavens. High above them, the great flagship, the *Wing of Vidar,* protected the group as a mother would its children.

Looking down through the glass floor, Khan Hayreddin marvelled at the sheer size of the fleet he commanded, reminiscing of the days when he first became the leader of the pirates. His close friend, Zelene, entered the observation room.

'Alexon,' the woman whispered as she approached, 'you look sombre. Is everything alright?'

The Khan looked up; his long dark beard trimmed neatly and smiled. 'I was just remembering the days of old, in the beginning.'

'That was a very long time ago, almost feels like another life.'

'It certainly does. I almost miss the small frigate I first commanded.'

Zelene couldn't help but let out a small giggle. 'It is humorous hearing you call a capital ship small. Compared to the Vidar everything is such.'

'Aye, the Vidar is a beauty and I sometimes forget she's a vessel and not a city.'

The Khan moved close to the women and took her by the hands. 'I'm afraid my agent could not discover any information regarding what happened to your husband,' he said sadly. 'I sent my operative to collect an item of importance on an enemy vessel, in which he succeeded. It didn't, however, contain any details of the event all those years ago.'

'What item was this?' Zelene asked curiously, 'and why would it contain information on that event?'

'I can't divulge all the information surrounding the object, but I can say what it holds is immense. We've finished decoding it, which has taken a long time, and we now possess invaluable details on Heridian tactics and plans. It didn't contain the location of their home-world, however.'

'This agent of yours, Stark, I believe his name to be? Is he good at what he does?' Zelene asked with a hint of spite in her voice.

'He is the best at what he does, Zelene. There is no equal. He ranks highest in the Dark Ops division.'

'So that division exists?'

'Just between you and me, yes, that division exists, and it doesn't.'

'I see, well he has been part of Xain's Reaper wing for years now and he still hasn't been able to find any information on my husband.'

'Be patient, Zelene. If he is alive, I believe he'll try to contact your son.'

'I hope you're right, Alexon. I hope you're right.'

The Khan let go of her hands and stepped away. 'They have called me to the bridge. Thank you for seeing me.'

'You're welcome, my Khan, and thank you again for all that you've done.'

Khan Hayreddin watched the woman leave the observation room and turned to the back corner.

'She knows only what I want her to,' he said.

The darkness shifted and drifted in front of him. *'See that she does,'* it whispered.

CHAPTER 18

From an Ancient War.

The currents of the Nebula Stream were strong against the hull of the two vessels as they navigated their way along. Dangerous gases and radiation pounded the nanite shielding causing arcs of electricity. Flares erupted across the armor, flashing a multitude of colors. The Nebula Stream was vast, covering thousands of light years in a circuit surrounding the anomalies center, with few entries and exits.

Both ships had entered the stream a day earlier in between the two giant statues and had since been fighting the currents of radioactive death. The *Dawn Eclipse* cruised relatively smoothly, its shape aerodynamic in a flowing environment of any gas. It avoided the hostile pockets of danger with ease, navigating and side shifting areas that would vaporize the vessel in seconds.

The *Arvernus* however, built by humans and elismorus, and although sleek, struggled even with the information being provided by the *Eclipse* remotely. It had sustained minor damage, losing a rear tail fin housing some electromagnetic countermeasures.

The exit was approaching and if a vessel missed it, the likelihood of that ship's escape was near impossible.

Draethus sunk further into his flight chair, deep beneath the liquid metal lake at the bottom level of the *Eclipse's* command deck.

Waving his hand through the liquid, he marvelled at the strange and mysterious method of piloting.

Why the liquid? Why not just a station on the command deck with the other consoles? He wondered if it was something to do with synchronising his body with the ship, which would explain being able to feel systems rather than just see them on his displays. Even those displays were strange, floating around him as holograms, unaffected by the liquid.

His controls felt cold to the touch with a flight stick on his right and throttle to his left, covered in buttons and flip switches. When he thrust the throttle forward, he could almost see the ship from the outside, flaring its engines.

Although he didn't understand his surroundings, it filled him with a sense of comfort and looked forward to leaning more about the ship. Making a mental note, he filed away the questions he had for the ship, and try to uncover its secrets.

Flicking his hands, he enlarged his displays until he could see the upper command deck where Raeson and Tremon were sitting at their consoles. The audio of their conversations came through clearly as a warning icon appeared in front of him.

'How are you faring, Slin? I see you lost something?' Raeson said over the coms as he manned his console on the *Eclipse*.

'Hilarious, remember this is your ship,' Slin laughed.

'Don't worry,' he mused, 'the repair bill will come out of your cut, and no, you can't start a tab.'

'Obstruction ahead!' Draethus yelled over the coms, interrupting the pair. 'Slin, evade twenty degrees to port now!'

Slin maneuvered the corvette as instructed and barely missed a twisted wreck of some long-forgotten vessel. As they passed, Draethus could see it was a graveyard of amalgamated ships that had collided together in a nightmarish display of death. The charred remains sparked with the particles of the Nebula Stream. He transferred the image onto the ship's display, and it rotated slowly, giving the bridge crew a close up.

'I don't recognise the configuration of those vessels,' Raeson stated.

'That's surprising. I would have thought a nomadic race would know all the ships,' Draethus said.

'If you hadn't noticed, space is enormous. I doubt anyone would see everything in his or her lifetime.'

'My respect for you is enormous,' Draethus said sarcastically. 'I mean that, honestly.'

'I might not know you well, but I'm pretty sure you're joking,' Raeson laughed. 'Don't worry, your feeling is reflected.'

We are coming up on the exit to the Nebula Stream, Commander Draethus. I'm transmitting the data to the Arvernus's systems now, the voice of the *Eclipse* said into his mind.

Very well Eclipse, I want you to mark the navigation curve for the corvette and we'll follow behind. If they mess it up, keep us in the stream with them for backup, Draethus replied.

You realize if we missed the exit, the pirates would probably just leave us behind? Why would you not do the same for them?

Because Eclipse, I'm an honorable commander, right?

You may find your morals broken by the end of this mission. Those who do not evolve will die, as is the way of life. The ship's voice faded from his mind before Draethus could question it any further.

He opened up the coms again to the bridge of the *Arvernus* and said, 'Slin, I've transferred the exit waypoint to your navigation systems. We'll follow you out.'

'Aye, we're setting course to follow the exit curve. Try not to get left behind, will you?' Slin replied.

'Just remember our weapons are forward facing,' Draethus finished, cutting the connection.

Raeson, who had been monitoring the radiation flow of the stream for the past few hours, glanced over at Tremon. 'You ready, paladin?' he asked.

'Ready? We are about to exit into unknown space. How can anyone be ready?' Tremon smiled. 'Still, I'm looking forward to a good fight. I haven't fired these guns in a while.'

Kicking its engines to full, the *Arvernus* burnt a curved light streak in a perfect vector needed for an exit. The golden ship trailed as both vessels finally left the gas flow, the solar winds to their rear continuing their violent storm. On the exit, both crews noticed the same type of statues seen on entry previously, though half of one monolith was missing. The damage looked smooth as glass, as if the giant had slipped away across the hips.

'What could have blown that away?' Tremon asked, leaning forward in awe. 'It was hundreds of kilometres high. Where is it?'

Raeson walked to the railing surrounding the liquid metal lake as the forward cameras displayed what lay ahead of the ship. 'Whatever caused it, probably did that as well,' he said, pointing. 'Welcome to Tiberous, everyone.'

Suspended in space, dead and motionless, the giant asteroids clustered together. The largest of the rocks, covered in a gray haze of dust, sat frozen with pillars of ruined buildings protruding like defensive spines of some prehistoric animal. The surrounding debris drifted in a disc like orbit, the remnants of what had once been the planet Tiberous. Mixed in the haze, an atmosphere of turquoise covered the area in an eerie light.

Walking onto the bridge of the *Eclipse*, Spect looked past Raeson and asked, 'Is that where the duel will take place? Is that Tiberous?'

'That it is, and for once I'm glad that I won't be going,' Tremon replied. 'Commander, I'm detecting a drive signature on the other side of the main surface.'

'I see it,' Draethus said. 'It's a Rid cruiser, and the ship tells me it's been sitting there a while.' The levitating platform appeared from below the liquid lake, on the bottom level, and lifted him onto the command deck. 'I'm headed for the dock. I'll take a fighter down to the surface and finish this.'

Raeson, never one to back down from a fight followed him out, 'Do you know how to pilot a fighter?'

Draethus waited for the command deck doors to phase out and replied, 'No idea, so I guess you're my taxi. I think I saw a two-seater in there?'

'Wait,' Tremon yelled after them, 'take this.' He handed Raeson his vibration sword, a variant to the one Draethus used, that was thinner with a slight curve. The ornate handle was chrome, covered in an embossed pattern of scales that weaved together to form a guard.

'Thank you, hopefully I won't need it,' Raeson said with a nod. The two men headed for the dock, and Draethus felt that closure was near. His friend was waiting, and it was his fault Johan was taken by the Heridians. If he'd only stayed, tried to force the door open and rescue him. Whatever happened next, they needed those co-ordinates to Heridia.

'You know this is a trap? Even though your duel is on the surface, there's nothing preventing the enemy cruiser from capturing the ship?' Raeson asked.

'This ship, Raeson, is a lot smarter than anyone knows, and I'd imagine it would have a contingency plan.'

'Are you saying it would leave us stranded on Tiberous if it came down to it?' the pirate asked, surprised.

Draethus glanced over to him and replied, 'That's exactly what I'm saying. It's better to sacrifice the both of us than have the ship fall into Rid hands. Besides, the Arvernus can collect us.'

'That's if the Heridians don't destroy it first.'

'Why not space us now?' Draethus laughed.

I've intercepted a transmission from the Heridian you refer to as Johan. He is waiting on the surface for you and sounds impatient, the *Eclipse* said into the soldier's mind.

Thank you. Hopefully this ends well, and we'll have the co-ordinates needed to reach the home-world of the menace. If it doesn't go in our favor, I'm guessing you know what to do?

Yes, Commander, this ship and your crew will be safe.

'I just had the weirdest sensation in my head,' Raeson said curiously.

*

The widowmaker class pirate fighter extended its landing gear and hovered above the surface of the massive asteroid. Dust kicked up from the anti-gravity turbines, causing a small whirlwind that, by the time it settled, revealed the two warriors exiting the cockpit.

'Don't expect me to pay you for the ride,' Draethus said, taking a step into the gray dust. 'Although, I'll have to learn to fly myself someday.'

'You can pay in compliments later,' Raeson laughed. 'Just warn me when you're training so I can ready the recovery craft. But yes, you'll have to learn and it's the most fun you'll ever have.'

'I think our versions of fun are a little different,' Draethus smiled, then twisted into a grimace. 'The feel about this place is ancient with a haunted sense of history don't you think?'

Raeson looked around for the dueling area, the co-ordinates of which were given to them by the ship earlier. 'I really don't know what this place is, Draethus. Those ruins in the distance appear older than anything I've ever seen. Do you think this pre-dates the origin world?'

Unconsciously feeling the pummel of his sheathed blade, Draethus replied, 'I doubt we'd even discovered fire when this race was alive.'

'Do you ever wonder about it? The origin world, that is? Some say all the alien races evolved from there, even the elismorus,' Raeson asked.

'It really makes no difference,' Draethus said. 'If the rumors are true, then leaving the dead was the best decision.'

As the two warriors came into view of their enemy, both men froze as their fight-or-flight senses took over. Draethus could feel his blood rising and fought the instinct to charge the beast. The fear was an invisible barrier, and the soldier wanted to smash through it, take the enemy by the neck and squeeze its last breath.

He glanced over at Raeson and saw the serious expression of a man who knew war. There was darkness in his eyes and an expression of pure hatred, ready to do whatever it took to kill the menace. For a moment Draethus thought of Johan again and wondered if he could be saved, or at least bargained with. Then he shook the thought from his mind because he knew nothing could cure the monsters.

They approached cautiously between fallen columns and onto a checkered floor covered in dust and debris. The surrounding walls had crumbled and showed signs of battle eons passed. On the other side of the open space, the Heridian leader stood ready to fight, its jaws open and claws flexing. It was everything that Draethus remembered: horrific, oppressive and terrifying. He was impressed with the courage Raeson displayed, knowing it was his first time seeing Johan.

'He's a big guy,' Raeson laughed. 'Can the thing even move? Surely that much armor would be better spent anchoring spaceships?' He stepped a few paces towards the enemy and then added, 'What is this place, anyway?'

'From an ancient war,' something whispered in reply.

'You heard that too?' Draethus asked the startled pirate.

'Yeah, does that happen to you often, hearing whispers like that? Alongside your other voices, that is?'

'You have no idea the things I've been hearing lately. The more it happens though, the fewer questions I ask, Raeson.'

'Draethus!' the Heridian leader roared. 'You dishonor yourself by bringing an ally with you, you coward!'

The giant beast slashed at the ground using the two claws on its side, kicking up a mass of dust that partially covered its dark crimson armor.

A strange wind passed over the crest beyond the ruins, before Draethus started towards his long-time friend turned enemy.

'This ends today,' Draethus said. 'Wait here.'

The Heridian roared at the approaching soldier, bearing rows of serrated fangs.

'At last, we face each other old friend, for the last time,' the menace said through its growl.

'I wish I could have been there for you, Johan. I thought you perished on the Dark Claw.'

The Heridian arched up to its full height and towered over Draethus, casting him in shadow. The creature's gears spun as the mechanised parts beneath its armor readied for the duel. Draethus could see the runes across the armor pulsing, slowly at first before becoming a constant glow.

'You could join me, Draethus,' Johan said in a low and deep tone. 'You could become one of us, but then you always were the honorable one, were you not?'

It roared and leapt into the air, stabbing the dirt where Draethus rolled from. The soldier thrust his vibration sword into the chest armor, hoping to score a hit inside the gaps, only to deflect away. He quickly side shifted again to dodge the claw that backhanded in his direction and took a face full of gray dust from the ground. It filled his eyes for a moment as he parried the incoming strikes.

The creature slashed at Draethus repeatedly with its massive claws, causing a strain on the defensive blade and the muscles holding it. The third claw aimed low at the human's feet but failed when he jumped over and began his own attacks. Strike after strike, he slashed with his sword into the Heridians' chest, so close that the creature struggled to parry as its claws were large and cumbersome.

Sparks flashed as metal connected. The creature's armor chipped away and fell burning to the ground, filling Draethus with some hope of victory. Johan, the creature, rushed forward and used its sheer size to knock the soldier off his feet and back into reach of the rusty, enormous claws. Draethus sprawled to the ground before quickly recovering to his feet.

*

From high above the battle, both crews, pirate, and paladin, watched the duel unfold on the displays.

Slin, Nash and the rest of the crew on the pirate corvette, sat at their stations in silence. They hoped Draethus would prevail despite the incredible size difference between the combatants. Rel, huddled in the corner of the docking bay on the *Arvernus*, watched the fight in tears, fearful of losing her new love.

Tremon and the scientist, Spect, sat in suspense on the *Dawn Eclipse,* observing the battle on the hologram display, so large it was like they were there in person.

'I commend his commitment,' Tremon said, 'it's not that long ago I would have been happy to watch Draethus die to the hands of a Rid. How things change.'

'The probability that he will win this duel is small, but as much as I would love to concentrate on the battle, I'm monitoring that enemy cruiser out there,' Spect replied.

'Keep a lookout for more ships just in case they attempt to sneak up on us,' Tremon replied, still transfixed on the fight taking place. 'Also, I've noticed you've been quiet lately, since we entered that mysterious room that is.'

Spect was silent for a moment before replying, 'I feel uneasy on this ship, and I think it's haunted.'

Tremon laughed and stopped when he realized the scientist was serious.

*

Draethus charged the Heridian leader again, slashing with his sword from a high right to lower left position. The rusty claw parried the strike easily but missed the second strike that flowed. It caught the creature across the face, dislodging one of its fangs, falling to the ground, and disappearing into the dust.

Johan let out a screech, more of anger than pain, and then attempted to stab Draethus in the chest. The soldier dodged again but missed the spiky tail from the creature and lost his footing. His sword flung from his hand and landed out of reach, buried in the dust, flat to the surface and hard to see.

Draethus rolled and scrambled towards the blade, but the giant creature's third claw emerged from under the dust and grabbed him. Johan lifted the soldier towards its fangs and tightened the grip.

'I never needed to ask your permission to join our ranks,' the Heridian said. 'I only need the parts inside that skull of yours.'

'Kill me now menace, or are you afraid I'll still win?'

Johan laughed, 'Even still you persist to taunt me and for what reason, to buy enough time for your rescue? No one is coming for you. You have lost and so has your ship.'

The creature screamed as a vibration sword entered through the back plates of its body, piercing the internals. Draethus dropped from the creature's grip to the ground and ran back for his sword as Raeson stabbed at the creature's back again. A dark liquid sprayed out of the Heridian and covered the pirate in the oily blood as a claw slashed at him. Raeson parried, then stepped forward to slash at Johan's side, which deflected off the carapace.

'Dishonor!' the Heridian leader roared. 'You are both dishonorable maggots!'

Three claws, a spiked tail and fangs the length of a man's arm, slashed and stabbed at the two warriors who were both engaged in the close combat battle. Again, sparks flashed as metal found metal. The two vibration swords struck and parried in a furious fight for the domination of the duel.

Johan's claws struck down at Draethus, finding only dirt as Raeson charged in from an angle. The pirate struck the mechanised body of the creature, causing more liquid to spray over the pair. The Heridian lunged forward and knocked the pirate on his back, lifted his enormous foot and slammed it down but missed thanks to Raeson's quick thinking. He shuffled across the dirt, sword still in hand, distracting the menace long enough for Draethus to strike a blow into Johan's head, beneath an armor plate.

Staggering back, whilst still slashing with its claws, blood drained from the wound before it fell onto his side. Both warriors tried to charge in but kept at a distance because of the ever-whipping tail.

The enemy got to its feet, then collapsed again in a wounded grogginess. Gray dusty rock beneath the dying creature pooled with the foul bloody oil as it thrashed, screeching into the night. Draethus approached cautiously, drawing a line in the dirt with his sword, exhausted from the duel. As he neared, the third claw slashed out for one last time but fell short, and then silent. The soldier could hear gurgling from the throat. Raeson joined him, jumped onto the chest, and thrust the blade through the monster.

'Not so lucky, are you?' Raeson spat out in spite.

'What are the co-ordinates to Heridia, Johan? You've lost, at least do something right.' Draethus felt the pain of loss for his friend. 'Will you tell me?'

The creature groaned and between clenched teeth said in pain, 'In all the duels we had in the past, never did you ever involve another in such a dishonorable way.'

'People change old friend, look what became of you.'

There was a pause as Johan struggled to say his words. 'We all change, but sometimes devolve. I'm not ashamed of what I have become, only that you were not by my side in the end.'

A piece of armor shifted under the chest-plate revealing something inside.

'Take this crystal, it will unlock the space-time co-ordinates needed to find Heridia. It will also give you the information needed for both invasion waves planned for Echelon. You need to take these so the Soldiers of the Void can prepare. But hurry, the Heridians might be back any moment.' Johan dragged his injured arm through the dust and pointed toward some ruins in the distance. 'Use it there.'

Draethus followed Johan's arm and peered into the dusty moonlight at their next destination before finally understanding. 'You're saying we were ready for the Rids because of the information I'll bring them?'

Dark blood began flowing out of the creature's jaws. 'It was always you Arcilous Draethus. You are the messenger and the reason we were ready for the Heridian invasion. Unless, of course, you cannot deliver the information.'

'Well, aren't you the important one now?' Raeson said, watching the creature struggle. 'Why would you suddenly help us?'

Johan glared at the pirate with hatred. 'All Heridians that have taken a mind also take on part of that persona. Mine is of honor, something I doubt you will ever know.'

'That explains why there wasn't a trap or interference from the Rid cruiser in orbit. Johan could have easily ordered an attack from the ship or even tried and captured the Eclipse,' Draethus stated.

Raeson shrugged and said, 'Let's get moving.'

The pirate pulled out the sword and started back for the fighter. It was thanks to his efforts, however dishonorable, that helped win the day. Draethus sat with his old friend until the power left its body; the runes flickered for a few moments before going dark.

'Goodbye old friend, I wish things could have been different, but I guess thanks to your part this message will reach Echelon.'

Draethus took the black crystal shard from the Heridian's chest and followed his pirate ally.

I guess the *Eclipse* was right. I had to put aside my morals for the greater good. If I had lost the duel, the space-time co-ordinates, the message, would never have reached the SOV.

*

Through his dying eyes, Johan, the Heridian leader and once Soldier of the Void, remembered the feeling of loyalty once more. He looked out into the distance and saw his childhood friend walking up the dusty gray dune, towards righteousness and towards a shadow that loomed in his path.

*

The Lords of Heridia cut the feed from the cruiser in orbit around Tiberous, archived the video data from the duel between Servatus and Draethus for later study, and then deactivated the array.

Although their bodies were physically part of the spire on their home-world, they could project their image to anywhere on Heridia's surface.

The Forth Lord stood on the edge of a mountain peak overlooking the distant blood ocean as wind howled through the rocks. As the Lord was a virtual projection, it couldn't feel its presence. The other two lords, both the Third and Fifth, materialized behind and joined in the internal conversation. To an observer, the three lords would have appeared as a shadow or a trick of the eye.

Fourth Lord: So, as predicted, Servatus failed us.

Third Lord: Servatus passed on the crystal as was clear in the video feed. The co-ordinates to the Link now exist in enemy hands.

Fifth Lord: This will give us the opportunity we have been waiting for to capture the Dawn Eclipse once it opens the Link.

Fourth Lord: If they decide to blockade rather than attack?

Fifth Lord: We will force them through using the fleets from the outside.

Third Lord: We need another protagonist to lead such fleets.

Fifth Lord: The one in command of the flagship is an ideal candidate.

Fourth Lord: He also failed in the ship's capture when it escaped the minefield. The idea of involving lesser life forms was in error.

Third Lord: I shall instruct this one to handle such matters in person, and upon failure, purge it.

Fifth Lord: Agreed.

Fourth Lord: If the enemy forces decide to attack Heridia they will face the full might of the orbital defence fleet. We must not reveal this until the ship has entered the Link and cannot return.

Third Lord: Suggest using the creature ship for its capture as it will nullify the Eclipses' ability to jump away.

Fifth Lord: I'll instruct its commander.

Fourth Lord: Then we are all in agreement?

Fifth Lord: Concur.

Third Lord: Concur.

The Third Lord vanished from the conversation, and its image disappeared from the mountain peak.

Fifth Lord: Why did you choose this area for physical manifestation?

Fourth Lord: It seemed appropriate for the situation.

Fifth Lord: How so?

The Fourth Lord directed a smile towards its counterpart before leaving the conversation.

CHAPTER 19

Theatre of Shadows.

A whirlwind of dust and dirt covered the landing area as the *Arvernus* pirate corvette detracted its landing skids and hovered above the surface of Tiberous. Slowly the ship descended, carefully setting down on flat ground that shook from the immense weight. From their fighter, Draethus and Raeson stood watching the large ship and wondered why it wasn't in orbit with the *Eclipse*.

'You realize we have our fighter here and can return to the ship ourselves?' Raeson said over the coms.

'We needed a closer look at the surface,' Slin replied with a crackle of the coms unit. 'We've detected a low frequency energy source emanating from a group of ruins nearby.'

'We know and are headed there ourselves,' Draethus said. 'You didn't want to miss out on the fun, right?'

Raeson smiled as he realized what was really going on. 'Pirates and their loot,' he laughed, 'we'll send a small team to check it out, understood?'

'Yes, sir,' Slin replied with a hint of disappointment. As the acting commander, he had to stay with the ship.

The outer doors slid open to reveal a distraught Rel who, armed with pistols and an emergency respirator, ran down the docking ramp. From behind her, Stark and Nash appeared with assault rifles and headed over, watching the young mechanic make tracks in the dust.

'Draethus!' Rel yelled as she fell into his arms. 'I watched the whole fight, and I saw you get knocked down. I was so scared of losing you.'

The soldier held the girl and closed his eyes with a smile. 'I'm fine Rel, I've just got some cuts and bruises.'

'I'm fine as well,' Raeson said, lifting an eyebrow. 'The two of you have gotten rather intimate.'

Rel looked away for a moment blushing, 'You're alright with Draethus and I, right?'

'Of course, why wouldn't I?'

Stark, with a sensor reader in hand, interrupted, 'The reading is two-and-a-half kilometres north-west of here. The Heridian cruiser left, but that doesn't mean it won't be back with re-enforcements. I'd rather not be in the open if that happens.'

'Agreed, let's get moving,' Draethus ordered.

Ten minutes later the team reached the edge of the ruins and noticed a host of stone and twisted metal. Strange winds moved the dust about the ground, revealing a mixture of intricate patterns displaying the remains of old roadways and paths. One such path led through fallen pillars, the direction Starks' hand-held scanner instructed the group to follow. Draethus knew they were headed for the same ruins Johan had pointed to.

'Watch your step. There could be anything around here,' Stark called out. 'Check your footing.'

'Showing care for others? That's not like you Stark,' Raeson replied, turning on a pocket light attached to his armor. 'Is there something else here you want to steal? My soul this time, maybe?'

'I'll leave that to the pilot,' Stark replied, referring to their new crew member. He continued on in front of the group, ducking under a pillar that had fallen across an entryway.

'Follow my footsteps, it's dangerous ground,' Draethus whispered to Rel, 'and be ready. I think something is shadowing us.' Unclipping the buckles of her pistol holsters, Rel gave a nod of acknowledgement and began looking around.

'Well, that's impressive,' Nash said as she entered what was once some kind of amphitheatre. 'This place is enormous.'

The team had found themselves amongst rows upon rows of seating, circling a large area with a podium at its center. Giant slabs of stone carvings covered the walls around the theatre, depicting battles between machine and beast, the same creatures that guarded the Nebula Stream.

'What do you suppose this place is?' Rel asked.

'A stadium maybe?' replied Raeson. 'Those creatures on the walls must have existed on this planet thousands of years ago.'

'Look who they are fighting, are they Rids?' asked Nash.

'I think so,' Draethus said, then added, 'there must be hundreds of battles depicted here.'

Stark kept moving away from the group and approached the center of the stadium. 'Look at this!' he yelled.

The podium's surface held a mixture of old dials covered in eons of dust.

'I'd say that crystal of yours goes here,' Stark finished.

Draethus stepped up to the podium, took the black crystal out from his armored compartment and pushed it into an opening. The area began humming with a faint vibration as light from emitters attached to the walls displayed a hologram in the center. Jumbled and fractured images shimmered, then combined. Draethus could just make out the image of a wormhole entry, spinning with blue and orange fire, orbiting a dense blackness, like a singularity.

'I'm guessing that's the Link we're looking for,' Draethus said puzzled. 'But how do we read it?'

'I will translate,' something said from behind them.

Nash quickly raised her rifle to shoot the floating Specter at the back of the stadium, but stopped when Draethus palmed the weapon down.

'Everything is alright, this thing's on our side. I think,' Draethus said, reassuring the woman.

'You think?' Raeson added, 'that's comforting to hear. What is it?'

Draethus approached the levitating shadow and stood inside the hologram. 'This is a Specter,' he announced. 'They have some part to play in all this and are superb at torture. They're not great conversationalists though, and have no sense of humor.' He looked at Raeson and added, 'The two of you would get on well.'

Raeson was about to reply when Rel stuttered, 'Torture?'

Draethus laughed. 'It's a long story which I'll tell you someday. However, right now we need an explanation.' To the Specter he asked, 'What does this read, shadow?'

The ethereal being drifted towards the group, its face covered by a tattered white mask with a vertical line carved down the center. Long ragged dark robes concealed any physical body underneath, and it flickered in and out of reality. 'What you see is the Link you have been searching for,' it said in a loud whisper. 'I will decipher the ancient language you need for its location.' The entity waved a jagged claw towards the podium, and the strange writing on the hologram changed. 'This is the location co-ordinates you need. The writing underneath is the two instances this Link will naturally open.'

'What about the Heridians' strength of force, how many ships are waiting on the other side?' Raeson asked only to realize the creature had vanished.

'They do that,' Draethus said with a grin. 'It's kind of annoying.'
'There are lots of things I find annoying right now.'

Nash handed a small cylindrical device to Draethus who looked at it with curiosity and asked, 'What's this?'

'A recording device to capture the images on the hologram. It's specifically designed to filter out the light transparency of holograms, unless you can remember all those numbers?' the women said sarcastically.

Draethus smiled and tapped the hilt of his blade. 'If you were in my squad back home, I would shoot you for talking to me like that, but thank you.'

'Really?'

'I'm just kidding,' Draethus grinned. 'I'd feed you to the dinosaurs. It's much more enjoyable to watch.'

Nash only waved her hand with a laugh as she began walking back with the rest of the group. 'Dinosaurs, sure.'

Rel stayed by Draethus' side and looked up in wonder as the hologram slowly rotated with the Link, or entrance at its center.

'You're really going to go through there, aren't you Draethus?' she asked sadly.

Draethus stepped to a different angle, finished capturing the images of the co-ordinates then safely put away the small device. 'We have to defeat the Heridians, Rel,' he replied.

'I wish you didn't. Just send the pirate fleet through and let them battle it out.' She looked down and added, 'We could run off together. I bet there is so much to see and explore.'

'After this is over, if I live, of course, I'll need to go back to Echelon and leave these co-ordinates for the SOV hierarchy to find. I'd like you to come with me, see where I grew up and then we can go anywhere from there.'

'Provided you live,' Rel replied with a tear. 'I will go anywhere with you, but please consider what I've asked.' She gave him a hug and began walking back to the ship.

Half an hour later, after the long walk back to the ship, Draethus approached the two-seater fighter to find Raeson leaning up against the cockpit. Draethus gave Rel a kiss on the forehead before they each went their own way.

'The two of you are officially a couple now I guess?' Raeson asked.

'Seems that way, she's an amazing woman,' Draethus replied.

'Have you had your first argument yet?' he laughed. 'Just wait until you see the fiery side of her.'

'I'm sure that'll come soon enough,' Draethus mused. 'You have something to say?'

Raeson shifted his weight to his other foot and asked, 'Tell me about this Specter. Can we trust it?'

'I believe so. I still don't know everything about them, but I think they have our best interest in mind. My crew, Tremon and Spect, had a leader that made use of the Specters as interrogators and was quite effective.'

'I see, but what exactly are they? Because I think I glimpsed one on the Arvernus once, like a ghost.'

Draethus began climbing into the fighter, using the hand holes on its side. 'I don't really know, but I think they watch events and interfere when needed, like guides, but I won't follow them blindly. I mean, how can you trust something that looks almost dead?'

'Good, trust is something that needs to be earned,' Raeson replied. 'I'm not sure about the whole dead thing. They kind of remind me of myself after a night out drinking.'

Draethus smiled at the image of an undead Raeson in his mind. 'You have earned my trust today, Raeson, and thank you for backing me up in the duel. I'd like to say I didn't need it, but there is more at stake here than just my pride.'

Raeson nodded in acknowledgement, finished climbing in, and lowered the cockpit canopy. Dust from the *Arvernus* blanketed the area in a visual blur as it lifted into the air followed closely by the pirate fighter. The two ships accelerated out of the atmosphere and disappeared into the distance.

*

It had been three days since both vessels, the *Eclipse* and the *Arvernus*, had re-joined with the main pirate fleet and moored inside the massive flagship, the *Wing of Vidar*.

On the garden deck, the off-duty crews were busy exploring new alien species introduced from a recently discovered world, as xeno-botanists added more to the small forest. Scientists gathered around the latest carnivorous plant, made sure its muzzle was secure, then pierced its leathery skin with syringes to extract its poison. Draethus and Rel watched the drama unfold as the large multi-colored head of the huge plant sent a scientist sprawling to the ground.

'This wasn't the uneventful and peaceful walk I was expecting,' Draethus said as Rel squeezed his hand in delight.

'It is fun though, watching grown men losing against something as simple as a plant. It's comical,' the girl said, giggling. 'Maybe you should join in?'

'I've had my fair share of killer plants, thank you,' he laughed, remembering the underwater terrors he faced on Echelon.

The pair watched for a while longer, then carried on through the man-made enclosure, heading towards the flower section, Rel's favourite.

'I help here sometimes, you know,' she said with a smile. 'That's why they allow me to take things home.'

'Hence the purple flower,' Draethus replied. 'I was thinking of bringing you the decapitated head of the Heridian leader, as a sign of how much I care for you.'

'Oh, please don't,' she laughed heartedly. 'That's disgusting. I'd rather… wait did you say you care for me?'

Draethus looked away and wondered if expressing what he felt might scare the girl, then replied with a simple nod.

Rel was silent, something she wasn't accustomed to being, before throwing her arms around the man. 'I do too! I'm so happy, but…'

'But?' he replied.

'Will you consider not going to Heridia for me?'

Draethus thought about it for a moment before replying, 'I haven't changed my mind on this Rel. I can't send my men on this mission and just sit back. There's a lot I have to redeem myself for, like the people who've died under my leadership, so I have to lead from the front and see it through.'

Tears welled up in her eyes as she buried her face in his chest, 'I know you have to, I do. Just please come back to me, please.'

*

With the Heridian forces now completely off their trail, the pirate fleet was free, at least for the moment, to find an area to anchor, rearm and refuel. Flying in formation, the vessels opened their solar sails and collected the energy from a nearby red giant. Silver glistened as the expanded panels consumed radiation in a glorious light show, metal behemoths basking in an ocean of fire.

Towards the back of the formation, the *Vidar*, its enormous sails expanded also, resembled an aquatic predator chasing food through the glowing waves as it trailed the smaller capital craft. The city ship would take four revolutions of the star to fill its buffers, transferring the energy to the building sized storage banks. Only then would the vessel return to full power, which it would need for the coming battle.

On the observation deck, Talon Commander Xain Raeson walked across the transparent floor and marvelled at the impressive display as a solar flare erupted and appeared to reach out to him.

'Thank you for coming, Raeson,' the Khan said as he entered through the sliding automatic doors. 'It was important for me to have this meeting with you.'

'You're welcome my Khan. How can I be of service?' Raeson replied, standing to attention.

'I've read your report on the journey to Tiberous, the duel with the Heridian leader and also the ensnarement. I'd like to hear your account of this, especially the detour,' the Khan asked. 'Why was this deemed necessary?'

Raeson relaxed his stance. 'Commander Draethus was piloting when we discovered a derelict vessel adrift. Not only did I find a missing crew member, but we discovered a set of co-ordinates written next to Draethus' name. He altered course to investigate, as it only added a couple of days to our journey.'

'And in doing so fell into a trap organised by a group of Scroungers in the service of the Heridians?'

'Yes sir, that's correct. My stranded crew member gave us the inscribed item with the location, so we deemed it safe. We did however scout ahead, but unfortunately Draethus ordered our ships to move in as the scouts missed the check in time.'

'What you should have done was advise Draethus to leave the scouts behind and proceed to Tiberous. Putting the ship at risk in such a reckless act could have cost us the advantage. If your crew member, Tek, wasn't such a damn war hero, I would think he aided the Rids by sending you on that path.'

Raeson felt the heat of anger reach his eyes at the mention of his crew accused of being a traitor. 'Tek doesn't remember how he ended up on the derelict vessel, but he is no traitor, sir.'

'Aye, that I agree with. I paid him a visit earlier to commend him for his actions in saving the fleet, something I should have done years ago.'

'Thank you. I'm sure he would have appreciated that.'

'He was thankful, in fact, although I feel being alone for so long has broken his mind. He was not, shall we say, himself?'

'Give him time, my Khan. I'm sure he will heal.'

Khan Hayreddin stroked his dark beard, and Raeson wondered what he was thinking.

'How many Scroungers were there?' the Khan asked.

'Dozens, I would say. I believe they stole the mines from our own arsenal, the ones we scattered along the trade lanes years ago.'

'That is what Stark tells me also,' the Khan replied. 'If the ship hadn't time-shifted, they would have captured both vessels.'

'You have already spoken to Stark?'

'I have indeed.' The Khan touched his small earpiece and activated his coms unit. 'You may enter.'

The sliding door opened again to reveal the man Raeson had grown to mistrust. Napier Stark, the member of his wing that continuously disobeyed orders and acted on his own initiative.

'I believe it's time to reveal information about your nemesis here,' the Khan said.

Stark stood to attention and saluted his leader with the customary nod of respect. 'Yes sir,' he said.

Raeson, now fully confused, felt the anger return to his eyes from earlier. 'What is this?'

The Khan nodded to Stark to acknowledge his salute and let the man relax before saying, 'I assigned Napier Stark to your Reaper Wing about five years ago now, I believe?'

'That is correct,' Raeson replied, 'so why is he here?'

'Stark's true purpose is to keep a watch on you and overall, for protection,' the Khan said.

'Protect me? Why would I need protecting? Why spy on me when others in the fleet are more dangerous?'

'I told you once that I knew your father and, as you know, I spend time with your mother.' The Khan began pacing along the observation window.

'Yes, I remember, and just about everyone aboard the Vidar knows you dine with my mother.'

'I was your father's closest friend before he abandoned the fleet. I made a promise to watch out for you, and I have, through Stark.'

'And why him?' Raeson asked.

'I'll let Napier explain that. For now, I have a ship to run. I wanted to tell you this in person as you have a dangerous mission ahead and I believe I owed you an explanation.' The Khan returned the acknowledgement from his men and exited the observation level.

'I didn't need you shadowing me all these years. I've been quite capable of looking after myself,' Raeson started.

'How capable would you have been if I hadn't intercepted the multiple assassins over the years?' Stark replied. 'You've seen only a few of them yourself, yet I am the one that stalks the shadows, protecting your life.'

Shock crossed Raeson's face as he asked, 'What do you know of such assassins?'

'I've intercepted a dozen assassination attempts on your life since being assigned to your wing. Most of which were family members of the crew your father left to die. I couldn't blame them really, however I disposed of them quietly. There were other more trained individuals, but I couldn't extract the information from them. They died before giving me their motive.'

'So, you're my babysitter in the dark?' Raeson asked sarcastically, glancing at the star again and forcing himself to swallow his pride. He felt like punching the man, but knew he was just doing his duty. 'I apologize for any grief I've given you. If I would have known sooner, things could have gone smoother.'

'If word got out, it would've made things more difficult for me.'

Raeson relaxed as events unravelled in his mind. 'I've had to deal with assassination attempts myself. Though I hadn't the patience to question their motives, I even spaced one of them. Was that all the Khan assigned you to do? What were you doing on the destroyer?'

'Heridian ships of that class and size contain an item that stores a library of information about their race. The Khan assigned me to steal it.'

'The core, you mean?' Raeson asked. 'That caused a lot of trouble.'

'It put you in harm's way, which was against my original mission but was never my intention. I read your report on the Sky Lord Theradin and your capture and I apologise for what happened. It was a failure on my part.'

'Accepted,' Raeson said as Stark headed for the door. 'Why would the Khan choose you, though?'

Stark smirked, a behavior that had infuriated Raeson from the day they met. 'Maybe I was just good at my role, Commander Raeson.'

'Or maybe you're Dark Ops.'

Stark grinned as he disappeared behind the sliding doors.

CHAPTER 20

In Honor of Actions.

Raeson winged over his widowmaker fighter, rolled over the top of Draethus, who was piloting his own craft for the first time, and levelled out beside him. They had decided that Draethus needed to learn how to pilot in case of emergencies, plus the pair needed some downtime. With the fleet refuelling, it was the perfect opportunity.

Draethus held the fighter steady, feeling every movement through the dual flight sticks on each side of him. Holographic lenses in his eyes displayed three-dimensional icons representing different systems.

The left side of his view showed navigation, and the right side was targeting. Glancing out of the cockpit, he ran his eyes over the sleek, forward swept wings and wondered why he hadn't done this sooner. His fighter bucked unexpectedly as the micro reactor pulsed energy into the buffers, causing the engines to scream and press Draethus into his chair.

'How does it feel Draethus?' Raeson asked, looking through his canopy across at the man.

'This is amazing. I might even hang up my boots and go full time.'

'You? Give up being a dirt pounder and join us in the skies?' Raeson laughed, rolling his fighter along its center axis. 'Can you imagine Rel's face if she had another fighter craft to maintain?'

'She'd kill me, and would be in the perfect position for it, too.'

Draethus could hear Raeson chuckling over the open coms as he said, 'She'd make sure you were grounded most of the time, I think.'

He lost himself in thought for a moment as something occurred to him. During his time with the pirates, he'd never seen them capture or destroy a civilian ship and wondered why. Obviously, they had been fighting the Heridians for some time, but surely there would be opportunities for plunder.

He put the question aside for the moment, then lost himself on a tangent. Did sacrificing all those people on Echelon set him on a downward path? Was his guilty conscience just an excuse to follow these Cygnians? He brushed the thought aside when he remembered their loss was not his intention, but the result of a poor decision. His poor decision.

Friend to an outlaw? Am I becoming one as well?

Raeson throttled forward and ignited his engines. 'There is a toggle button on your throttle to the left that will engage the engine burn and give you a little extra boost. Don't use it too often though, or you'll cause damage and end up stranded. I've set a way point on your navigation. Keep on my wing and try to match my speed.'

Although not nearly as smooth as the pirate, Draethus did as instructed, and kept on his wing. Both fighters screamed through the dark until the fleet was just a spec in the hazy distance.

'It's not as easy as you make it look,' Draethus said.

'All Cygnian Pirates grow up doing this. It's our way of life.' He jinked his craft from side to side then said, 'I'm going to perform some basic manoeuvres. Try to keep up.'

Raeson flipped his fighter on its back along its center axis, a perfect one-hundred and eighty degrees, and then pulled back on the stick, diving downward. Draethus mirrored the maneuver and then, in a wider arc, dove to the polar south and finished in a position behind. Draethus could almost feel the heat from Raeson's trail bursting into his cockpit, and fought the urge to cover his eyes from the glare before the canopy dimmed automatically.

Raeson then tipped his wing left and then right, swaying and dodging to each side, simulating a fighter being targeted from behind. Draethus tried his best to mimic the moves before the pirate disappeared underneath him.

'Hide and seek time?' Draethus said with a stupid grin on his face. 'What do I get if I find you?'

'Respect. Actually, scratch that, you can never get that,' Raeson replied sarcastically. 'You'll get to live, though.'

'If you said that to me a couple of months ago, I think I'd be offended,' Draethus said. He glimpsed a shadow pass in front of the star and spun his craft, pointing at Raeson.

'That was a standard bait and re-vector tactic. Give your enemy a false sense that they've got you, then strafe down and re-position.'

'That was fast. I barely even saw you perform the move. I'll try it.'

The left flight stick of a widowmaker fighter strafed a craft up or down and left or right regardless of the direction the fighter was facing. The right stick, however, was directional, and pointed the craft towards an intended target. Draethus pulled back on both flight sticks and, because he was still accelerating forward, spun out of control and lost sight of Raeson.

He lost his bearings, cut his engine and talked into his coms again. 'The gravity from that star is harsh, wait are you laughing?'

Raeson couldn't help himself, as it had been a long time since he'd trained anyone. 'I'm sorry, but if you saw yourself just then, you would laugh as well. I've got video of that.'

'No, you haven't.'

'Just you wait until I show the others.'

For a moment Draethus felt embarrassed, then laughed at himself and said, 'It's been a long time since anyone has trained me.'

'Next time, cut your engines with the kill switch on your left thumb; that will engage the manoeuvring thrusters and allow you to strafe using your left stick. In combat, that will give you an advantage as speed will limit how sharp a turn you can make. Fighting in the void can be a tricky task especially against the Rids, as their ships can match our vectors. The better the pilot, the more chance you have of surviving.'

*

The two fighters continued their training with Raeson at the lead and Draethus doing his best to keep up. As the pirate had been flying his entire life, he slowed down to let the soldier keep up and learn the tactics that might save his life one day.

'Good roll in,' Raeson said. 'Now try it in reverse as you cut engines and strafe to the high right. This will move your fighter off the line.'

'The line?'

'It's what we call the path your enemies' weapons will follow, from its guns to your hull. Once they fire, the plasma travels along a perfect line. By moving off that line, you avoid the danger and, if done correctly, will avoid their targeting systems and even their field of view all together.'

'Sounds complicated, but I understand what you're saying. Let's try it.'

Raeson strafed backward and down, then flew at Draethus, imitating a Heridian fighter veering in for the kill. He turned his targeting systems to active, locked on to the other fighter and rested his fingers on the triggers.

I could end this soldier's life right now if I wanted, maybe even claim his ship for my own. Rel would never forgive me, though. Is she worth more to me than something that could end the war? A vessel that could propel me to the highest ranks in the Cygnian forces?

Before he could brood further, Draethus disappeared from his field of view. The locking reticule turned from red to green and an alarm sounded in the cockpit. Draethus had performed the manoeuvre perfectly, as instructed, and the Raeson's lenses displayed an enemy lock-on warning.

'Finally performed it correct this time,' Draethus said enthusiastically over the coms.

'Well, it's about time,' Raeson replied. 'Let's simulate using weapons. Select your weapon load-out on your display and change it to training. This will alter the level of plasma in the guns to harmless, and only scratch the paint, but you will feel the hit.'

'I'm sure Rel yelling at us for scratching her fighters won't be harmless,' Draethus laughed.

Raeson accelerated away from the soldier to gain some distance before the fight, before replying. The subject of Rel was still on his mind. 'I've known Rel my entire life and I guess I just expected the two of us would make something of it. That was, until you arrived.'

'I'm shocked to hear you say that, but I wondered the same, being completely honest. Are you jealous?'

Raeson thought for a moment, remembering all the good times with his childhood friend. 'I think maybe in the beginning, though I realized I might just miss her company. I've never seen her this happy before, so I'm glad she's found someone that makes her feel that way.'

'I'm relieved to hear you say that. It's hard enough fighting the Rids without having to fight each other as well. I didn't want any animosity between us, especially with the mission ahead.'

'Know this though,' Raeson continued, 'if you hurt her, you won't need to worry about the Rids anymore.'

Draethus smiled and said, 'It's good to hear you'll protect her as well.'

Raeson charged in for the simulated kill, rolling his craft so the laser fire scattered over the area. Draethus strafed off to the side, and the weapon trail shot off into the darkness, missing completely.

Annoyed, Raeson followed up by performing an aggressive manoeuvre. He flipped his fighter onto its back, side strafed, and fired off another dozen rounds of heated plasma. He was surprised when Draethus returned fire blindly, and hit him with a single shot, slamming into his wing and sending vibrations through his cockpit. Blood rushed to Xain's head and excitement filled his soul.

Give me more!

*

Raeson's fighter touched down on the dock platform inside the great bay of the *Vidar*, with Draethus hovering behind in his own craft, waiting for clearance. The landing skids contacted the surface, then secured as claws locked them in place. The docking crane slid over quickly, ready to collect the craft, when it was abruptly halted by an angry mechanic.

'What do you call this!?!' Rel yelled, running over the deck. 'Look at this paintwork, it's ruined!'

'Don't be mad little one, we were only...' Raeson cut his words short as Draethus touched down on the nearby platform.

'Only what exactly?' she asked. 'Out to make my job harder by giving me more work to do?'

'I was teaching your lover over there how to fly just in case he needed to in the future. It would give him a better chance of survival. You know me, always the charitable one.'

'My what, my lover?' she mumbled as her face flushed red.

Draethus climbed down from his cockpit, removed the pirate helmet and walked over to the arguing pair.

'We've got to do that again, was quite a rush,' he remarked. 'Are you all right, Rel?'

'She's fine, Draethus, I was just telling her how I was teaching her lover how to fight in the empty.'

'Oh, I see.'

'I hate both of you,' she said as she began storming off, embarrassed.

'There is nothing wrong with people knowing that we are in...' Draethus said as the girl cut him off.

'Will you stop? You're making me go red,' she replied.

As Rel finished, Tremon ran down the steps towards them. The docking lights reflected off his white armor, giving an impression he had recently cleaned it. 'There you are. I've been looking everywhere for you,' the paladin yelled. 'Have you heard the news?'

'What news is this?' Raeson asked.

'To prepare for the coming battle and because of our efforts so far, the Khan has extended an invitation for us to join the Cygnian Pirates, officially,' Tremon replied.

'That's good news,' Rel said with delight. 'You'll officially be one of us.'

No smile reached Draethus' face.

'Nothing quick witted to say, Draethus?' Raeson asked. 'Nothing that's going to make me throw you across the deck?'

'I've been SOV for most of my life, and the idea of becoming a pirate doesn't really appeal to me. No offence intended, I just assumed I'd return to Echelon, eventually.'

'This person you think you are, would he have allowed another to step in during an honorable duel? Would he have aligned himself with a nefarious military fleet even for a greater cause?' Raeson asked, then walked up to Draethus, and with a cheeky grin added, 'After all, we are closer to your SOV than to pirates.'

Draethus peered into Raeson's eyes and knew the statement was loose at best. A pirate is just that, and no amount of humor would change his mind.

Tremon clasped his armored hand on his commander's shoulder and said, 'We haven't always agreed, especially in the beginning, but one thing has always been with us.'

'What's that?' Draethus asked.

'We've always done what we think is right and what we believe is the honorable way. The Cygnian Pirates may not be the same as the Paladins of Echelon or the Soldiers of the Void that arrived later, but they've shown us they are honorable. I believe their cause to be worthy and just. Besides, by the time we get back to Echelon, if we ever do, the SOV still won't exist, and I know the paladins have evacuated the planet.'

Draethus thought about Tremon's words for a moment. He could see the hope in Rel's eyes and swore she was going to cry. She wanted him to join them. 'When we met, Tremon, I thought you were a zealot.'

Tremon appeared shocked before saying, 'I was really hard on you when you appeared. Remember, I started as a nobody on the streets of Echelon. It took my whole life to become a paladin.'

'Yet you threw it away so easily by joining my crew and leaving.'

'My goals were never about rank or title,' Tremon said. 'I have a compulsion to protect people, which is why I was so angry when the city fell to the Rids. I couldn't do anything about it and saw you as the cause, which is why I directed my anger at you. My plan was to leave Echelon anyway, with the Senechal.'

'And not remain in stasis to help the SOV later?' Raeson and Rel looked puzzled at the conversation.

'I'll explain later,' Draethus said, referring to the precursory eleven captains in stasis on Echelon's Sky-Station.

Tremon looked down at the floor. 'No, I didn't like the idea of sleeping through the events to come. I saw our current goals aligned and followed my instincts. It doesn't matter what we label ourselves because we are here right now, fighting alongside the Cygnians.'

'It's hard to imagine doing anything different,' Draethus said. He stared out of the open dock entry and into the depths of the void, deep in thought. 'At this exact moment in time, the Soldiers of the Void haven't arrived at Echelon, as we currently exist in their past.'

Raeson added, 'If they haven't arrived, that will give you time to deliver the message, to warn the SOV of the coming attacks on your world.'

'Look at you paying attention,' Draethus said with a sly smile. 'I've realized that if I return to Echelon, I can't join their ranks as I could negatively affect the outcome of my progression.'

'You could get the Eclipse to time-shift you back to your present,' Raeson stated. 'Although you are fitting in well here.'

Draethus nodded and said, 'The ship tells me there is a price to shifting and it's only something used during dire times. Getting me home is not one of those.' He looked at Rel and smiled. 'I also have a good reason to stay.'

'So, you will accept the offer and join us?' Rel asked in delight.

'Yes, I'll accept the Khans' invitation to join,' he said as Rel threw her arms around his neck. 'I want an eye patch though, no deal without one.'

Rel kissed his cheek and giggled.

'What about you?' Raeson asked Tremon. 'Will you be happy here?'

'We're a team, Draethus and I,' he replied. 'As much as he infuriates me sometimes…'

'Most times,' Raeson interrupted.

'He really is that annoying,' laughed Tremon, before saying, 'I always thought I'd be protecting the people of Echelon, but they're gone. You should have seen Spect's face when I told him. He was more worried about changing the color of his lab coat. You'd think he'd at least wash it now and then.'

Raeson laughed. 'I'm sure we could organise something.'

'Your commander is annoying?' Draethus asked. 'That sounds like insubordination to me.' He made a cutting motion across his neck before changing the subject. 'What news of the fleet? Is it prepared?'

'The Vidar and support ships have refuelled and rearmed. The bombard ships arrived an hour ago.'

'What are bombard ships?' Tremon asked with a puzzled look on his face.

It was Raeson's turn for an explanation. 'A decade before the Heridian's appeared, there was a race of humans, actual zealots, that governed a small cluster of worlds. They believed only humans of their religion should live amongst the stars, so built enormous capital bombardment vessels to wipe out other human colonies. Genocide on a massive scale.'

'That's terrible,' Draethus added.

'We were full-fledged pirate's back then, not the military force of now. We kindly helped ourselves to their ships for our own purposes.' A small frigate floated silently past the group, who watched it for a moment before it disappeared further into the ship. Raeson continued. 'Unfortunately, we weren't fast enough to stop all the destruction but later traced the vessels back to their system and showed them the error of their ways.'

'You bombarded their worlds?' Tremon asked.

'That we did,' Raeson replied. 'We took everything of value first and gave any civilians time to escape. Actually, it wouldn't surprise me if groups of the zealots still exist, really.'

A huge smile crossed Rel's face. 'I'm to lead the mechanic crew aboard the lead bombard ship, so I can be there with you, Draethus.'

Draethus was silent for a moment as he gathered his words, then said, 'I want you here on the Vidar, Rel, where it's safe.'

'I don't think anywhere will be safe once we reach Heridia, Commander,' Tremon added.

Draethus wasn't happy but realized he didn't have a choice in the matter. If his girl wanted to be with him in battle, who was he to argue?

Raeson could see the pain on the man's face, so continued his story. 'The bombard ships are the slowest I've ever seen, but they are massive and covered in more armor than I would have thought possible. Once in orbit around Heridia, there will only be destruction for that forsaken planet. The Rids will die and with it, their hopes of winning.'

*

The four proud warriors stood at attention in front of the thousands of people in the arena, eager to glimpse the new honorary members of the Cygnian Pirates. Most had heard the rumours and stories of the golden ship traversing through the void, saving the crew of the *Arvernus,* and attacking the Heridians.

The word of the duel between Draethus and the Heridian leader Servatus, in all its details, including Raeson's part, spread throughout the fleet. It didn't take long for entrepreneurs to capitalise on the video sales of the fight, which had been running constantly on the vid streams in every location possible.

If there was ever someone with celebrity status amongst the group, it was the commanders who killed the Herician leader on Tiberous. One of these commanders, Draethus, stood in full SOV attire at the base of the stadium. His dark gray armor reflected the lights from the above stands, his powered vibration sword sheathed. To his right stood Tremon, his once rival turned friend, also adorned in armor, however white and much bulkier.

Next to him was the scientist Spectalin, almost cowering in his scruffy off-white lab coat. He seemed uncomfortable like he would rather be in his lab on the golden ship than in front of a few thousand people. He looked to the stands at the cheering faces, fists being thrust into the air, chanting their names, and wondered when the event would be over.

Lastly stood a warrior who, until recently had never seen acknowledgement. Tektar, 'Tek' Shahath, the hero of the fleet. People wanted to see the pirate in person, the man who sacrificed so much to save them from the Heridian trap all those years ago. He who had loathed himself for his actions. He was thought to be dead, only to re-appear in mystery. Vandals had spray painted his name all over the civilian parts of the ship. The Hero, it read, Sacrifice for Others. That he told no one of his actions only painted him more heroic.

In front of the group, the great pirate leader, Khan Alexon Hayreddin, adorned in his ceremonial armor, stood at a higher level near the podium. The shades of black and gray of his armored uniform were just visible through the dark cloak that draped his shoulders. The symbol of the pirates, an elismorus skull struck through by a sword, covered one side of the cloth.

'Warriors, workers and civilians of the Cygnian Pirate fleet,' the Khan began as the crowd hushed to a whisper. 'Behold before you, four warriors chosen in honor of actions beyond the normal capability of others.'

The crowd roared again, louder this time, as their leader stirred them into a frenzy, roaring and screaming.

'The first man, Commander Arcilous Draethus of the Dawn Eclipse, warrior and Soldier of the Void, has shown the strength and courage above and beyond the limits of normal men. I'm sure you have all seen him on the vids alongside our own Commander Raeson?' the Khan announced as the crowd cheered.

Three men from the side of the podium walked across to Draethus, each holding a piece of dark pirate armor, and knelt before the soldier.

'Please accept this gift as a formal gratitude and as a sign of your acceptance into the Cygnian Pirates. From outside you came, from inside you belong. Welcome to the fleet, soldier.'

Draethus nodded deeply in respect, as he had seen other pirates do in the past, and took the armor from the three men. A camera drone hovered in front of them, much to the curiosity of Spect, then relayed the video onto large screens scattered about the high ceilings.

'The second hero, gunner of the Eclipse and right-hand man to the last. Many of you haven't seen his actions, for he has fought in the background, well and true. May I present Paladin warrior Tremon,' the Khan announced. 'From outside you came, from inside you belong.'

The same three men from earlier, walked from their hideaway to Tremon, who was eager to receive his new attire. To his surprise, the pirates had replicated his paladin armor, but in their own colors of black and gray. Tremon, now beaming with pride, bowed his head and accepted the new uniform. Spect fidgeted and rolled around on the side of his boots as he knew his moment in the spotlight was approaching.

The Khan raised his hands to show he was about to speak again. 'And where would any of us be in this fleet without the hard work and dedication of our scientists? Let me introduce to you the scientist of the Dawn Eclipse, Spectalin. From outside you came, from inside you belong.'

Spect flushed red as the camera drone hovered in his face. He looked down, but the drone followed and tilted up so the crowds could see. Only one man this time walked across the podium, handing a dark gray lab coat to a surprised Spect. He gave a nervous bow before taking the attire from the man.

'The last man,' the Khan bellowed before hushing the crowd with his hands. 'The last man needs no introduction. By now, you have all heard the story of the warrior responsible for saving the fleet many years ago. A scout leader having to sacrifice his traitorous squad, so we all could live. Without his efforts, the fleet would have fallen into a trap prepared by the Heridians, ending in the deaths of everyone here.' The Khan considered his next words. 'I should have acknowledged this man many years ago, and I accept the responsibility for not doing so. I give you Tektar Shahath, famous pilot of the infamous Reaper Squadron!'

Everyone in the enormous arena jumped to their feet and shouted the hero's name. 'Shahath! Shahath!'

'For his bravery and sacrifice I award Tektar the Iron Skull medal, the highest award possible to any pirate, alive or dead,' the Khan announced loudly as he walked down from the podium. He revealed the medal; the Cygnian Pirate emblem carved from the rarest of metals and pinned it on Tek's chest. 'Well done warrior, I am honored to award you this medal and please accept my apologies for its lateness,' the Khan said.

A tear ran down Tek's face as all the emotion flooded into him. 'Thank you my Khan, thank you so much.'

'Let's hear it for our newest heroes!' the great Khan announced again.

The crowds leapt out of their seats again. Mobs of people ran up to the new recruits, wanting to meet their new idols.

'This is a strange feeling,' Draethus said as a woman got him to sign a vid stream cover for her son.

'I could get used to it,' laughed Tremon. 'I don't think Spect could, though.'

Spect had his lab coat up in his arms and was making a quick getaway when Draethus noticed a small red-headed girl headed his way amongst a group of familiar faces.

'Rel!' he yelled over the volume of the stadium.

The girl ran into his arms, causing him to drop the new armor at his feet and return her hug.

'I'm so happy you accepted,' she yelled into his chest. 'Things are really going well for a change.'

Raeson was about to say something when a group of young pirates ambushed him for an autograph. They handed him a physical photo, capturing the moment he had thrust the sword into Servatus.

'I don't plan on getting used to this at all. Sure, sure, I'll sign,' Raeson said with annoyance. 'Back off before I space you.'

Slin and Nash clasped forearms with the newest members and congratulated them, even their wingman Tek, who looked healthier.

'That's the happiest I've ever heard the Khan speak,' Raeson said, nudging Draethus. 'It's good to see even his spirits liven up.'

'You know him better than I do, Raeson. Every time I see him, I feel he's going to reprimand someone. There's no point getting too comfortable…'

'Yeah, we'll probably buy it on Heridia, if we ever get there.'

*

In the background, and blending in with the crowd, was the ever-watchful Napier Stark. The Dark Ops warrior scanned every person who approached Xain Raeson using a tiny, discreet hand-held device, looking for threats. The pirate commander could look after himself but was still a vital component of Stark's mission.

He glanced up at the Khan for a moment and noticed the normally dark and brooding leader looking happy, content.

You now have control of a ship capable of time-shifting, giving you access to the planet Heridia, and you didn't even have to steal it.

CHAPTER 21

Lost in Haze.

The *Arvernus* materialised from its quick translocate, a small skip across the emptiness of space where the bulk of the pirate fleet lay behind in wait. It was tasked with scouting the co-ordinates of the Link to Heridia, to fly ahead and make sure enemy forces didn't guard the gateway.

Despite the request of the newly titled pirate Draethus, the Khan had sent Raeson instead of the golden vessel, as it was too valuable.

'What do we have, Nash?' Raeson asked, getting up from his command chair on the *Arvernus*.

The woman in charge of navigation was busy activating the holographic buttons. 'Nothing on short range scans, sir, and I'm switching to extensive range now.'

There was a pause while the vessel opened its sensor ports, something only done in situations not requiring an active defence because of the vulnerable state it put the ship into. Large antennas extended from beneath the armor plates and sent pulses of electromagnetic waves that rippled out at the speed of light. If the ripples connected with anything physically, even that of an energy signature, the host ship would see the break in waves and a three-dimensional image rendered the results.

'Nothing on extensive range. There's nothing here Commander, not even an energy signature,' Nash announced from the back of the command deck.

'There's nothing at all?'

'That's correct, the Link isn't here,' Nash replied, the frustration in her voice clear.

'Open all visuals. I want a perfect eye on everything around us in case our sensors are faulty. There must be something out there we can't detect.'

A curve of displays appeared around the deck and began rotating to give the crew an image of their surroundings only to reveal nothing but darkness.

Raeson touched his ear to activate his coms. 'Arvernus to fleet, area is empty, reply to transmission,'

'Empty?' a confused reply from the Khan crackled. 'Very well, expect friendlies incoming.'

The first light sparked across the primary display like a glint of reflective metal drifting around a sun, a pirate vessel exiting its translocation jump. Another glint appeared with a warping of light and within quick succession the entire fleet had joined the corvette, physically, and in confusion. They had arrived at the co-ordinates found on Tiberous to find nothing but an empty void.

*

From within the liquid lake on the golden vessel, its leader, Commander Draethus, adorned in his new dark pirate armor, looked over the surrounding area and expected to see at least something spectacular.

Would you mind informing me why nothing is here, Eclipse? Draethus said into his mind. *Were the co-ordinates wrong?*

The entity that was the ship entered his mind in its usual warm and calming manner. *We are in the correct place, Commander Draethus, and even though your usual sensors are not detecting anything, the Link is here.*

Show me.

For that you need only to open the Link, on your command of course.

'My Khan,' Draethus said over the ship's coms. 'the Eclipse is detecting the Link and will activate it on our command.'

Sat at their consoles on the bridge, Spect leant over to Tremon. 'Isn't it weird hearing the commander call the Khan his leader? And I'm not seeing any sign of anything here in this space with us. Why is that? Can the ship tell lies?'

Tremon smiled and replied, 'Things will be different for a while around here. I'm sure you'll adapt. As for this Link, I'm wondering if it even exists at all. Maybe this has been a wild chase for nothing this entire time.'

The loud voice of the Khan boomed over the coms. 'We came here for a fight Commander Draethus. Your orders are to open this damn Link so we can crush the menace.'

'Received,' Draethus replied.

Open the Link, Eclipse. Let's make this happen, he ordered in his mind.

Monsters screamed through his mind, as visions flashed into his consciousness of a world covered in the dead and the dying. Creatures clawed from an ocean of blood to drag in the carved-up bodies of fallen warriors, rain falling from the dark skies, scorching their skin.

He looked down to see half of himself missing as one monstrosity bit him and was consuming the rest with giant, bloodstained teeth. Draethus screamed in panic, but no sound emanated. He wished for a quick death, for his life over so the pain would cease. As he lay on the ground, his spirit fading, he noticed a strange building way off in the distance, only just visible through the haze of rain. An enormous spike protruded from the red dusty surface, a spire reaching into the heavens.

The core of the *Eclipse* materialized in the protected room at the center of the golden vessel. A dark sphere that hovered, spun and abruptly froze at quick speeds, the ghosts on the other side howling and shrieking, trying to escape. The Tether Source then vibrated; dark violet and silver electricity arcing from its edges, connecting with the walls inside the room.

On the outside of the vessel, the armor plates slid backward and apart, revealing a red fiery glow from beneath, enveloping the ship. A swirl of radiation, gases and lightning began forming, ever increasing in speed until a disk tore the fabric of space and created the opening to the Link.

*

The sound of whispers spread throughout the entire fleet, haunting voices that began quietly then increased in volume until becoming a roar of many.

Khan Hayreddin stood on his command deck stunned by the visual beauty of the Link and like all the people in the fleet, tried to ignore the voices before giving the order.

'Bombard ships, I instruct you to move into the Link. Cruisers, frigates and other escort craft you are to keep pace but under no circumstance are you to leave those ships behind.'

The enormous bombard ships engaged their propulsion units. Fire bloomed behind, leaving a trail of thick orange smoke as the primitive vessels lumbered forward. Remnants of a race beaten by a war of their own making, the behemoths had only one purpose: planetary destruction. The pirate fleet had other orbit-to-surface artillery in their arsenal, but nothing near the magnitude of such ships.

'Three minutes until the first Bombard ship reaches the Link, my Khan,' said one of the navigation officers monitoring the fleet's progress.

The Khan remained silent. His officers would never expect an acknowledgment from their leader or dare repeat themselves. He ran his fingers through his dark beard, considering the many options and decisions needed in the moments to come. A wrong choice could be disastrous.

'Raeson, acknowledge,' the Khan said over his coms.

'The commander is unconscious, my Khan,' Slin replied. 'Those visions started when the ship opened the Link, and it has knocked him out. I've assumed command of the Arvernus until he awakes and can retake command.'

'So, it links Raeson to the Eclipse in the same way as Draethus?' replied the Khan. 'Very well, I want you to traverse the Link ahead of the bombard ships and if there is trouble on the other side, burn back and inform us.'

'Yes sir, right away.'

*

The pirate corvette fired up its engines, performed a rollover vector to the port side, and entered the tear. Inside was that of pure madness as a whirlwind of energy surrounded the *Dawn Eclipse*, connecting it to the Link. The *Arvernus* accelerated to full as it passed the golden ship and headed further into the corridor of energy.

'How are you holding up Eclipse?' Slin asked over the coms.

'The commander has passed out, something to do with the Link opening,' Tremon replied. 'Hope he wakes up soon. It's pretty shaky in here.'

'Copy that Tremon. The Khan has ordered us through, so if you don't see us again, it's safe to follow, or we are dead, either way.'

Tremon laughed. 'I'm uncertain how long this Link will be open, so you'll want to be fast.'

The pirate corvette raced through the tunnel of energy, sparks and lightning attacking the ship's nanite armor, but not enough to cause significant damage. Thirty seconds later the vessel was free and had made it through.

'Arvernus to fleet, other side is clear, do you copy?' Slin asked through the ship's communication system.

'This is Talon Commander Zekhal of the Dying Nova. We copy and are sending the rest of the fleet through, stand by.'

*

The first bombard ship entered the Link, the immense vessel vanishing alongside its cruiser and corvette escorts, followed closely by a cluster of six others, like a herd of giants lumbering to the destination. Behind them, the frigate, the *Dying Nova,* served as rear guard whilst running point for the next group of vessels soon to enter the vortex. As the frigate entered the Link the whirlpool of energy vanished, abruptly leaving again only an empty void behind it.

'Get it open!' the Khan roared into the coms system. 'Get that portal open again so we can reach Heridia!'

One officer approached the angry leader, steadied himself, and spoke. 'Sir, the Eclipse has vanished along with the bombardment fleet.'

The Khan gave the man an angry stare as the officer continued. 'Roughly twenty escort cruisers and frigates are with them, so that's something.'

'Something?' the Khan said angrily under his breath. 'We just lost the best chance we have at victory. Do you think with our fleet divided we can win? All we can do now is sit here on our hands and do nothing.'

*

The golden ship raced to reach the end of the Link, its engines white hot as a trail of plasma burned in its wake. Crimson streaks of energy, left over from opening the gateway, smoked off the now closed armor.

'Faster!' Tremon yelled, 'go faster for creator's sake. We have to make it to the end before the Link closes!'

Spect fiddled with some of his controls. 'I'm not piloting. The ship has control, Tremon.'

'It's what?' the paladin replied.

'The ship is flying itself. I have no control and what's worse, look behind us,' the scientist said as he rapidly activated the rear display.

An image of the frigate, the *Dying Nova*, was shrinking in the distance, as it too was in danger of getting caught.

'That frigate is too slow. It won't make it,' Tremon whispered.

The *Dawn Eclipse* burst out of the Link before the opening vanished, leaving the pirate frigate trapped behind.

'What will happen to it do you think?' Tremon asked the scientist.

Spect ran a finger across the frame of his glasses and shrugged. 'It will probably stay trapped for eternity I would imagine, lost in whatever realm that Link belongs too.'

Tremon felt a pain in his chest with the thought of losing one of their own, but knew that in the end, before this war was over, there would be a lot more casualties.

'Let's join with the bombard fleet,' Tremon said, 'and get the Arvernus on coms. We have to do something about our unconscious commanders.'

From under the liquid metal lake, Draethus lay unconscious, floating as a corpse would in an ocean lit by fire.

*

The capital ships that successfully made it through the Link had carried on with the mission under the combined command of both Raeson and Draethus. Though outranked by any of the cruiser commanders that were escorting the bombard vessels, the joint vote put the two in charge. This meant that none of the eighteen cruiser commanders could try to pull rank and kept animosity between the pirates to a minimum. Draethus thought it may have something to do with their new fame, however.

The fleet moved painfully slowly because of the sheer mass of the bombard ships, and for the last two hours they had been fighting off waves of Heridian fighters emanating from an unknown source. Red cloud enveloped the area, a nebula of gases that made seeing the way ahead impossible and with the hundreds of derelict vessels scattered throughout, very hazardous.

Are you detecting anything on long range scans Eclipse? Draethus asked the ship in his mind, *and are you sure we can't activate the Link again?*

The entity that was the ship entered his mind in a peaceful and in-evasive manner. *The interference from the energy within this area is disrupting all scans. We can detect no planet and cannot activate the*

Link for another few days because of the limitations between the ship and the Tether Source.

Understood.

'What about you Spect? Can you see anything on visuals yet? I'm sure a planet wouldn't be that hard to find,' Draethus asked the scientist who was busy at his console.

'I've been scanning the area since we started this gauntlet,' Spect said, squinting into his displays. 'All I see is a red cloud, not even a star in sight.'

'Any idea what these derelict wrecks are doing here? Do they have a configuration we've seen before?' Tremon asked, hoping that someone on the open channel could answer the question.

It was Slin who spoke first. 'They seem to have similar features to the ones in the Nebula Stream we almost collided with a couple of months ago.'

'There must be hundreds of destroyed vessels here, including Heridian capitals. Must have been one hell of a battle,' Tremon finished.

'I would love to salvage them,' Spect said, looking up from his scans. 'Even if we could reconstruct the schematics and manufacture them ourselves, they would make a great edition to the fleet.'

'Let's worry about making it to the end first before we think about rebuilding, shall we?' Draethus said from under his lake of liquid metal. He held his head and wished for some painkillers. Knowing that Raeson had suffered the same fate made him feel a little better.

*

The Heridian fighter activated its frontal weapons and took a shot at the pirate fighter craft as it banked a hard turn to evade. Flares burst from behind the dark ship as the Heridian fired its missiles, only to have the countermeasures lead them off into the distance. Hot plasma burnt into the pirate fighter as the enemy projectiles connected and ricocheted, then repaired on the fly by the nanites embedded in the armor. Both fighters strafed from side to side, the front runner burnt for his life, trying to reposition and break free from his pursuer.

'This guy is a pain in my stern,' Stark said into the coms as he looked over his shoulder at the red fighter trying to target him.

'I'm on it, pull down now!' Nash yelled as she flew between the two, hoping to confuse or at least distract the enemy.

Her plan worked. The Heridian fighter hesitated just long enough for Stark to spin his craft on its center and fire his guns. His cockpit display blinded him as oxygen inside the enemy craft ignited along with its fuel. The remnants of the enemy burst outward in all directions.

'Thanks, Nash, you're becoming quite the pilot,' Stark said thankfully.

'Shut up,' she replied. 'The commander might have given you a pass on what you did, but I haven't.'

Stark thought about replying, but let it lie. He could see her point and after all, he put her in harm's way.

'Stark, we have more fighters' incoming from the front. Reform your squads and don't let them get to the bombards,' Raeson ordered from the command deck of the *Arvernus*.

Positioned in front of the fleet, Stark fired his weapons at the crippled Heridian fighter and watched it spiral out of control then crash into the wreck of a derelict. He quickly rolled right to evade the twisted metal of another wreck that appeared from nowhere and squeezed through the gaps in its hull.

Damn, that was a gutsy move, even for me.

The last enemy fighter exploded as Nash and her wingman launched a combined arsenal of missiles that streaked through the night.

'Scans are clear,' she announced over the coms. 'No, wait there's something else.'

Four Heridian cruisers emerged from the fog of war, beasts launching themselves from the mist, hunters searching for prey.

'Shit, they're going for the lead bombard vessel and look at their speed,' Nash announced.

The voice of three cruiser commanders escorting the bombard vessels, chattered over the coms, before each left their assignments and headed on a collision vector with the approaching hunters. A mass of laser fired out from the enemy capitals and cut the lead pirate cruiser in half. It buckled from the middle and exploded into two enormous pieces that separated into opposite directions.

Stark could hear the orders from Raeson over the coms being ignored by the two remaining cruiser commanders to the front. The pirate vessels, although powerful, were no match for the speed, agility, and sheer firepower of the four Heridian cruisers that now bore down on them. Another pirate capital ship exploded without even firing a shot, white hot gases erupting in a spectacular light show. The third vessel decided he couldn't take on all four of the enemy and retreated, running back to the main fleet, something Raeson had already ordered.

'Cruisers four to nine form up around the front bombard, star formation and keep it tight. The moment the menace is in range I will give the command, understood?' Raeson ordered.

The fleet commanders acknowledged, and the pirate vessels began as instructed but were too far behind the lead bombard before the enemy opened fire. Light gleamed from the four enemy monsters and connected with the lead bombard vessel. Its armor held for longer than Stark had expected, then began melting, its thick plating giving most of the crew time to evacuate. Pods separated from the back of the vessel and drifted away with their beacons flashing. The enemy lasers fell silent as the lead bombard broke apart and exploded. Large chunks of debris drifted apart as the core at their center sparked and erupted, the enormous bombardment weapon at its base disappearing into the distance.

*

Draethus watched from the back of the fleet and knew the vessel Rel served on was now the next ship in the line of fire. 'I'm not just going to sit here, fire engines, and let's get into the thick of it,' he said.

'About time I got to shoot something,' Tremon exclaimed as he ran a check of his weapon systems.

'Raeson, we're going in for interdiction to see if we can draw fire,' Draethus reported over the coms.

'I'd ask you to hold back,' Raeson said, 'but I know your intention.'

The golden vessel accelerated forward, easily overtaking the rest of the fleet and spiralled in towards the incoming enemy vessels. Pulses of energy pushed the vessel as it strafed from one side to another. Enemy weapons fired at the smaller ship forming crisscrossing patterns, deathly lines of plasma, but were too slow to hit their intended adversary.

'Time to explode some shit,' Tremon yelled gleefully as he triggered his holographic guns at the targets displayed in front of him.

Spect looked over in surprise as he was not used to hearing the paladin curse. The pirate's vocabulary had been rubbing off on him.

Silver lasers erupted from the sides of the golden ship, hitting one of the enemy ships on its bow, stripping away some protective armor. Pieces of plating curled away and spun, but not enough to penetrate the hull.

'We are coming around again, get ready,' Draethus ordered.

The *Dawn Eclipse* aimed to the heavens, rolled over and came in for another pass. The distraction plan was working and gave the pirate cruisers enough time to form around the new lead bombard vessel. Draethus knew the fleet was almost in weapons range.

The ship strafed across the four enemy cruisers again, the silver laser peppering across the bow of two, but again inflicted minor damage.

'Get clear Draethus!' Raeson yelled over the coms.

Combined weapons' fire from the six pirate cruisers cut the first Heridian vessel from dorsal to bow, severing its head, and causing it to erupt in an enormous explosion. The three other enemy ships attempted to evade by scattering in multiple directions, the second enemy moving too slow, running headfirst into the pirate weapons fire. A line of illumination hit the vessel, connected from bow to stern, and evaporated the Heridian into nothing more than scrap.

The last two Heridian cruisers raced in opposite directions trying to get out of the death, then arced back around and engaged the back of the fleet. Before they reached the rear, the pirate cruisers had reformed and performed the same tactic. The battle was over, and the victors resumed their slow progression through the clouds.

*

'More fighters are coming. Cruisers resume your escort cover over each bombard,' ordered Raeson.

Hundreds of enemy fighters emerged from the clouds, a swarm of insects covering the eerie sky, ready to unleash devastation. They burst in from every angle. Weapon's fire blanketed the bombards and cruisers alike, luminous streaks engulfing the ships, which combined would eventually penetrate the hull. The pirate fighters, totalling thirty-seven now after hours of losses, engaged the swarm in a mass of chaos and confusion. Explosions signalled the end of either a pirate or an enemy fighter in the smallest flash of light.

Stark twisted and turned, his fighter covered in scorch marks and even a small fire on his back fin. He knew if he held a predictable line he would die, so didn't concentrate on any one fighter and prolong the engagement. Two pulses of the trigger, if it connected the enemy would explode. If not, then move to the next target. A straight line meant death.

'We can't keep this up, Raeson,' Stark reported. 'Thirty odd of us against hundreds. Even with cover fire from the cruisers anti-ship fire, we won't last long.'

'There's no choice. We have to reach Heridia with the bombards intact if we are to win this war,' Raeson replied.

'I suggest we dock the fighters and repair, let the capitals take the fire for a while, they can take it,' Stark said.

'Negative, keep up the pressure and...' Raeson stopped when Slin yelled out from behind him on the bridge.

'Planet ahead, it's Heridia!' Slin yelled.

The crimson world of Heridia appeared as the fleet exited the hazy clouds of destruction. Its surface was familiar to both Raeson and Draethus, dark rocky continents swimming in oceans of scarlet fluid. Mountains stretched across the land and continued into the liquid as islands protruded like spines. The ominous clouds in the upper atmosphere drifted with what seemed to be an intelligent intent, moving in multiple directions casting acid to the surface.

'All fighters dock,' Raeson ordered. 'I say again, all fighters dock. Fleet set waypoint to the following position I'm sending you now.'

By the creator, I know this evil place.

The pirate widowmaker class fighters flared their engines, disengaged their fight, and headed for their respective ships. Destructive energy completely engulfed the fleet as the Heridian fighters strafed and circled. Anti-ship lasers from the cruisers continued their defensive attempts, but were far too slow to keep up with the tight turns of their targets.

Raeson's coms chimed as Draethus asked, 'You recognise this planet, don't you?'

It took a moment for Xain to respond with the realization. 'This is the world from our vision, isn't it? How can that be?'

'Maybe it was the Eclipse readying us for what lies ahead? I'm not sure, but we shouldn't worry about that now. I don't believe the Rid fighters are atmospheric, so we should set up in a low orbit.'

'Confirmed. Let's bombard this hole back to the hole it came from.' Raeson switched back to his fleet coms and ordered, 'Prepare to set up orbits, bombard ships begin immediately, cruisers create covering fire.'

*

The enormous lumbering vessels arced their way into a low orbit. Flames from the atmosphere covered the bow and ignited the front armor plating, creating a furious glow.

Most enemy fighters followed, exploding without the required trajectory or protection against entering orbit. It only took a few dozen Heridians to die to convince the rest not to pursue. The fleet had reached its destination.

The *Dawn Eclipse* flew on point, positioned at the front of the fleet in a low orbit. The vessel streaked across the sky, a golden angel leading the pirates to victory.

'By the creator,' Spect said in shock, 'it's coming for us.'

'What are you talking about?' Tremon asked as his smile quickly vanished. 'Um… Commander?'

'I see it Tremon, there isn't anything we can do,' replied Draethus.

The incredible and enormous Heridian creature ship, a capital vessel that would cast a shadow over any other in existence, was on an intercept course. Like the enemy flagship the crew had encountered previously, it resembled a prehistoric ocean monster, covered in dark red plated scales with multiple tails. The tip of each tail held a capital weapon of immense proportion, and its hull was lined with an arsenal of smaller weaponry.

It was the bow that caused the crew to panic. Rows of giant teeth surrounded an opening, a physical anti-ship weapon that could clamp down on helpless capitals in close quarters or swallow them for capture. The bridge of the *Dawn Eclipse* grew dark, as it had nowhere to run.

The creature ship closed its enormous jaws and captured the time-shifting vessel.

*

Raeson looked on in terror, knowing what losing the golden ship meant. 'Begin bombardment of the surface,' he ordered the fleet.

'Slin, you have command of the Arvernus. I'm going to take a fighter and try to board that monstrosity.'

CHAPTER 22

A Monster Within.

Stalking through the corridors, the Heridian soldiers pushed forward, searching for the humans on board.

The enemy "creature" ship had captured the *Dawn Eclipse*, and then restrained it using countless gravity waves and physical grapplers. Bombarding it with a variety of electronic warfare, waves continuously invaded the ancient victim, draining its power as minute nanites attacked its hull like microbes feasting on a carcass.

Eclipse, are you there? Draethus said into his mind. *Damn it, where are you?*

Secured on the command deck, the three crew members readied themselves. Weapons primed, they sat in darkness, waiting for the enemy to breach the door. The dim cyan emergency lights flickered intermittently, creating silhouettes across the consoles. Their projectile weapons rested over the top with eyes aimed down the sights.

'The Eclipse is not responsive, we are on our own. Shoot everything that comes through that door, and we'll try to break for the docking bay,' Draethus ordered.

Tremon, armed with the biggest rifle possible, was unflinching. 'Death comes today. Let's make sure it's the Rids and not us.'

The scientist Spectalin tried to hold his pistol steady and aimed in the general direction of the white door, but remained silent. Draethus guessed he was inexperienced in combat, and an engagement in such a tight space removed the option to run.

'You'll be alright, Spect,' Draethus assured him. He understood how the man must have felt, knowing that death could be minutes away. 'Just aim at the door and squeeze the trigger when they cut through.'

Spect looked over with a nod and laid his other hand over the gun to steady.

The cutter started with a flash of sparks as the Heridians worked their way through the white metal. With the ship disabled, the nanites that normally repaired such damage were offline, making the breach possible. Smoke bellowed into the bridge from the cutting and created a haze that Draethus hoped could give them some advantage.

Not long now.

As the Heridian cutting torch finished its work, the door blew inwards, skidding across the floor before toppling into the lower lake below.

Draethus ducked as projectiles flooded the bridge, one sparking the console above him and catching fire. Crimson armored beasts, covered in runes and wielding rifles, ducked through the opening and then ran towards the men in pure disregard for their own safety.

Tremon fired first, catching one soldier in the chest, turning the creature into a smouldering pile of twisted metal, spraying a mist of dark liquid over the floor.

Draethus hit an enemy in the shoulder only to have it spray random fire in his direction as it spun wildly away, surprised at being struck. It turned again to aim, clicking its extruded jaws at the team before dying to a second shot from Tremon.

Spect fired his pistol repeatedly into the smoky opening the enemy was emanating from, hoping to shoot something. As another enemy burst through, the scientist hit it in the head and, although the bullet didn't penetrate, gave Tremon enough time to aim and end the creature's life.

'You only sent three?' Draethus yelled, reloading his rifle. 'I'm insulted!'

Spect looked over to him with fear beaming from his eyes. 'Do you have to encourage them?'

Draethus stood up from his position and stormed for the door. 'Let's go. Follow behind and we can reach the docking bay.' He watched in slow motion as a grenade rolled onto the command deck before detonating. Pain and searing light blanketed his mind in a familiar sensation, one he never expected to experience again, and the three men fell to the floor. Through his fading vision, Draethus glimpsed the mechanical menace standing over him, the barrel of a rifle pressed against his temple.

*

Following the creature ship down through the atmosphere, Xain Raeson pushed his fighter further.

Pulling out of the trajectory needed to compensate for orbit entry, he changed his systems into an atmospheric configuration. The wings of the widowmaker class fighter swept backwards, making it more aerodynamic, and engaged the front intakes to accept the oxygen in Heridia's atmosphere.

His coms re-connected with a rush of static voices that deafened him for a moment before altering the communication settings to filter out the garble.

'Talon Commander Raeson,' Slin said from the command deck on the *Arvernus*. 'We are in position and request permission to begin operation.'

'This is Raeson. You are free to engage the planet's surface. I want everything levelled, do you hear me?'

When the Khan discovers I left my command position for an ill-fated rescue mission, he'll have my head. Get in line.

'Command accepted. All vessels begin bombardment of the planet and leave nothing untouched.' There was a pause before Slin continued. 'Sir, what is happening with the Eclipse?'

'It's gone Slin, but I'm going to follow this beast down to the surface, if that's even where it's going. What do you think the chances are I can kill it with good looks and sarcasm?'

'Can I have your skull collection when you're gone?'

Raeson watched the strange cloud formation and wondered if it was trying to surround him. Although the planet below looked scorching, his cockpit was freezing cold. With a chuckle, he replied, 'You could join the collection if you want? Raeson out.'

The Heridian creature ship continued its downward vector towards the planet's surface. Contrails covered much of the vessel as Raeson manoeuvred his craft inside to hide himself from any ground defences. He gently dodged through a pair of morbid spikes on the vessel's back and felt a chill when they reacted to his presence.

This is the stupidest thing I've ever done in my life. What am I doing?

The ground was quickly approaching and although he couldn't see through his canopy, his systems displayed he was running out of time. Landing with the ship, he knew, would be a terrible idea and probably get him killed faster. He banked to the left, quickly picked out a mountain range in the distance, and decided it was time.

The creature ship pitched upward, changing its orientation from nose first into belly first, then headed for a dark patch on the surface.

It was only then that Raeson saw the Spire for the first time, in reality at least, and felt himself gripped in fear. The enormous spike protruded from the ground on a heavy slant, reaching into the heavens. Its rusted exterior gave the impression of rock mixed with hull plating, and Xain noticed thousands of lights across its surface. Small craft hovered and flew about, orbiting the structure like a busy city. The brief distraction caused him to miss the object headed his way, as anti-air artillery struck his fighter and cut his wing clean off. He streaked towards the creature ship that was preparing its own landing.

Blood covered Xain's face, his eyes stung, and with his head throbbing he prepared to make a crash landing. Impact jolted him forward in his seat, and the straps across his chest held him in place as the fighter contacted the ocean. A body of liquid he guessed wasn't water.

The world began to fade as he fought the need to pass out, the desire to sleep. His craft floated in place for a few moments before it slipped below the waves. He unclipped his harness, opened the canopy and with a groggy effort, pulled himself free.

Barely had he the chance to jump from his fighter when a hovering Heridian craft, open topped and piloted by three mechanical soldiers, reached his position, and held him at gunpoint.
If you're here to offer surrender, I accept.
Raeson's words never reached his lips before he passed out.

*

Hours later, the dimly lit sky above was filled with thunderous clouds rolling and swirling together, a battle of supremacy for the next acidic downpour. Draethus lay restrained on his back, thin metal filaments binding him to the hovering Heridian craft.

He raised his head to get a glimpse of what lay behind and saw the creature ship landed in the vermillion ocean. The vessel blocked out the sky and the world behind it, a beached predatory creature resting in the shallows.

To his front, a Heridian soldier piloted the craft, its back turned and obviously confident the prisoner was secure. Draethus ran his eyes over the dark armor, plates of metal over lacing gears and cogs beneath. A feeling of hatred ran through his body, making him shake involuntarily. He'd killed so many of the creatures, for so many years, yet it made no difference. The hatred turned to helplessness as he struggled to break free, the filaments only squeezing tighter.

Rel. I wish we could just get away from this place.

The hover craft shuddered as a wave splashed over him, drips of the red liquid covering his face. Draethus licked his lips and realized the craft wasn't flying over water but blood, an entire ocean of it. He struggled to comprehend how such a place could exist.

He tried to put the thought out of his mind. 'Any chance of a bathroom break?' he yelled at the pilot.

The pilot didn't respond and kept its eyes forward, either from ignorance or a lack of intelligence. The pirate noticed the runes across its body unlit and decided it mustn't have a biological mind contained inside.

Just a stupid follower.

He forced a look to the side and noticed two more hover craft flying alongside and skimming the liquid. Although he couldn't see them, he knew his crew had suffered the same fate and his helplessness turned into guilt. The images of all the people who had fallen under his command threatened his mind's eye before he pushed them down.

Both men, before he appeared in their lives, were happy with the world they lived. Tremon, an ex-ganger turned paladin, protected his city, walking the streets in his mechanized chicken. The man had come so far in his life and stood up for what he believed in. Draethus remembered how they fought to begin with, how he'd won Tremon's trust and became friends.

Spectalin, the scientist, worked vigorously in his lab whilst fighting off that small lizard of Varican's. It was this scientist who created the displacement device that started this mess. If it wasn't for his actions, however, there may never have been a fighting chance against the Heridian forces to begin with.

Draethus craned his neck to see the driver again and saw the spire, the enormous structure reaching into the skies. He expected to feel a sense of dread, but instead felt calm, almost serene. Was he accepting his fate finally? Has the creator finally finished tormenting him like a grand puppeteer throwing away the profession? He didn't understand why they were still alive, why his mind wasn't beneath the armor plate of a foul mechanical monster. He lay back down and stared once again into the dark heavens.

I wish I'd eaten something before the battle.

*

Darkness, silence, and the void.

Draethus felt pain constricting his body. They'd taken away his armor, and he knew the metal filaments still bound his torso and limbs. All he could see was blackness. He blinked a few times to determine if his eyes were open, and if it wasn't for the pain under him, thought he was floating. Memories of his interrogation on the Sky-Station flooded back, when he first met the Specter.

'Damn you,' a voice echoed next to him. 'I'll kill you all.'

'Raeson, is that you?' Draethus asked, turning in the direction the voice originated.

'Draethus? Yeah, it's me. I guess you got captured too, eh? What of the other two?'

'I'm here, Commander,' Tremon voiced. 'I don't know what these restraints are, but they get tighter the more you struggle.'

'Oh, Tremon's here,' Draethus chuckled. 'Please keep the lights off.'

'I hope you're tortured first so I can watch,' Tremon said.

'These restraints are probably designed as a torture method and escape deterrent,' Spect said into the darkness.

'That makes four of us then,' Raeson replied. 'Spect is right, though. These filaments will hurt more if you struggle. I found myself on a Rid destroyer once and was tortured with them. The Rid's name was Skylord Theradin, and a real evil piece of shit. I'm pretty sure it died.'

A vibration hummed through the room, with a sound of hydraulics hissing and the contact of metal on metal. There was a dull illumination from the ceiling as hatches opened and three cylindrical tanks slowly descended from above. Draethus could see wires connecting the top of the tanks to the space where they originated from. The lack of light in the room made it too difficult to make out what was inside.

'So Theradin is no more,' a voice said, emanating from one tank. 'How did you purge it?'

'Purge it, you mean kill it?' Raeson replied.

'Indeed,' another voice said.

Draethus interrupted. 'How about you tell us what you are first, are what is this place?'

'You are in no position to give orders, human,' a third voice said.

The filaments holding the men tightened. 'How did you purge it?'

Raeson was adamant to remain stubborn until he saw the pain on Spect's face in the darkness, illuminated by the tanks. 'Something killed it and I couldn't see what because the fight happened behind a closed door.'

'I see,' the second voice replied, 'then you shall have your questions answered. If you cooperate, you shall receive.'

'Isn't that generous of you?' Draethus said. 'What would we receive exactly?'

There was a pause, and it became apparent that they ignored his question.

'You are in the depths of the spire, one of the deepest levels closest to the planet's core,' the first voice answered. 'Who amongst you knows where the golden ship originates?'

Spect stuttered an answer before Tremon interrupted him and replied, 'It just appeared on our world one day. First it wasn't there, and then it was, so we don't know where it originated from.'

'What is the spire?' asked Raeson.

The voices seemed to chatter amongst themselves before the second voice said, 'The spire is the structure at the center of our world that is Heridia. It serves as a base, city and communication with all that exists outside of the Link. Who of you integrates with the time ship?'

'I am the Commander of the Dawn Eclipse, the ship you refer to as the time ship,' Draethus answered.

'Then it is you who will join our army, you that will lead our fleets from this prison and you that will submit to our will,' the first voice announced in a sinister tone.

Draethus made a face and mouthed several mocking, silent words, before laughing.

'What is humorous?' asked the first voice.

'Did you star in one of those cheesy action vids? You know, the one where the evil lord floods our ears with grand threats of domination and oppression? I would sooner end my own life than allow myself to become Heridian. I saw what it did to my friend, Servatus, and I will die first.'

The second voice laughed, 'Oh, we won't harvest your mind like the rest of the legion. I very much doubt the consciousness of the ship would allow access to its systems.'

'No, you will stay as you are, human, and we will hold your friends until the day we purge you,' said the third voice.

Raeson struggled against his bindings and said, 'He won't let your filth escape just to save the three of us. We all sacrifice for the greater good.'

'And what of you, Scientist, would you agree to sacrifice when you could study the race that is Heridian?' the second voice asked. 'Could you, given enough time, be able to gain control of such a ship?'

'I can't,' Spect whispered. 'Not again. I couldn't kill thousands of people just to save my own life.'

The first voice laughed. 'I think we could tear the paladin's mind from his body and have him torture the scientist until he builds us one.'

Tremon fought his restrains, hoping to find a way free, and glared at the dark tanks. 'What can we do Draethus?' he whispered between gritted teeth.

'There is nothing you can do, soldier Draethus,' the second voice interrupted. 'You have, after all, already joined our ranks.'

'That will never happen!' Raeson yelled. 'Someone get me a stick. I want to beat them with sticks!'

'You want the ship to control the Link and release your forces,' Draethus stated, trying to stall and think of a way out of the situation.

The tanks hissed and buzzed for a few moments, the cables above swaying as if a chemical was being pumped into the enclosures. An acrid smell filled the room.

The first voice said, 'With control of the vessel, we no longer have to wait for the natural occurrence when the Link will open unassisted. This will give us complete access to the outside universe. We can import resources to build our fleets and freely attack any world we chose. It will also enable us the ability to travel to any time and place of our choosing, therefore giving us more choice in our targets of interest. We will also be able to transport multiple versions of our fleets from different timelines and bring them to Heridia for its defence.'

'By import, you mean the biological minds of other sentient races?' Raeson asked.

'That's correct,' replied the third voice. 'We can strike any race on any world and at any instance in time. Whether that be at the beginning of a race's evolution or the middle, either way we will cause the extinction of that species.'

'But without our cooperation the ship will be useless,' Tremon said.

'Yes,' replied the first voice. 'We need the ship to open the Link.'

'Then all we have to do is die,' said Raeson angrily, 'and you lose access to the Eclipse and remain trapped here.'

The first voice laughed deeply. 'We are the Lords of Heridia, and we know you don't die.'

The three dark tanks illuminated as lights on the inside ignited within the liquid. Oxygen bubbles behind the glass streamed to the top, as the lords contained within revealed themselves. Corpses hung suspended like lab experiments in a nightmare. In the first tank floated a skull with an attached spine, the lower jaw missing, with wires connecting to a device above. The bone was fragmented and scared, the eye sockets dark with decay and a sense of emptiness.

The second tank held the top half of a decaying torso, with a full rib cage and an intact skull set in a permanent facial expression of terror. The torn flesh on the ribs drifted gently in the liquid, revealing bite marks and abrasions. Cables protruded from the chest and ran through the skull, then into the top of the tank.

The last tank contained a third corpse, half a rib cage attached to a short section of spine and a flesh torn face. It, too, connected to the monstrosity that was the machine.

Shocked, Draethus could only ask, 'Well, you three have a face for audio only coms channels. Were you human?'

The first tank lit up as it spoke. 'Once we were human, but that was long ago.'

Raeson's eyes widened as he realized what was going on. 'Draethus, look closer at the second tank.'

As Draethus did, his world changed forever. Around the neck of the corpse, in the second enclosure, hung a golden amulet embossed with a dragon.

'No, it can't be!' Draethus screamed. 'That thing, that abomination cannot be me!'

Although the corpse lay still, the second tank flashed to life as a light surrounded the enclosure. 'You see proud warriors, you all join us in your future, and it is inevitable.'

'That amulet is not the one I wear now, monster,' Draethus replied.

'It matters not,' the second tank replied. 'We are the same entity, you and I.'

Spect, who had been quietly trying to keep the attention off himself, asked curiously, 'If you are in fact our Commander then why have us killed? Why send Servatus on our trail? Wouldn't that mean you would cease to exist had Draethus died?'

The third tank laughed. 'Heridia and everything that exists beyond the Link, in this area of space, exists apart from time.'

'What does that mean, exactly?' Draethus asked.

'It means,' continued the lord, 'what happens in the space-time outside of this realm does not interfere with what's inside. We could kill you now, and as we are apart from time, there would be no consequence for us. We would still exist.'

'Meaning if you had access to time-shifting you could bring an unlimited amount of your fleets to protect this world and not have the timeline outside changed?' asked Tremon.

'Correct. We would have an infinite number of forces, including biological specimens to increase the competency of our armies.'

Draethus went quiet as he soaked up the information, pieces in his mind joining and completing the puzzle. 'You targeted Johan to lure me here with the ship. That's why he gave me the co-ordinates because you wanted us to find Heridia.'

The third tank illuminated. 'Yes, Servatus was the best candidate to complete the task. I also wanted a reminder of the insect I once was, the brooding and pathetic pirate commander. Tell me Xain Raeson, how does it feel to look into your own reflection and see the hatred you've been fighting all these years?'

Raeson stared into the corpse's dead eyes and knew it to be true. A piece of flesh broke away from the face and sank to the bottom of the tank.

'I recognised you... me,' Raeson said darkly. 'If my life ending doesn't destroy your existence, then I'll make sure I erase you completely.'

The third corpse, also known as the Fifth Lord of Heridia, cackled at the thought of an insect trying to kill a god. 'Fly closer to me and you will burn.'

Draethus leaned over to Raeson, gestured with his chin towards the third tank and said, 'You need to eat a little more.' The comment seemed to calm Raeson as he tried to not smirk.

'You do not see the intention behind revealing who we are. All of you could escape and never become the god-like beings you now see before you. It matters not,' the first tank, the Third Lord of Heridia said.

'In some timeline, at some instance, the three of us joined the Heridian race, to become the three lords. We exist apart from time, and we shall always exist despite your actions,' said the Fourth Lord of Heridia from the liquid encased in the second tank.

'What about your assassins?' Raeson asked, 'where did you recruit them from?'

'Assassins?' the Fifth Lord asked in a questioning tone. 'What assassins?'

Raeson fell silent and Draethus made a mental note to ask what he meant, if they lived of course.

Tremon spoke up, still in shock with the knowledge of the Heridian leader's identity. 'So who are you?' he asked the entity in the first tank, the Third Lord. 'Do I become you?'

The Third Lord bellowed its reply. 'You insult me with your question. No, you do not become me. I am more than any of you!'

*

Rel stood against the transparent plating of the lead bombard vessel and peered down at the dark crimson planet below. The shelling of the world's surface had been going smoothly, leaving devastation and craters in their wake.

She stared into the distance at the giant spike piercing the skies and wondered what had become of her lover, Draethus. She knew the enemy had captured his vessel, and saw the creature ship swallow and fly them down to the surface.

The fleet agreed to still bombard the planet, including the area around where the enemy vessel landed, as even a hero was expendable during the war.

Pain filled her heart as she imagined never seeing Draethus again, to never hold him, to never stare into his eyes once more.

Tears welled up as she imagined what he was going through, if he was even alive to begin with.

As she turned to walk back to her post, a bright white light blinded her from the side and the red-haired girl felt no more.

CHAPTER 23

Shrouded Intentions.

The orbital bombardment of Heridia sent vibrations through the massive spire, reaching deep into the world's core. Fire rained from the skies as the unopposed pirate fleet continued, despite their leaders' capture.

Draethus knew he and the others were expendable, that no personal connection would halt the attack, and wondered what the end was like. Would the spire collapse and kill him instantly? Maybe the Heridian lords would order his execution instead of fulfilling their plans. Which ever the path, the outcome was the same. He just hoped he'd done enough to redeem himself in the eyes of the fallen.

'You feel that, filth?' he said, glaring at the three corpses in their liquid chambers. 'Soon your world will die, and with it, any hope you have of freedom.'

The Heridian Lords laughed in unison, the Fifth Lord cackling hysterically, causing the chamber's speakers to hiss and pop with static.

'Do you think we would leave Heridia defended by such meagre forces? We may have multiple fleets roaming outside of the Link, but we are far from defenceless,' the Fifth Lord said. 'Behold.'

The filaments around the four captives feet pulled them towards the ceiling, giving them an unobstructed view of a holographic display, now flickering above. Draethus could see the curvature of the planet, dark clouds swirling and distorting, and the pirate orbital bombardment ships unleashing their deathly power. Fire erupted from the enormous cannons under the vessels, streaking down to the surface, and finishing in a colossal explosion, throwing dirt high into the air.

'What you are seeing here is, in actual time, puny ships unleashing your so-called destruction on our world,' the Third Lord said.

Without warning, massive streaks of projectile fire launched up from the planet's surface as Heridian space artillery began firing on the fleet from hidden positions under the ocean. The armor encased around the bombard ships fractured, burned, and then melted. The once slow-moving behemoths of destruction became fireballs falling from the upper atmosphere.

Draethus watched as the lead bombard received a hit directly through the habitable section and exploded. He knew Rel served aboard. Metal and reinforced glass shattered outward as a huge chunk of the ship broke away, separating from the main body ending in several large pieces descending to the planet.

'Rel!' Draethus yelled, thrashing against his restraints. 'You bastards, I'm going to break into those chambers and strangle you all!'

The man roared in fury, screaming at the menace uncontrollably as the filament binds tightened, almost cutting off his circulation. As his oxygen ran out from the metal around his neck, the lords loosened the restraints, as they still needed Draethus alive.

Raeson stared in horror, watching the bombard ships fall from orbit in a blaze of death, tears falling from his cheeks.

With a flicker, the hologram changed to display the pirate cruisers in a higher position above, fighting for their lives against a Heridian capital fleet. Enemy destroyers pounded the vessels in a grand and terrifying light show. Fighters interlocked in a mess of swarming trails, pinpoints of explosions marking the destruction of a craft from both sides.

'You had a hidden fleet,' Raeson said defeated. 'You waited for us to begin our attack and then hit it from both sides.'

The Fourth Lord, in a smug tone, replied, 'Do you think there was no consequence to your assault?'

'We have been building our forces for many years, if that term even exists in this pocket of space,' said the Fifth Lord. 'After we destroy your fleet and gain control of the Link, we will continue our rampage against your forces waiting on the other side.'

'You can't open the Link without my help,' Draethus said, out of breath. 'There's no chance for that to happen.'

My quick death would solve this. I could see Rel again.
'Even if we somehow lost control of the time ship,' stated the Fourth Lord, 'the Link would open naturally eventually, and our forces will continue to spread throughout the galaxy. We are eternally patient.'

'Now tell us, scientist, how did you build the time device?' demanded the Third Lord.

Fire reflected from Spect's glasses as a pirate cruiser exploded, taking with it a corvette that was in proximity.

'I scanned the ship and found enough designs to construct a crude version of a time-shifting schematic,' Spect answered.

'Say nothing!' Tremon said angrily. 'What are you doing?'

'We've lost Tremon, and besides, nothing I tell them is any good because I can't scan the ship again without my specific equipment. Nor can I construct a displacement device from memory, let alone create our own Tether Source.'

'What did you say?' the Third Lord yelled. 'You brought with you a Tether Source?'

'Why yes, it's what powers the Dawn Eclipse and gives it the ability to time-shift,' Spect replied.

The tank enclosing the Third Lord went dark as the sound of gears and pistons activated, causing the cylindrical pod to disappear back the way it came, up and into the ceiling in what seemed to be a rush of panic.

'Why have you abandoned this conversation?' the Fifth Lord questioned, knowing the Third Lord could hear.

Before there was a reply, the lights within the room flickered hysterically, and the space around the captives howled in whispers.

Dark ghosts swirled, phased and shifted eerily, attacking the remaining two containment cylinders. Glass and liquid exploded in a mixture of noise and pain as the Heridian lords, both fourth and fifth, fell to the floor, their cables severed. The entities of shadow quickly crushed the skulls of the corpses, revealing a mixture of brain matter, blood and cybernetic implants once imbedded within. As the two gods fell silent, the enclosures sparked out and darkened, void of life.

'Whatever you are, set us free!' Tremon yelled.

The thin metal filaments slowly unravelled and lowered the men to the wet floor. They each stood covered in the unknown fluid that had exploded from the tanks, and looked around the room in astonishment.

Seven entities, which Draethus now recognised as the Specters, floated in front of the men in their ethereal state. Each wore a white mask with various symbols that hid their faces, worn and void of any eyes or mouth. The ragged black robes swayed in an invisible breeze, torn and tattered, their claws dripping with the enemy's blood.

'We need to leave now,' they whispered. *'The Third Lord has escaped and will send soldiers to intercept us.'*

'Get me a weapon,' Raeson said. 'I want to shoot something.' Draethus, still in shock and overcome with rage, stormed up to the lead Specter, liquid splashing on his boots, and asked, 'How do we reach the Eclipse? And why didn't you help us sooner?'

'It took time for us to reach here. As to your first question, when we are in line of sight of our destination, we shall be able to take you there.'

A slight variation of the voice continued. *'Three rooms from here are the items taken from you. We go there first, then onto the main elevator to the surface.'*

'If the Third Lord still has control, won't they be able to lock us out?' Spect asked.

The Specters ignored his question.

'Time is up, we move now,' one ghost whispered.

The door to the room burst forward as the Specters telekinetically forced it open, releasing the men from their prison. The entities glided ahead of the exhausted pirates who hadn't slept in days, and headed toward the men's equipment.

*

Draethus fired again down the long walkway and tore away another Heridian soldier's body, severing it clean. He could feel the steam emanating off the cooling module, keeping the gun at temperature, as he reloaded. 'We have to storm this walkway soon,' he said to the team who were busy firing their own weapons from positions of cover nearby at the approaching enemy.

The Specters were busy in close quarter combat with some larger Heridian drone soldiers further down and created an obstruction for the pirates' shooting.

'Move up,' Draethus ordered, 'let the Specters do their work. We need to get to that elevator now.'

The former SOV warrior sprang up from his position and charged forward, hoping his armor would deflect the laser fire that was soon to start. Tremon shouldered his oversized rifle and followed with

Raeson at his side and Spect towards the rear. Pistols weren't much good at the range, so the scientist had kept himself hidden for most of the engagement.

'It's times like this I really miss my lab back on Echelon,' Spect said. He reached into his dark gray lab coat and made sure his pistol was still secure in its holster.

Three of the Specters dispatched their Heridian opponents with a flurry of slashes and strikes from their long claws, hastily joining the team.

Draethus felt vertigo as a circle of darkness appeared around the men, followed by unsteady feet as the entities enveloped the group in the Tether's energy. By the time he realized what had happened, they were at the base of the massive elevator, transported in an unworldly manner.

'Where there is a line of sight we can take you,' one Specter whispered. *'Once at the top, call in your ship to pass.'*

'You can get us on board with a low-level fly over just by seeing it?' Raeson asked.

'Correct. There is still the matter of the time ship, we must rescue or deal with it,' replied the ghost.

'If you can call in a fly-by, I'll make for the Eclipse and try to get it out,' Draethus said.

Tremon wasn't so keen on the idea and said, 'You're not having all the fun. I'm coming with you.'

'After this is over we'll have a chat about your stalker-ish behavior,' Draethus grimaced. He felt a pang of guilt for smiling when Rel had only just perished.

Such a familiar feeling.

'The important thing is to get us out of here,' Draethus added. 'One man can go unnoticed, but that chance lowers the larger the group. I want you to look after Spect. The Heridians can't have him.'

Tremon looked as if he was going to argue then thought against it, acknowledging with a nod.

They entered the elevator as heavy doors slid open, revealing a grated floor that was large enough to fit a vehicle. The doors closed behind, leaving them in the dark, low lit room. Without warning or preparation, the Specters transported the men again using a small clear window in the elevator ceiling. They found themselves at ground level in an open loading area covered in dead Heridian soldiers from the Specter's entry earlier. Replenishment forces of Heridians walked amongst their fallen.

Raeson glanced up through the clear domed ceiling, then touched the coms in his ear. 'Slin, do you copy?'

Nothing but static replied.

Lights from explosions in orbit reached his eyes as white contrails from falling debris streaked across the already blazing sky. More Heridian troops entered the area from the front as the docking gates opened, soldiers followed by the walking armored vehicles.

'Get to cover!' Draethus ordered. 'Those walkers will shred anything that moves.'

Again, Raeson tried his coms as he hid behind a large cargo crate but received no connection. 'Where are you Slin?'

*

The pirate corvette, the *Arvernus*, rolled to avoid an incoming torpedo launched from a Heridian cruiser, and only barely evaded. Slin knew that had the incoming fire been guided missiles, they wouldn't have been so lucky.

'Hard to starboard, thirty degrees, now!' Slin yelled from his chair on the command deck.

The vessel cut half of its rear engines and increased the remaining, causing the ship to bank to starboard sharply before spearing away from the enemy cruiser. More torpedos sped towards the pirates, but good piloting took the *Arvernus* off the line of trajectory.

'Get us amongst the wreckage of that cruiser ahead. Maybe we can throw them off and give the other ships time to escape,' ordered Slin.

'Slin,' Nash yelled out, 'I mean Commander, I'm picking up a voice in the static on the coms.'

'There's a battle going on Nash, I'm sure there's a lot of chatter between the ships.'

'This is on our personal channel, the one reserved for internal crew only.'

'Link me into it,' Slin asked. 'See if you can clean it up a little.'

Slin concentrated on the voice in the static and instantly realized who it was, more from reprimands than anything else. He stood from his chair and rushed up to Nash, making a mental note to apologise to her later for being abrupt. 'That's Raeson. Can you target the source and create a connection?'

'You think he's alive?' Nash asked. 'I can try. We would definitely have more power behind the signal from our end, so it might work.' She did as instructed, filtering out the interference from the planet's magnetic field and the surrounding battle.

'This is the Arvernus, Raeson can you hear me?' Slin asked into his coms.

'Slin? Are you taking my ship on a leisurely cruise? I've been trying to reach you.' Raeson replied. 'Listen, I need you to perform a low-level fly over of the domed facility at the base of the spire. Can you do that?'

'A fly over? You need a distraction?'

'Something like that. I need you here now as the Rids have us pinned down.'

'Give us three minutes Commander, you'll hear us coming,' Slin said, smiling to himself.

'Make it two minutes or we won't be here,' Raeson answered as the sound of gunfire ricocheted nearby.

Slin cut the coms and, turning to his pilot who was busy evading weapons' fire through a wrecked cruiser, ordered, 'These are your new waypoints, boy. Take us in low and fast, and make as much noise as you can.'

'Yes, sir,' the pilot replied with a frown. Still, no one referred to him by name.

The corvette blasted out of the wreckage, heading towards the planet at its fastest pace. The pursuing fighters couldn't keep up as their small engines reached maximum thrust, and watched the pirates disappear into the upper atmosphere. Fire erupted along the bow, spreading across the outer hull of the *Arvernus* as it ignited like a fireball burning across the sky. Diving directly down, it increased in velocity before pulling up and heading towards the spire in the distance.

'How long, Nash?' Slin asked patiently.

'Another thirty seconds and we'll be over that spike structure. Add a few more if we have to evade any ground fire.'

The pirate corvette kicked up a dust storm behind it, dirt spiralling along as the vessel skimmed above the surface, the sonic boom reaching the spire in a thunderous introduction.

*

Draethus snapped off another couple of rounds at a Heridian soldier hiding amongst some loading equipment. The first struck the creature in the arm, the second, to its benefit, deflected harmlessly off the machinery.

He never got the chance for a second attempt as the world around grew dark with swirls of ghostly energy. When the swirls abruptly vanished, he quickly found his bearings and realized he was inside the creature ship and meters from the *Dawn Eclipses'* entry. Draethus was far from his team and wondered if he'd made the right decision venturing out alone, but seeing the golden ship squashed that vulnerability.

'The ship may not fly again,' a voice whispered. *'If you cannot reactivate the systems, we will have to scuttle it.'*

The idea of destroying his ship, not because it was his first, but an ancient vessel he was still discovering, was a gut-wrenching thought. He had already lost the woman he loved and the fight against the menace. Sacrificing his ship, he knew, would bring him closer to breaking point. The ship represented freedom and gave him the ability to make a difference, to make choices, and to answer the call of the fallen.

'She'll fly again,' Draethus said, turning to the Specter next to him. 'Besides, there's no other way out.'

In a flash, the ghostly apparition flickered into the distance, its claws slashing and cloak diffusing the surrounding light. An enemy squad shrieked in horror as they were torn apart by the Specter, their blood splashing through the ghost and onto the floor.

Draethus realized his jaw had dropped at the sight, and quickly regained his composure. 'How do I get claws like that?' he asked, swiftly moving up to the Specter's position.

The Specter ignored the question and said, *'I will make sure the Tether Source is still functioning and you can wake up the ship. We disarmed the electronic warfare on our way to rescue you, but there are more enemy soldiers approaching, so you need to hurry.'* It flew ahead and phased through the closed outer door.

Draethus placed his palm over the side panel and to his surprise the door phased out of existence, allowing him entry.

'There must be power running through her for the door at least,' he said to himself. 'Actually, the breaching damage is gone too.' He moved further in and, in a raised voice, said, 'Sleepy time is over,

Eclipse. Let's go.' He knocked on the walls, hoping to create some noise, then sprinted for the command deck.

Wake up already.

*

Back at the docks, Tremon grabbed Spect by the coat and dragged him behind the remains of a Heridian walker, destroyed by the Specters.

Spect coughed and sputtered as the smoke from the ghostly teleportation reached his lungs, but was glad to be out of harm's way.

He rubbed his glasses to clean them as the sonic boom struck, the wreckage over him vibrating profusely. Glancing up into the high domed ceiling, he jumped as a black corvette darted over them, its engines burning a bright azure.

There was a sense of longing for the safety of a warship, able to defend itself or jump away if needed, and the scientist wished he were aboard. As the stable feeling of the ground left him, the vision in his eyes darkened. He felt himself being shifted and realized they had granted his wish. Tumbling into a corner, he lost his balance, and his lunch threatened to reveal itself.

'So that's new,' Slin said startled, looking at the three men who appeared on his bridge. 'How did you do that?'

Raeson straightened his armor and replied, 'Magic Specter dust and a lot of luck. Is there any sign of the Eclipse?'

'Nothing yet,' replied Nash from the back. 'We're going back to the main body of the fleet.'

'Good,' Raeson said. 'Slin, you're still in command of the Arvernus. I want you to message all the ships left alive to regroup on us.'

'Yes, sir, but where do we go if the Eclipse doesn't make it? That ship is our only ticket out,' Slin asked.

'Set a waypoint for the group of wrecks near where the Link opened. We'll have to keep on the move until we figure out our next move.'

Sat in the corner, Spectalin regarded the pirate with awe. To be so confident and self assured was something the scientist never thought possible.

I can build a time displacement device and any weapon imaginable, but I can't hold myself steady.

Levering himself up, he composed himself and brushed off the dirt from his lab coat. The pistol almost fell from its holster before Tremon caught it and secured the buckle.

'I feel like your mother,' Tremon grinned. He noticed Spect's expression and then added, 'Sorry, I didn't mean to bring up any bad memories.'

'It's alright,' Spect replied. 'They're only good ones.'

Tremon nodded, turned to Raeson and then asked, 'What of Draethus? We can't just leave him down on the planet?'

'A Specter is with him,' Raeson said. 'If he can't get that ship working, then he's just as stuck as we are. Don't worry, if we don't hear from him we'll mount a rescue.'

'Damn right we will,' Tremon said. 'You know, we had bets on you Cygnians stealing the ship and killing us all.'

Raeson laughed and said, 'Don't worry, there's still time.'

The dark ship reached into the skies, burning its way into the heart of the ongoing conflict in orbit. Capital ships on both sides traded weapons fire as laser and missiles alike slammed into each other's hulls.

The area was blanketed with horrific wrecks, tumbling, spinning, and streaking to the planet below. As the pirate corvette joined the remaining vessels, Slin transmitted the area wide broadcast for retreat and watched as another pirate cruiser explode in a spectacular fireball.

'All remaining ships are disengaging and falling into formation behind us,' Nash announced. 'There aren't a lot of them left, Slin.'

Tremon walked up to the forward viewing display. 'Can you switch to the rear camera?' he asked, rubbing his left arm where a bullet had grazed him.

The rear display showed how intense the battle in orbit had been. Twisted wrecks covered the field of view as fires and explosions raged from both sides, and of the remaining pirate vessels, none were unscathed.

'The number of lives lost today is intolerable,' Tremon stated flatly, watching the pirate escape pods being captured or destroyed by the enemy. 'This menace needs eradicating. I just wish there was something more we could do.'

Spect thought about voicing his role in the grand scheme, how every life lost since he built the device was his fault. He felt a sickening feeling envelop his mind and oppress his conscience. As he moved up to Tremon, he slid his hand deep into his coat and made sure the Heridian implant was still there.

Before any of the crew could reply, Nash bolted out of her chair in excitement and exclaimed, 'There's another signature headed our way amongst the Rids.'

On the display, Spect spotted something glint in the ambient light around Heridia. It looked like a firefly, weaving and dodging through the torn wreckage before streaking towards them.

The Heridian fleet ceased its pursuit of the pirates and concentrated all their attention on the glowing ship who only shrugged off the attack. Like an angel of fire, the golden ship burst through the enemy lines, leaving them far behind. The pirate fleet flared their engines, causing the display to dim, and headed for the last known location of the Link.

'I hope one of you guys paid the tab?' Commander Draethus said over the coms. 'We're going for the Link I assume?'

Raeson spoke first and replied, 'Tremon was just saying how much he was going to miss you?'

'I don't miss,' Tremon chuckled.

'Watch your back with that one,' Draethus replied. 'He has a tendency to knock men unconscious and drag them back to his sky cave.'

'That was…' Tremon began and gave in. 'Sure, sure. So how do we get back?'

'The ship says we've just enough energy to open the Link for us to escape.'

Spect ran his finger over the frame of his glasses and let out a sigh of relief.

The red clouds of the surrounding nebula enveloped the pirate fleet, and despite the Heridians on their tail, had enough interference to vanish.

*

The conference room aboard the *Dawn Eclipse* was narrow. Down the center was an ornate, dark wooden table with a glossy surface covered in holographic displays of the space around the ship.

Draethus and Raeson sat on one side, whilst Tremon, Spect, Stark, and a holographic Slin sat on the other. At the head of the table was the entity, a Specter, with an oval, bone colored face mask with a single vertical line carved down the middle. It was silent, but watchful.

'I have summoned you here to share our joint purpose against the enemy race that is the Heridians,' the Specter said, floating above the floor in its invisible eerie breeze.

'What is your purpose?' Raeson asked.

'We protect the vessel you refer to as the Dawn Eclipse. Scattered throughout time and space, we exist where the ship is, has or will be,' it whispered.

Slin, who connected with the meeting remotely from his personal viewing display in his quarters on board the *Arvernus*, asked, 'So, who built the ship?'

The ghostly apparition turned to the holographic representation of the corvettes' acting commander sitting next to Tremon. *'An ancient race built the vessel long before even our masters existed. It trapped the Heridian forces in a pocket of space that exists apart from time, the space we currently travel in. The Dawn Eclipse is the gatekeeper, the method used to open the Link and to seal it.'*

'More space magic,' said Draethus. 'I don't see how one ship could create a pocket of space and trap an entire planet. If its purpose was only to open the Link to it, then I could understand.'

'There is much you do not understand. You are not the first races to fight against the Heridians over the thousands of years,' said the Specter. *'The long-ago war with the reptilian race you saw evidence of on Tiberous played a major role in the enemy's entrapment.'*

'So those were the wrecks we've seen scattered throughout this area?' Spect asked. 'I really want to get my hands on those schematics.'

'That is correct,' the Specter replied, its cloak suddenly shifting in the non-existent breeze. *'The war caused the lizards extinction, but to the benefit of all others, and halted the enemy's advance.'*

Stark, who had sat quietly until now, asked what many of them were wondering. 'What exactly are you, Specters, and who are your masters?'

The entity paused, as if it was deciding how much information to reveal. *'The name of our masters shall remain unknown to you for their protection. As for the Specters, like Draethus, we were once*

Soldiers of the Void. We were lost long ago during the great voyage to Echelon.'

Draethus sprung to his feet at the statement. 'You were SOV, but how? What detachment were you in?'

'The Link is approaching,' the entity stated, and with no sign of it ever being present, vanished.

Tremon looked over at his commander and asked with a sly smile, 'Didn't see that coming did you?'

Draethus gave him a silent expression of shock.

Raeson stood and said, 'There's still the matter of the lord who escaped during our interrogation.'

'The Third Lord?' Slin questioned. 'Will anything even change if the Rids are commanded by only one of them?'

'We won't know for a while,' Draethus said. 'I think we can discuss this in further detail later.' He glared at Tremon and Spect who knew what he meant. If word spread that Draethus and Raeson became the Heridian lords, chaos would follow.

As the room emptied, Tremon, with his arm now bandaged, stopped both commanders, and said, 'I'm sorry for your loss. I know Rel meant a lot to both of you.'

Both commanders nodded silently, exchanged glances, and left for the command deck.

*

A swirl of fire erupted as the whirlwind of energy appeared around the golden ship and opened the Link to normal space. The remnants of the pirate fleet, a handful of cruisers escorted by corvettes, entered first, descending into the gateway. As the last capital vessel passed, the ship began the Link's closure, hopefully for the last time, and accelerated to the exit.

'I am so sorry, Rel,' Draethus said through tears from the privacy of his command position under the metal liquid lake on board the *Eclipse*.

CHAPTER 24

The Departed Fallen.

The Cygnian Memorial, a converted space station used solely for burying the dead, orbited the barren home-world of the pirates. Once used as a hub for planetary exportation now served as a skyward graveyard where a warrior's remains could lie to rest.

Five enormous domes surrounded a central structure, each one a unique ecosystem and self-contained, maintained by robotic drones that saw to their cultivation. Dome four contained the lush growth of trees entwined with exotic plants taken from different worlds around the known solar systems.

The bright colors of greens from the foliage and purples of varied flower species created a calm atmosphere around the quiet group of people standing to attention. Rows of pirates, soldiers, and civilians remained silent as someone sounded an instrument signalling the end of the special service for the fallen heroes.

Talon Commander Xain Raeson, dressed in full formal attire, approached one of the many statues erected in honor of each fallen ship. A pillar of marble, a meter square at the base, then tapered to a small square at the top, stood taller than any human. It held a bronze plaque with all the names of the deceased. A hologram above the monument gently rotated, depicting the ship with its name clearly labelled underneath.

Draethus, the commander of the ancient vessel, the *Dawn Eclipse*, stood next to his friend and eyed Rel's name on the plaque.

'She should never have been there,' Draethus said sadly.

'No, she shouldn't,' Raeson replied, 'but she was strong willed and neither of us could have stopped her.'

Draethus laid down a purple flower against the monument, closed his eyes and wished Rel would be in front of him when he looked up. In his mind, he could see her standing in the distance, waving and running towards him.

'Rel used to give those flowers to me, before you came along,' Raeson said.

Draethus snapped out of his vision and replied, 'I didn't know that. She was an incredibly caring woman,' then whispered, 'and we left her body on Heridia.'

Xain turned to the grieving man. 'We can't afford to think like that Draethus, besides there was nothing left of her as the ship burned up in the atmosphere. A better end than what happened to your friend Johan.'

Draethus nodded as he fought the choking feeling in his throat. 'So what of your friend, Zekhal was it?'

Tremon heard the name mentioned and joined the two. 'Is there a chance we'll find him?'

Raeson shook his head and said, 'The void holds many wonders, but in that place, whatever plain of existence the Link exists, is new to me. I'm not sure if the Dying Nova frigate will ever find its way out.'

'But they have enough food and water to survive for years at a time, so there might be hope for them, however slim,' Draethus said.

'Always the optimist,' Xain smiled briefly. 'We have Spect scouring through the data we captured while passing through the Link. If anyone can uncover something, it's him.'

'Speaking of Spect,' Draethus said, 'where is he?'

Tremon pointed off into the distance. 'He sends his condolences but had to rush off, something to do with a few new ship designs we found amongst the wrecks near Heridia.'

'For a genius, he really has a short attention span,' Draethus added.

A group of men near another monument saluted, then parted, allowing Khan Hayreddin to walk between. The man had spent most of the hour giving the eulogy, the send-off that would immortalise the fallen men and women so their legacy would live on. Dressed in an armored uniform reserved only for the ceremony, the man stood tall, proud yet sombre.

'Commanders,' he started, 'it's sad to see you here today, but I'm relieved you survived.'

All three men nodded deeply to their leader, eyes lowered and stern.

'You can relax,' the Khan said. 'There are some things we need to address. I would like to have done this later however it cannot wait.'

The bearded man looked at Draethus and a smile reached his eyes at the sight of the Cygnian badge on his shoulder. 'It looks great on you, on both of you,' he finished, turning to Tremon.

Draethus felt pride with a feeling of belonging before he realized he couldn't stay, for now at least.

'My Khan, do you know of the message I have to deliver to my old allegiance?' Draethus asked.

The pirate leader nodded. 'Aye, I know of it and before you ask, I think you have a duty to honor it.'

It surprised Draethus, and he asked, 'Will you allow me to fly to Echelon, to deliver the co-ordinates the SOV need to fight the Heridians?'

'If it means more of the menace will die, then yes, I will allow it on one condition.'

'The Eclipse,' Raeson added.

'That's right,' replied the Khan. 'We need that ship, but on your return, you will again be its commander.'

Tremon interrupted. 'What ship will he take?'

The Khan grinned. 'I believe your scientist has something in mind.'

Tremon frowned and said, 'I'm not sure I like the sound of that. I guess we'll find out.'

The Khan slapped his hand on Tremon's shoulder. 'That reminds me, how would you feel about leading a new class of warrior, in the image of what you were?'

'What did you have in mind?'

'The fleet needs more structure with internal security. I was thinking you could lead and train what I'm calling the Cygnian Paladins. What do you say?'

The look on Tremon's face gave away his answer. 'It would honor me, my Khan.'

'I'm glad to hear it. You start tomorrow and will report directly to me,' the older man replied. 'For now, I have things to attend to.'

The men nodded deeply in acknowledgement as their leader vanished into the crowd of people.

'Congratulations,' Draethus said to Tremon as Raeson slapped the man on the back.

'I was wondering what my role here would be. I thought it was on the Eclipse, but I guess you have a mission to achieve,' the paladin said, looking at his former commander.

'You could come with me. Echelon was your home after all,' Draethus replied.

'It was, but it lays abandoned now and it looks like I have a security force to form. It is a tempting offer, though.'

Draethus smiled and said, 'Then I better get this message to its destination and come back to help.' He looked at both men intensely. 'We should keep what we found on Heridia secret.'

'You mean the identity of the lords?' replied Tremon.

Raeson nodded. 'I agree, that information would be trouble for us in the future. Although I don't mind the idea of being called a lord…'

'I'm sure there are a lot of titles we could call you,' Draethus grinned, then with a serious expression added, 'it's settled then, that information stays with us. Tremon, please relay the request to Spect.'

Slin, Nash and the young pilot whose name everyone forgot, appeared from behind a monument further down the line. A holographic fighter slowly rotated behind them.

'Commanders,' they said.

'And newly awarded paladin we hear,' Slin said with a wide grin.

Tremon beamed with excitement. 'Better watch yourselves now that I don't throw you in the brig. Actually, maybe now you can pay me your debt.'

'What debt?' Nash laughed. 'You got that the wrong way around buddy.'

Tremon walked up to the young pilot and gave him a cheerful slap on the side of his shoulder. 'You know, we never got to find out your name.'

'I don't see how anyone could forget it,' the red-haired human replied.

Draethus gave the boy an assumptive stare in anticipation.

'My name is Killiax Lasser.'

'That's horrendous!' Tremon yelled. 'How could anyone forget a name like that?'

Killiax just shrugged. 'I get used to it, and I'm not that memorable… you could call me Kill for short?'

Nash laughed, rubbed her hand through his ginger hair and said, 'that's not happening.'

'So, what now?' asked Slin.

'Now we rebuild our fleet,' Raeson answered. 'We launch reconnaissance missions to track the Rids, then attack them again as the Third Lord is still out there. We might plan another attack to finish him.'

'And I have a message to deliver to my former soldiers,' Draethus said. 'I better get back to the ship and inform it I'll be absent.'

Draethus looked back at the monument and into the distance, hoping to see his vision of Rel once more.

*

Talon Commander Arcilous Draethus, warrior, soldier and recently recruited pirate, stood at the center of his command deck, running his gaze across its elegant design. Sleek lines interwove the metallic white surfaces of the consoles as the holographic interface floated above each station. Strange shapes marked the various controls linked to the ship.

How are the repairs coming, Eclipse? he thought in his mind, knowing the vessel was with him.

The repairs are complete, Commander Draethus. The damage inflicted by the Heridian electronic warfare is no more, as are the invasive nanites.

Draethus could sense there was more to say, a curiosity lingering in the background of the *Eclipses'* consciousness.

Eclipse, he thought with a stern tone, *is there something else you are not telling me?*

There was silence for a moment as the ship considered its options, deciding to go with the truthful question. *Are you leaving?*

He smiled to himself and sent in a thought, *For a short time, yes, I will leave. I have a mission to complete which involves delivering a message to the SOV on Echelon.*

He felt a sadness emanate from the entity inside his mind, a sense of abandonment with a need to follow. *I would take you along, of course, however I have agreed with the Khan that you would stay here.*

I see Commander, and how long will you be absent for?

The scientist, Spect, thinks that it's a ten month round trip depending, of course, on how long I stay on Echelon. I don't see the need to stay long, just enough to leave the details for the SOV to find.

The ship didn't seem happy with the decision, but gave the Draethus the sense of acceptance. *Very well, Commander.*

Draethus walked off his command deck when he realized he'd never asked about the ship's involvement with the Specters. *Did you know the Specters would help us on Heridia?*

Did the Eclipse know it was smuggling the deadly ethereal beings called Specters into the military center of the Heridian race to slay their leadership?

I'll take that as a yes.

*

The scientist Spectalin ran his fingers quickly over the long console in front of him, calibrating the controls of his new creation. He had obtained a massive amount of data within the Heridian pocket of space and had been compiling it into ship schematics ever since their return.

Spect had scanned every wreck within the ship graveyard with enough detail to construct plans to recreate the vessels. It was this idea the Khan had liked the most, to rebuild the fleet using ancient designs from the large capital vessels down to the smallest of fighters. In the foreseeable future, the Cygnian fleet would comprise Heridian designs alongside the unknown reptilian race.

As he finished the last of the calibrations, the soldiers he had fought alongside, men and women he'd grown fond of, were ready to give their commander a send-off.

Draethus leaned against the ship he would call home for the next twelve months. He ran his hand along its nose, admiring the rugged appearance. Unlike the widowmaker class fighters, the craft wasn't sleek and resembled a winged reptile. He imagined the race that designed it to share similarities. Spect had the ship painted the black and gray of the pirates, as opposed to the khaki green of the original design.

Draethus looked over his group of friends and felt great pride in what they had accomplished. Tremon and Raeson stood next to Spect, with Slin and Nash on the other side.

'She's the first of her kind,' Spect started, 'well, built by us that is. I've taken to calling the race who designed it the Tiberous because of their former planet.'

'Looks fast,' replied Raeson, 'and it's designed for translocation I hear?'

Spect ran a finger across the frame of his glasses and realized he was the center of attention. His face flushed a bright red as he said, 'In a limited capacity yes, the craft can make short distance translocates but also has stasis capability. Commander Draethus can sleep for months at a time if he so wishes.'

'Have you named the class of ship yet?' Slin asked.

Tremon laughed. 'This is Spect we're talking about here, and he's probably named the whole damned fleet by now.'

'Now hear this,' Spect started before catching his temper. 'Alright, maybe I have named the entire fleet and the new ships we'll be building soon, but I give them illustrious names.'

'That you do old friend,' Draethus added, 'and we call this?'

'An Aspen class long distance fighter. Although not as manoeuvrable as the standard pirate craft, it's designed specifically for long journeys and will be perfect for your mission. As mentioned earlier, I have fitted it with a stasis module, as the fighter can only support one person. The darkness out there is lonely and can be hazardous to a pilot's mental state, so this is the solution.'

'So the sleeping princess can deliver his message,' Raeson laughed as he gave Draethus a shove.

'I'd give you a shove back if you weren't so delicate.'

Spect tapped on some of his controls and a door behind the canopy opened. It slid to the side as a crude ladder extended down to the docking platform.

'We have stored all your belongings aboard as requested. I've also run multiple systems checks and you are safe to fly,' Spect announced.

Tremon was the first to clasp forearms with Draethus, and they locked each other in a stern gaze. Old rivals turned friends.

'Be well, friend,' said Tremon.

'And you Tremon, the new paladins won't know what hit them.'
'I'll try not to hit them, but no promises.'

Raeson faced him and said, 'It's been a long road, an unfinished one, but we've done well. Come back soon, there's still Rids to kill after all.'

'Look after these soldiers for me, Raeson,' Draethus replied as they clasped arms. 'They'll need your leadership in the next battles.'

They nodded before Draethus slapped the scientist on the shoulder. 'I'm proud of you too, Spect. You're quite the warrior now.'

The scientist looked down and smiled. 'Thank you, sir.'

'And thank you for the ship. It means a lot.'

Draethus finished his goodbyes with both Slin and Nash before he climbed the ladder, turned, and bowed his head in salute. His team, his colleagues and friends, returned the salute as the door closed.

After settling into his cockpit, he ran his pre-start check and the fighter's engine burst to life. The clamps released him off the dock and, with a burst of radiance, headed out into the void. He glanced back at the fleet and reassured himself.

I'll return once I've left the co-ordinates on Echelon, so the SOV will find them, along with the exact times the Link will open. They'll be ready for when the Rids arrive.

He settled back into his chair and missed the warm feeling in his mind that was the *Dawn Eclipse.* An ancient and mysterious star vessel that could reach into the corners of his consciousness and he didn't even discover more about it. As he set the autopilot to the route Spect had plotted to Echelon, he noticed something hidden under his console. It was a strange bottle with a note stuck to the front that read:

'A friend to keep you warm on your journey—Tremon.'

As he lifted the note off, Draethus noticed writing underneath and engraved on the bottle.

FANG.

*

Back on the docks the group watched as the fire from the Aspen class fighter's engines disappeared into the night.

'I feel I should be alongside him,' Tremon frowned as Raeson punched him in the arm.

'You have a paladin army to train now.'

'With the route I calculated, Draethus will arrive at the time specified. We'll see him again soon, if we survive the coming war. There are Heridian fleets still out there,' Spect added.

'Always the optimist,' Slin chuckled.

Nash held Slin's hand and pulled him in close. 'Could we go check on Tek? We haven't seen him in a couple of weeks?' she asked him.

Before Slin could respond, klaxons screamed, echoing through the docks, a warning that a vessel was making an unauthorized entry. Every flashing and rotating signal transformed the open area into a yellow haze as pirate guards began running towards the danger.

'What's going on?' Raeson asked a guard as he approached.

'That gold ship has disengaged the docking clamp somehow and is trying to leave,' the man replied out of breath.

The group followed the guard to the dock in question, and it wasn't hard to guess what ship he was talking about.

When they arrived, the golden ship was indeed unsecured from its mooring but hadn't engaged its engines. The majestic vessel floated still and looked ready for an escape.

'Raeson to the Eclipse, what are you doing?' the pirate commander yelled into his coms. 'I know you can hear me.'

The Eclipse is sorry, the ship replied into his mind. *This is the only way.*

Xain's mind reeled at the sound of a voice in his head other than his own.

The Tether Source within the core of the vessel spun into action as external armor plates slid back, revealing the glow within, light pulsing and swirling as an intense energy erupted like azure fire around it.

Everyone on the docks shielded their eyes from the blinding light, and Raeson feared they would be vaporized. The vibrations in the air were almost too much to handle, and the noise of a thousand engines shrieked through the docks of the *Wing of Vidar*.

As the noise vanished, Raeson removed his hands, uncovering his face, and felt the pain from his ears ringing. He looked up, expecting to see the empty dock and a missing ship, only to see that the *Dawn Eclipse* was still in the same position.

'Eclipse, what's going on?' he asked as the noise in his ears faded. 'You better have a good explanation for this, and why did it look like you executed a time-shift?'

His coms crackled to life with a voice that he didn't recognise but felt familiar. 'Raeson, as in Xain Raeson?' the man asked.

'Yes, who is this?'

'Well, if you're truthful, then I guess that makes you my son.'

Epilogue

Draethus awoke to a screaming alarm originating from the cockpit of his Aspen class fighter.

It took a few moments for the stasis gas to clear in his horizontal chamber, the blanketing mist covering his body dissipating as the containment glass lifted.

Running into the cockpit, he was startled to see a fast-approaching surface through the canopy. His consoles flickered with warning holograms informing him of imminent danger combined with a full systems failure. Fear raged through his mind.

'Not now,' he yelled. 'I haven't come all this way to fail now!'

He ran back into the mid-section of his craft and rapidly put on his armor. If he were going to crash, he would need all the protection he could find. His helmet automatically flipped over his face from behind and created an air-tight seal as he strapped into the flight chair. The control stick was unresponsive, and nothing Draethus touched had any effect.

The Aspen fighter slammed into the dusty gray surface, carving a three-kilometre-long crater as the craft skidded through the rock. Wings tore away as the body became a shell-like projectile, then after what felt like an eternal hour, slowed to a fiery halt. The remaining oxygen burned off, leaving him with only the limited supply contained within his personal armor.

His head throbbed as he fought the urge to pass out. His hands ran over the console to make sure his message was still intact only to find it partially corrupted.

'The co-ordinates to the Link are missing,' Draethus said to himself, 'but the invasion dates are intact. I guess that's something.'

He stabbed a finger repeatedly at the locater graphic on the floating display until it finally worked and discovered where exactly he had crashed landed and laughed. 'Echelon's moon and thousands of years too early. So that's what the SOV found up here... me.'

Looking around, he found a sharp piece of debris and, knowing the ship's systems wouldn't last the thousand years, began etching the co-ordinates into the console.

Draethus knew his oxygen supply was dangerously low because of a small rupture in the armor. He could see the vapor emanating from multiple locations, too many to cover all at once. The reading inside his helmet displayed he hadn't long to live, and as he finished the co-ordinates, felt a sense of peace.

Hopefully, the fallen can rest now.

His vision faded into darkness. The image of his lover appeared in the distance, standing quietly in the gray dust, smiling, and holding a purple flower.

'Rel,' he whispered.

Arcilous Draethus held the locket, gifted to him by Rel, in his hand and caressed it with the thumb of his armored glove, wondering if fate had finished with him.

TO CONTINUE...

Milton Keynes UK
Ingram Content Group UK Ltd.
UKHW041025260124
436571UK00007B/87/J